Saving The Dark Side

Book 1: The Devotion

Joseph Paradis

Cover design and interior
www.ebooklaunch.com

Edited by Mike Waitz of Sticks and Stones Freelance Editing
www.stickandstonesediting.net

Author Website:
www.AeneriaIsComing.com

FROM THE WORLD OF AENERIA

For all Hate mail and love letters:
www.AeneriaIsComing.com/contact/

This book is dedicated to those to braved it first.

Mike Waitz
Timothy Charest
Trevor Hornbeck
Melanie Kasparian
Terri Paradis
James Miller
Lydia Gill

And to Brandon Courcy,
who showed me just how real Aeneria was.

CHAPTER 1

RIDICULE

"I can't breathe, I can't breathe."

"Miss, miss look at me. Jesus she's really losing it here. HEY! There we are, okay? My name is Officer Daniels. I need you to tell me what's going on. Why did you call 9-1-1 tonight?"

"I can't breathe, I... I..."

"Daniels look at her, you're spinning your wheels right now." Sergeant Brady sighed, taking off his cap and tossing it onto the kitchen table. Two decades on the department taught him this girl wouldn't be much help. Her bony frame sat like a crumpled umbrella on the floor. Her bleach-blonde hair covered her face and eyes, though it did nothing to muffle her wailing. Annoyed, Brady turned to his partner, "The EMTs will be here in five minutes. Let them have a go with her. Look, there's a stroller in the corner, why don't you look around and see if there's any other kids in the house."

"Alrighty then," Daniels said and took his hand off the girl's shoulder. Scowling, he started his scan of the first floor.

Sergeant Brady watched out of the corner of his eye as his partner left the kitchen. He hoped the house could tell them something. There were signs of kids all over the apartment. Hopefully they weren't in a bad way. Brady had seen more than his fair share of hurt kids in this neighborhood. The Tree Streets were not a safe place in broad daylight, let alone at 3 o'clock in the morning. This neighborhood held the record every year for the most calls. Domestics, drugs, noise complaints, shootings, and other things associated with this caliber of 'ghetto trash'.

"Got a kid over here in the pack-n-play. Six months or so, but he looks fine," Daniels called from the living room. "Might be another one upstairs." He held up a cheap ninja sword that Sergeant Brady recognized as having come from the dollar-store down the street. "Heading up now."

Unbuckling his portable radio, Sergeant Brady waited for the girl to quiet down so he could make the call. Her wailing seemed to be on the rise however, so he cupped his hand over the microphone, "Twenty-Eight on scene at Blossom Street. Got a female, early twenties, no injury. One child, six months, no injury. Searching the rest of the house now." He rubbed his eyes with his thumb and forefinger as he turned the volume down on his radio. Judging by her hyperventilating sobs, he guessed the girl was no closer to telling him what was wrong. He took a look around the first floor, which didn't take long considering it had two rooms and a closet. The place was a bit messy, but not dirty. There were dishes on every counter and blankets on the floor, but the small apartment didn't have that stink that you found in most places around here.

Careful not to wake the little one, Sergeant Brady sidled past the couch to see if the room could tell him what the girl couldn't. He bent low and gripped a family photo off the end table. There was the girl and what looked like the infant, but there was another boy as well, three maybe four years old. They all had matching white collared shirts. The older boy reminded Brady of his nephew. He frowned, wondering what kind of low-life the boy would turn out to be. This damned neighborhood did it to them. Nearly every kid in these streets had their wings clipped before they ever had a chance to be someone. Brady said a silent prayer for both boys, hoping they would amount to more than his nephew had.

Sergeant Brady made his way back into the kitchen as Officer Daniels came stomping down the creaky stairs. Daniels reached out to grab the banister, but seemed to think better of it after a quick glance at the broken spindles.

"Do you have to be so loud?" Brady hissed as his mouth disappeared behind his moustache.

Officer Daniels rolled his eyes, motioning around him as if to showcase that there was no point keeping quiet. Red and blue lights flashed through the apartment and another squad car's siren could be heard screaming down Pine Street nearby. A few neighbors started to pop up like alley cats perched on their front stoops, eyes peering for a better view into the apartment.

"You think I'm going to wake anybody up on *this* street?" Daniels whispered as loudly as he could, "These people don't wake up for nothin' less than a gunshot. And if you haven't noticed, the chick is belting out a pretty good tune for somebody who can't breathe." Daniels winced as the infant in the living room started crying softly. "There's no one upstairs, but I think another kid lives here," Daniels whispered, quietly this time.

Sergeant Brady's moustache twitched as he held Daniel's eyes with an iron glare. The kid was still a rookie, but he had the attitude of a jaded detective. "Come on then," Brady grumbled.

The girl was still fighting for air as though choking on tear gas. Daniels craned his neck. Sergeant Brady adjusted his belt under his ample belly and squatted down next to the girl, who sat with her legs straight out like a doll's. It was as if she didn't even know he was there. Gently, he placed a finger under her chin and tilted her head up just an inch. He held out the family photo and her sobbing stopped abruptly.

Sergeant Brady adopted a voice which he normally reserved for his granddaughter: "Sweetie, where is your other son?"

She looked as if she was going to break down again as she grasped the hair at the sides of her head. Shaking, she squeaked, "He's gone."

Brady's wispy eyebrows came together, "Honey, I need you to tell me exactly what you mean by that. Where is your son right now?"

His gentle voice seemed to calm her as she unraveled her fingers from her hair and wrapped her arms around her middle. "I...I woke...I mean... Joshy woke me up a couple hours ago because he was hungry. I went into the boy's room to feed him and Cole was...Cole wasn't... I can't... I can't breathe." The incoherent sobbing stole her voice and wracked her small frame.

Sergeant Brady's eyes went wide as he stood up. Daniels was looking intently at him, his flashlight at the ready. "Check the exterior." Daniels nodded and rushed outside, leaving the door open.

• • • •

Two days passed in a riot of activity. The girl's name turned out to be Tara Carter. Her little apartment was visited at all hours by crime scene investigators and a detective from the state. Though they assured her they were doing everything they could to find her oldest son, they didn't have much to go off of, and she seemed to know it.

Investigators discovered the windows and doors were locked from the inside, and no one else had a key to her apartment. There was no sign of a break-in and Tara didn't have any close friends, relatives, or enemies who might want to cause her family harm. With her permission, the local news offered what help they could. Cole's big smile and neatly combed hair could be seen several times a day on the broadcast channels. Her neighbors, with whom she had never said a word to, offered a hand as well. Every night they went out calling his name, poking through dumpsters, cars, garages, sewer drains, every place an imaginative toddler might crawl into.

Tara had eventually stopped crying, but she also stopped eating, sleeping, and showering. Her upstairs neighbor, a matronly woman known for her heavy hand when dealing with troublemakers, offered to take Joshy for a night or two while they sorted this out. Tara, however, refused. She claimed she couldn't bear to be without her remaining child. Brady and Daniels stopped by a few times a day to offer condolences and what little updates they had.

On the evening of the third day the department had yet to make any measurable progress. Brady and Daniels stopped by Tara's apartment at the beginning of their shift. Both officers were determined to get something out of her. Their window for finding the child alive would soon come to a close.

The smell of cleaning sprays and fresh coffee permeated through-out the small apartment. The kitchen gleaming, Tara set aside two mugs for her two guests. She looked as unkempt as ever, as if she had done nothing but clean the place for the last few days. Her short blonde hair looked like a toothbrush that was long overdue for replacing. Daniels held Joshy in his arms as he jiggled his keys in front of his wiggling, chubby fists.

"Do you fellas want any milk or sugar?" Tara asked. Her voice was empty and monotone.

"Black is just fine for me, hon," Sergeant Brady replied.

"Extra-extra for me, please and thank you," said Daniels. "No-no-no Joshy, not in your mouth. That's for Officer Daniels, yes it is. Do you want to be a cop someday too? You do don't you?" The squirming Joshy had just unfastened Daniels's badge and immediately tried to gum it.

"So, Tara..." Sergeant Brady spun his hat awkwardly in his wrinkled hands. "The state's detective wants you to come down to the station tomorrow. It's not an interrogation or anything of the sort, he just wants to go over some details. Work history, past boyfriends, known relatives. You know, little pieces of the puzzle. To be honest hon, you've been mighty quiet the last couple days. Help us bring Cole home."

Tara placed two red mugs on the table with a dull *clunk*. "We're at sixty-eight hours. When I talked to that detective guy he told me if missing children aren't found within seventy-two hours, the chances of finding them alive is..." her voice trailed off for a moment. "I don't know the 'how's or the 'why's or any other questions you've been asking. I've told you everything. My baby is gone. He just vanished." Her tone shifted from hard wood to brittle glass, "I've never felt so helpless. He's probably angry with me for not being there for him. He's never gone more than a few hours without me. He must be so scared. I just want my Cole back."

She walked back to the counter and grabbed another mug, but she merely held it in both hands close to her chest as she gazed out the window. "Cole took his first steps right out in the driveway, right in the middle there next to the crack. He was so nervous, but he trusted me. He would fall and start crying, but then I was always there to pick him back up. He would give me the biggest smile and try over and over. He barely ever smiled too. I thought there was something wrong with him, never smiling you know, but now I think he was just busy trying to figure things out. Now he's all alone in the dark somewhere and I'm not there to pick him back up. I'm never going to see him smile again."

Sergeant Brady rubbed the stubble on his chin, trying to find the words. She was right of course. At this point the odds were pretty long.

"Tara don't…don't think like that. We don't have any leads yet but that certainly doesn't mean Cole has been harmed in any way." Sergeant Brady cut his hand through the air. "We've only just started looking and forensics haven't finished their bit. There's no sense carrying on with that talk. What Cole needs now is for you to get a solid night's sleep so you can hit it hard in the morning with the detective."

"Come on, Brady, be real with the kid," Daniels cut in, plopping Joshy down in his walker. "You know as well as I do that things ain't looking good. We've got nothing and she's clamming up whenever we push her too hard." Daniels raised his hands defensively as Sergeant Brady gave him a look that indicated he had better change his tone. "Now I'm not saying that she's a suspect or anything but I'm telling you she knows something. Doors locked, windows locked, not to mention this neighborhood doesn't have a stellar reputation. Somebody came in here, I'm telling you. She needs to come clean with who she knows or who she's protecting. Maybe she's got a pissed-off boyfriend or something. Do you even know who the kid's father-"

"Dammit boy that's enough!" Sergeant Brady leaped to his feet, his face flushing the same color as his mug. "You're-not-helping." He jabbed a finger into Daniels's chest with each word. "How is she supposed to keep a level head with talk like that, you hot-headed fool."

"She needs to hear it!" Daniels pushed back against Brady's finger. "The kid's gone and the friggin clock's ticking! The sooner she rolls on whatever friends she's trying to protect, the sooner we can track down the crack head responsible."

Sergeant Brady placed his mug down as slowly as he could, keeping his eyes locked on his partner. "Go."

"Go where?" Daniels asked, crossing his arms.

"Question the neighbors, wait in the car, I don't care. Just go before I reconsider your probationary status," Sergeant Brady responded in a quiet voice.

Daniels looked as if he was about to throw a punch, but seemed to think better of it. He cast a poisonous look at Tara's back and stepped towards the door. As he reached for the handle an empty mug smashed on the linoleum floor.

Thump-thump, thump-thump

With eyes as big as blooming lilies, Tara turned her head towards the stairs.

Thump-thump, thump-thump

A boy stood at the landing, one hand curled around the broken spindle. His little belly poked out from under his dinosaur t-shirt as he greeted the room with a smile.

"It's time for fruity peeeebels mommy!"

• • • •

Over the next week Tara's little apartment was swamped with neighbors, all demanding to see the boy with their own eyes and share their relief. Reporters stopped by to request information so they could write up their pieces. It's not every day that stories like this turn out with a positive ending. Tara had no new information to give them, however. Over and over she told them she was deeply disturbed by the whole ordeal and just wanted to move on. The reporters were tactful enough not to press the subject, and agreed to make it seem like Cole had just turned up in the middle of the night, which he had, sort of.

The local police department as well as the state detective were very curious as to how the boy could show up out of nowhere. They couldn't completely rule out Tara as a suspect. After all, who else could have provided a three-year-old with the means to disappear and reappear? There was some deliberation, which culminated in a shouting match between a red-faced Sergeant Brady and his command staff. All things considered, there was no proof of foul play so the investigation was closed, and Blossom Street shone just a tad brighter for a time.

With the reporters gone and the investigation finally over, Tara was able to get back to her normal life. She couldn't afford to take any more time off from work, so she took her neighbor up on her offer to watch her boys. The woman, who preferred to be called 'Nana Beth', had been retired for a few years and had all the time and attention in the world. Furthermore, Nana Beth was much cheaper than daycare, at the cost of a few nice cozy dinners a week, which she usually cooked for anyway. Nana Beth was sweet as could be and definitely had enough fire in her bones to protect the boys. The old woman was also unusually tall and impossibly strong. Groceries never took her more than one trip, and she shoveled the whole driveway by herself in the winters. There was a rumor that she had been a champion boxer in her youth, back when there were no women's leagues. It was only a rumor, but her towering frame and hard-as-nails attitude were enough to stop trouble before it started. More than one mischief maker in the neighborhood had felt her massive bony hands across their backside at one time or another. Even the teenagers straightened their backs and filtered their language around her. Still, despite how safe the boys were in Nana Beth's capable hands, Tara called every few hours just to be sure.

Several weeks had passed and the world had all but forgotten all about Tara and her lost boy, and that was just the way Tara preferred it. Nana Beth turned out to be a steadfast and reliable friend who was always good for a story or sagely advice. Things were indeed looking up for Tara's little family. Cole stayed within sight, and Joshy became more mobile by the day as his chubby legs began to find traction on the carpet.

While they didn't have time to visit very often, Sergeant Brady and Officer Daniels did make frequent passes down Blossom Street. Brady still felt a sense of custodial responsibility for the family while Daniels still didn't buy the whole 'look who just happened to turn up all on his own' story.

Officer Daniels's reservations were all the more vindicated when they were called back to Tara's apartment not six weeks after the incident, and again a month after that. Cole was making a habit of disappearing in the middle of the night. Each time he would vanish without a trace, only to be heard coming down the stairs a few days later with a soft *thump-thump*.

The neighbors, who were so helpful during the first occurrence, now turned their noses to Tara as if she was something revolting that a dog had dragged in. Headlines in the paper now read 'MOTHER LOSES CHILD IN OWN HOUSE…AGAIN!' and 'BLOSSOM STREET MOM TO LOSE CUSTODY AFTER THIRD OFFENSE'.

The case was reopened and a social worker was assigned to Tara's family. Brady and Daniels were reassigned since they were too closely involved with the first incident. The state detective and social worker both seemed hell bent on taking Joshy and Cole from her.

The small apartment had been scoured by forensics teams from the town, state, and even the FBI after the third occurrence. Cole had supervised visits with a pediatric psychologist a few times a week who, try as he might, couldn't get the boy to divulge anything regarding his little adventures. None of it made sense. The landlord installed top-notch child-proof fittings on every window and exterior door. Questioning the boy amounted to nothing, just as each thorough search of the apartment. Only one explanation remained; Tara must have something to do with it.

Tara was charged with criminal negligence and child endangerment. Her saving grace was a firm testimony given by Nana Beth, as well as Sergeant Brady pulling every string he could in the department. As a result, Tara retained custody of Cole and Joshy, but was placed on a suspended status until both boys were adults. The social worker visited twice a week thenceforth, and if Tara so much as missed a doctor's appointment the state would take her children for good.

Nana Beth was a saint throughout the whole ordeal. When the world turned against Tara, the old matron was as resolute as ever. Reporters ceased all visits after Nana Beth heard them bringing Tara to tears with their rapid-fire loaded questions. Without warning the old woman swooped down on one reporter like some ancient bird of prey. After a black eye and losing a very expensive camera, Channel 7 decided to pursue stories that were more financially practical, leaving Tara to raise her boys in relative peace.

Chapter 2

Breaking Point

"Cole wake up. Lights. Cole, I want lights please."

"There are no lights, Joshy. The sun's up. There's your light," Cole mumbled from under his blankets. "Go back to bed, Joshy. Wait, what time-aww Joshy come on! Why do you have to wake me up five minutes before mom does? I want to sleep!"

"Sorry," Joshy said plainly.

Huffing, Cole whipped his blankets off and jumped out of bed. He walked over to his door as if to leave the room but instead rapped the wood with his knuckles. "Mom! Mom we're up, can you let us out now? I have to pee."

A moment later, shuffling footsteps came from the creaky stairs, followed by the clacking of a latch being undone.

"Good morning boys. How'd we -whoa Cole, where's the fire?" She raised an arm as Cole darted under it, sprinting for the bathroom. "At least he's *here* this morning. How'd you sleep, Joshy? Did you see Cole come in last night?"

Joshy sat up and laughed, "Lights, ha ha ha!"

"The lights again huh? What color were they this time?" Tara asked, snatching up a rogue sock.

Joshy gave her a blank stare and shrugged, "I dunno."

"Well you're a big help aren't you?" Tara chided with a hand on her hip. "Why don't you come down to breakfast and we can talk to Cole about these lights. You keep bringing them up when Cole goes away."

Cole was now ten years old and the disappearances had returned, this time far worse than when he was a toddler. His vanishings now happened as much as twice a week in the last month alone. The school principal questioned Tara on her son's truancy and made several threats, which he had yet to follow up on. Tara ran through every excuse in the book; stomach bug, night terrors, common cold, chickenpox, just to name a few. Tara nearly called the police when it first started happening again, but after Cole reappeared in his room hours later, she knew what she was in for.

Aside from his vanishing acts, Cole had grown up to be as normal as any kid his age, though his teachers would say he was too rough at recess. Before Cole's most recent bout of vanishings, the principal would call to scold Tara for Cole's behavior, stating that he seemed to find his way into every scuffle in the school. The reason was always the same. Cole was very protective of his younger brother.

It wasn't until the first grade that Cole began to realize his brother was not like the other kids, right around the age when children are first capable of cruelty. Joshy was born with low-functioning Down Syndrome. During preschool and kindergarten Joshua's mental handicaps were not so prevalent. The other kids thought no differently of him. However, it became more and more apparent every year that Joshy was not keeping pace with his friends' mental and social developments.

Coming home from school one day, Cole asked his mother what an orangutan was. Not thinking anything of it, Tara replied, "An orangutan is an orange monkey that lives in the jungle. Are you learning about jungle animals in school?"

Cole frowned and fidgeted with his coat's zipper, "No. Mommy the kids in my class said Joshy looked like an orangutan. Why would they say that, Mommy? Is it because Joshy has orange hair like an orangutan?"

Tara always tried to be strong in front of her boys and would never let them see her cry, but this was too much. Wiping off the tears she crouched down and gently grasped Cole's shoulders. "Colton, Joshy is… different. Joshy is never going to be as big or smart as you or the other kids in class. To us, Joshy is just Joshy. But to everyone else Joshy looks and acts different. There are lots of awful people out there, Colton, and they're going to be mean to Joshy and try to hurt him. That's just the way the world is. You need to be a good big brother and protect him. Will you protect Joshy from the mean people?"

The then seven-year-old Cole took these words to heart, and from that day onward he became Joshua's sworn guardian in the halls and at recess. Unfortunately this meant Cole frequented the principal's office with a bruised face and raw knuckles as Joshua's bullies got more creative and specific with their remarks.

Downstairs, the now ten-year-old Cole was pouring himself a bowl of Fruity Pebbles. Sucking on the inside of her lip, Tara dragged a chair right over to her oldest son and sat next to him. "So Colton, do you know what day it is?"

Cole didn't look up from the puzzle on the back of the cereal box. "Friday," he replied in between bites.

"No Cole, it's Monday," Tara's voice was low, though Cole could sense her anger rising. "You've missed a day of school and been gone all weekend. Any idea where you were this time?"

"No idea." Cole looked up from his puzzle and squinted. "Had a dream about whales though. They were flying and singing to me. I got to ride one."

Tara's eyes shot to the ceiling, as though praying for patience. "Colton you were gone for over three days this time. You know what's going to happen if someone finds out you were missing, right?" Cole buried his face in his cereal. "You and Joshy will be taken by the state and you'll go off to a foster home and I'll be put in jail. Is that what you want?"

"Mom it's not my fault!" Cole pleaded. "I really don't know where I go. I don't remember anything and it's not my fault, no matter what you say." He sniffed, willing his tears to stay put. "I don't want to go away. Can't we just tell people I was sleeping at Nana Beth's?"

Clearly unimpressed, Tara cocked her head and looked down at her son. "After school you and I are going to have a talk. I don't care how long it takes. You're going to sit there and try until you remember something. No TV or video games until you remember something." Tara crossed her arms and gave Cole a glare only mothers are capable of.

"How are you going to punish me for something that I can't even control? I didn't do anything wrong. I haven't gotten into any fights in a while and I've been doing my chores," Cole bargained. The video games were a low blow in his eyes.

Tara swept across the kitchen and straightened out Joshua's outfit. "No, pull your pants up. Up I said. No not that high. C'mon Joshy you look like an old man with high-waters. There you go, now have a seat while mommy gets you some cereal." She stomped to the cabinet and set to Joshua's breakfast. "Relax Cole, it's just a talk, not torture. Spyro will be there when we're finished. You've been on those video games too much lately anyway." She ignored Cole's moans as she poured Joshua's cereal. "This affects everyone in the house and it's been getting worse. If we can't figure something out we're going back to the therapist."

Cole knew it was an idle threat. The last trip to Doctor Garvey had been risky to say the least. He'd kept asking Tara weird questions when she brought up the 'sleepwalking'. She had seemed to forget to mention he had been missing for forty hours at a time. When Doctor Garvey had started talking about the safety of her children, Tara had quickly changed the subject to an innocent case of nightmares.

Cole stomped out of the house, weighed down by his backpack and foul mood as he led his brother to the bus stop. Tara's talks were dreadful at best. She wouldn't take no for an answer and never seemed to run out of questions. His mood lightened somewhat when the bus arrived. Ashley was on this bus and she always saved him a seat.

"Hey Cole! Good morning Joshy. I saved you a seat right next to me, Cole." Ashley shuffled her bag under her seat to make room, slapping the vinyl seat next to her.

"What's up, Ashley? Did you do anything fun this -hey Joshy, no Joshy, you sit here next to us." Cole put a hand on Joshua's shoulder, stopping him.

"Sorry, ha ha ha!" Joshua's laughter filled the bus, halting conversations and drawing amused looks.

Joshy frequently tried to sit in the back of the bus. Cole knew it was because that's where the cool older kids sat and Joshy wanted to be one of them. Unfortunately, the cool older kids were also the mean older kids, and Cole had to protect his little brother from them.

"Where were you on Friday?" Ashley asked, scrunching her nose. "I had to sit all by myself. Were you sick again? You get sick a lot you know."

"Yeah I had the uh… ear infection. So, did you do anything fun this weekend, Ashley?" Cole asked, ignoring the laughter coming from the back of the bus.

Ashley leaned back over her seat and fixed Joshua's hat, which was tilted in such a way that drew even more attention to his grinning face. "There Joshy, now you look cool too. Um, yeah my parents brought me and Sarah down into Boston to the aquarium on Saturday. Cole It was so cool! There were cute little penguins that you could throw food to and there were sharks as big as a car and stingrays with pointy stingers." Her curled fingers shot up to her lips as her eyes looked past him. "The deep sea exhibit was scary though, I didn't like that part. All the deep sea fish look like monsters. What about you, did you do anything fun?"

Cole fidgeted with the zipper on his jacket. He didn't know what he had done this weekend. He wanted to tell Ashley about the whales from his dreams but that didn't seem as exciting as a day out in Boston, not to mention it would probably get him in loads of trouble. He wasn't supposed to talk about his vanishings. "My mom was working all weekend so I had to watch Joshy. Pretty boring weekend for me."

"Aww Cole you're so *cute* the way you take care of Joshy." Ashley smiled. "Really though, I think it's very responsible of you. Isn't your big brother just the best, Joshy?"

"Yah, ha ha ha!" Joshy giggled.

Cole could feel his chest swelling with pride. He liked Ashley, he knew that for a fact. She was the prettiest girl he knew, and she had a way of making him feel like he was more than the poor loser with the retarded little brother. *And* she said he was cute. If only he knew how to ask a girl out.

"Thanks, Ashley." Cole grinned sheepishly. "I guess I am a good brother. It bothers me sometimes though, having to take care of Joshy all the time. I want to go out and make friends. I want to go to aquariums and stuff…*with you*," said Cole, saying the last part in his head.

Ashley listened, eyes drooping with concern. Her eyes suddenly lit up as she smiled and punched Cole in the arm. "Well Cole thanks for *not* noticing, but you have a friend right here next to you! I can be your friend outside of the bus too. Next weekend we are going back to Boston to check out the museum of science. It's supposed to be amazing! They have a big lightning machine that shoots lightning all over this room and you're only protected by a metal fence. You should ask your mom if it's ok."

Cole could hardly believe what he was hearing. He let her words sink in for a moment before the bus hit a large bump that lifted everyone from their seats.

"Hey Joshy! Hey buddy where'd you get that hat?"

Mark Sullivan, a sixth grader with the loudest, dumbest laugh Cole had ever heard was waving to Joshy amongst his nearly equally loud and dumb friends. Joshy stood up, actually shorter than sitting, took off his hat and waved it back and forth as if it was on fire.

Mark and his friends exploded with laughter. They did this almost every day. Joshy was an eager source of entertainment for them and they also took pleasure in goading Cole, a two-for-one deal. Cole could feel his face getting hot as he clenched his fists.

"Joshy sit back down!" Cole shouted. "I said sit down Joshy, those guys are trying to make you look dumb." Cole grabbed his brother's arm and wrestled him back into his seat.

"C'maan Cole! That's my friend," Joshy protested, cramming his hat back on, crooked of course.

"They are not your friends! Those kids are making fun of you, and I'm really getting sick of it..." Cole trailed off, taking a step towards the back of the bus.

"Cole don't, you'll get in trouble," Ashley pleaded, grasping at Cole's sleeve, "And there's like, four of them and they're huge!"

"Hey Cole, that's a sweet jacket, man," Mark called out. "Where'd you and Joshy pick out your threads, the thrift shop on main street?" Mark laughed his high-pitched machine-gun laugh. "You know you're not supposed to buy *all* your clothes there, that place is only for Halloween costumes. At least you'll be all set for Halloween, right? You can go as a poor person."

The hot anger in Cole's cheeks curdled into shame as the sixth graders howled with laughter, waxing on not so eloquently about the state of his and Joshua's clothes. Tears dripped from the corners of his eyes as he sat down next to Joshy and buried his face in the collar of his second-hand coat. Joshy looked confused at his big brother's behavior.

"What's wrong Cole? You sad? You cry?" Joshy poked his big brother with his little fingers. "I know, I help. Joshy protect you, Cole."

Joshy wrapped his arms as far as he could around Cole, who shrugged him off. Joshy was not supposed to see him cry. *Ashley* was *certainly* not supposed to see him cry.

Cole wouldn't speak to Ashley the rest of the way to school, despite her best efforts to console him. He was too ashamed, and those kids were right anyway. He didn't want to be seen in his lame clothes while everyone else strutted around in nice jeans and polos from the mall. He twisted his stupid jacket in his hands, wishing he could tear all his clothes off. When the bus arrived Cole hurried off, dragging his little brother behind him before Mark and his friends could find something else to laugh at.

Even though the day started off rough for Cole, he was back to normal by mid-morning. Unlike most ten-year-old boys, Cole enjoyed school. Maybe not the lessons and curriculum, but the atmosphere had a certain appeal Cole couldn't find anywhere else. Here, during group projects and recess, it was like having friends. Because of Cole's history he lived a fairly sheltered life. As he grew older he began to suspect that his mother kept him from getting too close with anyone because then they might find out about his problem. He understood, but it was no easier a pill to swallow. The other kids were always talking about the fun stuff they had done after school. Cole had no such stories to share.

The morning was a breeze for Cole. Fortunately, Mrs. Cutler put on a movie first thing, which gave him some time to dry his eyes and collect himself. By the end of the movie he had all but forgotten about stupid Mark Sullivan. During morning recess Ashley found Cole and let him know just how stupid she thought Mark Sullivan was, and she just so happened to like his jacket. As usual, Ashley had a way of making Cole think he was something more, someone bigger than himself. She then officially invited him to join her family on their trip to the museum of science this weekend.

Cole was a little less attentive the rest of the day. The prospect of an entire day with Ashley set a flock of butterflies dancing about in his belly. Was it a date? Would they be boyfriend and girlfriend after this? No, probably not, but maybe someday.

Mrs. Cutler was droning on about something to do with how the American government had borrowed money from France, and that put Cole's thoughts on the topic of money itself. He would need some new clothes if he was to be seen in Boston, and some money for lunch, and some more for a ticket. He had never asked his mom for money since she was always complaining about how they were broke. Cole sank lower in his chair as his hopes sank somewhere down around his shoes.

On the bus ride home Ashley couldn't stop talking about their weekend plans. Cole put on a smile and feigned interest, not allowing himself to believe it could really happen.

"Oh, and Joshy can come too," Ashley said, fixing Joshua's hat again.

Cole stumbled, searching for words, "Yeah, um, Joshy doesn't like crowds and the last time he was on the train he threw up. I'll ask my mom but she might not let him go." Cole cast a sideways glance at his brother, who laughed absentmindedly.

Truthfully, Joshy would probably love the museum of science, but this meant his trip just got twice as expensive.

"So did you end up getting a lot of homework today?" Cole asked. "I hate it when Mrs. Cutler gives us homework. If I'm doing school work I feel like it should be at school. I've got better things to do with my time."

Ashley picked up her legs and tucked them crossways so she was sitting on her feet. Cole picked up his legs too. "Not too much. Just some reading and one sheet of math. I'll probably do it before basketball practice. You should try out for basketball, Cole. You're kind of tall, and I've seen how quick you are at recess. Are you too busy after school or something?"

Cole sat up as tall as he could in his seat. "Um, no not really. I mean Joshy needs to be watched until my mom gets home from work but nowadays he pretty much looks after himself. I've seen him watch the Spanish channel on mute for a couple hours once. I guess I could find some time for sports. When's the next tryouts? Baseball and soccer in the spring right?"

"Oh yeah you should do baseball!" Ashley said, bouncing in her seat. "I love going to my dad's softball games. And you'd probably play at the park by my house. I could come watch!"

Cole swallowed, a bit dumbstruck by the idea. The way she looked into his eyes made him feel again like he was ten feet tall. She could have suggested he try out for bull-riding and he would have asked his mom for cowboy boots tomorrow. It was decided. Cole would become a baseball player.

The bus screeched to a halt at the end of Blossom Street. Cole grabbed his bag and made to get up but he bumped into a very stiff shoulder. Mark Sullivan and his friends were getting off here? This wasn't their stop. Frowning, Cole tapped Joshy on the shoulder, who seemed to be distracted by a man he recognized coming out of the corner store.

"C'mon Joshy, stop waving, you don't even know that guy," said Cole in a loud whisper. His breath caught in his throat as he noticed someone missing from her seat. Ashley was almost off the bus. He felt he should say something to her. "Bye, Ashley. Good luck with your… your practice tonight." Stupid. She didn't need luck with a practice.

Ashley didn't seem to notice his blunder. "Bye Cole! Don't be sick tomorrow and make me ride alone okay?"

Positive that Mark Sullivan and his gang were waiting for them, Cole grabbed Joshy by the arm and muscled his way through the group. He wanted to get out of there before they had a chance to really get going on him.

"Where are you going Cole? The thrift shop is back that way," Mark called out with his signature rapid-fire laughter.

"Let's go, Joshy." Cole yanked on his brother's arm. Joshy seemed to want to join in on whatever the sixth graders were laughing about.

"Oh, I know!" Mark continued. "You guys must be headed to the circus. Little Joshy is performing tonight right?"

Cole walked faster, or as fast as Joshua's small legs could go. To his dismay, the jerks were now following them, and their long legs had no problem keeping up.

"Steve, give me that. Joshy, hey Joshy, I know you love these. You want one buddy?" Cole jerked his head around to see Mark produce a banana and start dancing around. Like a monkey.

"C'mon Joshy don't you want the tasty banana?" asked Mark, who was now on all fours and hopping sideways.

Joshy, who was very good at imitating people, started making monkey noises and waving his arms around. Thinking he was a part of the fun, he laughed and contorted his face into the most ridiculous shapes.

"JOSHY NO!" Cole bellowed, "Stop that right now! I'll tell mom you're acting up and you'll be in big trouble. Let's go, now!"

"C'maan Cole!" Joshy started crying now. Cole was twisting his arm in frustration. "That's my friend!"

"Ha-ha-ha-ha," Mark could barely get the words out, "Steve you're right, the little retard looks just like a monkey."

"Joshy they are *not* your friends!" Cole barked over Joshua's obnoxious sobs. "They're making fun of you, don't you understand? Come on!"

Cole only made the situation worse as Joshy broke down into a full-blown tantrum, showing his true mental age of a four-year-old. He flopped on the ground and cried as if being flayed alive. Joshua's tantrums were rare, but very embarrassing for even the passerby. Mark and his friends however were indulging in the pitiful sight.

Cole couldn't hear what they were saying now as the cacophony coming from his brother drowned out their jibes. He didn't really care at this point. He just wanted to get Joshy up and home as quickly as possible. He would carry him if he had to, but he didn't want to resort to that just yet.

Sour guilt coated the inside of Cole's mouth. He didn't need to be so harsh. He took a deep breath and calmed himself. Joshy would only get worse if he was wound up too. "Joshy, I'm sorry for yelling." Cole started rubbing his back gently. "I was being mean, Joshy, I'm sorry for yelling at you. Cole was being bad. Can we go home now?"

"Don't-yell-at-me," Joshy squeaked in between sobs.

"Okay Joshy, I'm sorry all right," Cole said in a gentle tone. "Let's get you up." Cole grabbed Joshy under the armpits and hoisted him to his feet.

SMACK

A broken banana landed at Joshua's feet just as he planted them on the sidewalk. Joshy stopped crying altogether and rubbed his face, confused. Chunks of mashed banana adorned Joshua's hair and face as a thin line of blood crawled down from his lower lip. Mark and his friends doubled over with renewed howls of laughter. Joshy bent down and picked up the remains of the banana and offered it to Mark, as if it had been simply dropped by accident.

The sixth graders were laughing too hard to notice Joshy, who had turned around and said something to Cole. Cole didn't hear what it was, however. A loud ringing accompanied by the accelerating drum of his heart filled his ears. Before he knew it he was walking directly towards Mark, who was laughing too hard to see him coming.

• • • •

"Tara I'm telling you I've never seen anything of the sort. Carrying on like a bunch of animals over a scrap. Heavens, even *my* boys… and Colton! Your son has a temper in him, Tara. He was so blind with it he couldn't even tell I was there, let alone three other boys twice his size walloping him. If I wasn't putting the trash out I guarantee Colton would have ended up in the hospital too." Nana Beth bobbed slightly on her toes as she held a crying Joshy, patting his back. "Shush now Joshua, Shush now," she cooed in a sweet tone. "We're all right sweetheart, we're all right."

Tara slammed the front door, dragging Cole into the kitchen by the collar of his coat. Sulking, Cole wiped the tears from his face and opened his mouth.

"Colton Carter, I don't want to hear it!" Tara roared, looming over him. "You put yourself *and* your little brother in danger! Real danger! How can I trust you when you pull stuff like this? If Nana Beth hadn't been there those boys would have killed the both of you. And that one kid is now in the hospital! What did you do to him?"

Fumbling with his zipper, Cole looked at the floor. "I…I don't remember."

"Oh, 'I don't remember'," Tara laughed maniacally. "The famous words of Colton Carter, 'I don't remember'. We'll see what you remember when the kid's parents have the cops showing up at our door because you hurt their son. Are you trying to get you and your brother thrown in foster care? We have no more strikes, Colton. If we have even a little hiccup this family will be torn apart. What were you thinking?" Her voice broke and tears welled in her eyes.

Cole winced as his mother's words fell like hammer blows. He hadn't thought about getting in trouble with the court. "They were making fun of Joshy because he has Down Syndrome, calling him a monkey and a retard. Then Mark Sullivan threw a banana and it hit Joshy in the face and hurt him. I got mad and I fought them. I'm sorry."

Tara seemed to deflate as she looked over at Joshy, who was now in the living room being serenaded by Nana Beth.

"Are you ok?" she asked, brushing Cole's hair aside and inspecting his face. "They got you pretty good on the nose, and your ear."

"My hand hurts the most. I think I punched Mark in the head. Ouch!" Cole cried out as Tara took his puffy appendage in her tender hands.

"Dammit Cole, that looks broken," Tara hissed as she ran her fingertips over his swollen flesh. "Looks like you're going to the hospital after all. I have to go call out of work. I hope Danni can cover for me. We'll put some ice on it till we get there."

Tara cracked some ice cubes out of the tray, and a plastic bag from the drawer. Cole took the ice pack and nursed his injured hand while his mother called in to work. His hand hurt pretty badly. He could feel his heartbeat inside it, each pump sending a spike of pain up his arm.

Cole made his way into the living room to see how Joshy was doing. A shaft of golden light from the setting sun blinded him momentarily as he passed the front window. Nana Beth was cradling a snoozing Joshy in her vast arms. It was funny, Cole thought, how just five minutes ago those arms were easily managing a street brawl, and now they were rocking Joshy to sleep.

"Busted hand huh?" Nana Beth must have been listening while she was singing Joshy to sleep. She usually heard everything within a mile. "Never punch someone in the face without gloves on. If you're that close, use an elbow or go for a choke."

Cole was taken aback. He had expected a good telling off from his pseudo grandmother. And what did she know about fighting?

Nana Beth laughed at Cole's bemusement. "What, didn't think Nana Beth knew how to fight? I've been in my fair share of rumbles before even your mom was born. You need to keep your hand above your heart by the way. The swelling's getting worse."

Holding gently onto the ice, Cole lifted his hand up as instructed. The pain was getting much worse now and he couldn't move his two littlest fingers at all. Through his teeth, Cole asked, "Nana Beth, where'd you learn how to fight? You're really good for…for someone your age."

"Oh on these streets of course, but your hand will be the size of a basketball before I could finish half the stories." Nana Beth laughed again. Cole liked her laugh. Her talking voice was deep but it went really high when she was laughing or singing. "You know, there's no shame in what you did, Colton. I saw the whole thing. I could have stopped it sooner, and I probably should have, mind you, but I wanted to give you a chance to show those boys what you were made of."

Cole managed a small smile through the growing pain in his hand. "Really? But what about the police? What if Mark is really hurt and they come to arrest me?"

"No one is getting arrested today, Colton. I know Mark Sullivan's parents and when he wakes up in the hospital his father will knock him out again for what he did. I'll have a talk with Randy and Patty tomorrow and make sure we're all on the same page. Tormenting a person without the mental capacity to defend himself is a low thing. Those boys deserve worse than the bruising we gave them. Maybe not a K-O punch, however." Nana Beth finished with a wink.

A stuttering laugh escaped Cole's lips, which were now turning a bit pale. At Nana Beth's instruction, he lay on the couch next to her with his legs and hand elevated.

"They make fun of me and Joshy every day," said Cole, staring at the ceiling. "Every day it's something. Either my clothes, or Joshy, or how I have no friends. I can't take it anymore." Cole shook his head as tears flowed from the corners of his eyes and tickled his ears.

Nana Beth ran her fingers through Cole's damp hair. "Trust me Colton, these aren't the only bullies that life's going to throw at you, and that's a Nana Beth Guarantee. Most will be bigger than you, some may even be smaller. Some will even be your best friend after you square up. Everyone has their breaking points and today you hit yours. You won't hear me say that you did wrong by standing up to them. Do you know where bullies get their power from?"

Cole thought for a moment. "They are big, and have stupid friends."

"Very true, very true," Nana Beth replied, tapping her fingers on a sleeping Joshy. "But that's not where they get their power from. Marcus Sullivan relies on you and others like you for his power."

"But...but how? I didn't give that jerk-," Cole stammered.

Nana Beth flicked Cole on the forehead, silencing him. "You gave him something if I say you did. Bullies get their strength from the people they torture. You gave Marcus Sullivan power and influence because you gave parts of yourself to him. You gave him your anger, your shame, your impatience, and he used these parts against you. When he gets a rise out of you, Marcus and his friends have a good laugh and then they all join in. The bully grows stronger. People will even give bullies their fear, which makes them the strongest."

Cole scowled, ashamed at the truth in Nana Beth's words. He dismissed them, however. At the moment he was too angry to say something nice.

"It's okay, Colton. No need to think on it overmuch right now. You'll understand when you're a bit older and wiser like me." She paused as Tara wrapped up her conversation on the phone.

"Danni can't cover for me but Chelsea doesn't mind working a double," said Tara as she threw her Jacket on. "All right Rocky Balboa, let's get you to the doctor's."

CHAPTER 3

TIME TRAVEL

As Nana Beth had predicted, the police did not call at Tara's apartment. Once Mark Sullivan had recovered from his mild concussion, he and his gang seemed to think that Cole had enough going on with his broken hand. In fact, they never bothered him or Joshy again after their sidewalk brawl. Cole had several more disappearances over the next few months, though his broken hand made for a good excuse as he needed a few surgeries to fix it.

Eventually Cole's hand healed up and he hadn't experienced a single disappearance in several years, though his bad luck with injuries had only just begun. The following year he broke his leg while trying skateboarding. A couple years after that, the same leg cracked under the pressure of learning how to ride Nana Beth's old dirt bike. The next year was even worse as he broke his hand on a machine in shop class, only to break his collarbone a month later during a sledding accident.

Cole's injuries, while not life-threatening, were certainly life-altering. All those months of recovery weakened him to the point where he was useless for most physical activities. He was almost always cut first from tryouts. The sports themselves didn't matter to Cole as much as the missed opportunities to make friends and be a part of something. The popular kids all played sports, not to mention they had no problem getting girlfriends.

Aside from his bad luck, another constant in Cole's formative years was Ashley. Besides Joshy, she was the closest thing Cole had to a friend. The two could be found playing video games on weeknights or seeing how fast Cole's wheelchair could go through the halls at school. She meant more to him than Cole would admit, though he never could pluck up the courage to tell her how he felt. Years passed and Ashley began to make new friends, and she eventually fell in with the popular kids. Every year she seemed to have less and less time for playdates and trips to the Museum of Science.

Cole would find himself pushed out of social circles more often than not, which resulted in cries for attention that landed him in the principal's office at least once a month. Tara would have to listen to the staff's complaints about Cole dropping stink bombs, going over the intercom and saying vulgar things, or throwing snowballs at the principal herself. To Tara, the offenses were highly embarrassing and drew entirely too much attention to their family. To Cole, the stunts were a way for him to get a quick laugh and some recognition from the kids at school. The punishment seemed worth it if it meant someone would strike up a conversation with him in the hallway afterwards.

As Cole entered high school the pranks had lost their appeal, as the school was so large that even the popular kids he'd grown up with didn't give him much notice. Ashley stopped taking the bus and started riding to school with other guys. Cole had picked up a few friends by now, though they never seemed to remember him when someone threw a party. If popularity were measured by how fast you could beat a video game, Cole would be prom king for sure. All of this was about to change, however, because today was basketball tryouts.

Cole had been training all month for this day, shooting hoops at the YMCA, running the track, and watching basketball on TV, which bored him nearly to death on several occasions. This was it though, it had to be. This was his final chance to get out there and make some real friends and be a part of something. He had the sense not to go for varsity, but he was a senior now and pretty tall for junior varsity. Besides, he saw a JV game last year and they didn't look all that amazing. He had been sinking shot after shot no problem at the Y.

Cole entered the locker room feeling very out of place, but determined. He found an empty spot in the corner and began to change into his gym clothes.

"My dad says I'm good enough for varsity," said a tall redheaded boy Cole recognized as a freshman. "It's a shame they're making me try out for JV. At least I'll look pretty damn good this season next to all the midgets."

"I just hope they don't hold three cuts again," said an equally tall black boy who looked like he could play for a state university. "Last year they smoked us for all three cuts until they weeded out all the failures. You wouldn't believe how bad some of those kids were. It's like they'd never touched a ball before."

Cole inched farther down the bench, hoping he wouldn't be recognized. He had never made it past first cut and from what he heard, each round was more grueling than the last. He knew this time would be different though, there's no way these guys trained as hard as he did. Cole left the locker room and joined the rest of the crowd on the court. Mimicking the others, he began stretching.

"All right all right gents, listen up!" Coach Connelly shouted. He was a barrel-chested man and carried a megaphone, but his voice was so loud he seemed not to need it. "Go ahead and start running laps. Watch out for the bleachers in the back corner, they're stuck open at the moment."

The whistle blew and the crowd dispersed to the perimeter of the court, forming a rectangular train of testosterone and squeaking shoes. Cole sprinted ahead, trying to pass as many people as possible. One lap, no problem. Two laps, too easy. On the third lap Cole was no longer passing anyone. By the fifth, he was now the one being passed. He could barely catch his breath as a cramp stabbed at his stomach.

"Control your breathing, dude," said a short chubby kid who was slowly passing him.

The only way Cole could have caught his breath would have been to start walking, which was out of the question. He would be first cut for sure if the coach saw that. Where was the coach anyway? Shouldn't he be watching this part? Cole lost track of the laps as well as time. After what seemed like an hour, Coach Connelly returned to the gym as the door slammed behind him, echoing throughout the gym. The whistle blared again.

"Now that you're all warmed up, I want you to line up against the back wall there and get ready for jump drills." Coach looked around at the group as they began to migrate towards the back wall. Cole couldn't help but notice Coach's gaze fall on him. "Some of you need to do a bit more running. Running is half of what you do during a game. A twenty-minute jog ain't nothing compared to four quarters against a team like Pinkerton."

Hot shame flood Cole's already sweaty face. Twenty minutes! He could have sworn they had been running for at least twice as long. The next event should have gone much better since he had been practicing wall jumps too, though not after a twenty-minute run. Cole had to stop several times to catch his breath and wait for the burning in his calves to subside. Coach was definitely watching this one. The next event was-.

"Suicides! You know 'em and we all love 'em," Coach Connelly barked. "Give me ten lines at the end of the court. Ready!"

The tryouts wore on for what felt like hours. After suicide-sprints, it was all Cole could do to keep himself upright. His training at the YMCA seemed childish. Even when it was time to shoot a ball he missed every time. When the final whistle blew he would have cried in relief if he had the breath.

"That's enough, gents, that's good for tonight," Coach Connelly's voice rebounded throughout the court. "Put the balls back in the rack and stack the cones up by the door please. And I'll need two of you to hit this floor with a mop before you all go."

Was that it? How would they know if they made first cut or not? Coach Connelly didn't even know his name and it's not like there was a sign-in roster. Confused, Cole placed a ball back in the rack and made a beeline for the man with the whistle.

"Um, excuse me. Coach Connelly, can I ask you something?" Cole said, suddenly noticing how soft his voice sounded.

"Sure, sure. What's up?" Coach asked, punching the squealing megahorn into submission.

"I was just wondering how we, uh, I mean how will I know if I made the first cut? You usually tell us on the first night..." Cole's voice trailed off at the end as he felt Coach Connelly's eyes examine him from head to toe.

It was as if Coach could sense Cole's lack of confidence. He took a step closer and put a heavy hand on Cole's shoulder. "You've tried out every damn year for the last four years and you've never made first cut. Yeah, I remember you. That right there says something about a person.

The fact that you get back on that horse and keep giving it everything you've got shows some spine. I wish my team last year had half the dedication you have. Tell you what, rest up and make sure you hydrate over the next couple days. I have a good feeling that you're gonna make the first cut this year."

Pride, something he was not used to feeling, blossomed in Cole's chest. This could be it! This could be his ticket to friends, parties, meetups, and hopefully a girlfriend. Tired and sore as he was, Cole could barely sleep that night as he fantasized about his new life. When his dreams eventually came for him, he greeted them with a sleepy smile on his face.

A gentle nudging roused Cole the next morning. "Cole hon, wake up. It's quarter to six already and if you miss the bus today you're walking," Tara's voice swam into Cole's mind as though from another world.

Cole stirred, feeling as if his brain were stuck in mud. Tryouts took more out of him than he thought they would. His legs seemed to be filled with rusty splinters. A groan escaped his drooling lips as he forced himself upright. But the prospect of walking to school was motivation enough to take his mother's threat seriously.

"Cole honey, you look awful. And why didn't you come say hi when you got in last night? I didn't even know you were home. You weren't up all night playing video games again were you?" Tara asked as she fixed Joshua's pants. "Dammit Joshy why do you pull them up so high? Look at your belly button, see that? Put your belt right below your belly button."

"No, I crashed right after I got in. I don't even remember hitting the bed. Coach told me- ouch!" Cole gasped as he burned his finger pulling a pastry out of the toaster. His head was still foggy with sleep. "Coach said he thinks I'll make first cut. I find out at lunch today when they post the list."

"Cole that's so great!" Tara chirped, quickly sipping her coffee. "I knew you'd do well this year. See, all that hard work you've been putting in is paying off. When's the tryouts for the second cut?"

"Tonight," Cole groaned through a mouthful of pastry. "I'm so banged up from last night though. My legs barely work. I don't know if I'll have it in me to survive tonight's tryouts even if I do make first cut. Can I have some coffee? I feel like I could pass out."

Tara gave Cole a suspicious look. Cole never drank coffee. "Yeah sure, I've got a little left in the pot. I wouldn't worry about tonight, I know you'll do fine after you loosen your legs up. And Coach Connelly sounds like a good guy. If he says you're gonna make first cut then you're gonna make first cut. Oh I can't wait to go to your games!"

Cole smiled as he allowed himself to indulge in the idea of him playing a real game. "Mom, I wouldn't get all excited yet. There's still a third cut and a lot of these kids have been playing their whole lives. This one kid had to have been six-four, and he's only a freshman!"

"I know you're gonna make it this year, Colton. Call it 'mother's intuition'." Tara set her coffee down and started fussing over Cole's bed-head. "You need a haircut there shaggy. And you better run a comb through this before you head out. No one wants a slob on their team, especially when you have to wear an actual shirt and tie on game days. Maybe it's time to retire this old hoodie?"

Cole shooed away his mother's fingers as she picked and combed through his messy hair. He liked his old hoodie. He would never admit it, but having long messy hair was something the popular kids did, so Cole's hair would be long and messy as well. Scowling, he pulled his hood over his head and yanked on the strings until only his nose poked out.

"Oh stop it! What, am I embarrassing you? Oh I forgot, it's cool for teenage boys to look like teenage girls nowadays," Tara gave her son a playful slap on the back of his head.

"Watch it old lady. What do you know about cool anyway? You're what fifty now? When you were my age all the guys had girl's hair and wore makeup for crying out loud. Hey!" Cole laughed as Tara's hands made a loud *thwap thwap* on either side of his head. He pulled his hood off so he could see the next blow coming.

"Excuse me, you little punk!" Tara exclaimed as she loomed over Cole. She was barely taller than he was sitting in his chair, but like all moms she had the ability to appear eight feet tall when necessary. "I'm a thirty-four-year-old bartender at a nightclub. I'm pretty sure I've got a decent idea of what all the cool kids are doing these days.

Besides, you've never seen the way the light hits Brett Michaels on stage, and behind the stage." Tara's eyes shifted focus as she had clearly just left the kitchen for a moment.

"And that's my cue to leave," Cole snapped from his chair and grabbed his and Joshua's coats. "You ready Bud?"

"Yahah! Cut your hair Cole!" Joshy giggled as he reached up and shook his hand through his brother's very cool hair.

"C'mon Joshy I'm good, I'm good. Here, throw your coat on and let's get going. Mom's right, you look like an old man with your pants up so high." Cole tugged Joshua's pants down to an acceptable level, knowing full well they would go right back up to his chest as soon as they started walking.

"Bye, boys. Joshy be nice to your friends today, I don't want another call about you being mean to Kyle." Like every morning, Tara hugged and kissed both her boys goodbye. Her arms squeezed Cole a bit longer this morning as she whispered in his ear, "I know you can do it. Go show them."

By the time Cole and Joshy arrived at the bus stop his legs did feel better, though he found that throughout the day he couldn't get up from a chair without a moan slipping through his gritted teeth. He gave Joshy a pat on the back as he dropped him off at the special education classroom and rushed to his first class. If he was lucky he might catch Ashley in the halls, but his legs seemed determined to hold him back. To his fiery annoyance, Cole had somehow managed to make a wrong turn and lost several precious minutes. The early morning fog was still thick in his mind. The bell rang a full minute before Cole walked into Mrs. Webster's class.

"You know you are not getting another freebee today Mr. Carter." Mrs. Webster's stout figure stood at the front of the class, who were all in their seats and now looking at him. "Attendance is *ten percent* of your grade. All you have to do is show up on time and you get a guaranteed ten percent. Pass your homework up after you find your seat."

Cole stuttered something inaudible as he fidgeted with the zipper on his jacket. Hoping no one saw the heat radiating from his cheeks, he slumped into his seat. He knew he was late, she didn't need to call him out like that. He shuffled through his backpack, pretending to look for his homework.

U.S. History never ceased to put Cole into a stupor, especially with the old woman's monotonous, dry rant. Cole imagined she started every day off with a bowl of plain, flavorless oatmeal and a glass of bitter tomato juice. Just shy of ten minutes into the lecture Cole could feel his chin slipping off of his hand, as though his head was magnetically attracted to the desk. He shook himself awake and redoubled his efforts, but the old woman's voice sounded like the back seat of his mom's Chevy Lumina on the highway. Does she even need to breathe? How can she go on and on like that without pause? Cole jumped awake as the bell sounded the end of the class. He could hardly believe he'd dozed the entire period. At least he got some decent sleep though. He should be able to stay awake for the day now.

Mrs. Webster caught his arm on the way out of class. "Attendance isn't just showing up on time you know. You have to actually sit through the whole thing. Do you have last night's assignment?" Her eyebrows met, creating a wrinkled 'W' on her forehead as she accepted Cole's vacant stare. "You're not doing well in here, but I don't need to tell you that. Bring it in tomorrow and I'll only knock off ten points. I'm putting up some extra credit assignments on the website tonight. You should take a look at them."

Cole shifted his backpack higher on his shoulder. "Mrs. Webster, I'm sorry. I didn't mean to sleep through the whole class. Last night was basketball tryouts and it took a lot out of me. I'll do the extra credit tonight before tryouts, I promise."

Mrs. Webster paused as her face took on an irritated look. "You weren't sleeping Cole, at least not in here. Your seat was empty. Just bring the assignment in tomorrow and get yourself to your next class on time."

Cole mulled over Mrs. Webster's accusation as he departed. How could she have missed him? He dismissed it however. Probably just old age getting to her. She was right about one thing, he needed to hurry. Not to his next class though, not just yet.

The halls of Stonebrook High School fell into no discernable pattern or design. Every freshman fell victim to its whimsical layout, as if the building was originally a mental institution designed to make escape impossible. The students' complaints were often met by the rebuttals of older teachers who remembered the school as it was before its many additions. Cole had been late to every class for the first month of his freshman year, but he was a senior now, and knew the most efficient paths to navigate the school's halls.

Cole nearly took a spill around a corner as his foot slipped on a puddle of what he hoped was water. He looked to a nearby clock. He only had another few minutes to get to where he was going, and then to class. He sped off as quickly as his sore legs would carry him, now accompanied by an annoying *squeech* coming from his left shoe. After he hobbled a few minutes, his knowledge of the school's shortcuts paid off. Cole's face broke into an irresistible smile as he came squeaking around the final corner.

"Oh, Ashley, what's up?" Cole said, trying his best to appear as if he wasn't out of breath.

"Cole!" Ashley returned his smile, stunning Cole somewhat. She seemed to have the ability to make him forget his own name when she looked at him like that. "How did tryouts go last night?"

"Not as bad as last year, and Coach kind of hinted that I made first cut. I'm not getting my hopes up too high but I think I'll be taking part in second cut tonight." The morning's lingering torpor suddenly melted, as though her smile were made of straight caffeine. Cole's eyes wandered as he took in her hair. It was almost black, fastened in a high bun held by two obsidian chopsticks. He walked his eyes down a free lock that bordered the left side of her olive-toned face.

Ashley didn't seem to notice Cole taking inventory of her. "I knew it would pay off. All the training you've been doing. Not to mention you haven't broken a bone in the last five minutes. You're getting your body to where it should be." She took his hand in both of hers, fingering his surgery scars. "You still can't feel…"

"Yeah, nothing in between those two fingers. I've got almost full range of motion back in the index finger though." Cole flexed his hand as she held it, massaging the scar that ran in between his first and second knuckles.

Ashley returned his hand with gentle grace, placing it over his abdomen as if it were still injured. "Well, keep massaging it like the doctor said. Break up the scar tissue. How's Joshy liking his new classroom?"

Cole relished the lingering touch of her warm hands, though he wasn't quite ready to change the subject to one that didn't involve her massaging his scar. "Oh you know Joshy, he would be happy anywhere as long as he has somebody there talking to him. He's got a lot more one-on-one time in this room, which is good but I don't know if it will help him learn anything. Honestly I don't know if he can learn much more. He seems to be stuck in the five-year-old stage."

"Maybe he doesn't *need* to learn anything else. If Joshy is happy with less than what we have, then maybe in a way he's smarter than us. He doesn't worry about what other people think of him, or how to get ahead. Joshy just loves. He practically radiates it." Besides Cole, Ashley was the only person at this school who truly appreciated Joshy and what he had to offer. Cole couldn't help the stupid grin that took hold of his cheeks. Ashley reciprocated with a grin of her own.

Cole felt a closeness to Ashley that he couldn't describe with words, mostly because he would end up tripping over his own tongue. His smile fell apart as he searched for the courage to change the subject to one he had been pining over for weeks; the Fall Ball.

"So I don't know if you've got somebody in mind, I mean I'm sure you do, but have you given any thought to who you want to go to the Fall Ball with?" Cole held his breath and winced inwardly, preparing himself.

Ashley's eyebrows met as she shifted her backpack higher up on her shoulders. "Yeah I've been asked by Kyle and Drew. They're really cute and I'm friends with both of them. I don't want to offend anyone, but I know I've got to make a choice. Who do you think I should go with?"

Something heavy and queasy fell from Cole's chest down to his stomach. "I don't know. I've never been in that predicament before. They're both on the football team right? I'm pretty sure they are close friends." An idea suddenly popped into Cole's frantic mind. "Maybe...maybe you shouldn't go with either of them. I've seen Kyle get into fights over girls, and Drew is known for trying to hook up on the first date. It may end up hurting their friendship if you go with either of them, you know?"

"That's a good point, I didn't think of it that way. But what else can I do? No one else is asking me." Her look of concern changed into one of almost pleading.

An alarm went off in Cole's head. This was it! This was his window, he just needed to push through his fear. "Well if, you know, you can't decide in time. I'll just go with you, all right? So no worries, you won't have to go alone." He could tell before the final word came out what the answer would be.

"Oh my God Cole, you're too cute!" Ashley gushed.

Cute. Cole was being Cute. He certainly didn't feel cute. He felt as if somebody had just tossed a bucket of ice water in his face.

When Ashley's giggling subsided, her eyes lit with an answer: "I know what I'll do though, yeah this will work. Sarah doesn't have anyone yet so I'll just ask her to go with me. Then the four of us can go double-date style and figure it out that night. Yeah that will definitely work."

"Yeah but you know Drew is going to-," Cole jumped as the one-minute bell blared from the speaker right above his head.

She turned on her heel. "They really don't give us much time between classes, do they? Thanks for the help, Cole. Sarah's going to love it. You'd better start thinking about who *you're* going to ask."

Ashley disappeared into the queue before Cole could explain what exactly Drew would do to her.

Cole's tardiness might have gone unnoticed if not for his squeaky shoe announcing his arrival to the whole class. Mr. Scroy didn't make a big deal of it though. Cole was one of his favorites in this class. Zoology was one of the few subjects Cole found interesting. Unlike most of his other classes, which bored him to death and resulted in slightly less than mediocre grades, Cole was near top in this class. Today they were talking about the different layers of rainforest canopy, a subject that would normally have him enthralled, yet Cole threw his bag down in a solitary seat in the back of the classroom and proceeded to brood over his exchange with Ashley.

If only he could call Nana Beth. She would know exactly what to say to make him feel better. He recalled a late night on her couch many years ago, when he'd been upset for not having any friends outside of school. Ashley was on vacation with her family, leaving Cole alone for two weeks in the summer. As usual, Nana Beth had regaled him with stories of her youth while imparting her sagely advice to him. He couldn't remember the stories, but one bit of advice stuck in his mind: No matter what life throws your way, you keep moving.

The bell rang, jolting Cole alert and signaling the end of class. He didn't know how he was supposed to keep moving, so he took it literally and decided to take the long way to lunch and stop by Joshua's classroom to check up on him. The special education department was on the third floor and by the time Cole climbed all those stairs he was out of breath, though slightly less winded than he thought he would be. He felt a little more confident about tonight's tryouts.

"Colton, come in, come in. Joshy look who came to visit you," Joshua's one-on-one, Mrs. Walker, patted him on the shoulder to get his attention.

"Oh it's you, hahaha!" Joshy beckoned to Cole in a theatrical carefree manner, as if he'd been expecting Cole's arrival.

"Joshy, show Colton what you're working on today." Mrs. Walker then dropped her voice in feigned undertone: "We're learning about heroes today and Joshy wrote an essay on who his hero is. No Joshy, your essay, it's right here silly."

"I know," Joshy said plainly as he proffered the essay to his older brother.

The essay was very short, only a paragraph, and it included a neatly written translation below due to Joshua's dreadful handwriting. Cole didn't need the translation, however; he was one of the two people who could understand Joshua's handwriting as well as his garbled speech.

Colton is my hero. He walks me to the bus stop and protects me from the mean kids. Colton is my brother. He sleeps too much but he takes care of Joshy. Colton is my best friend. Colton is my hero.

Cole felt a swell of gratitude for his little brother, as well as a modicum of pity. Joshy loved so much, but he'd definitely never find a girl to reciprocate those feelings, except for their mom and Nana Beth of course, but that was different. Cole thought he was better off this way. Joshy wouldn't ever have to deal with the heavy sack of disappointment Cole was currently slugging around.

Throwing an arm around his little brother, he squeezed him as hard as he could, causing Joshy to emit a breathless giggle as he fought to escape. "Thanks Joshy, I didn't know I was your hero! You know what, I think you're my hero too, Bud. You're the one who always wins when we play basketball. Here, you'd better put this in a safe place. It's got to be the best essay you've ever written."

Joshy flicked his hand dismissively. He put on his cool-guy pouty face, as if the essay were a trivial matter not worthy of his attention. "No, you keep."

Cole was the one laughing now, securing the essay in his bag. "You are *definitely* my hero, Joshy."

Just outside the cafeteria was the school bulletin board. Here you could find information on the school dance, a flyer on the new parking policy, signup sheets for the Latin club, and most importantly the list of who made first cut from last night's Junior Varsity basketball tryouts. Cole hesitated with his sweaty palms and racing heart. It wasn't until this moment that he realized how high his hopes had risen. Holding his breath, he finally examined the list. It was there. Third from the top. His name. Cole released the breath in his lungs with a loud *whoop*, punching the air.

The cafeteria was a madhouse as usual. The school had staggered lunch times but even after Cole showed up ten minutes late, the line was still out the door. At least with the din of conversation no one could hear Cole's still-squeaking shoe. With tryouts now a definite, Cole had grabbed a double lunch to be extra fueled up for tonight's round of suicides. Walking past Ashley and her friends, Cole had hoped to get a wave or at least a smile from his crush. She was too busy laughing at whatever that idiot Drew was going on about, however. Cole picked up his head and kept moving.

Cole joined his friends at the usual table. 'Friends' was a grandiose term for people he ate lunch with and reminisced with about all the pranks they used to pull in middle school. The stories were hilarious, but Cole would throw himself out the window if Ashley overheard the anecdotes passed around the table like trading cards.

Cole sat down mid story-battle, knowing exactly which one they were on. Everyone at the table was trying to one up each other with their tales from middle school.

"No-no, it's really easy. You just take the two paper clips and stick them in the socket. Make sure they don't touch though or else you might get electrocuted," said Kevin Fitzgerald, a tall, chubby kid still sporting a bowl-cut. He was in the middle of a narration in which Cole himself had been the main character. "Class was just about over and we were working on a stupid poster or something in the hallway. Cole said he once saw an electrical outlet shoot sparks if you connect the wires, so we found a couple paper clips and Cole stuck em right in there, the idiot! I thought he was going to get shocked for sure. Me, Jay, and Little-Kevin formed a human wall so no one could see. Cole told us to take a step back and we didn't friggin listen, did we, Cole? Anyways, Cole takes his notebook and touches the two paper clips together and BOOM!" Kevin threw his arms out as wide as possible, knocking over Little-Kevin's soda. "Sorry Little Kev. So, BOOM! Sparks everywhere like a fourth of fucking July! Must have been eight feet tall. The notebook got toasted of course. It was still on fire when all the retards came running out of the sped classroom. Apparently Cole knocked the power out in half the wing. Imagine all those retards screaming in the dark!"

The table erupted with obnoxious laughter and fists slamming on lunch trays. This was a pretty good opener. While it would be hard to top that one, Cole could already think of three other stories that would put that one to shame. Cole was about to start when he heard Ashley's voice from a few tables over. He remembered the laughs he had gotten from the exploding socket, but he also remembered poor Joshy running out crying his head off because he was so scared. Shame clamped his mouth shut. Little-Kevin took the next one however, weaving an epic about a Halloween night when Cole had pulled a mailbox up and thrown it onto the roof of some unknown neighbor's house.

Cole's next class was Astronomy, and it was easily his favorite. It wasn't due to the teacher being cool, which he was, or the class being easy, which it wasn't. Cole loved astronomy because the school had just installed a million-dollar planetarium last year. After pouring over basic astrophysics, the class would spend a portion of the block in the starlit room. The planetarium was small, but Cole found it fascinating.

"All right guys and gals, come on in and find some floor," Wayne Johnson corralled his students into the dimly lit room. Everyone quickly found their favorite spots and got ready for the show. "We don't have as much time this week so we're going to skip the intros and get right to it. Lights are going off. Please, *please* no funny business. I swear I heard two of you slurping on each other yesterday."

A smattering of childish giggles peppered the room, which was now pitch black. Wayne Johnson was definitely not an authority figure. At twenty-eight years old, Wayne had thick glasses and a beautiful ponytail that swept his upper back. Try as he might, he could never get the students to call him 'Mr. Johnson'. It wasn't out of disrespect, far from it in fact. Wayne was just so likeable. It was as if he was their awkward, cool-in-his-own-way older brother they took pity on, yet gave him a gentle ribbing from time to time for his own good.

Cole adjusted his backpack under his head as a makeshift pillow, and gazed at the domed ceiling, which was now full to the brim with stars. Unless he were out in the desert a hundred miles from the nearest street light, Cole would never otherwise see such a show. Today Wayne planned to shift the sky to the southern hemisphere and go over the foreign constellations. Cole loved hearing about the different tales each culture made up to go along with the seemingly random pattern of dots. Today however, Cole was having a difficult time paying attention. Yawning over Wayne's narration, he shook himself and took off his hoodie, hoping the cold air would rouse him. Why was he still so tired? He had just slept for over an hour in Webster's class.

The bell rang, waking Cole with a jerk. The room was empty. Confused and chilled, he put his hoodie back on, wondering why nobody had woken him. He wasn't the most popular kid but still, was it too much to give him a kick?

The lights in the hallway were blinding. Cole stood for a moment wincing like a vampire emerging from his coffin. When his eyes adjusted, Cole notice the hallways were empty as well. Terror gripped his heart. That wasn't the bell for the end of class; that was the bell for the start of the *next* class! Cole took off running, only to be halted by his aching legs. There was no point running anyway, he was already late. The entire school was eerily quiet. As he squeaked through the barren halls, Cole's imagination spun up a post-apocalyptic zombie scenario where he was the sole survivor living in the school. By the time he reached his next class, he had rescued Ashley from the hordes and the two of them chased the sunset in a commandeered school bus. Cole was about to imagine what he and Ashley would do after the sunset until he opened the door and his dreamy smile fell from his face. There was no one in the room.

Cole swore as he looked at his watch. Five o'clock? How was that possible? Disoriented, he took inventory of his thoughts. He could miss one class, he was doing fine in Statistics so this wouldn't set him back too far. He could walk home from school. It would be cold and dark but he'd done it before. Joshy was okay as his mom should have picked him up today on account of Cole's tryouts tonight. The tryouts! Cole swore even more loudly this time. Cursing his rusted legs, he ran as fast as he could to the locker room. If he was very lucky, Coach wouldn't notice him coming in a few minutes late.

Cole was not lucky, however, not even a little bit. Tryouts were well underway by the time he emerged from the locker room. Hoping Coach could see past his tardiness, Cole approached the man with the megaphone and asked where he should fall in.

"You're kidding me right?" Coach Connelly didn't bother looking at him, but there was no doubt that Cole had his full attention.

Cole was ready for this. He had a rehearsed an entire sob story involving his mentally handicapped little brother getting sick all over himself and needing a change of clothes. It was quite a tale considering Cole had less than ten minutes to think it up. This was low and he knew it, but not even Joshy would begrudge him this life-changing opportunity at the expense of an embarrassing fib. "Coach I know I'm late but there was-"

Coach Connelly interrupted him without taking his eyes from the court: "You're what, eleven minutes late now? You know I could work with you, for being late. Hell I'd give you the benefit of the doubt if you were twenty minutes late, but there's one thing I can't work with. Do you know what all my student athletes have in common?"

Cole froze, unable to think of an intelligent response. If only Coach would let him explain.

After an appropriate pause in which Cole was supposed to respond, Coach Connelly drove on, "All of my student athletes are just that, *student* athletes. Damn good ones too. Your responsibilities as a student come before your responsibilities as an athlete." Coach brought his gaze down into Cole's eyes now, boring right through him. "You show up late for your first class and leave for an hour of lecture, then you show up late for your second and third, then you don't even bother showing up for your last class. We all have our priorities but I have no use for someone with yours. Leave my gym."

There was no room for misinterpretation or arguments. Cole turned on his heel and left. A wave of nauseating shame washed over him as he shrunk to the size of a small child. Rebellious tears leaked down Cole's cheeks as he changed back into his squeaky shoes and day clothes. Luckily the locker room as just as empty as his Statistics class was. Cole wondered how Coach knew about his lateness. He also wished he would have let him explain that he'd never left his classes. He was sleeping because he was exhausted from the stupid tryouts. Cole finished changing and started the long walk back to Blossom Street, berating the stalker of a coach all the while.

It was fully dark by the time Cole reached his front door. Even from outside he could smell one of his favorite meals wafting through the drafty door. Under the orange glow of the street lights, Cole paused for a moment on the front steps. It only just now dawned on him how worn-down the front porch was. He remembered it being so much cleaner, and the paint was supposed to be brighter. Now the steps were down to the wood, chipped and scuffed by thousands of scraping footsteps. His sticky shoe had accumulated a layer of sand and rocks beneath its gluey layer. Cole removed his shoes at the bottom of the steps so as not to rub off even more of the paint. The screen door screeched his arrival even before he opened the main door. At least he was in time for dinner. Nana Beth, a very messy Joshy, and his mother were at the table.

"Hey, Honey. I thought you wouldn't be done for another hour. I hope somebody dropped you off?" Tara raised an eyebrow. Cole was old enough, but he knew she wasn't crazy about him walking the tree-streets alone after dark. "How did second cut go?"

Cole walked to the hallway and avoided Nana Beth's eyes, stuffing his backpack in the closet. "Much quicker than first cut. I guess Coach thought he beat us up enough last night."

"So when's third cut? Or will there even be a third cut?" Tara asked. She had bought it.

"I don't know. I'll find out tomorrow at lunch." He needed to change the subject and fast. Cole was not a good liar, especially with Nana Beth's eagle-eyes upon him. "That's a nice look Joshy, I think you've got more food in your hair than on your plate."

Betrayed, Joshy dropped his fork and gave Cole a look of deepest loathing, as if dinner was going perfectly fine until Cole had to open his mouth and sell him out. Cole never told on Joshy. Cole was his hero after all.

Tara gasped at the mask of chicken and rice that caked Joshy's face and hair. "Oh Jesus, Joshy how many times do we have to do this? Come on get up. GET UP!"

"Camaan!" Joshy bellowed, kicking his chair in protest.

Tara put a firm hand on Joshua's arm. "Get up now, come on, there we go. We're going to the bathroom to wash that off. I thought you wanted to be a big boy, Joshy. Big boys don't wipe food all over their faces! They use napkins!"

Cole fixed himself a plate as his mother's tirade faded up the stairs. He couldn't help but noticing Nana Beth's eyes still on him. He took a seat as far from her as he could on the little table. A minute passed. She was clearly waiting for him to speak first.

Cole finally broke the silence: "I was kicked out of tryouts."

Nana Beth cocked her head slightly, her scrutinizing gaze raking over him. "You're almost a grown man, Colton. You needn't tell me anything if you don't want to."

A reluctant grin tugged at the corners of Cole's mouth. He winced slightly as his chapped lips cracked. As if she was expecting it, Nana Beth pulled a jar of Carmex from her cardigan. The warm goo soothed his cracked, scratchy lips. "Nana Beth, you know I can't keep anything from you. There's no point in me trying to hide it."

"True, true," Nana Beth said and replaced the Carmex in her pocket, and crossed her hands over her lap in a matronly pose. "But I feel the need to at least give you the chance to keep your secrets to yourself. Everyone deserves the rights to their own secrets, even if they have a terrible poker face."

Cole laughed. "Yeah I should probably work on that. Maybe you could help me with it sometime?"

"Maybe," Nana Beth inclined her head to him. This was Cole's indication to say his piece.

Cole's smile faded as he dropped his gaze to his half-eaten plate. "I was late to every class today and I completely slept through my last one. Coach Connelly found out and kicked me out of tryouts."

"And do you think his verdict was fair?" Her tone wasn't patronizing, but Cole felt foolish all the same.

He knew the right answer, though it was hard to feel it through the hot lump of anger filling his head. "Yes, but he doesn't know I've been sick. I must be coming down with something, I mean I feel like I could fall asleep right here at the table. No matter how hard I fought it I couldn't stay awake in first block, and I completely passed out in the planetarium for a few hours. No one bothered to wake me up at the end of class. Though I guess being sick doesn't excuse me from being late to the three classes I did attend."

Nana Beth looked slightly bemused as she mulled over his words. "Sleeping that much *is* unusual for you. If you still feel lousy tomorrow then you really ought to get checked out. Have to make sure it's not something nasty like mononucleosis. My boys had it one right after the other, all from the same girl too. Have you been kissing all the pretty girls at school?"

Cole let out a derisive chuckle. "Yeah, I wish. Or at least there's one girl I wish I was kissing."

"You know, I have some experience in this matter. Believe it or not I used to be a pretty young thing myself. Would you like some advice?" Nana Beth leaned across the table. Cole could smell her perfume. It was nice, like a Yankee Candle. Not the typical old-person potpourri.

Cole met her gaze, feeling a warm familiarity replace his chilly vulnerability. "From you? Of course."

"The heart is a stupid and powerful thing. When it yearns for something it's going to let you know, day and night. It only gets worse from here on out and boy is it going to stick you in a few jams. Get to know your heart, Colton." Nana Beth reached her vast arm across the table and gently tapped Cole's chest. "When it wants something that you also want, you'll do whatever it takes to get it. At the end of each day if you didn't get it, then you clearly didn't want it bad enough."

CHAPTER 4

QUESTIONS

Even though Cole went to bed early, he was still just as tired the next morning. More so perhaps, and he didn't even have the tryouts to blame this time. Though he couldn't stay awake in any of his classes he did manage to show up on time to every one. Joshy hadn't forgiven him for the previous night's betrayal at dinner, and wouldn't sit next to him on the bus. Ashley was still ambiguous with her plans for the Fall Ball. Unable to muster the courage to ask, Cole managed to dance awkwardly around the subject whenever they talked in the hallway.

After a couple sluggish days, his lethargy only seemed to be getting worse. Heeding Nana Beth's advice, Cole had his mother schedule him an appointment with their family doctor. After several tests the doctor didn't have any answers other than a possible late-pubescent growth spurt. Cole felt like he was spending more time asleep than awake, but more than that he was less connected. He kept forgetting simple yet important things such as money for lunch, or seeing that Joshy got on the bus after school. Hopefully he could shake whatever this was before the Fall Ball on Friday night.

A gentle hand shook his shoulder. "Wake up hon, you're gonna be late for school again."

"What time is it?" He coughed, clearing the gunk from his throat.

"A little after seven. You sure you're ok to go in today?" Tara sat on the edge of his bed and placed a hand on his forehead. "At least you don't have a fever."

Cole groaned, covering his eyes with a pillow. "I'm already late. There's no way I can make it to the bus in time."

Tara rose to her feet. "You get a pass today. I'm going in late so I'll bring you and Joshy in. You gotta boogie though, chop-chop."

Cole would rather have walked. It was embarrassing enough to be one of the only seniors without a car, but to be dropped off by your mother was a whole different level. Cole did his best to hide the fact that he took the bus, slipping off quickly and joining the crowds funneling in from the student parking lot. It was a weak ploy, but he was pretty sure it worked. He always wanted his own car but for that he would need a job, which was impossible while he had to watch Joshy after school. His mom worked her bartending job most evenings, and Nana Beth was now in her eighties. It was up to Cole to be Joshy's hero.

"I'm not dropping you off from the parking lot. It's too cold and you're being stupid. Do I embarrass you that much?" The car's engine whined as Tara pulled up to the main entrance.

"It's embarrassing to be the only one in my grade being dropped off by his mommy because he doesn't have his own car." Cole stretched his neck, trying to see who would see him being dropped off.

Tara's tone became icy, "Well whose fault is that? And don't you dare say Joshy."

Cole ducked his head down. They just passed Ashley and her friends. "Then I don't know what you want me to say."

Voice rising, Tara brought the car to an abrupt halt. "I don't know, how about the person who decided to play video games and run around harassing the neighbors all summer instead of getting a job? How about the person who has two nights a week and weekend-days free but still doesn't go out and find a job? Who do you think that might be, Cole?"

Hot anger sparked through Cole. "I'm going to get a job all right? I won't go to third cut and I'll go get a job. Then I'll have my own car and I'll be looking for my own place this summer. Then you can find someone else to babysit your son five days a week."

"Do what you want, Cole. I'm telling you you're in for a rude awakening once you hit the real world. The real world is gonna hit back, hard." Tara looked past Cole, donning a smile that did not reach her eyes. "You better hurry up and get inside before Ashley sees you getting dropped off by your mommy."

"Ashee?" Joshy chimed in. It was as if he hadn't heard a word of their argument until her name popped up. Without waiting, he shot out of the car door towards Ashley.

"Bye Joshy, have a good day sweetie," Tara called, and blew her youngest son a few kisses, which he returned with enthusiasm. "Bye Cole, have a-"

Fearing the pet name and kisses Tara was likely to toss his way, Cole shut the door. "Let's go Joshy, stop doing that, it's embarrassing." Joshy was still smooching the air. Cole grabbed his brother by the arm and dashed towards the crowd, hoping he could blend in before Ashley saw them. He was not quick enough, however.

"Ashee!" Joshua's bullfrog voice cut through brisk morning air like a crusty knife over silk.

Cole swore. Of course Ashley heard him.

"Joshy!" Ashley glided towards them. Cole admired the confident grace with which she moved. "Joshy you're looking awful dapper this morning. And I love your haircut. Did your mom cut it?"

"Yahahah!" Joshy was practically bouncing out of his Velcro shoes. He wrapped his short arms around Ashley's middle and buried his face awkwardly in her chest.

"Joshy calm down bud. Hey that's enough, you don't need to smother her. Sorry Ashley." Cole seized his brother by the back of the coat and yanked.

"Camaaan Cole!" There was Joshua's famous scream again.

"Oh, Cole be nice to him. He's just saying hello, right Joshy?" She locked eyes with his little brother, who beamed up at her with a cartoonish, toothy grin. "You don't need to be so high strung with him. Let the poor guy be will you?"

"You don't have to live with him every day though..." Cole stuttered. Clearly this was not what she wanted to hear, so Cole changed gears: "Besides we're brothers, we give each other a hard time. It's part of the job. You wouldn't understand."

Ashley gave him a curt nod. "Okay, Cole. Brother-stuff, got it." She bent down and gave Joshy a kiss on the cheek. "Bye Joshy, I'll come swing by this afternoon okay? I hope you have a present for me again."

"Let's go Ash, we need to stop at the store before the bell and grab one of the new school shirts. Didn't you want to grab a bagel too?" Kyle Summers, one of Ashley's statuesque suitors for the Fall Ball flicked her ear. He was a full head taller than Cole and had six-pack abs since elementary school.

"Hey!" Ashley laughed, punching Kyle in the stomach with a very solid *thunk*. Cole thought that six pack might be a twelve pack at this point. "Alright, let's make moves. Bye Joshy, Cole."

Thankfully, Cole made it to Mrs. Webster's class on time this morning. He was determined to stay awake through the whole thing. He was getting sick of the strange comments from his teachers about his leaving the classroom. His grades were slipping as well, just as his head was currently slipping off his hand. Shaking off the mental grog, he took off his hoodie and sat as tall as he could in his chair. At this point if he were to doze he would have to fall out of his seat. It seemed like a fool-proof plan. If only the subject were more interesting, he would have an easier time of it. Or maybe it was just Mrs. Webster's droning voice. Twice, the students next to him had to stifle giggles as Cole nearly did fall out of the chair. By the end of the block he couldn't tell if he had actually fallen asleep or not, but he certainly couldn't recall what the lesson was about. He vaguely remembered something about the nineteen-twenties; jazz music, prohibition, and the invention of penicillin. Definitely not going to cut it for the quiz at the end of the week. At the end of the block Cole passed in his homework, his late homework, and extra credit assignments. Not that he was expecting Mrs. Webster to be overly pleased with him, but he was annoyed to see her confused expression when he approached her desk at the end of class. He got that same befuddled look at the end of every class, it seemed.

"Thank you Mr. Carter. Um, excuse me but were you just in the bathroom...oh never mind," she huffed as she waved Cole out of the room.

The hallways were packed shoulder to shoulder. Cole meandered towards his next class. In the fuzzy corners of his mind he felt the urge to take the longer, less crowded route so he could catch Ashley before her next class, but couldn't recall how to get there. Cole thought that if he were driving he would certainly be pulled over, appearing under the influence. This was what being drunk must have felt like.

"Ouch, that's my foot! Watch where you're going!" squeaked a petite freshman girl, who had just received a flat-tire from Cole.

"It's too crowded in here," Cole mumbled.

The girl shot him a venomous glare and disappeared with a swish of her ponytail. Cole realized too late that he should have apologized, and made a mental note to do so the next time he saw her. He was proud of his moment of almost-chivalry, but by the time he made it to his destination he had completely forgotten about the frazzled freshman.

Cole was too late to see Ashley, which was for the best because he would now be on time for Zoology. Cole may have been on great terms with the teacher Mr. Scroy, but his good credit was running low after a few days of sleeping through his lessons. Hopefully he could remain alert enough to at least appear to be paying attention.

The topic of the day was certainly interesting enough to stay alert for. They were still in the rainforest, this time discussing the different food chains and how illegal logging had a ripple effect throughout the ecosystem. Cole was unusually alert. He answered every question Mr. Scroy asked and even chimed in with some well-educated input. Feeling particularly engaged, Cole even took it upon himself to step up to the front of the class. Everyone, even Mr. Scroy himself hung upon his every word. By the end of class the girl sitting next to him slipped him a piece of paper with her number on it. Looks like he had a date to the ball after all.

WHAM

"Have a good nap?"

Heart racing, Cole jolted upright as Mr. Scroy reopened the textbook he had just slammed on Cole's desk.

The class exploded with laughter, but Cole was too disoriented to feel ashamed. "I, I thought I was awake!"

"Why don't you step outside with me for a minute? You and I are going to have a little chat." Mr. Scroy stood over him, arms crossed. "Leave your bag, we're not going that far."

Cole was expecting a scolding, but Mr. Scroy seemed more concerned than anything. After Cole explained several times over that he wasn't on drugs, Mr. Scroy led him back into class.

Before reaching the door, Mr. Scroy dropped his voice to a low whisper: "If you're gonna nap then nap, but if you leave the room again just give me a heads up, okay?"

Something significant clicked in Cole's mind, but he wasn't quite sure what it was. "Sure thing Mr. Scroy."

Cole managed to stay awake and in his seat for the rest of the block. He tried to pay attention, but something else kept nagging at him. Every teacher had accused him of leaving the classroom while he knew he was only sleeping. He wondered if this was his childhood disappearing act all over again, but he dismissed the idea at once. When he was a kid he'd vanished for days at time. People would have noticed if he had been missing for that long now, or at least he hoped they would. Cole checked the date on his watch just to be sure.

The bell rang and Cole hurried out of the class. Ashley walked past him without noticing. She seemed troubled. Sneaking up behind her, Cole stretched his arm out and grabbed the two ornate chopsticks holding her hair up. The dark sheet of hair flowed and bounced like one of those shampoo commercials.

"Hah, gotcha!" Cole's smile curdled into alarm as Ashley whipped her head around and glared.

"Oh, hey Cole. I thought you were Kyle." With a deft motion, she snatched the chopsticks from his grip and wound her hair back into a high bun. The way she moved never ceased to leave Cole star-struck.

"You feeling okay? You look like something's wrong." He didn't expect her to divulge what was really wrong, but he was genuinely concerned all the same.

"I'm fine. You don't look so good yourself there Mr. droopy-eyes. Did you just wake up? You know people have been talking about you. About how much you've been sleeping in class." To Cole's satisfaction, Ashley now wore the look of concern.

Cole opened his eyes in an attempt to look more awake. "I think I might be coming down with something. I've been super tired all week and sleeping something like fourteen hours a day. And no, it's not mono. I went to the doctor's yesterday and had some tests done. Are you headed this way?"

"Yeah I was actually about to swing up to Joshua's classroom to say hi. Do you want to come with? Maybe you can make up for being such a jerk to him this morning." Ashley gave him a playful jab in the gut. The sound it made was much less impressive than when she had punched Kevin earlier. And it hurt.

Cole looked away, hoping his face wouldn't betray the dull queasiness radiating in his belly. "Yeah I've just got lunch next. I guess I could come up and say hi."

"As if you weren't just about to ask me anyway," Ashley beamed, turning on her heel. "Well come on then. I can't wait to see what Joshy has for me."

This was the most time they had spent together in Cole's recent memory. It was only a short walk and an even shorter visit with Joshy, but Cole would take what he could get. Joshy had made something for the both of them. For Ashley, he had written her name several times in his best penmanship on a nice piece of parchment paper, still illegible of course. He then gave Cole another one of his essays, highlighting Cole's better attributes such as his strong grip and loud voice.

Cole and Ashley wrapped up their visit and made their way to the cafeteria. This was a first. They were *going* to lunch together, so did that mean they would be *sitting* together? He was too nervous to broach the subject. Ashley however, was not. She invited him to come sit with her and her friends. He did his best to hide his excitement for the rest of the walk.

His giddiness was short lived, however. The table was crowded by the time they got there. Ashley of course sat in the seat Kyle was saving for her. Cole squeezed in between Ashley's friend Sarah and some hulking mass who played on the football team. His name might have been Dave, or was it Dan?

Cole felt very much out of his element. He couldn't hear Ashley, and none of the conversation at the table was relatable. So Cole did what he did best and sat there invisible, save for the occasional sideways glance from Sarah. Did he smell bad or did she always have that look on her face? At the end of lunch Cole sidled up next to Ashley, intent on walking her to her next class. She already had an escort, however. Cole faded back into the crowd as she wound her arm through Kyle's.

His time with Ashley left him with a bittersweet longing. When he was with her he was wide awake. He truly felt connected to the moment. Cole knew he was holding on to false hope that she might eventually see him in a romantic light, but he couldn't help how he felt. He was reconciled with his lot, yet it did nothing to quell the sick jealousy he felt when she was hanging all over Kyle.

After lunch Cole went right back into his stupor. He took a nice long nap in the planetarium and managed to sleep with his eyes open in his last class. He was getting pretty good at this walking dead thing. The final bell didn't even startle him when the blaring tone woke him. Cole tossed his backpack over one shoulder as he set off to Joshua's classroom.

"Hey Bud, you ready to go?" Cole yawned as he stretched his arms over his head. The massaging rumble of the bus seat was calling to him.

"Oh you strong!" Joshy reached up and squeezed Cole's biceps. "You bet. How was the rest of your day?" Cole helped Joshy put on his backpack before stepping out into the hallway.

"I dunno." Joshy shrugged his shoulders as if to say 'just another day at the office'.

"Always a conversationalist, aren't you, Joshy?" Cole put an arm around his brother as they wound through the flowing crowds. "Hey Joshy, I'm sorry for being so rough with you. And the yelling. I've been doing it too much lately. Next time I do it go right ahead and smack me, will you?"

Joshy raised his arms above his head, flexing his biceps, "Yahahah, I strong!"

"Oh I know you are! Just don't smack me too hard-I don't want the girls to see me getting beat up by my little brother." Joshy laughed as Cole jumped back in a feigned look of alarm.

As usual, Cole took them the long way to the bus pick-up to avoid being seen. Joshy never questioned it. Cole could have walked them home and Joshy would have followed like an obedient little soldier.

"Hey Joshy, I'm gonna take a little nap. Will you wake me up when we get to our stop?" Cole rearranged his backpack and sprawled himself over the bus seat.

"I know," Joshy said plainly.

"Thanks Bud," Cole yawned as he made himself comfortable. The soft bumps and steady vibrations of the big diesel engine lulled him into a heavy sleep. He always liked sleeping in cars.

When Cole woke there were no bumps or hum from the engine. There was no noise at all in fact, or anyone else in sight. Cole shivered, peering out the windows, seeing nothing besides a sea of yellow parked all around. His heart drummed faster as he realized where he was. This was the parking lot where the buses were dropped off at the end of the day. Why didn't Joshy wake him? Why didn't anyone wake him?

Cole grabbed his bag and made his way to the front of the bus. The doors wouldn't budge. Feeling trapped, he pushed and kicked, but the doors remained solid. Fumbling in the dark, he pulled every lever and pushed every button on the dash. Nothing. He realized the bus must need power to open the door from the inside. Panicking, Cole looked around at the windows. It was difficult in the dark, but he found and yanked on a small handle on one of them. He was about to crawl through and brave the drop when he saw something in the soft glow of a street light: **EMERGENCY EXIT**.

Cole swore, stomping to the back of the bus and cranking the red handle. He probably would have fallen on his face crawling out of that window. The back door swung free and Cole hopped down. He shut the door as far as it would go but couldn't latch it from the outside. That would definitely look suspicious in the morning.

Cole walked until he found a fence with barbed wire at the top. He looked up, considering the spiked wire for a moment. Definitely not. This place had better have an unlocked gate. He was going to kill Joshy when he got home. He followed the fence around and eventually found an exit over a climbable gate.

After nearly an hour's walk in the clammy fall air, Cole finally shuffled his tired feet up the front steps of the apartment. He couldn't help but wonder how much paint he was rubbing off with each step, as if part of his childhood were fading away. The door was unlocked and the lights were on. Joshy was on the couch watching the Spanish channel on mute and Nana Beth was at the sink. She must have made dinner. The smell made Cole's stomach whine.

"Lasagna's in the fridge. You'll have to re-heat it." Nana Beth didn't bother looking up from the pan she wrestled. "So Colton, funny thing happened today. Would you care to hear it?"

Though his stomach felt as if it was eating itself, Cole didn't dare grab himself a plate just yet. Nana Beth sounded just a hair away from unleashing her formidable temper. "Nana Beth, Joshy didn't wake me up on the bus! I told him to wake me up when we got to our stop but he just let me sleep right through it!"

"I was upstairs on the phone with my granddaughter when I heard a little knock at my door," she continued as if Cole hadn't said a thing. Her fury was restrained, like a loaded bear trap. "Can you guess who was at my door, Colton?"

Cole remained silent this time.

"Joshua was at my door, cold, crying, and alone. I asked him how he came to be at my door, cold, crying, and alone. He was in such a state I couldn't get a word out of him. I had planned to go visit my youngest son and his family tonight, but instead I've been playing host to little Joshua for the last four hours. Now don't get me wrong, I love Joshua as one of my own, but I'll be damned if my granddaughter wasn't looking forward to seeing her grammy tonight. I don't like disappointing my grandchildren without cause, Colton. I know you wouldn't have me doing such a thing without a very good reason, so I'm not going to bother interrogating you. You will, however, tell your mother the very good reason as to why I had to miss dinner with my granddaughter this evening. Do we understand each other, Colton?"

"Yes, Nana Beth." He wished she had hit him. This was much worse.

Nana Beth finished drying the pan and set it down gently on the counter. "Very good. I am going back upstairs to enjoy the rest of my night." The floor creaked as she strode over to Joshy and gave him a kiss on the top of his head. "Not that I didn't enjoy my night with you, Joshua. You were an exemplary gentleman as always. Goodnight boys."

Furious, Cole waited until he heard Nana Beth's heavy footsteps travel all the way back up to her apartment before rounding on Joshy. He wanted to yell and shake his little brother. It was his fault Cole had missed their stop and now Cole had to explain the whole thing to their mother, who was probably still angry from this morning. Joshy didn't even look up from the TV as Cole stood over him. He was oblivious and smiling, though his eyes were still raw from crying. After a moment, Joshy finally looked up at Cole. There was no trace of resentment, only love and adoration. Joshy was pathetic, and Cole took pity on him in that moment. Deflated, he collapsed on the couch next to his little brother.

"Mind if I turn the volume back on?" Cole asked, settling himself in for a marathon of the Spanish news.

Tara came home shortly afterwards, and true to his word Cole explained what had happened. He'd learned long ago not to go back on a promise made to Nana Beth. Tara was mad of course, but seemed more worried for Cole's health in the end. She agreed to get him checked out again after he fell asleep right there at the kitchen table. Tara took Joshy upstairs for a shower and Cole started on Nana Beth's lasagna. Even though the old woman had been furious, she had still put all of her love and expertise into the dish. It was delicious. Before his second bite the phone rang. Who would be calling at this time of night?

"Cole honey, get that will you?" Tara called from upstairs, clearly engaged with Joshua's nightly routine.

He swallowed dry before picking up the phone. "Hello?"

"Cole?" It was a girl, and it sounded like she was sobbing.

"Um, yeah? Who's this?" he asked, checking the windows.

"It's Ashley," said the voice.

An odd mixture of elated confusion filled him. "Ashley! Hey how's it going? I mean are you okay? You sound like you're crying."

Ashley, to Cole's guilty elation, had just been dumped by Kyle. He loathed to hear her anguished sobs over the phone, but she was now dateless for the Fall Ball.

"I know this is last minute but please Cole, I don't have anyone else to go with." She sniffed and blew her nose.

"Wait, are you asking me to go with you?" His heart seemed to stop, waiting for her answer before it was safe to resume beating.

"Well yeah, unless you're already going with somebody else," Ashley mumbled.

Could it be true? This must be a dream, but he felt more awake now than he had in a week. Ashley hadn't called the house in at least five years. Was this actually happening?

"Cole? Are you still there?" Her voice was shaking.

"Yes! Yes I'm here with you-, I mean I'll go with you. This is just so… What time does it start tomorrow and when should I pick you up?" He was talking so fast he nearly tripped over his tongue.

Ashley laughed, "Aw Cole this means the world to me! You've always been such a good friend. I should have just gone with you in the first place. Mark's *such* a scumbag. It starts at eight tomorrow, so pick me up at seven?"

Her words were music to his ears. Hopefully she couldn't hear how big his smile was over the phone. "Seven it is then."

They talked for a long while. Ashley eventually apologized for having grown distant over the years. She claimed it hadn't been intentional and not something she had noticed. Cole didn't care though, he had his Ashley back, for good this time. They stayed up late into the night reminiscing about the good old days in elementary and middle school. While she chastised Cole for all his pranks, she still laughed and asked to hear just one more story. He left out a few of the more nefarious tales, however. Best not to overdo it. Strangely enough, Cole felt wide awake, even after midnight. It was odd, as if she anchored him to the world. He would have stayed up all night talking, but Ashley eventually nodded off, leaving him in silence.

Cole went to bed with a grin that nearly touched both ears. Careful not to wake Joshy, he sneaked under his blankets with ninja-like stealth. He was too excited to sleep, though he was content with fantasizing about all the implications of his date tomorrow evening. Ashley and him! His hopes, now somewhere near the stratosphere, suddenly dropped to the mud when he realized he had less than a day to come up with a suit. Suits were expensive.

Cole didn't remember falling asleep, but at some point his dreams melted into something else entirely. He felt himself being pulled. It was gentle at first and without direction, as if he were being drawn into himself. The pulling waxed with every exhalation until it was no longer a gentle tugging, but a steady falling sensation. He couldn't tell where he was falling, but he was definitely moving. Someone else was falling with him. He couldn't see this other person but *His* presence was obvious. It was definitely a *He*, and *He* felt familiar. It felt as if this person had been there with Cole throughout his entire life, watching and observing at the edge of his thoughts. Unsure but unafraid, Cole reached for the familiar presence. Cole could sense that *He* was hesitant to make the connection. Inch by inch, or it may have been mile by mile, they were slowly drawn together by strands of curiosity, falling all the while. Cole faltered. This person, however familiar, was immensely powerful. *His* presence was overbearing now, it was too much. Cole could sense that *He* somehow knew everything about Cole's life; everything Cole feared, everything that incited his rage, all of his passions, everything that made Cole who he was today. Cole's own memories rushed from *Him* like a storm. Cole tried to pull back, kicking and screaming. It was too much. *He* wouldn't let go. *His* presence enveloped and engulfed Cole until neither of them could tell where one began and the other ended. They were the same, they were one.

They were no longer falling, but moving with purpose. They were no longer in their bodies, but comprised of a single orb of life and light. They were no longer directionless, but flowing onwards and upwards as if flotsam in a river. They were no longer scared or overwhelmed, but very much aware. Others were with them, glowing and pulsing like a river of multichromatic fireflies. Together, Cole and *He* glowed with them. Some roared, cherry red with terrible fury. Others dripped with unsettling tones of bruised flesh which seemed to scream in agony. Cole steered clear of them, and in the act of steering found that *He* had no problem with Cole guiding them along this river. They were together now, and *He* made the two of them glow and pulse fantastic colors of lavender and white snow. They felt great, as if their deepest desires were actively fulfilled and they had eternity to appreciate it. They found others that hummed similar songs with their lights. Some were golden diodes that blared with pride. Others were throbbing flames, baying with euphoric bliss. Cole and his new friend found themselves dancing with these other lights, creating an aurora of emotion with too many colors to count. Even the darker motes danced with them, contributing their morose tones to the symphony. The tempo rose to a feverish pace as the river flowed faster, onwards and upwards. Cole found himself at the fore of the throng, and the others were following. With *His* help, he would lead the river to their destination. Cole was unsure exactly where they were going, but *He* knew they were heading in the right direction.

Time was not a factor on this journey. It may have only been seconds, or perhaps years, but they had arrived. The pulsing mass of the river broke upon a meadow like a heavy rain. The meadow and surrounding forest were unlike anything Cole had ever seen. The plants were foreign and the sky glowed with strange hues coming from a massive moon. The moon seemed like it couldn't make up its mind as to what color it wanted to be, and that amused Cole to no end as *He* changed their color to complement the moon's shifting fancies. This place was alien to Cole, but it felt as if he'd been here before. *He* certainly felt comfortable here, as if *He* were visiting an old haunt. Together they danced and reveled with the other lights. The meadow was their stage, and this was their show. The odd plants and even strange animals joined in before long. The whole place felt alive, as if it were being born anew and Cole was helping with the energy from his soul. Every tree, shrub, vine, and stalk of grass blossomed with flowers, adding to the spectacle. Critters large and small jumped and twirled through the lights, mad with life. Cole wove in and out of a stream that twisted through the meadow, determined to touch every orb of light along the way. Dizzy and careless, he gave himself fully to the beautiful chaos.

Cole would have stayed in that meadow forever, but eventually *He* decided it was time to go. Cole resisted, but *His* influence was too strong. Together they slowed the music and dance of orbs until they were all ready to go. With *His* gentle yet firm nudge Cole led the river upwards and onwards, but not before something caught his attention.

There was a person at the edge of the meadow, not a creature or speck of light, but a person. She stood there transfixed, staring directly into Cole's orb of light. *He* pulled, harder this time, but Cole would not be denied his curiosity. Cole was now in control and moved them towards the woman until his entire being was right before her gaze. He could only make out her eyes as the rest of her was cloaked from his awareness. Equal parts of intelligence and ferocity radiated from them, but within them Cole also found a sadness so deep that he could feel her drowning. Throwing caution to the wind, Cole asked *Him* to change their color to one of comfort and compassion. *He* obliged, and together they cast out their healing song into her. Cole held her for a moment, bathing her in a soft lavender glow. Tears of gratitude leaked from her sweeping lashes, masking her in a terrible beauty that left Cole numb. Satisfied, Cole allowed *Him* to pull them to the front of the river; it was time to go.

Chapter 5

Fading

When Cole woke the following morning, he recalled the entire dream, which was unusual because he barely ever remembered his dreams. The whole thing felt so vivid and real. He looked around for the strange yet familiar presence, peering into every shadow. He would have sworn *He* was still in the room. Perhaps *He* still *was* there, just out of sight, quietly observing. Frustrated and exhausted, Cole threw off the blankets and forced himself upright. He felt as if he had spent the entire night running instead of sleeping. Even worse was his feeling of disconnection, as if he were not entirely there. After having to return to his room for mistakenly putting on Joshua's shirt, Cole joined his family down in the kitchen for breakfast.

"Are you feeling any better this morning?" Tara looked up from a magazine and inspected him.

He seemed not to hear her as he stared transfixed down the hallway.

"Cole, I said are you feeling any better this morning?" she said, more loudly this time.

Cole's voice was gravelly and rough: "Yeah. I mean no, not really. I feel even worse than yesterday."

Mild concern laced Tara's voice. "Worse like you're catching the flu or what? Do you want to stay home today?"

Part of him wanted nothing more than to stay at home and sleep the day away in the comfort of his own bed, but after talking with Ashley there was no way he would miss out on seeing her. His mother wouldn't let him go to the dance later that night if he was too ill to sit through class.

"No I'll go, today should be an easy day anyway. I think we're just watching movies," he said trying to find a way to smoothly segue to the topic of tonight's dance; however, his grogginess slowed his mind down too much. "Mom, there's a school dance tonight and I want to go."

Cole could see the empathy in her eyes. "Colton you know I work Friday nights. Who's going to watch Joshy?"

"I'll ask Nana Beth if she will. If not then I'll figure something out. I really want to do this." Just the thought of a dance with Ashley opened his eyes a little wider.

A slight smile tugged at the corners of Tara's mouth. "And who is the one that makes you want to go so badly?"

"Ashley asked me to take her," Cole said, noticing the pride in his tone.

"I figured as much. You two were chatting pretty late on the phone last night. Go ask Nana Beth before you head out, and see what she says. I'm sure she wouldn't mind the company." Tara reached over and ran her fingers through Joshua's hair. "Do you want to watch movies with Nana Beth tonight Joshy? Cole has a big date with Ashley."

Cole laughed and gave Joshy a false-glare, daring him to make fun. Joshy didn't poke fun at Cole, however. He showed no response at all in fact, which was highly unusual seeing as Nana Beth and Ashley were two of his favorite people. Instead, he looked up at Cole with pleading eyes.

"I want lights please," Joshy whispered in a quiet garble.

Tara's magazine fell to the floor.

"What did you say?" Cole put a hand on his brother's arm. Joshy hadn't talked about the lights since Cole's last bout of vanishings seven years ago.

"I want lights please," Joshy repeated the words more slowly so Cole could understand.

"Joshy look at me," Tara sat straight up in her chair. "What lights are you talking about? Where did you see these lights?"

Joshy casually jabbed his thumb towards his big brother. "Cole lights."

Tara's eyes shimmered wide. "Cole, what's Joshy talking about? Did you...? Is it happening again? Oh my God that's why you're so sleepy. No no no..."

"Mom relax, please!" Cole raised his hands as if she were a bomb about to go off any second. "I was in the room the whole night I swear. It's definitely not happening again. I was gone for *days* last time, remember? I went to bed last night on a Thursday and today is Friday, right?"

Tara checked the calendar then snatched Cole's wrist and scanned his watch. "You're sure?"

Cole lowered his voice, trying to instill calm into her: "I'm sure. Joshy's probably just talking the same nonsense about the fireworks we saw last week from the stadium."

Joshy shrugged, nodding as if this were a perfectly good explanation.

Relief and color flooded back into Tara's face. "Oh Joshy, you really had me worked up for a second there. I'm still calling the doctor today. We need to get you in first thing Monday morning for a second opinion. The sooner we find out what's wrong, the better I'll feel."

"And who knows, I may even kick this thing over-," even as he said it, a big yawn took the words right out of his mouth, "-the weekend."

"Hmm." Tara raised an eyebrow, clearly not impressed.

The day couldn't go by fast enough. Cole even stopped fighting the urge to sleep so as to jump through time a little quicker. A half hour here, an hour there. He was getting good at this. Each time he woke he could feel the strange and familiar presence of his friend from the night before. He found himself checking his surroundings, certain he would find *Him*, though he still had no idea what *He* looked like. Cole could even feel *Him* while he was walking through the halls in between classes, as if *He* were following just out of sight. When he was with Ashley however, his lethargy as well as his friend seemed to disappear.

After having a nice visit with Joshy, Cole and Ashley walked to lunch together yet again. This time, however, they sat alone at their own table. It was like the good old days; the conversation flowed effortlessly, peppered with belly laughs and jokes only they knew. At times Cole thought she might have been pulling his leg because she seemed to break down in a fit of giggles even when he wasn't trying to be funny. He forgot how easy it was to talk with Ashley. He felt safe with her. This was how things were supposed to be.

"So what are your plans for after the dance?" Ashley stopped massaging Cole's scarred hand, "And don't tell me you're going back home right after, the thing ends at ten and it's a Friday night."

"Well, that depends on what *you're* doing after the dance. If you're about to invite me to something boring then maybe I *should* call it a night." Cole raised his chin and looked away as if she were the most boring thing in the room.

Ashley laughed, fast and breathless. Was he really that funny? "Oh stop it! You know you're coming with me to Sarah's right? Her parents are away for the whole weekend and she's having a few people over."

"Do these 'few people' include… I mean it's fine if he is. I'll still come, obviously," Cole held his breath, waiting for the let-down.

Ashley's smile disappeared. "Kyle and his goon squad are definitely not going."

Cole took a deep breath, hoping she didn't notice. "Well that's good I guess. Wouldn't want any competition eh?"

Ashley's eyes connected with his for a long moment. "Trust me, there's no competition." She resumed massaging his scarred hand, "And make sure you pack a sleeping bag."

The elation from their lunch date carried him all the way through his next class. Cole had no urge to sleep whatsoever, even when the lights dimmed in the planetarium. Anticipation of the night's events filled his head like a hot air balloon.

Cole wasn't the only restless one in the class, either. Wayne seemed to sense the atmosphere in the small room was not very conducive to learning about much of anything today. It was a Friday, and the Fall Ball was merely hours away. Instead of teaching, Wayne took music requests from the impressive library on his laptop, and invited the class to chill out and 'take in the stars, man'.

After astronomy, Cole's lethargy returned, and so did *He*. Cole could feel *Him*, stronger than ever, calling and pulling. *He* was enticing, tempting Cole with vivid memories and surging emotions from the night before. If only Cole would lay his head down for but a moment, *He* would take him there again. The orbs of light were with him as well, beckoning with their lustful songs. Cole shook his head, bringing himself awake and sending *Him* away. *He* laid an understanding hand on Cole's shoulder and agreed to leave, for now.

The final bell rang as Cole took off at a trot, hoping to outrun his drowsiness and connection to *Him*. He collected Joshy and the two of them took their circuitous route to the bus circle. Cole would not sleep on the bus today. In fact, he would not sleep the rest of the day at all, no matter how tired he was. Cole felt a wave of weariness as the bus's motion sent vibrations up his legs. Mustering every ounce of willpower, Cole took to teasing and playing with Joshy to keep his mind occupied. He would need Joshy in a good mood for what he was about to pull off anyway.

As the bus rolled to its first stop, Joshy looked confused as Cole rose from his seat. "Let's go Bud, we're getting off here today."

Joshy sprung up from his seat. "Yahahah! Okay!"

A surge of gratitude gushed within Cole. Joshy's loyalty was unwavering as ever. The little guy really would follow him anywhere. He clapped Joshy on the shoulder and led him off the bus.

This stop was only a few minutes' walk from a mini mall where Cole intended to buy a suit for tonight. He wouldn't have time to get it tailored of course, but hopefully he could find a cheap one that would be under his meager budget. Gently coaxing his brother down a cobblestone alley, they walked as fast as Joshua's little legs would allow. As long as Joshy didn't fuss too much in the store, they would be back long before Nana Beth noticed they were late. She certainly wouldn't approve of taking Joshy for a late stroll through the Tree Streets, especially with the days getting shorter and the nights growing colder. This wasn't the best neighborhood, but as long as they kept to themselves there should be no cause for trouble. Besides, Cole was Joshy's protector.

The alley opened up into a parking lot adjacent to the mini mall. The whole lot exemplified the ghetto trashiness of the Tree Streets as it was a hub for its denizens. Out-of-towners were easy to spot because they usually wore jeans and shoes instead of filthy sweatpants and flip flops. A small trash tornado of fast food bags and cigarettes skittered across the pavement. Though they were nowhere near a body of water, fat seagulls patrolled the area, demanding their next handout with as much fervor as the wandering homeless. Even though Blossom Street was only a couple miles away, Cole couldn't help but feel judgmental of the people here. It certainly made him appreciate how his mom had raised him and Joshy.

"Almost there, Joshy. How are you doing, Bud?" Cole placed both hands on Joshy's shoulders and sidestepped a pile of something that smelled terrible.

"Good," Joshy said plainly.

"That's good." Cole felt his pocket for what must have been the hundredth time today. All day he had been carrying ninety-two dollars in his pocket, vestiges from birthdays and holidays. This was definitely not the best place to be walking around with that amount of cash.

Cole pushed open the door to Larry and J's Tux. The smell reminded him of the first day of school mixed with strong cologne. On display was a meager selection of dress slacks, jackets, shoes, and hats for formal wear. Slightly out of place in such a low-income area, Larry and J's managed to stay in business by advertising ridiculously low prices on their stock. There was no staff to be found, so Cole went to work searching for an ensemble while Joshy busied himself watching the TV behind the counter.

Cole knew nothing about suits or what size he might be. He tried on a few jackets, most of which were far too big. A door slammed in the back of the shop, startling both him and Joshy. He crammed a champagne colored blazer back onto the rack before the racing footsteps got too close.

"Hey lil' guy. Uh, can I help you find sumthin?" The man addressed Joshy, clearly not aware that Cole was standing right next to him. "What the hell are you doing in here, where's your…handler? Parent?"

The man had a disheveled look about him. His patchy stubble was not flattering and he was overdue for a haircut. Cole would have pegged this guy as a stray from the parking lot, had he not been wearing a suit identical to the one on the mannequin in the window.

Joshy pointed to the TV and mumbled a request for the Spanish channel, but his words were lost to one not fluent in Joshuan-English.

"Joshy we're not here to watch TV." Cole stepped into the man's view. "That's just my little brother. I'm looking to buy a suit."

The man gave an audible sigh of relief. "Man, I thought the kid just wandered in by himself. I'm no good with kids, especially special-needs ones, no offense. I'm J."

"Don't worry, none taken." Cole was used to people not knowing what to make of Joshy. "So I've got a dance tonight and I need a suit, except I have no idea where to start."

J chewed his lip and rubbed the stubble on his narrow chin. The scratching sound irritated Cole for some reason. Walking a full circle around Cole, the man appraised him.

"What are you, about a thirty-eight, maybe a forty?" J asked.

Cole shrugged, "I don't know. I was hoping you could tell me."

Pulling a measuring tape out of nowhere, J set about measuring Cole's arms, neck, chest, waist, and inseam. "Pretty average, won't have to do much tailoring."

Cole checked his watch. "Wait, how long does it take to tailor a suit?"

J snapped the measuring tape back into its reel. "Can have it ready for ya by Monday night. Any idea which one ya want?"

"Just a plain black one is fine. And a white shirt and black tie and shoes. Monday doesn't work for me though, I'm going to a dance tonight. Does a suit have to be tailored?" Cole asked, feeling stupider by the minute.

"Of course not, but ya might look a little chubby with an uncut suit." Then he seemed to see the worry on Cole's face, and reconsider. "But maybe we can get ya pretty close. Besides, dances are pretty dark right? No one will notice a thing. Lemme look at what we got in the back. Hey, customers ain't allowed behind the counter ya know."

Joshy had taken full advantage of the moment's distraction and was now standing on a chair behind the counter, trying to find the Spanish channel on the TV.

"Dammit Joshy get down from there! I told you we're not here to watch TV!" Cole grasped his brother by the belt and yanked him off the chair. He would have fallen if he weren't being held up by Cole's wedgie grip.

"Camaan Cole!" Joshy bellowed like a bullfrog, yanking himself free and rubbing his backside, "I want TV!"

"Listen to me you little asshole! I told you we're not here for that! This needs to be a quick trip so just stand there and shut the hell up for five minutes!" The words were out of his mouth before Cole could bite them. Between his yelling and the wedgie, Cole had just incited a full-blown, top-tier, Joshy tantrum of the highest order.

J cupped his hands around his mouth, shouting to Cole, "I'll just give ya a minute to deal with that, huh? I'll be in the back room picking out a few pairs a slacks for ya."

Joshy was in full swing by the time J left the room. He even melted onto the floor, screaming all the louder when Cole attempted to pick him up. There was no hope for it; Cole would just have to wait it out. He looked outside to make sure no one was coming. The streetlights were coming to life as the sun sank behind the opposing buildings.

After several minutes ground by, Joshy had screamed himself hoarse and calmed down enough for Cole to get a few words in. Standing up by his own volition, he allowed Cole to lead him over to the hat rack to pick out one of his very own. It had been years since Tara had allowed Joshy to wear a hat as he never wanted to wear it properly, the end result making him look even more foolish and mentally challenged. Unfortunately these were all tacky fedoras and trilbies. Their mother would without a doubt be confiscating it. But satisfied that Joshy would keep himself busy for at least ten minutes, Cole rang the bell and summoned J from the back room.

J was laden with several variations of shades and styles. The options were cut down significantly when Cole told the man his budget. He certainly wouldn't have the nicest suit at the dance, but it was going to be dark in there anyway. Ten minutes and ninety dollars later, Cole and Joshy strode out of the store with a full complement of men's fashion accessories, to include one pin-striped fedora. Cole checked his watch again. They hadn't much time now.

The sun had fully set now and had taken its warmth with it. The wind had picked up too, so they hurried across the parking lot for momentary solace in the cobblestone alley. Cole paused for a moment. There was a man in the alley, lit by a soft orange glow. He appeared to be arguing with someone, but as they got closer it was apparent he was alone. Probably one of the crack-heads who plagued the dingier parts of the neighborhood. Cole seriously considered turning back and going around the mall, but it was freezing and that would add at least another twenty minutes to their trip. He couldn't be late for Ashley. Determined to ignore the stranger, Cole placed Joshy on the opposite side of the alley and trudged onward. Judging by the man's rambling, and the fact that he was talking to the wall, he was definitely high on something.

"Don't tell me what I'm owed! You know what I did to the last motherfucker who tried to short me? Don't nobody walk away from shortin' Ricky, baby. Sets a new standard, and there's only one standard up in this motherfucker and that's mine! Me, *my* standard!" The weirdo was clearly out of his mind, but hopefully he would be too preoccupied with yelling at the brick wall to notice two boys sneaking by.

As Cole rushed Joshy behind the lunatic, he noticed the man wielding an object with which he alternated between beating his chest and striking the wall. Cole could hear chunks of brick chips skittering across the cobblestone. Joshy seemed to sense Cole's urgency and they doubled their pace.

"Hey! Don't think I don't see you there!" The man directed his sunken eyes in their direction.

An icy hand tickled Cole's insides, but he didn't stop. He heard the man's footsteps scuffle down the alley. Towards them.

"I see those bags you got. That's my delivery ain't it? You tryin' to short Ricky again this week?" The man broke into a sprint.

Before Cole could grab Joshy and run, the stranger was on them.

A stench of body odor and ammonia breathed down Cole's neck. "Don't you take another fuckin step or I'll stomp both your heads in."

Cole froze.

"Keep walking, Joshy," he whispered into his brother's ear, "He's one of the mean kids. Keep walking so Cole can protect you."

If there ever had been a time for Joshy to obey a command from his older brother it was now. He hesitated, but thankfully took one baby step at a time, watching Cole all the while.

"Keep walking Joshy," Cole repeated.

"Give me them bags, you little bitch." The man stepped close and ripped the bags free. Cole stood there, rooted to the cobblestone.

"Please keep walking Joshy," Cole breathed, closing his eyes.

"Where's it at? Where the fuck is it?" The stranger tore the bags open and sifted through the clothes, throwing them in a puddle. "What'd you do with it? Did you sling it your damn self? You better make with the stuff or make with the money real quick 'cus Ricky sure as shit don't got a lot of patience these days."

Still unable to speak, Cole reached a quivering hand into his back pocket and pulled out his wallet. The wallet slipped out of his fumbling fingers. He bent over to pick it up but the man shoved him. Cole stumbled and fell into the puddle his clothes had landed in.

"There's nothing in here!" the man screamed as he pulled a few loose bills from Cole's wallet. "There should have been at least five hundred in there! What the fuck did you do with it all? Where is it?"

Cole never shied from his fights in school, even when the odds were stacked against him, but this was real. This was danger and fear in their purest form. Cole didn't dare get up from the puddle, especially when this psycho still had that heavy thing in his other hand.

The man was now so close that Cole could smell a strong odor of crotch funk mixed with chemicals. He could count what was left of the individual blackened rocks that were once teeth and see the raw sores that pocked his cheeks. Spit flew from the man's crusted lips as his breath threatened to knock Cole unconscious. The fear was as nauseating as it was debilitating, but there was something else happening inside of Cole; he felt tired.

Sleep pulled at his eyes as the alley faded in and out of focus. Even as the man stood over him screaming his head off, Cole's head bobbed and his eyes drooped. It was as if something or someone were trying to take his mind away from here.

Walking down the alley, *He* was silhouetted by the orange glow of the street lights. Though the world seemed to slow, *He* walked along at an urgent pace. A few orbs of light trailed the familiar presence. No, now was not the time. Cole shook his head, sending *Him* away. Grabbing hold of his fear, Cole used it to bring his focus back to the babbling lunatic.

The man had stopped screaming and looked not to his left where *He* was, but to his right, where Joshy was walking towards the three of them. His little fingers grasped the brim of his pinstriped fedora as he offered it to the man. Joshy gave Cole a proud smile, as if he were about to set everything right and they'd soon be on their way.

"I know," Joshy said plainly.

The man appeared to move in slow motion as he took a step towards Joshy. He swung his arm and with a sickening *crack*, clouted Joshy in the head. Joshy's little Velcro shoes left the ground as he sailed through the air. His arms were still reaching even as the hat flew from his tiny fingers. It seemed to take a lifetime for his little body to fall. If he made a noise when he landed, Cole didn't hear it. The screaming coming from Cole's own mouth drowned out everything else.

The world continued to slow as he emptied his lungs. The flow of time ceased, leaving the grizzly scene in freeze-frame. The man's arm was still in the follow through and Joshua's feet had yet to meet his body on the cobblestone. Cole found that he could still move, though very slowly as if he were trapped in a jar of cold honey. A deep pulsing sound shook the alleyway, jarring his teeth. It came from *Him.*

Boom
Boom

With every throb Cole felt himself falling, just as he had in his bed the night before. He resisted, but the sensation was overwhelming.

Boom
Boom

He could no longer fight it. Cole was falling now, fading into himself. The next pulse would take him for sure. He looked to his right to see *Him* striding smoothly over. Little orbs of blue light dancing about *His* feet. *He* knelt down, offering a hand.

Boom

CHAPTER 6

EGRESS

C ole was back in the river. He and the familiar presence had joined once more, leading the throngs far away from the world. Far away from the pain. Their colors were not so varied this time. Following Cole's lead, they were all some shade of sad blue, weeping a mournful melody. Cole had chosen their color this time and *He* was now steering. Upwards and onwards they flowed through the river, swirling and coalescing like a flock of starlings. After a minute, or perhaps an eon, they arrived not at a meadow, but a lagoon. The pulsing spheres crashed into the water without disturbing the surface. The same opalescent moon from Cole's dream loomed above, bathing the lagoon in gentle hues of sapphire and violet. Below, shoals of fish darted about, startled by the sudden appearance of the glowing motes.

While the other orbs started changing colors and dancing, Cole remained a dark blue, letting himself sink to the bottom. *He* didn't object. This was a terrible moment for both of them. They continued their descent like a falling leaf until they nestled into a patch of undisturbed sand. Others came by and attempted to make contact in hopes of cheering them up; however, their grief was utterly unshakable and consuming. Cole's orb radiated such palpable sorrow that the others avoided him entirely for risk of being infected.

After a time the fish returned, unable to resist the tempting euphoria emitted by the others. Larger creatures were also drawn towards the gathering as they twirled amongst the dancing orbs. The coral and plants swayed and quivered with new growth as they bloomed with spectacular displays of flowers and spores. The celebrations filled the lagoon with romantic undulations of color, lights, and song. The lagoon and its reef were now their stage, and this would be a show to remember.

For all its beauty, the symphony could not pierce the shroud that *He* and Cole had placed upon themselves. They would stay there alone on the bottom forever, for returning to that cobblestone alley meant facing a crippling truth. With no urge or desire to speak of, they wallowed and sobbed, saturating the surrounding sand and water with fetid sorrow.

There was an abrupt pause in the festivity as a shadow swept over the lagoon. Above, something immense had blocked out the moonlight. A hulking whale broke the surface from the air above. The whale emitted a beautiful moan that ended with a high echoing note. The fish as well as the other lights were not alarmed by the whale's appearance, they merely parted the waters and allowed it to pass. Its massive size belied how fast it was moving, and its movement was directly towards Cole. The skin of the whale was adorned with colorful growths, but as it got closer Cole could see they were actually decorative jewelries. The stone and gem accents embellished the flowing curves of its body and fins. The whale alighted upon the sandy patch and brought its stunning eye to Cole's morose blue orb. Cole's despair seeped into the whale, but it drew closer, unaffected as it continued baying its song of terrible beauty. The song was wretched, yet perfect, as if the whale had made it just for Cole and his loss. He could feel it touching upon every facet of his grief, drawing it painfully out of him. Within the eye Cole could see intelligence and empathy as it blinked in understanding. A low hum bellowed from deep inside the creature as the cloud of azure sadness swirled and siphoned into its gargantuan eye. When it was finished, the whale blinked once more and, with an audible swish of its tale, rose to the surface and left the water. As the whale's shadow moved across the reef, Cole could feel his color changing from sad blue to a pale, empty grey. The pain was still there, but it was no longer overwhelming. With a gentle nudge, *He* steered them back towards the others. By unspoken agreement, the other diodes rose to the surface, waiting for Cole to lead them back. Cole wasn't ready, but how could someone be ready to face such a truth? With *His* consent, they rose out of the water to the fore of the river, upwards and onwards.

• • • •

The first thing Cole noticed was that he was wet. Wet and very cold. Slowly, he raised himself up and out of the puddle, spitting out the dirty water that had crept into his mouth. He was alone, save for the small figure lying a few paces away. Fear joined the cold that shook limbs as he approached the tiny figure that lay prone in its own dark puddle. He knew what he was about to see. Bending down, Cole pulled back the red hood and moaned. He pulled Joshua's limp body into himself and sobbed into his jacket. Cole couldn't help but notice how cold and light the body felt. Somewhere in the back of his mind, a whale's song played a mournful tune.

• • • •

"Tara dear, he's waking up."

"Colton! Oh Colton, honey how are you feeling?" Tara plopped herself onto the bed and placed a hand on his cheek.

Disoriented, Cole pulled himself upright. "Mom?"

Tara hugged her son, barely able to speak through her sobbing. "Colton, y-you're in a hospital, honey. An ambulance brought you in last n-night. D-do you know what happened?"

Cole's face fell as the memories came flooding back; the suit, the alley, the crack-head. It couldn't be real, it must have been a dream. "Where's Joshy?" Cole demanded, looking his mother square in the eye.

Hyperventilating gasps wracked her chest. She tried to speak but couldn't get a word out. Nana Beth rose from her chair and joined them on the bed.

"Colton, look at me. Joshua is dead." Nana Beth's voice was steady and sure. "A woman phoned the police when her husband found you and Joshua on their doorstep this morning. You were delirious with hypothermia and Joshua had sustained some sort of trauma to his head. The police found Joshua's blood in the alley by the strip mall. You are now in the ICU at Saint Judith's and it is four-thirty in the afternoon."

"No, no, no, no," Cole buried his face in his hands, digging his fingernails into his forehead. "It was my fault. Joshy shouldn't have been there, but I made him. I killed Joshy."

If Nana Beth was disturbed by Cole's words, it didn't show on her face. Stoic and gentle as ever, she waited with her hands on her lap for Cole to finish crying. After a few minutes, she spoke with a voice solid as granite: "Colton, when you're ready, you're going to tell us what happened after school yesterday."

Cole blew his nose and slowed his breathing. He needed to be strong now. It was difficult at first. He found he couldn't remember much from yesterday before the incident. Slowly, he told them about how they got off at the first stop and went to the strip mall where he bought a suit. He elaborated about his time in the store; Joshua's meltdown, the salesman, Joshua's hat. He was afraid to come out of that store again, even in narration. He was stalling.

"By the time we left the store it was pretty dark out. We took the alley over by the dollar store to save time. There was a man. He was crazy, doped up on something. He was screaming and yelling at no one and beating the wall with a pipe or something. I should have gone around. Why didn't I just go around?" Wracking sobs consumed Cole as he twisted the collar of his hospital gown.

Tara had stopped crying now, her watery eyes piercing and un-blinking as she gripped the blankets with white knuckles. Nana Beth continued to listen politely, as if she were merely talking to a stranger on the bus about the weather.

When Cole was ready, he continued, "I put Joshy on my right side and tried to sneak by the guy, but he saw us. He thought we were somebody else, thought that my bags from the store were a package of drugs or something. I told Joshy to keep walking, and he did. The guy took my bags and dumped them. When he didn't find what he wanted I gave him my wallet, but dropped it. I bent down to pick it up and he shoved me. He was screaming his head off, swinging that pipe around. I was so scared he was going to hit me with it…" Cole paused. This was it. This was the part he didn't want to say. He could hear the snapping, crunching thud. He could smell the crotch-funk and chemicals. His eyes looked off into nowhere as his breath raced away. He was no longer in the hospital room.

"And that's when the man hit Joshua with the pipe?" Nana Beth spoke in a loud, clear voice, breaking Cole from his trance.

"Joshy tried to give the man his hat." Cole's tone became eager and defensive, as if he needed to defend Joshy's actions. "He loved that stupid hat. You should have seen the smile on his face when he picked it out. He crossed his arms and did his cool-guy pose in the mirror. Probably thought he looked like one of the actors on the Spanish channel. He loved that hat but he thought that the man in the alley needed it more, so he tried to give it to him."

"And what happened after the man hit Joshua with the pipe?" Nana Beth asked before Cole could go too far into his tangent.

Cole made to speak, but something caught in his throat. He threw off the blankets and jumped out of bed. His hand was barely on the bathroom door before vomit shot from in between his fingers.

"Oh Cole! Here, here take the trash can. There you go," Tara patted his back. "We don't need to talk any more just now. Let me go get the nurse in here."

"No." Nana Beth stood from the bed.

"What are you talking about, Beth? He's had enough for now, obviously." Voice rising, Tara rounded on Nana Beth. Her fiery eyes were barely level with the old woman's navel. "We're taking a break."

"No, we're not," Nana Beth's voice was as calm as ever. "Colton is going to finish vomiting, and then he's going to sit back down on this bed and finish telling us what happened. There is something missing from this story." Seeing that Tara was about to become unhinged, Nana Beth reached down and placed a hand on her shoulder. "Tara, in my years I've seen tragedies and horrors that still haunt me. It has been my experience that it's best to pull these things all out at once. He might not be able to start again if we put it off. Now that he's awake the police will be in shortly to question him. He may need us to help him retell it." Her eyes sharpened as her gaze turned to Cole, "And I believe Colton has been keeping something from us for some time now."

"Mom she's right. I need to do it now." Stepping around the puddle on the floor, Cole returned to the bed, legs shaking.

Deflated, Tara joined Cole on the bed. Nana Beth remained standing, keeping an eye on the door.

Cole waited a moment, unsure. Just as Tara was about to speak, he blurted, "It's happening again."

Mouth agape, Tara asked, "*What's* happening again?"

Cole searched the floor in front of him, looking for a way to explain it. "In the alley, after…after Joshy…got hit, I got real tired and…I went somewhere."

"What do you mean you *went somewhere*? Did you leave him in the alley?" Tara said, horrified.

"Yes. I disappeared, just like when I was a kid. It's happening again except this time I'm remembering it all. It happened the other night too and I think it's been happening in school. It's worse this time though. It's more than once a day now. I feel like I'm not all here, like I'm fading. I lied about the lights. The lights Joshy talks about. I saw them. I was the lights." Cole looked at his mother, heart sinking.

The distress and color drained completely from Tara's face, looking like she might be sick herself. "I knew it. I've been feeling it too, in my heart. It's like you're not in me anymore. My heart is empty now. I'm going to lose both my sons."

Nana Beth shot Cole a shrewd look. "Colton you know you may have only passed out. What you saw in that alley may have just put you into shock. Are you quite sure?"

Cole nodded. "I'm sure. And I don't know how to explain it…but I have this feeling. Like I'm not supposed to be here. Like I might not come back next time."

The room went quiet. Even Nana Beth was shaken, letting out a small gasp. There was a knock and the door inched open. A young female nurse walked in, only to be halted by Nana Beth's towering frame.

"Not a good time," Nana Beth spoke as if there was no other alternative.

The nurse gave a weak smile as she craned her neck to meet Nana Beth. "Just wanted to let you know that there's two detectives on their way up. They're here to talk to Mister Carter."

"I appreciate the forewarning. You may go now." Not needing a second telling, the nurse turned heel and exited the room. "Tara, we should go head them off. We need more time with Colton before they interrogate him."

Tara stood up, eyes ablaze, "You're right. They'll never believe the vanishing thing. We need a better story. Cole, honey, clean yourself up. We'll be back in a minute."

• • • •

Nana Beth and Tara had only just closed the door to Cole's room when they were approached by two men in suits. One was even taller than Nana Beth.

"Gentleman, you'll find that young Colton is in no fit state to play host to interrogations. I'm terribly sorry but you'll both have to come back later." Nana Beth's voice was calm, but carried with it the severity of an executioner at the gallows.

The shorter detective stepped forward, unaffected by Nana Beth's imposing glare. "Miss Carter, we need to talk to your son. Now. There's been a development in the case and we need to hear his take on it. And you, are you his grandmother or something?"

"Why yes, I am." Nana Beth crossed her arms, now locked in a staring contest with the taller detective.

The taller man spoke, "It's only going to be us and the boy's guardian in the room. You'll have to wait outside."

Spreading her arms, Tara stepped in between the detectives and Nana Beth. "No. We told you he's not ready. He's still asleep and he's not stable right now."

"The hospital staff told us the boy was stable. It won't be long, just a half hour or so, and you'll be in the room with him." The shorter detective sounded cheerful, as if he was offering them a good bargain.

"No," Tara said in a low voice.

The shorter detective sighed, shaking his head before nodding to his taller partner. With no apparent effort the man gently pushed the two women out of the way. Nana Beth crowed indignantly and Tara clung to his arm, completely suspended off the floor. The shorter detective strode into the room, only to come out a moment later after Tara spouted off the most colorful insult that her upbringing in the Tree Streets had taught her.

The shorter detective filled the doorframe, teeth bared. "Miss Carter, we are trying to find your son's killer. This is time-sensitive. Protecting Cole is not in your best interest right now!"

Breathing heavily, Tara shrugged off the huge arm that was wrapped around her middle. "Fine! Let's get this over with."

The man didn't move.

Tara stared at the man, furious. "What do you want? An apology from me or something? Move your ass so we can get started."

The detective jabbed his thumb over his shoulder: "There's no one in this room."

Chapter 7

Arrival

Cole opened his eyes, blinded by the blazing sun. He could hear birds and little creatures scurrying around him. When his eyes adjusted, Cole found himself in the middle of a forest. Some of the plants there were oddly familiar but he had absolutely no idea where he was. Rubbing his eyes, he took inventory of his most recent memories.

He was in the hospital bed, Nana Beth and his mother were arguing with some detectives outside the room. And then... *He* showed up. Cole remembered the concussing *boom* that filled his mind and the fading-falling sensation. They were in the river, but it was just the two of them this time. He couldn't recall how he'd gotten here though. This was unlike every vanishing before. This time there were no dancing lights and he was in his own body. Perhaps this was part of a dream?

Cole held his breath, trying to force himself to wake. Nothing. He pinched his thigh. The pain was real enough. He called out into the forest, but the only answer was the offended cries of the birds above. The chilly breeze that caressed his exposed backside felt real as well. Looking down, Cole discovered he was still in the hospital gown, complete with wrist-tag and sock-shoes.

A slight panic set his heart fluttering as Cole stood up, looking about. He was alone, half naked, and in a strange place. He spoke to himself as calmly as possible: "It's ok, it's ok. I just need to wait it out. After an hour or so I'll reappear back in the hospital bed. I'll just tell everyone that I went downstairs to the café or something."

The thought of food made Cole's stomach gurgle. He hadn't eaten since lunch the day before. After tightening the back of the hospital gown and brushing the dirt off his rear, Cole walked towards what he hoped to be uphill. He intended to find some kind of elevation point or a good tree to climb so he could see if there was a nearby town. There was no telling how long he would be here, so he may as well find some food and water too. He wondered if some of the plants were edible, though they could just as well make him sick or worse. The trees, as it turned out, were closer to ferns. They had no bark and towered higher than Cole could even guess. Their branches ended in evergreen spikes, like pine needles back home. Some of the smaller bushes were patterned with odd colors, and bore fleshy flowers that wafted a tempting sweet aroma. Cole stepped on what he thought was a rock, only to have his foot sink right into it. Alarmed, Cole yanked out his foot, which was now sockless and covered in warm, pink goo. He used the other sock to clean his foot, hoping it wasn't some kind of flesh-eating acid.

"Maybe exploring isn't such a good idea," Cole admitted to no one.

The squishy rock gave a sharp hiss as if it agreed. Annoyed with being even more naked, he looked around for a safe, or at least comfortable, spot to wait out his stint in this weird place. A change in the pattern of greenery flicked his periphery. There was something big and solid a little farther up the hill. Cole crouched and snuck towards the thing, careful to avoid every rock. As he approached, he could see it was actually some sort of structure the size of a one-room cabin. The exterior was made of a stone-colored moss and there were no features save for a flat spot that may have been a door. He took one cautious step after another, ready for anything. As he approached he realized the structure was made for someone twice his height.

"Hello?" Cole called out to the cabin, "Hello? My name is Cole. Is there anybody in there?"

There was no answer. Slowly, Cole took one careful step at a time towards the door. There was no telling what would be on the other side. He thought it might be best for him to just hide behind a fern and wait, but the cabin intrigued him. Cole rapped his knuckles against the door, testing it. The door gave a little, almost giggling. Pushing harder, Cole could find no opening. The door just bent in around his fingers. With a loud *pop* the material snapped around his hand, encircling his wrist with cold, flexible stone. Cole tried to pull his hand back but the door held fast. Struggling, he put a bare foot against the door for leverage, but it too went into the door with a loud *pop*. He yanked harder and harder, careful not to touch the door with anything else.

"Help! I need help! Can anybody hear me?" he cried into the empty air. Once again the only answer was the birds above.

After exhausting himself, Cole resigned to simply lean back and catch his breath. The panic begrudgingly faded as he realized he was in no immediate danger. He was very much stuck, but the door was not about to kill him. This was as good a spot as any to wait it out.

Cole's standing foot began to ache, and his leg cramped from its awkward position. He tried shifting his weight, but stopped quickly when more of his wrist and foot were pulled into the door. It felt like a Chinese finger trap. He could only get himself more stuck the more he struggled.

"This is so stupid!" His voice broke as he screamed at the top of his lungs, hoping someone would hear him.

Nearby, something responded with a high-pitched *coo cha?* Cole stilled himself, craning his neck around to see what it was. There was nothing behind him, but he could hear something land on the roof of the cabin. Cole looked around, hoping for a stick or a non-squishy rock nearby, anything that could be used as a weapon. Small, crunchy footsteps moved across the top of the cabin. As Cole jerked his head up, a face appeared.

"Coo cha?"

There, a few feet above was what appeared to be a monkey, or perhaps a cat. Its fierce ruby eyes considered Cole for a moment, sniffing the air with its stubby snout. The creature hopped down, landing behind him. Not sure what to expect, Cole prepared to defend himself with his free hand. The creature was only the size of a small dog, but it might prove to be a formidable opponent with him in his current position. Cole twisted his neck in an attempt to size up the critter. It had red eyes, striped brindle fur, a short tale, and long canines that descended below its jaw. A crest of white fur on its head gave it the appearance of sporting a little mohawk. It was unlike anything Cole had ever seen. The creature watched for a moment with expectant eyes, as though it was waiting for something. When it became apparent that Cole was not about to make the first move, the monkey-cat nodded and strode confidently forward. Without hesitation it reached for the hem of Cole's hospital gown. Clawed black fingers pulled the cloth to its snout as it sniffed aggressively. With a snort of satisfaction, it sat back on its haunches and looked at the door, then to Cole, then back to the door.

"Coo Cha?"

"Yes I'm stuck in a door. Are you going to help me or -hey! What are you doing? You better not freakin bite me!" Cole hopped on one foot as the monkey trotted under his stuck leg, pressing its nose into the door.

"Stop that, you'll get stuck too," Cole said. There was another *pop* as the creature's head was swallowed by the door. "I told you. Can you even breathe?"

The thing didn't struggle as Cole expected. Instead, it pushed itself farther into the door until its stubby tail disappeared with a tiny *pop*.

A muffled shriek came from the other side of the door: "Coo Cha!"

Considering his options, Cole pushed his hand deeper into the door. His fingers eventually wiggled into open air. He hoped this wasn't a one-way trip, but what choice did he have at this point? Cole held his breath and pushed his face into the door, which gave a powerful snap, ringing his ears. Once he committed to moving, getting through the door was easier than expected. With a final *pop* he pulled his aching foot through the door and massaged it. Inside, the room was illuminated by sunlight trickling through moss-covered holes in the ceiling. The sparse glow showed a few bookshelves against the back wall, a round table and chair in the center, and a humongous sleeping mat off to one side. Everything seemed to be made for someone much larger than he. The walls were covered in what looked like fist-sized bells. Squinting in the dim light, Cole flicked one of the bells experimentally, making a rubbery *thud*. Steadily, the bell glowed with a gentle turquoise light. After a moment, Cole realized it was no bell, but a speckled mushroom growing right out of the wall. Cole flicked a few more, bathing the room in a soft glow. His new friend appeared at his feet, looking up at him expectantly.

"Coo Cha?"

"Yeah, yeah I'm ok now. Thanks for asking," Cole said, shuffling away. He still didn't trust the critter.

The animal nodded and scooted across the room, jumping up on the table. Cole inspected the cabin, turning on a few more mushroom-lamps. The shelves held dozens of books and a few empty containers. The sleeping mat felt stiff, yet comfortable. The monkey-cat pulled something from a bowl on the table and started munching. Hunger clawed at Cole's stomach.

Cole stood on his tiptoes, barely able to see the top of the table. "Whatcha got there?"

The creature paused, snatched another nugget out of the bowl and rolled the lump to the edge of the table. Cole eyed the long canines as they went to work on whatever it was chewing on. Slowly, Cole reached for the nugget, relieved when the creature gave no reaction. He took an experimental nibble on the thing, and to his delight it tasted edible enough. It had the consistency of a banana but tasted like nuts. Cole decided to wait a few minutes before eating another, just in case the first made him sick.

"Can I have another?" Cole asked, wondering why he was talking to an animal.

The monkey pulled a nugget from the bowl and held it in its sharp teeth, then grabbed two more and pushed them towards Cole. He was even hungrier after three, and before long the two of them finished the entire bowl. Each time he asked permission and each time the creature obliged. Slightly less hungry, Cole looked about the room for more food. Nothing looked edible and he decided against risking one of the glowing mushrooms.

"I guess this is as good a place as any. Do you mind if I hang out here for a bit?" Cole asked his new friend.

The critter snorted, but otherwise didn't object. To pass the time Cole inspected the books on the shelves. He didn't recognize any of the letters or symbols, though each book appeared to be printed in a different language. He flipped through a few more volumes until he found a book with nearly the same alphabet as English, however he couldn't make out the language.

"I think I found a name for you. How do you like 'Goran'?"

The creature perked its ears, gazing at Cole with an intensity that made him look away first.

"Or how about, Ishme-something. Never mind, I can't even pronounce that one. Alrighty, Goran it is," Cole said, snapping the book shut.

The monkey-cat took a long breath, swelling to nearly twice its size. After a moment it lost interest and curled up on the table, closing its eyes.

"I'm pretty tired too. I think I'll use the bed though. Well Goran it was nice meeting you, but I might not be here when you wake up," Cole said with a yawn. He was tired, though not with the unusual weariness that had plagued him over the last week. This was a normal sort of tired.

Cole stretched out on the sleeping mat, barely taking up half the padded surface. To his surprise, and slight annoyance, he couldn't fall asleep right away. His mind was simply too active to shut down. It seemed determined to busy itself with darker thoughts. He tried thinking of other things, but as soon as he relaxed and let his guard down, the dark thoughts bubbled up to the surface. Cole hugged himself and cried quietly, waiting for sleep to take him back to cruel reality.

Cole woke refreshed, yet disappointed to find himself still half naked in the cabin. Goran was nowhere to be found, and all the mushrooms had gone out. Guided by the shafts of sunlight, Cole flicked a few mushrooms on. To his surprise, the bowl had been refilled with the same type of nuggets as before. It was a good thing too as his stomach was growling angrily at him. He wolfed down most of the bowl's contents, leaving a few in case Goran came back.

Cole hopped up into the chair and waited. For what, he didn't know. There was no plan other than to simply wait for himself to reappear back in the hospital bed. Maybe *He* would show up and take him back. Cole looked around, trying to sense *His* presence lurking in a dark corner. Nothing. He was alone.

Growing restless, Cole took to the books again. He looked through every page but nothing was recognizable, except for the one with Goran's namesake. Where did his friend go anyway? And who refilled the bowl?

Time passed in quiet ambiguity. He placed books on the ground to mark the movement of the shafts of light, but after what seemed like hours they hadn't moved a hair. Cole tried sleeping again, but to no avail. Irritation urged him to make an attempt at the strange door. Holding tightly to the fact that Goran had managed to leave, he begged the door to allow him passage as well.

The process was still unsettling, but the door swallowed him through. Cole walked the perimeter of the cabin, careful to not step on any rocks. During his second loop, a very loud *COO CHAAA!* Rang from far away.

"Goran?" Cole turned his head, trying to find the source of the cry.

It sounded again, but with more urgency. Cole trotted off towards the cry, eyes raking the ground for some kind of weapon, but found nothing. After he ran for what felt like several hard laps around the basketball court, the dense fernery gave way to a sandy grove completely devoid of plant life. Cole stopped at the edge of the clearing. Something about it seemed off. The crusty surface was completely flat and decorated with several large circular patterns, each with a neat little hole in the center.

"COO CHAA!"

Cole jumped back, clutching his racing heart. Across the clearing, clinging on to the branch of a fern was Goran. A taut, flesh-colored rope wriggling from one of the holes was fastened to one of his feet. Cole took a step forward, but as he did, a similar tendril wandered out of the hole nearest to him. Cole jumped back and watched in disgust as the pink, veiny thing quivered its way towards him. Avoiding the sand entirely, he ran around the edge of the clearing, getting as close to Goran as he could without triggering the creature in the hole.

As gently as he could, Cole put a bare foot on the sand. As if it were expecting him, another tentacle shot out of the nearest hole. Cole removed his foot and took a few steps back. Goran was struggling now, readjusting his grip on the branch. Cole could tell he wouldn't be able to cling on much longer. His tiny ribs puffed in and out at a rapid pace.

Cole scanned the area for anything that might be of use, but the forest floor looked as if someone had just cleaned it. A small boulder caught his eye. It would have to do. Cole heaved the boulder off the ground and, as he suspected, it was of the same hissing, jelly-filled variety he had stepped on before. He hauled it back to the edge of the sand and, with his best shot-put throw, tossed the thing at the open hole. It was too heavy, however, and the squishy rock fell short. The quivering tentacle shot out of the hole again, wrapping itself around the rock, which flexed and hissed as it attempted to scurry away. The tendril pulled more of itself out of the hole and threw a few coils around the rock, dragging it slowly towards its home.

Hoping the rock would keep the tentacle busy, Cole approached Goran, who was now holding on by only one clawed hand. Cole wrapped his fingers around the pink rope and felt it flexing and pulsing under his grip. He yanked, trying to give Goran some relief. The tendril didn't budge and it was too slippery for him to get a good grip. Goran screeched, his grip failing entirely as he flew through the air, arms waving. Cole caught him like a football as they both fell to the ground. Feeling the weight of an even larger meal, the tendril pulled harder, dragging the two of them steadily towards the hole. The crusty sand was none too forgiving on Cole's more sensitive parts not covered by the gown.

He had to think fast. They were mere feet from the hole now, which was beginning to stir. Afraid to see what else the hole had to offer, Cole took a hand off Goran and brought the tendril to his teeth. The thing tasted foreign and metallic, like a mouthful of soft pennies. Hot, coppery blood spurted onto Cole's tongue as he gnawed it. With a final yank, the tentacle broke. Goran clung to Cole's chest as he ran back towards safety. In his panic, he ran not the way he'd come, but rather took a different, quicker path. Before his feet left the sand he felt a halting tug on his hospital gown. Another tendril had its grip on the cloth and threatened to pull him off balance. Cole threw Goran as far as he could, landing him safely outside the sand. Grabbing his own handful of the gown, Cole pulled with all his might. The tentacle threw more coils around the cloth and inch by inch dragged Cole towards its hole, which he was now almost on top of.

The sand erupted, spraying Cole's face and eyes. When he opened them a fat, hairy grub the size of a couch emerged from the hole. Long spiky hairs covered its skin, which quivered with perverse excitement. It flexed and wrestled the tendril back into its car tire-sized mouth, wiggling a tunnel of barbed yellow teeth. It had no eyes, but Cole felt the thing looking at him like a piece of juicy, vulnerable meat.

Without conscious thought, Cole twisted about, surrendering the hospital gown. Gasping, shaking, and bleeding, Cole joined Goran at the edge of the clearing. Luckily, the grub seemed to be anchored in the hole and did not pursue. By unspoken consent, Goran and the now entirely naked Cole bolted for the cabin.

Even though there were no people around, Cole felt embarrassingly exposed. Not that the gown did much, but at least it concealed his front side. He tried to cover himself the best he could, but abandoned his modesty when his hands could be better used to navigate the dense foliage. He hoped none of the plants had any poison ivy-like qualities. Along the way, Goran stopped to scale a particularly large fern. Cole waited on the bottom, searching the canopy. Something struck him in the face.

"Ow! What the hell?" he blurted.

Something else fell next to him. Rubbing his cheek, Cole bent down and picked up one of the soft seed things he and Goran had been munching on earlier. A dozen more landed around him before Goran descended from the fern.

"So you're the one who filled the bowl. Thanks," he said, picking up the rest of the lumps.

Rain twinkled up in the canopy as the cabin came into view. Urged by the thought of being naked, cold, *and* wet, Cole broke into a run. Once inside he deposited the seeds into the bowl and slumped down onto the mat. He couldn't tell if he was shaking from the cold or from the shock of almost being eaten. Goran pulled another bowl off the shelf and placed it under one of the holes in the ceiling.

"You know, you're pretty smart for a cat, or even a monkey," Cole quipped, and grabbed another bowl and followed suit. Goran gave him a look that clearly said, 'You know, you're pretty dumb for a human'.

"So are you a boy or a girl anyway?" Seeing the quizzical look on Goran's face, Cole stood up. "Do you have one of these?"

Goran stood on his legs and looked down.

"Yep, you're a boy like me. I was hoping you were. Wouldn't want to be naked in front of a girl. Though I guess you're just as naked as I am…" Cole paused, wondering once more why he was talking to an animal.

With nothing better to do, Cole told Goran all about life back home. He explained about the dreams and disappearances, growing up poor, his feelings for Ashley, his mom, Nana Beth, and even his some of the stories he'd learned in the planetarium. He avoided one subject in particular, however; he was not ready to talk about that, even to someone who couldn't talk back. Goran sat on the table the whole time and listened intently. Seeing the rain trickling through the holes in the ceiling, Cole readjusted the bowls. Goran watched every move, analyzing and learning. When enough water had collected, they each drank their fill.

The sky darkened, though Cole couldn't tell if it was from the sun setting or the clouds from the storm. He flicked every mushroom on the wall, illuminating the cabin with their turquoise ambiance.

"No wonder the floor is still dry, look at the roots!" He shuffled his feet as if the floor were covered in spiders.

The mushrooms had sprouted thin roots that crept down the walls and covered the floor. The sight was eerily familiar to what they had just barely escaped earlier in the day. When it became apparent that the roots were only interested in the water, Cole perused the library on the wall again, this time looking through every word. While he didn't find any answers, he did find one large volume with a cloth cover and threads in the binding.

"This isn't your favorite book is it?" Cole held up the large book for Goran, who didn't bother looking up from the water bowl he was currently lapping at. "Ok then…"

Cole pulled at the thread bindings, careful not to snap them. Once the binding was undone, the cloth came apart easily. The material was old and not certainly not ideal, but it would work. Cole was no tailor or master of bookbinding, but after an hour or so he had a passable loincloth wrapped around his more delicate parts.

"So how'd I do? Not bad, I think." He spun around, proudly displaying his work for Goran. Goran sniffed, but was otherwise disinterested. "Gee, thanks Goran. I for one am pretty damn proud of my handiwork. I think it makes my butt look good too."

Cole plucked a small rock from the ground and flicked it at Goran. The pebble smacked Goran's flank, and the creature twitched in surprise. Goran inspected the rock and looked up at the ceiling. Unable to discern where the rock had come from, he laid his head back down on the table and closed his eyes. Another pebble struck his flank, a direct hit this time. Goran jumped up on all fours and scanned the ceiling, sniffing the air with bared teeth.

Cole stifled his giggles and pretended to inspect the ceiling as well. "What's wrong Bud? Is the ceiling coming apart?"

A menacing growl leaked out through Goran's needle-sharp teeth. After a minute of searching, he hopped down and nestled himself under the table. Not wanting to overdo it, Cole laid himself out on the sleeping mat and let his friend sleep. Now that the adrenaline had worn off, he was tired enough to sleep as well. He couldn't tell if it was night time yet as the light coming from the holes hadn't changed. Just as he felt himself slipping into a dream, something hit him in the stomach. He bolted upright and found a smooth pebble next to him. Goran was fast asleep.

The next day, or perhaps it was the same day, Cole woke before Goran. The rain had stopped but the sky was still overcast. How long was he supposed to be stuck here? The novelty of the cabin had worn off entirely, but the dangers that lurked in the woods were even less inviting. Yet after a few handfuls from the bowl, Cole decided to brave the forest. Popping out of the door, the first thing he noticed was how sore his feet were. He hadn't run around barefoot since he was a kid, and even then that was only at the park. He adopted a tender gait and set off. Before Cole took more than a few steps he heard the door pop behind him.

"Coo Cha!"

He turned to see his friend galloping towards him, seed in mouth. "Welcome to the land of the living. You know you snored all damn night? Are animals even supposed to snore?"

The pair set off, Cole taking a slow lead with his raw feet. They walked in ever larger circles around the cabin, exploring for a while and taking breaks when Cole needed it. Goran seemed content to follow him. During their breaks he would show Cole things, mostly edible things. There were some flowers which had thick flesh that tasted similar to plums. Under the fake-jelly-filled rocks there were usually a few beetles, though Cole let Goran keep those for himself. Cole even learned how to tell the difference between the real rocks and the jelly ones; the jelly rocks never stayed still too long, eventually wiggling or letting out a quiet hiss. Sometimes Goran would wander off just out of sight, but he always came running back within a few minutes. Cole wondered why Goran always came back. He was a solitary wild animal. Why would he be attached to a random stranger that showed up out of the blue? Whatever the reason was, Cole was grateful for his company.

After one of Goran's tangents, he returned with a struggling rodent in his jaws. It squeaked and kicked madly, but there was no hope of escaping Goran's long canines. Cole watched with morbid interest as Goran brought the creature over to a real rock, picking up a smaller stone along the way. With practiced motions, Goran held down the rodent with a hand and one foot, then proceeded to bludgeon the creature's skull. He brought the stone down again and again, each time producing a sickening crunch. Cole went sickly pale, suddenly sweating and out of breath. He clutched his ears, wincing at the noise.

"Stop it! Stop! Leave him alone!" Cole screamed.

Goran looked up from his kill, which was no longer struggling. He clamped his jaws on one of its legs and dragged it over to Cole, placing it at his feet. Cole took one glance at the creature and vomited. Still gasping for air, Cole ran for the Cabin. He dove through the door and fell into the table, knocking it into the bookshelf. His breath now rapid and shallow, Cole hugged himself to keep from falling apart. Goran came through the door shortly afterwards, without the dead rodent. His ruby eyes were wide with concern.

"Coo Cha?" he barked.

Cole continued his fit, curled up in a ball on the floor. Goran shoved him in the back, but to no effect. Cocking his head, Goran snorted and sat back on his haunches as Cole's spasm eventually gave way to uneasy silence.

When Cole woke with no memory of falling asleep, the whole left side of his body was senseless. He pushed himself up into a sitting position as his numb side exploded with pins and needles. Goran was still sitting, eyes fixed.

"I don't want to talk about it," Cole grunted, wiping the tears and spit from his face.

As the days passed, Cole realized there *were* no days because this place never had any nights. Once he tried staying up for as long as he could just to see if the sun moved. He eventually gave up after Goran went through two full bouts of sleep while the sun hadn't deviated an inch from his book markers. With no other means of tracking time, he counted the times he slept, though that was unreliable because he had no idea how long he dozed off for. It was the best option however.

Weeks went by, or at least by Cole's estimate. The surrounding area had more than enough edible plant life for Goran, but with Cole's appetite they had to venture farther as their food sources diminished. Cole even tried some of the small game Goran caught. The first few times were more of an exercise in failure than anything else, seeing as Cole had no idea how to make a fire, and he had no means of dressing the kill. After trial and error, the two devised a foolproof system that would almost always work. Cole would sneak around a dense patch of undergrowth and push his way through, scaring any small creatures towards Goran's capable canines. While Cole was much too slow to catch his own prey, his newly sharpened rock and knack for creating friction-fires proved to be a boon for the duo.

Goran had apparently never seen fire before, as he hid on top of the cabin for an hour after Cole had miraculously made his first. While Cole found Goran's reaction amusing, he refrained from laughing or poking fun. There were countless occasions when Cole found himself paralyzed with a sudden panic attack, and Goran was always there for him. Certain triggers consistently brought about these debilitating fits, such as a puddle he fell into by accident, and when Goran cracked open a hard fruit with a rock, and even a hearty whiff of Cole's own body odor. Each time Cole found himself on the ground shaking and unable to breathe, he would wake to find Goran by his side patiently waiting for his friend to be okay.

Eventually, their foraging brought them to a path. This was an unusual discovery for Cole at the least. Goran on the other hand seemed quite at home no matter where he was. Inspecting the trail, Cole realized this was no game path for rodents or other small creatures. This was a road clearly made for a reason. Real rocks lined the edges of the trail, and there wasn't a single weed or shrub encroaching within its limits.

Cole hopped down from a ledge bordering the trail, landing sloppily. "Goran, what is this thing?"

Goran landed next to him and continued down the trail as if he owned the place.

Cole took a long breath, looking behind him. "We're already a good ways from the cabin, but I kind of want to see where this goes. You up for a little walk?"

Goran answered his question by trotting at a steady pace down the trail.

"Well you seem to know where you're going at least. Hey, not so fast, my feet are still a little sore." Cole winced and started after him.

To the left of the trail a steep slope dropped off towards a valley. To their right was higher ground and their cabin. Goran picked up a faster pace than usual, making Cole jog to keep up. He seemed to be doing this more and more since their first trip into the woods. Cole didn't mind though. For the first time in his life his body was becoming accustomed to running. He had no mirror to judge with, but he could tell he'd lost a great deal of weight. He never got winded as long as they weren't sprinting. The wounds on his backside had healed up and his feet were callusing up nicely. He imagined he looked quite good, though his tattered book-binding loincloth could do with replacing.

"What are you in such a hurry for?" Cole said in between breaths. "If we keep going we're going to have to sleep outside again. I can't sleep in a tree like you and I'm not trying to get eaten by a pissed-off worm today."

Goran quickened his pace.

Cole groaned, "This better be worth it."

If only he had Goran as a running coach. Cole would have made any team he tried out for. They maintained their pace for a while, Goran eventually slowing. This was the first time in Cole's life when he was the fastest runner in a group. Grinning, he dropped his head and lengthened his stride. Without warning, Goran skidded to a stop.

"What's the matter Bud, getting a little tired?" Cole let out a haughty laugh while he bent over, catching his breath.

Goran was dead still, eyes wide and straight ahead. Cole couldn't tell if he was ready to flee or pounce. With a grunt, Goran shot off like a little bullet and scaled the nearest fern.

"What the…" Cole arched his neck, losing sight of his friend in the canopy.

The path and surrounding forest were eerily silent. Even the birds had ceased their usual gossip.

In the quiet, Cole could hear something farther down the trail, animal cries or perhaps human voices. Something didn't feel right. The air was too still. Cole darted to the left side of the trail, stumbling downhill as he fell into a flowery shrub. The voices grew louder. They were definitely people and they were definitely coming his way.

CHAPTER 8

NIGHTFALL

Peeping through the leaves, Cole spied two children on the trail. A rosy-cheeked girl skipped alongside a boy who had the same nose and hair, possibly brother and sister. The language they spoke was just as foreign as their clothes, which appeared to be no more than strips of earth-toned cloth wrapped tightly like gauze. While the boy carried a severe look and walked with a military-like stiffness, the girl was carefree, as if any moment not singing and dancing was a moment wasted.

Cole wished his hiding spot was a little farther off the trail. The two children were close enough now that he could hear the swishing of the girl's garments. As they neared, Cole noticed that even though they were the size of children, their faces were crinkled with lines both deep and light, giving them a contrasting aged look. Cole held his breath as the girl twirled past without notice. The boy, however, saw Cole immediately, crying out in alarm. Cole emerged with raised hands, dropping his sharpened rock in plain sight, a decision he regretted instantly when the boy pulled out a jagged dark blade from the folds around his middle.

"It's okay, I'm not going to hurt anybody." Cole's voice was as soft and gentle as he could manage.

The girl stopped dancing and hid behind the boy, who held out his blade and shouted something. Cole tried to make himself look as unintimidating as possible, but he was nearly naked and almost twice their size. The boy repeated himself, taking a step forward with a white-knuckle grip on his weapon.

Cole shook his head slowly, palms facing outward. "I'm sorry, I don't know what you're saying. Everything is okay, I'm not going to hurt you guys."

Cole's gaze darted from the boy's eyes to the knife. The boy took another step forward, jabbering all the while. Cole hadn't the slightest idea as to what the boy was getting at, but it didn't sound friendly. Another step forward. Cole widened his stance, confident he could overpower the kid and take the knife. He was wrong. With his other hand, the boy whipped a rock at Cole's head. Cole ducked, hearing the rock whoosh by his ear. His head rang like a bell as his face was met by the boy's foot. Stunned, Cole fell to his knees. As he felt the blade on this throat, his hand found the boy's wrist. They wrestled for a few seconds as Cole's other hand found the boy's free arm. The boy was very strong for being so small, but luckily Cole was much larger and twisted his arm behind his back. Cole wrenched on the boy's wrist, gaining a pained cry as the knife dropped to the dirt. Half blind with watery eyes, Cole spun the boy, tossing him as far as he could. His little body landed heavily in the dirt and didn't get up. Cole would have felt terrible if he hadn't been nearly murdered.

"I told you I didn't want to hurt you!" Cole's voice cracked. He snatched the blade from the dirt. "Why would you attack me like that? I was no threat!"

The boy answered with a groan as the girl rushed to his side. To show he was no danger to them, he held the blade behind his back and helped the boy to his feet. The girl watched, still as a statue.

Cole adopted a sincere tone and brushed the dirt from the boy's front. "I'm sorry, I shouldn't have been so rough. Are your shoulders ok?"

The boy didn't speak, but the girl chimed in. She appeared to be pleading with the boy. Without breaking eye contact with Cole, he responded to her with a short, fiery words. She continued to bargain with him, her hands tugging lightly at his. He answered with a quick nod and the tension seemed to evaporate from the air. Smiling, the girl threw her hands up and spun on the spot. Without fear, she snatched Cole's free hand, beckoning him.

"You want me to follow you?" Cole guessed.

She responded in a pleasant manner and pulled at him. The boy deliberately pointed at Cole and then himself, then down the trail toward where they came from. Cole gazed up towards the canopy. Goran was nowhere to be found.

"Goran! Come on down, it's safe now!" Cole shouted through cupped hands. There was no response. He called again but the only reply was a bird cawing angrily back at him. "Huh. I'm sure he'll turn up sooner or later. You probably just spooked him."

The boy looked up, confused. With a face of wrinkled stone he nodded down the trail, indicating they should be going. He held his hand out expectantly as they stepped off.

"I think I'll hold on to the knife for now." Cole wiped some blood from his neck, showing the boy. The boy huffed and quickened his stride.

As their legs were much shorter, Cole had to restrain himself from walking too fast. The girl held his hand the whole time, swinging it back and forth as she chirped away, explaining this and that as though Cole could understand. The boy remained silent. Goran never appeared, though Cole wasn't worried. He probably just had gone back to the cabin.

The trail gradually rolled over to a grassy blanket. The cool blades soothed Cole's battered feet as the forest thinned to a windswept field. A welcoming breeze rippled through the high grass, making it look more like an ocean. Without the shade he was accustomed to, Cole had to squint under his hand to see. In the distance, a group of tall buildings poked up from behind a lone hill. The girl laughed, bouncing on her feet as she pointed towards the structures. Even the boy smiled.

The group of buildings turned out to be a dumpy village. It was hard for Cole to tell, but if he had to guess this was a poorer section of town. A musty stink hung in the air, reminding Cole of a homeless person in the summer. The buildings were a few stories tall and so crooked that Cole was hesitant to walk too close. Insects swarmed in the gaps in between houses, which seemed to be the dumping spot for their refuse. Tiny people popped from the doorless thresholds. They all wore the same wrappings and none of them were taller than Cole's chest. Apprehension painted each of their wrinkled faces when they saw him.

A woman approached the three of them with her hands on her hips. Her hair and neck were wrapped tight, giving her a mummy-like appearance. She gestured towards Cole's naked body, barking at him with spit flying from her jowls. Cole gripped the knife a little tighter. The children talked with the woman, hopefully putting in a good word. Cole had overpowered the boy but his confidence waned as the adults circled close. After some deliberation, the woman stepped uncomfortably close to Cole. Without blinking or dropping her gaze, she held out a hand and demanded something of him. Her voice was harsh and raspy, pushing Cole a step back. He was completely surrounded now by more than he could count. The little girl took his hand and spoke in sweet, reassuring coos. Cole relinquished the knife to the older woman, who passed it off to another, her eyes stabbing him all the while. The small knife wouldn't do him much good anyway, not against so many. At the old woman's command, the crowd dispersed. The two children from the trail remained.

When the children didn't move, the old woman scolded them, or at least that's what it sounded like to Cole. The boy seemed to be reasoning with the woman as the girl chimed in, still holding Cole's hand. Without a word the mummy-lady undid the wrappings from her hand as the boy began pleading. With heavy knuckles, she smote the boy across the face, causing his feet to leave the ground. His body seemed to take a lifetime to fall. Chilled worms tickled Cole's insides, taking his breath away. He felt the girl's fingers slip from his as she was dragged away. Cole couldn't hear her cries as the pulse in his ears was deafening. He was having another panic attack. He hugged himself, steadying the shakes before they set in.

Not remembering having closed his eyes, Cole opened them and slowed his breathing.

Surprisingly, the boy was back on his feet. Blood drooled from a split under his eye. He had his arms around the girl, consoling her quietly as she bawled. He whispered in her ear, coaxing as he guided her away. She looked back at Cole and reached for him, but the boy nudged her along. The old woman said something to a few men Cole had just realized were standing behind him. They each held a pole taller than Cole, each with a jagged dark blade at the tip. Cole winced as she poked him in the chest, then made a walking motion with her stubby fingers before pointing at her own chest. The signal was clear enough; *follow me.* Cole didn't need much convincing after seeing the three pike-men, who trailed behind silently. The mummy-lady led him deeper into the village. The buildings grew taller and less shabby as they went. The dank aroma was replaced by a sterile smell not unlike that of a hospital. This new district was much cleaner. The dirt roads eventually became stone polished to a mirror finish, which blended seamlessly into the buildings. There was no trash to be found and the doors were all solid. The people here were much taller than Cole, and lacked any sort of wrinkle or blemish on their faces. Their wrappings were darker with a silky sheen, some even laced with shiny metallic threads. Unlike their shorter counterparts, the people here took no notice of Cole. They were too busy in conversation or rushing around as if late for an appointment.

Cole began to feel very self-conscious about his near nakedness when they stopped at what appeared to be a shop. The mummy-lady signaled to one of the guards and he went inside, emerging a few minutes later with a large roll of black cloth. He tossed it to Cole, who caught it, dumbfounded. The guard let out an impatient sigh before passing his pike off to his partner. Before Cole could stop him, the guard ripped off his loincloth, tossing it aside. He didn't have much time to be embarrassed however, as the guard snatched the cloth and set to wrapping it around Cole. The fabric was chilly and loose but as it soaked up Cole's body heat it snugged gently to him, like a second skin. There was thankfully enough to wrap several layers around his feet for shoes. When the guard was done Cole was completely covered from the neck down. He flexed and bent testing for gaps, but the fabric seemed to have adhered to itself. It was seamless, yet breathable.

"Thank you." Cole did his best to make a gesture of gratitude.

The guard responded with a grunt and resumed his position behind Cole. Satisfied, the old woman snapped her fingers and they resumed walking. They came to a structure that looked more like an office building than a residence. Its stone walls were veined with a brilliant white material, and shone with a gloss that put the surrounding areas to shame. The steps leading up to the door were very tall. Cole could barely reach his legs high enough, and the others had to jump up each one like children clambering into their parents' bed. The main door was of equal proportion. Without a backwards glance the old woman pushed her face into it and disappeared with a tiny *pop*. Grateful that this was not the first time he had seen such a door, Cole followed close behind.

Once inside, the first thing Cole noticed was the large furniture and very tall ceilings. The décor was dark and imposing, as though the curator had hand-picked each piece to make its viewer feel inferior. The building had no windows, or any discernible light source, yet the interior was lit by a harsh ambient light that produced no shadows. Pained faces adorned the trim on the wall and the arched thresholds. There were hundreds of them, each with its own unique expression that resonated within Cole. It was as if each face was intentionally carved to exemplify a specific horrible emotion. Cole wondered if the artist worked a second job as a torturer.

He was made to wait in the atrium with the guards as the old woman's padded footsteps echoed off down a hallway. The guards gave Cole the feeling he had better not make any sudden movements. He was content to stand there silently, disturbed and intrigued by the architecture. In the center of the room was a statue of a giant grotesque figure. It was as if the sculptor kept switching his mind as to whether he wanted to make a human or an insect. At the foot of the statue were smaller carvings depicting a crowd of the childlike people. Adoration gleamed in their eyes and, to Cole's disgust, all of them were mutilating themselves in one way or another. One was pulling the skin off of her bare chest while another was cradling his self-eviscerated bowels, smiling longingly all the while.

Cole was just starting to feel nauseated when the atrium echoed with the woman's padded footsteps, this time accompanied by a loud clacking partner. From around the statue appeared the small old woman. Behind her in stark contrast followed a man so tall that Cole now felt like the child, based on the fact that the top of his head would barely meet the man's belt.

The giant man wore a suit so white it seemed to darken everything around him, making the pristine marble appear dirty. The old woman spoke, but the man was drawn to Cole as though he was the most interesting thing he'd ever seen. The giant ignored the woman, crouching low and bringing his eyes level with Cole's. His face was smooth alabaster and lacked any imperfections - not a single blemish, vein, or hair out of place. When he spoke Cole couldn't understand a word, but the voice that came from his chiseled lips was so charismatic and reassuring, Cole felt a sudden urge to do something impressive.

"I'm sorry, I don't understand a word you're saying," Cole muttered, fixing his posture to stand a little taller.

The man's eyes went wide with delight as he clapped his hands together rapidly. Cole had no idea what he'd done to please him, but he felt proud and hoped to please him again. With a dismissive wave of his huge arm the towering man clicked his tongue. The guards as well as the old woman obviously took this as their cue to leave, and did so without a word. The man was clearly annoyed at how long it took for them to find the exit, following them with a look of disgust. Cole found himself irritated with them as well, scowling at their little backs. When the final *pop* sounded, the man aimed his fascination back to Cole. Crouching lower, the man brought his thumb and forefinger to Cole's Jaw, tilting his head up. Cole shut his eyes as the man kissed his forehead. An electric sensation trickled through Cole, leaving him confused and disoriented, as if he were experiencing profound déjà vu,

"That's better, isn't it?" The man laughed, his voice rich and clear like the polished marble that surrounded them.

"Y-you can sp-speak English?" Cole stuttered, tripping over his words. His mouth seemed to move too slowly for his thoughts.

The man laughed again, hearty and genuine. "Of course not. I've no idea what 'English' is. My friend, it is you who has picked up a new language."

"B-but, how? I d-don't know any other l-languages." Cole knew he sounded foolish now. Why was he stuttering so badly?

"Well, you do now. I've implanted in you a cypher that will allow you to speak my language, which is Aenerian. Light-side dialect to be precise. It will take some time for your tongue and lips to grow accustomed to the movements." His eyebrows twitched up as his grin widened. "I see a thousand questions blooming in your eyes. I have several of my own, but as you are my guest here, please, take your pick." The man crossed his legs and sat on the floor, now eye level with Cole. "Just speak slowly if the stuttering bothers you, trust me, I have all the time in the world for you."

Cole hesitated, wondering if his words would come out in their tongue or his own. He searched his mind for a switch or memory that would allow him to speak in this 'Aenerian'.

"My friend, it's best if you don't think on it overmuch. Just look at me and speak freely." His big hand pattered on Cole's shoulder. "Come now, give it a go."

Cole took a breath and spoke as slowly as he could: "Where am I? And who are you?"

"Your second question is easiest, so I will answer it first; my name is Kreed. I oversee this municipality and all of its inhabitants. As for your first question, that is a tricky one. I suppose we should start with the obvious. You are here, in my home, which is located on the edge of the city Costas, which is located Light Side of Aeneria. You are lucky, we are currently in the house Terra, and so we have strong sunlight for a little while longer. Ah I see I've planted another question in you?" Kreed talked slowly so Cole could understand, but it only made his voice sound silky and enticing.

"W-what do you m-mean 'house Terra'?" Cole had to force himself to speak at a snail's pace, "And where is Aeneria? And what's the Light Side?"

"Your questions grow like weeds!" Kreed chuckled, growing more excited. "As soon as I tend to one, three more sprout up! So you don't know what Aeneria is, or much of anything about it. From what I can tell you haven't been here long or else I would know you. Forgive me, but I could require a bit of context before I answer your questions further. Where did you come from?"

Well, I grew up in Nashua. It's a city in New Hampshire." Seeing Kreed's confusion, Cole rushed on, "New Hampshire is a state, in the U.S.? Have you heard of the United States? In North America?"

"My friend, I haven't the slightest inkling as to where those places are. Hmm. On what planet would I find these places?" Kreed asked, tapping his chin.

Cole frowned, "Well, that would be Earth, right?"

Kreed's eyes popped wide. "Ahh now there is a place I *have* heard of. We call it Terra, but that is most interesting. Most interesting indeed." For the first time, Kreed's eyes left Cole's and searched the polished stone floor, as if he'd lost something very important. "How is this possible? What is your name and how did you come to this planet?" Kreed's voice was no longer polished and kind, but accusatory and steely.

Cole's mouth fell open. A sickly worry bubbled in his gut. "What do you mean 'this planet'?"

Kreed relaxed, a curious smile returning to his face. "Why, Aeneria of course. Terra is up there." He pointed up towards the high arched ceiling. "Well, not there exactly. Come, follow me outside. And you said your name was?" Kreed rose to his feet in one fluid motion.

"I'm Colton Carter," Cole said, joining him.

"Interesting. This is your only name? Are you sure of it?" Kreed looked sideways down at Cole.

"Um, I'm called 'Cole' for short, but that's it," Cole replied.

Kreed pursed his lips and squinted. "I'm not so sure that it is, but we will see, Colton Carter."

Kreed led him deeper into the building, down hallways decorated with more disturbing scenes and incredibly lifelike paintings. Cole kept his head down after seeing one that displayed hooded figures placing infants inside an open cadaver. He hoped he was seriously misinterpreting their art. They wound their way through a series of dizzying turns, higher and higher into Kreed's house. Eventually, Cole felt the light and heat from the sun on his face. Kreed gestured to an open balcony, bringing Cole's gaze down to a garden. Flowered vines crawled over every statue, making the figures look as if they were being choked by nature. There were a few of the wrinkled child-people in white wrappings tending to the shrubs and wading through a brook that sprawled throughout.

Kreed lifted Cole by his middle and sat him on the edge of the bannister. "The courtyard is beautiful, isn't it?"

"Yeah, it is," Cole said in a dreamy voice, captivated by the living art. He couldn't tell if they grew in such patterns on their own or if they were painstakingly manicured in such a way. As if to answer his question, one of the child-people pulled out a short white staff and waved it over a shrub, which flowed and undulated at its coaxing. To Cole the bush now had a more pleasing form that flowed better with the bend in the stream. The tiny groundskeeper tapped the shrub in several places and flowers crept out from its depths.

"Our caretakers are very skilled, but if I may direct your attention elsewhere, you will see your Earth, or Terra. It's just there on the horizon, exactly opposite your star."

Cole hardly needed Kreed's arm to point it out. There, peeking over the horizon, was the blue marble itself; his home. It was the size of a grapefruit held at arms-length. "How the hell!" Cole wobbled and his heart dropped as he almost fell from the balcony. Kreed's hand held his shoulders steady. "How is this possible? There's no way! We would see another planet this close!"

"It's true, you would see another planet at this distance, but not this one. Even with its small size, Aeneria should still be quite visible day and night from Terra. Aeneria however is not at all like other planets. While we are certainly here on this planet, which is without a doubt very close to your Earth, we are also at the same time *not* here." The befuddled expression on Cole's face seemed to make Kreed even more excited. "Ah, I can see the confusion. How do I put this? Aeneria is a transient thing. It is ethereal in nature. It Travels, like a wraith, unseen through different realities. Right now we are in your reality; the house of Terra. Shortly we will move to the next; the house of Pastori, which has its own sun that is unfortunately not visible from Costas."

This was too much. Feeling lightheaded, Cole asked Kreed to place him back on the polished stone floor. Cole had hoped all along this was a weird dream he would eventually wake from. Now after hearing things explained by an apparently sane person, it became real.

"How is this possible?" Cole's vision blurred as tears leaked from his eyes.

"I was hoping *you* could explain that part, Colton Carter. I can see you are distressed. Naturally this has come as quite a shock to you. I admit I am very disturbed myself. You need rest, but before I let you retire I need you to explain everything you remember. Your situation is unprecedented and my superiors will require a full report." Kreed crossed his legs again and joined Cole on the ground, lifting his chin and wiping his tears away.

Cole looked into Kreed's eyes and felt an unprovoked urge to please him. He had no idea why, but he trusted Kreed. Before he knew it, Cole was retelling his entire life's story. Everything was in vivid detail, from his first memories of the police showing up when he was a toddler, all the way up to his arrival on Aeneria. He waxed for hours, saying things that surprised him because he hadn't remembered them until now. When he finished, his throat was sore and his eyes heavy. He wanted to continue, but there was nothing else to say. He looked eagerly at Kreed, hoping he'd done well.

Kreed blinked for the first time in hours. "Thank you, Colton Carter. I know that was very difficult. And you have my most heartfelt condolences for the loss of young Joshy. You've done so well for me. Now, my friend, it's time for you to rest. When you wake up we'll see what we can do for you."

Kreed rose, scooping Cole up in his arms like a child. His embrace was gentle and warm, and Cole felt safe for the first time in weeks. He fell in and out of sleep, vaguely aware of someone carrying him through the halls of Kreed's place. They eventually arrived at a door, passing through with a deep *pop*. Barely awake, Cole felt himself land on something soft.

"Sleep well, Colton Carter. When you wake we will have much more to discuss," Kreed said in a soft tone.

Cole stayed the sleep just a little longer: "Kreed?"

"Yes, my friend?" Kreed brushed Cole's hair aside.

Cole felt like he was talking from the other end of a tunnel. "Is this place magic? Is that how they shaped the flowers in the garden? And how you made me speak your language?"

Kreed smiled. "Yes, but to us it is nothing more than a different set of rules we live by. Rules that perhaps you may come to learn one day."

"Could you send me back home?" Cole pleaded.

"We shall see. Now sleep, Colton Carter." Kreed placed his first two fingers over Cole's eyes, closing them and pushing Cole into his dreams.

Cole woke, warm and whole, indulging in a nice stretch. He sat up and found himself in complete darkness. He was perched upon something soft and pleasantly cool to the touch. Fumbling in the dark, he found a wall and used his hands to search for a light switch. Did they even have light switches on this planet?

"How am I supposed to see anything with no light?" Cole said to the darkness.

As if in response, a sourceless white light illuminated a room filled with pillows from wall to wall.

"Um, a little brighter?" Cole guessed.

The gentle glow intensified so that Cole had to wait for his eyes to adjust. When they did, he found the room had a large bay window with bars over it. Stepping over the pillows, he pulled himself up to the window sill and peered outside. The sky was pitch black. Where had the sun gone? Were they no longer next to earth?

He reached his hands through the bars and felt a significant drop in temperature. It was as if there was an invisible barrier keeping the cold out. A few stories below, he could see a winding street with closely-packed buildings. Blue oval lanterns accompanied each solid door, making the street look like a river. There were a few people walking the streets, appearing from the solid doors like phantoms in the ghostly hue. Cole thought he saw a shadow moving across the rooftop directly below him, but after a few minutes he didn't see it move again and lost interest.

A high-pitched growl broke the silence, startling him. He searched for the source of the noise, only to discover that it was his stomach. Thankful that no one saw him jump, he hopped down from the sill, landing bodily on a larger pillow. He clutched his stomach again, attempting to stifle another growl. He hoped Kreed had some food besides flowers and seeds. He approached the door and pressed his face into it. The door was very much solid.

"Ow!" Cole swore, rubbing his nose. He pushed his hand into the door, but it may as well have been a wall. "What is this, a one-way door? Wait! Am I stuck in here?"

He frantically pushed on every part of the door he could reach, then ran his hands over every part of the wall, then yanked and tugged every pillow into a corner of the room, searching the floor beneath. There was no way out. He jumped back up to the window and was about to shout to the people below, but stopped himself mid breath. Kreed probably had a very good reason for locking him in here. Cole knew nothing about this place, and for all he knew the bars and solid door were for his own safety. Shaking his head, he laughed at his own foolishness. He was in no danger at the moment. There was nothing to fear, not even giant grubs.

To pass the time, Cole examined the mural that wrapped around the entire room. Taking it in from left to right, he realized the mural showed a story. There were people gazing longingly up at a planet on the horizon. A few of them blinked away into orbs of light, not unlike the ones from Cole's dreams. The lights gathered to form a colorful swarm that flowed up into the sky towards the planet. The next scene showed the lights arriving on a new planet and greeting the people there, who lived in trees and had clothes made from animal skins. The light-people could be seen helping and sharing with the primitive ones, either healing the sick or creating tools. The light-people pointed back towards the sky, becoming orbs once more. The primitive ones seemed to adore the light-people, appearing to beg to be taken with them. The final scene showed a swirling river of lights, twisting and twinkling its way up into the night sky.

The story depicted a striking resemblance to Cole's more recent dreams. He was convinced that this had something to do with his vanishings back home, and decided to bring it up to Kreed when he saw him next.

A scraping noise from outside the window drew Cole's attention. It grew louder, as if something were coming up the wall.

"Lights, shut off!" Cole whispered to the room. "Um, dim the lights, cut the lights, turn them down?" The room ignored him.

The scraping sounded as if right outside the window now. Cole dove into the pile of pillows, covering himself and peeking through the tasseled edges of a particularly frilly one. The scraping came to an abrupt halt as something clanged against the metal bars. Cole sank deeper into his hiding spot, afraid that his pounding heart would betray him. He waited, breathing as slowly as possible so it wouldn't appear as if there was a pillow breathing by its own volition.

"Hello?" said a little voice.

Cole clamped his mouth shut and held his breath.

The little voice called again, "Naked one, are you in there?"

It was the voice of a child. Cole inched his head forward, daring a glance through the tassels. It was the girl from the trail. Her curly hair poured over the window sill as she squeezed her head in between the bars.

Her eyes searched the room. "Naked one?"

"Y-yes?" Cole lifted the pillow.

"Aha! There you are, naked one." The girl dropped her voice to a whisper after looking over her shoulder. "Naked one, you are not safe. You must leave this place. Word has spread and things are changing."

Cole emerged from his hiding place. "How am I in danger? This is the safest place I've been in a while. How did you get up here?"

Ringlets of hair bounced as she shook her head. "No, this is not a safe place. No one is safe here. You must leave. Please, naked one." Her voice took on a tone of pleading. "The Aenerians are talking about you. Bad things are coming. Bad people are coming. They are coming for you, naked one."

"I'm not naked, I'm Cole. I'm not from this planet, I've only been here a little while. I'm from Earth, I mean Terra. Kreed has been the only decent person to me so far and I trust him. You and your friend attacked me at first sight, remember?" Cole crossed his arms, cocking his head.

"Habbad was scared. He thought you were one of the Dark Ones. The Dark Ones are evil beings from deep in the forest." The girl's voice became defensive: "Besides, Habbad is my brother and *I* trust *him*."

"Well I'm not a Dark One, whatever that's supposed to be. I'm just Cole, from Earth." He took a step closer to get a better look at her.

"That is why you must leave. You came from Terra, that's important! Bad people are coming for you Cole, they are outside now. Kreed is one of them. Kreed hurts kids. He promises them food and light and soft pillows. He hurts them Cole, he hurts them in this room! But the bad people are worse than him. I don't want you to get hurt." She was crying now, but her fear kept her sobs quiet.

A sick feeling illuminated something not quite right with Kreed. It wasn't until now, after seeing the fear on this girl's face that he knew he really was trapped.

"What's your name?" Cole asked, approaching the window.

"Lexy." She sniffed, rubbing her nose on her wrists.

Cole jumped, scrambled up the window sill, and sat close to her. "Lexy, I believe you. I would leave, but the door is solid and I can't fit through the bars. Do you know a way out?" He placed his hands over hers, which were wrapped around the bars.

A tiny smile popped onto her face as she nodded. "Yes, Cole! Yes!" She looked over her shoulder again. "Habbad is in there with you. He is coming to get you out. Habbad is going to steal a shaper-stick from the garden. He should be here soon." She paused, mouth agape as if she had forgotten something. "Darkness, come to me."

The sourceless light dimmed until Cole could see nothing but the faint blue glow from the street below. He loosened his grip on Lexy's fingers as he realized he was crushing them.

"How will Habbad get me out of here?" Cole whispered.

"With the shaper stick. Habbad can use Wisdom, though it is not allowed for us. He knows how to use the shaper stick too. You can't tell anyone he is using it." Her voice dropped until Cole could barely hear it: "He comes."

A circle of blue light appeared low in the door, growing larger as if an invisible hand were scooping the material away. A figure crawled through, crouching and holding a blue lantern.

"Naked one?" the figure whispered.

"Are you Habbad?" Cole asked.

"You must leave, naked one. They are here." Habbad turned on the spot and waved a short staff over the hole in ever smaller circles, filling it in. He patted the smooth door, satisfied.

"Habbad did they see you?" Lexy whispered, a little too loudly.

"No," he replied, approaching the window.

"Did you use Wisdom?" she asked. "You know they can smell it."

"No one could see me. Naked one, help me up." He tapped Cole on the leg.

Reaching down, Cole hoisted Habbad up to the window. "My name is Cole. Thanks for helping me."

"Move over," Habbad shooed Cole with a flick of his hand and offered him the blue lantern. "Hold this."

Cole grabbed the oval lantern. It looked like the ones mounted outside, except this one was wrapped in wire and had a handle. Habbad placed the shaping stick against the metal bars, wincing as they groaned and screeched. After a few seconds there was an opening large enough for them to fit through.

"Lexy, go down so we can follow," Habbad ordered.

Habbad touched the surface of the lantern with a finger, and the lamp dimmed until the blue glow was barely noticeable. Cole shivered as he followed Habbad out of the window. There was definitely some kind of invisible barrier keeping the chilled air out of the room. He placed the lantern in his teeth and descended the ladder, limbs shaking.

"Move faster. They are inside," Habbad's whisper called from the roof below.

The ladder wobbled uncomfortably as Cole's hands jerked from rung to rung. The ladder was clearly not intended for anyone heavier than these children. Once on the rooftop below, Habbad lowered the ladder, hefted it over his shoulder, and lowered it once more at the edge of the roof.

"Lexy, go first." Habbad placed a protective hand on her shoulder as she hopped light as a feather down the ladder.

"You next." He pointed to Cole.

Cole peered down the ladder as he planted his feet as firmly as he could. The ground below was pitch black.

Cole whispered into the darkness, "Lexy, watch out. I'm-"

A mournful howl shattered the silence. Cole lost his footing and slipped down a rung. Light erupted through the bent bars of the window.

"They are upon us! Go, now!" Habbad shouted.

Fear dulled his fingers, which slipped haphazardly down the rails. Another howl jarred his teeth. It sounded as if a dozen old men were being tortured, screaming for death from the same mouth. The lantern slipped from his mouth, shattering in a flash of blue light on the ground. The ladder seemed several times longer this time around.

"Lexy, where are you, I can't see anything," Cole hissed.

"I'm here Cole." She found his hand. "Habbad are you- oh!"

Something struck the ground beside them, making Cole jump.

"You dropped the lantern," Habbad stated. "Here, let me touch your eyes. This will slow me down so don't run too fast."

Cole bent his head down without hesitation. He could feel Habbad's hands walking their way up his neck until a finger planted over each of his closed eyes.

"Open them," Habbad demanded.

Cole's eyes twitched. He forced them open as wide as he could, only to clamp them after something like static jolted his pupils.

Cole gasped, "Ah! What did you-"

"Keep blinking. Lexy where are you? Let me do yours." The words flew from Habbad's mouth.

Cole blinked several times as he felt the strangest thing in his eyes, almost as if they were growing bigger. With each blink, however, his vision became more and more clouded with smudges. Slowly, he realized those smudge marks were actually Lexy and Habbad standing next to the ladder. He could somehow see in the dark.

"Habbad it's not working!" Lexy cried, "We have to go! They can smell you using it!"

"I'll carry her. I can see." Cole stared wide-eyed at Habbad, who replied with a curt nod.

"Follow me," Habbad said, darting away.

Cole hoisted Lexy into his arms and trotted after Habbad. Another sickening howl pierced the night, followed by a crash Cole felt in his feet. Not bothering to see what had just landed behind them, Cole instinctively bent down and scooped up Habbad as well. He resisted at first, but after feeling the fear and adrenaline that drove Cole's limbs, Habbad scrambled up onto his back. Instead of slowing, Cole surged faster with the extra weight. He had no intention of letting himself or his new friends fall prey to whatever horror had released that howl.

"Turn right after the barrels." Habbad's voice shook with the pounding of Cole's feet. "Run to the end of this alley, then turn left."

Cole obeyed without hesitation, acting as the vehicle while the voice in his ear was the driver. A few turns later, they heard another howl. It was farther away this time, though no less mortifying. Eventually Cole had no choice but to slow his cadence as his body refused his will. Panting, he set the two down behind a wagon and dry-vomited.

"We cannot stop here. Can you still move?" Habbad crouched, peering around the next corner.

"Yes," Cole heaved again. "But slower, at least for a minute."

"Keep up with me. They are very angry." Habbad disappeared behind the corner with Lexy in tow.

Wiping his mouth, Cole stumbled after them, grateful that their little legs weren't capable of anything faster than a steady jog. He couldn't seem to catch his breath and hoped with all his heart that his ragged breathing wouldn't give them away. Habbad seemed to be weaving them through the darkest alleys, which was a good thing since the blue lanterns were now so bright that they hurt Cole's eyes.

Though the situation was dire, Cole's body didn't seem to care as it gradually began to shut down with every stride. His legs screamed for fuel, which he had none of. He needed food. The last meal he'd had was with Goran before they set out from the cabin.

"I-can't- run- anymore," Cole panted. "Have- to- walk."

Habbad stopped, breathing heavy as well. Lexy on the other hand seemed as if she were only out for a leisurely walk.

"I think we are far enough anyway, though we must keep moving." Habbad rubbed his eyes. "We can't go back to our home. They saw me before I jumped from the roof. They know my face now."

"No Habbad!" Lexy pulled at her brother's arm. "You said you wouldn't let them see you. They will punish you now and I'll be all by myself forever and ever! The others are so mean to me without you Habbad. I don't want to be alone." She rubbed her cheeks into her brother's arm, soaking the cloth with tears.

Habbad's eyes bored into the ground at his feet. "What's done is done. We cannot go back. We have to leave."

Cole slumped back against a wall, wiping the froth from his mouth. "I know a place. Can you get us back to the trail where you found me?"

CHAPTER 9

PROPER INTRODUCTIONS

"We aren't allowed to leave the village when there's no sun. We could be punished you know!" Lexy rubbed her eyes and blinked after Habbad worked his trick on them once more. "It worked this time, brother. I can see."

"If they catch us we're dead anyway. Well, Cole might not be, they have other plans for him I think. From what I overheard they wanted to bring him to Decreath." Habbad inspected his sister's eyes before stepping into the tall grass. "This trail runs alongside the main one here, it's longer but we'll be under cover."

Cole ducked his head as he entered the grassy tunnel. He recognized the grass from the fields they had passed on the way into town. He could see stars through the shoots above, though the constellations were completely foreign to him. A different reality indeed. He suddenly felt very homesick. "So we're not near Terra anymore?"

"We are in the house of Pastori." Lexy's whisper took on a melody as she skipped through the grass tunnel, running her fingers along the stalks. "Terra is gone, gone, until the cycle repeats, repeats."

"What is the house of Pastori, and what's a cycle?" Cole asked. The concepts of different realities gave him an unsettling, sinking feeling. He couldn't wrap his mind around where exactly he was.

"Lexy, don't touch the grass like that. If they're in the sky they'll see it," Habbad said, falling back so he could walk next to Cole. "You have no idea, do you?"

"I've been on this planet for only a little while. How long exactly, I have no idea. I can't tell how you measure time. My sun was in your sky for what felt like weeks with no nights, and now you tell me we're somewhere else. I knew nothing about Aeneria until I woke up here one day. How do you measure time here anyway? Kreed said he planted a cypher in my mind so I could speak your language, but I wish he explained a bit more. This is all so strange to me." Cole kicked at a loose rock, sending it skittering into the grass stalks.

"Kreed touched your mind?" Habbad stopped, gripping Cole's forearm. "That is bad, Cole. Do you feel well? Does anything feel…off?"

"Well, I can't figure out if I'm scared to death or starving to death, but other than that I feel about as normal as I can." He didn't like how Habbad was looking at him. It made him feel even more out of place.

Habbad frowned and continued walking. "Then it is true, you really are from Terra." Habbad was silent for a moment, apparently deep in thought. He shook his head. "I don't know much about the other planets. Learning about them is forbidden so I don't know what your meaning of time is. We measure time by the passing of houses, or local planets. That is as specific as it gets for us. The Aenerians like Kreed have other ways of measuring time, though that too is forbidden for us. They keep knowledge from us. It makes us easier to control."

"So how long will it be dark?" Cole asked. The prospect of weeks or months of darkness was unsettling.

"Until it is light again," Habbad said. "We won't see a sun again until we enter the house of Cigni, which is a few planets ahead of Pastori. Even then it won't be bright here like it was in the house of Terra. Cigni's sun is low in the sky from here."

"So what is a cycle then?" Cole asked.

"A cycle is complete when this planet, Aeneria-," Habbad slapped his hand on the dirt as if he were explaining to a child, "-passes through all the houses. It repeats itself over and over. We just left Terra's reality and now Aeneria is passing by the planet Pastori.

"How long until we are in the house of Terra again?" Cole was afraid to hear the answer.

"There are twenty-one houses total, so twenty more including Pastori." Habbad replied, unconcerned.

Cole pondered for a moment, trying to do the math in his head. "So it's going to be…a long time before we are back in the house of Terra?"

"A full cycle, yes. That is a long time for you, is it not?" Habbad asked.

"It's a very long time," Cole's voice broke as his vision blurred. It would probably be years before they saw Earth again.

Habbad remained quiet, ignoring Cole's sniffling.

Cole broke the silence after collecting himself: "Habbad, how is it that you made me see in the dark and you can use that staff? Can you use magic?"

Habbad hefted the staff in both hands. "It is forbidden for most Underkin, but I have some skill with Wisdom."

"What is *Wisdom*?" Cole asked, taking in Habbad's wrinkled face and tiny stature, "And I'm guessing you're an…Underkin?"

"Yes, all the smaller people that you've seen are Underkin. The ones bigger than you are Aenerians. Wisdom is one school of magic. There are others, but I don't know what they are. Wisdom is the physical manipulation of the world around you. If you are skilled enough, and truly understand something, you can change the rules of how that thing works." Habbad sounded as if he were reading directly out of a textbook.

"How did you learn to use the Wisdom?" Cole asked, zealous curiosity taking hold. Maybe while he was here he could figure out how to use magic as well.

"Kreed showed me." Habbad's voice became quiet and morose. "Not everyone has the disposition. He sensed it in me and tempted me with many promises. Kreed is a master liar, but he is very skilled with the different magics. I learned quite a bit when I was with him. Some things I wish I could unlearn. He trapped me in the same room you were in. That's how I knew where to find you."

Cole changed the subject: "Do you know if there's any way I can get back home? Back to Terra?"

Habbad's wrinkles deepened on his brow. "You should never have been able to cross over in the first place. That's what makes you special. No one for a very long time has Traveled between the local planets. That is why Kreed was so interested in you. He wants to know how you did it so he can Travel too. He uses the worst kind of magic to hurt people, even when it's not necessary. If anyone breaks the law, he punishes the family instead of the lawbreaker."

A morbid curiosity itched its way to the fore of Cole's thoughts. "How are the families punished?"

Habbad slowed and spoke in a whisper so that Lexy was out of earshot: "There is a woman who lives under the markets. She is many lives older than she should be. She would have died of old age many cycles ago, but Kreed put a curse on her, granting her everlasting life. She was caught telling stories of what it was like before the war with the Dark Ones, telling secrets about the Dark Side, which is of course forbidden. Kreed used his magic on her, forcing her to murder her children right in the street in front of everyone. He also cursed her with fertility so that every cycle she can repeat the process as a reminder for everyone to obey his law. He doesn't even let her use any weapons, just her hands and teeth. I'm confident Kreed is working for the Dark Side. It's not right, what he does to people. Kreed was going to turn you in to Decreath, he's one of the leaders of the Dark Ones. The howling thing that chased us down the alley was one of Decreath's minions. By the sound it was making I think it was a Corpulant."

Cole didn't want to know what a Corpulant was. Its terrible moan still rang in his ears. "What do you mean when you say Light Side or Dark Side? Isn't it dark here now?"

"True, but we see the local stars on this side as we pass by them. On the Dark Side, they never see the suns. We move into the next house before the sun can fully rise over there." Seeing that Cole still wasn't getting it, Habbad stopped and carved two circles in the dirt with his foot. "This circle is your planet, and this one is your star. Think of Aeneria as having a back side and a front side. It appears in a reality, then moves in-between the local planet and its star." Habbad then illustrated the point by dragging his foot in between the two circles. "Aeneria travels without rotating, and just as the local star's light touches the Dark Side, Aeneria leaves that reality and appears in the next. The back side, or Dark Side, will only ever see a sunrise for but a moment."

"I think I get it now. Aeneria shifts into another reality before the sun gets a chance to shine on the back side." Cole watched Lexy twirl and dance ahead of them in the tunnel. "How old is everyone here? You and Lexy would pass for children on my planet."

"We are considered children here on Aeneria. I am just shy of my second cycle and Lexy just went through her first with the passing of Terra. No one knows how old Kreed is, as we Underkin only live for about ten cycles. He has been in charge of Costas for all of our recorded history. Books of our past are locked up in Kreed's home, where they are combed and approved by him before we are made to learn them."

"What *do* you know about your history?" Cole asked. Aenerian history sounded much more interesting than his own. Cole stifled a pang of homesickness, wishing he could talk to his mom about all this.

"I know very little. Though after having spent time in Kreed's house, I do know more than most. Aeneria used to be a peaceful planet, except it was only the Aenerians and they didn't know how to use their magic at first. Eventually a war started when the Dark Ones began using evil magics. Almost all of the Aenerians were killed off from the fighting. The Light Side was winning and trapped the Dark Ones on Aeneria's back side. Victory was certain for the Light Side; however, the Dark Ones had learned many uses of magic, and they used a tainted form of Wisdom to change the rules on Aeneria. They banished the rest of us to the Light Side. The Dark Side is much smaller than the Light Side, so we have had room to flourish and recover since the banishing. In their madness, the Dark Ones trapped themselves on the back side and have been festering ever since. Since the banishing there has been a barrier keeping the Dark Ones trapped, and no one has Traveled between the local planets. No one since *you*." Habbad gave him a significant look.

"Didn't you say all the Dark Ones were banished to the back side? What about their leaders and that Decreath guy?' Cole asked, eyeing Habbad as the Underkin pulled a blade from his wrappings and started cleaning under his nails.

"I don't know how the magic of the Dark Ones works, but they managed to keep their most powerful generals on the Light Side. The Three, as they are called, have been growing in power ever since, feeding and preying on the inhabitants of the Light Side. They are Grotton the Hungry, Decreath the Feared, and Sorronis the Hated and Despaired. They've been here so long that they've worked their way into our governments. I believe Kreed has been working for them for some time now. I spied him communicating with Decreath in his chambers. Luckily, Decreath is far away or else he would already have you. Kreed thinks that you hold a secret that will allow the Dark Ones to escape their prisons and infect all of Aeneria as they once did. That is why Decreath's Corpulants are after you."

Cole was silent for a moment, rolling another question around. "Why did you help me escape? You risked Lexy's life to help me. If we get caught…" Cole's chest flooded with chilled dread. "Why would you risk Lexy? What if Kreed makes you kill her like that lady killed her kids? That was stupid!"

Habbad didn't answer. He watched his sister dance up ahead. His crinkled cheeks stretched into a little grin as she plucked a blade of grass and waved it around like a ribbon. "I was aware of the risk, and so was Lexy. It was her idea in fact. When I was trapped in Kreed's home, I disobeyed him. He wanted me to do something disgusting, but I refused. He could have forced me with magic, but he wanted me to do it on my own. He locked me in a chest in the pillow room and told me to listen carefully, because he was going to teach me something important. He seemed happy, and for a moment I thought I wasn't going to be punished, that perhaps the chest was just another test to bring out my Wisdom. I waited and listened. Finally they popped through the door. I could hear my parents and Lexy, as well as Kreed. In that moment I knew it wasn't a test. I was being punished like the woman under the markets. Kreed placed me in that chest so that I could hear everything he would do to them, but not see it. I listened. I still listen to it every time I shut my eyes for too long."

"Habbad, I'm so sorry." Nausea bubbled in Cole's stomach.

"Don't be sorry for me. Be sorry for Lexy. She had to watch it," Habbad turned his head and looked into Cole's eyes. "That is why we risked saving you. We have set ourselves against Kreed and The Three. You are special. They would use you to hurt more people. We cannot let that happen."

Cole watched Lexy farther down the grassy tunnel. He felt a newfound level of respect and empathy for his new friends. "You would never know by looking at her. She always seems so happy."

"She hides it well. That is why she never stops singing and dancing. She says it keeps her full of good thoughts so the bad ones will have no room to grow…I think we should change the subject."

Lexy's whimsical dancing had twirled her within earshot. She took Cole's and Habbad's hands in each of hers and swung them back and forth as she hummed a tune.

"So Cole, what is Terra like? We know little of our own planet, and nothing of the local ones. I am curious," Habbad asked, cracking a small smile for his sister.

"Yes Cole, tell us about Terra and your family. They must miss you so." Lexy nuzzled her cheek against Cole's hand. Her face was cool to the touch.

"Well, I have a mother and a grandmother, and I never knew my father." Cole didn't want to talk about his other family member just yet. "I have a few friends at school, which is where we send our children to learn things before they become adults. My mother works every day, real hard, just to support us - I mean me. She's tough on me sometimes, but it's usually because I'm being lazy. My grandmother is tough on me all the time though, but she does it because she loves me." Cole looked up with watery eyes at the foreign stars through the grass. "I have a friend at school, her name is Ashley. I've loved Ashley since I was a kid like Lexy, but she never seemed to feel the same way until recently. She finally chose to be with me, but then I came here. I just disappeared and left her and everyone else."

"So you don't know how you came to Aeneria? No memory at all?" Habbad's eyebrows went up.

"No idea at all. I remember a dream with lots of lights and a river moving through the sky. When I woke up I was here, in the woods not too far from where you found me." Cole looked to Habbad, hoping this might reveal some answers. Habbad showed no reaction, however.

"Ashley must be an interesting person to catch your eye, no?" Habbad asked.

"She must be pretty too!" Lexy giggled, looking up at Cole with big, fluttering eyes. She was cute, even with her wrinkly little face.

"Ashley is the prettiest girl I've ever met." Cole smiled down at Lexy, who was overcome with a fit of laughter. "And yeah, she's interesting. She…" Cole wracked his brain, he had never thought about what exactly made Ashley so intriguing, "She can play a couple musical instruments, she's really good with sports, and when I'm with her I feel really full inside, like I have a piece of me that I was missing. She's also one of the few people that are nice to Josh-… she's just nice to everyone." From the corner of his eye, Cole felt Habbad staring at him.

Lexy's eyes shimmered with wonder as the starlight poked through the grass, dancing across her lined face. "I hope *I* fall in love someday."

Habbad let her statement hang for a moment. "And what of Terra? What can you tell us about your home planet?" Cole was grateful that Habbad changed the subject.

"I haven't seen much of it to be honest, not even one percent. Terra spins so our days are much shorter than what you have here. It also travels around our sun, and when it completes a full orbit we call it a year, which I guess would be like your cycle. Our location around the sun gives us our seasons due to Terra's tilted axis that it rotates on." Seeing that Cole was quickly losing Habbad with his rudimentary astronomy, he changed the subject: "We have over six billion people and all kinds of different plants and animals. Our people live in different countries which all have their own government. They fight sometimes, actually it's more like all the time. There's always war going on someplace or another. We also have technology. We create machines that allow us to do all kinds of things like talk to each other from any distance, fly, build things, or cook food. I wish I could show you some of the stuff we have, it looks like Aeneria hasn't advanced too far with technology yet."

Habbad released Lexy's hand and tucked his knife back under the wrappings around his middle. "We have technology, but only Aenerians are allowed to use it. When permitted, we use magic for menial tasks like trimming the gardens, but we are primitive in Costas compared to the bigger cities. Sometimes other Aenerians come to Costas riding machines that fly and carrying weapons that kill."

"Why aren't you allowed to use technology or magic?" Cole asked.

JOSEPH PARADIS

Habbad's eyebrows twitched together. "Kreed says it is because the Underkin aren't smart enough and we will end up hurting ourselves. I think it's because it makes us easier to control."

"Why doesn't your government do something about Kreed? He must answer to someone? Can't somebody report him?" Cole asked.

"He *is* the government in Costas. Besides, would you risk your family to report him?" Habbad took Cole's silence for an answer. "We could try to leave, but the nearest city is very far away and no one knows how to get there. The only ones that travel between the cities are the big people on their flying machines." He pointed down the trail. "We are near the end. We should not talk if we can avoid it. Kreed may send soldiers out to patrol the main roads."

Cole nodded and Lexy stopped her humming. When they reached the end, Habbad placed his head low to the ground before peeking out from the grass. Once he was satisfied that the way ahead was clear, he motioned for the others to follow. The walk back to where they met seemed longer to Cole due to the lack of sunlight and his crippling hunger. Even though Habbad had altered his vision for the darkness, Cole had a hard time seeing through the shade of the trees.

Cole blinked with wide eyes. "Habbad, I can't see a thing. Can you change my eyes some more?"

"I cannot. It's taken all of my focus to maintain the spell for this long. My mind and body are weary from it." He rubbed his forehead and grimaced as if he had just picked up a whiff of something foul. "I must release it now, from all of us. The spells have gone sour. I've never maintained three spells at once. There should be enough starlight for us to see anyway."

They halted on the trail, blinking and rubbing their brows. From his eyes Cole felt a great relief of pressure only now apparent due to its absence. Habbad's weariness lifted from his face as Cole's vision brightened, revealing the starlit trail and trees around them.

"This is the place where I attacked you." Habbad walked over to the edge of the trail and picked something up, tossing it to Cole. "This is yours."

Cole snatched the object. His fingers embraced his sharpened stone like reuniting with an old friend. Tucking the stone under the wrappings behind his back, Cole looked at the surrounding area. "Thanks. Yeah there's the bush I was hiding in. Hey I'm sorry by the way, for hurting you. I shouldn't have thrown you."

"It was necessary. If you hadn't defended yourself I would have killed you. Lucky for you I was too startled to use Wisdom. The Dark Ones may have been banished from this side, but they have been rumored to cross over. I've never actually seen one, but you looked so strange that I thought you were one of them."

"You were foolish, Habbad," Lexy chimed in. "You always tell me to think first and act second. You should apologize you know."

Habbad looked to Cole and shifted his feet uncomfortably. "I...I did what was necessary at the time. For all I knew he was a Dark One. I wasn't going to give him the chance to hurt us. I regret nothing."

Lexy crossed her arms. "That's not how mother and father taught us to behave. Even if he was a Dark One you should have given him a chance to be nice first."

"Well, mother and father are not here anymore, are they?" Habbad's voice was robotic and cold.

Lips quivering, Lexy looked as if she wanted to respond, but couldn't find the words.

Cole bent down and put his hands on their shoulders. "No apology needed. You made the right choice, Habbad. You two have to look out for each other." He gave Lexy a gentle shake, "And it looks like I'm stuck here so there's three of us now. I'll take care of you like you've taken care of me."

Lexy's face stretched into a toothy grin. "You are in our family now, Cole. You are our new big brother." She threw her arms around Cole's middle and squeezed him tightly.

Habbad gave Cole an approving smile. "So, big brother, where are you leading us?"

Leading them from the trail, Cole found the woods were difficult to navigate under the starlight as everything looked different. They went slowly at first but eventually Cole found a familiar game trail and they quickened their pace. Fortunately this trail also had a few edible flowers, though Cole felt somehow even hungrier after eating a few.

When they finally reached the base of the hill where the cabin was, Cole broke into a run, eager to see if Goran was waiting for him.

"Goran!" he shouted outside the cabin. "Goran I'm back! Are you in there?"

There was no response.

"Who is Goran?" Habbad asked when he reached the cabin a moment later.

"Goran's my friend. He's an animal, I'm not sure what kind though. Maybe you can tell me when you see him. Goran are you in there?" Cole pushed his face into the door and popped through.

Cole flicked on a few mushrooms and discovered the cabin was empty, though the nut bowl was full. Habbad and Lexy popped through the door and looked in wonder at the glowing mushrooms.

"Oh my stars! These mushrooms look like lanterns! They are beautiful aren't they, Habbad?" Lexy stroked one of the glowing blue bells.

"Don't touch it!" Habbad slapped her hand. "They might be poisonous."

"The glowing mushrooms? Really? They're harmless as far as I can tell. I mean, I wouldn't eat it but…well go ahead and flick one, like this." Cole snapped his fingers over a rubbery mushroom close to the ceiling.

Lexy gasped in wonder, then ran around the cabin touching every mushroom she could reach. Habbad squinted as his eyes adjusted to the bright turquoise lights. After grabbing a handful of nuts, Cole offered the bowl.

"Those I recognize. They are deka seeds. How did you get them?" Habbad asked as he sniffed one of the seeds.

"Goran climbs up and throws them down to me," Cole replied through a mouthful of seed.

"The animals on Aeneria are typically feral. How did you train one to get food for you?" Habbad asked.

"I didn't train him. If anything Goran's been training me. The first day I appeared here I got myself good and stuck in that door. We don't have anything like that on Terra, so it scared me and I tried to pull myself out. Don't laugh, Lexy! I didn't know any better!" Cole gave Lexy a playful swat. "Goran heard me yelling and showed me how to get myself unstuck. He kind of saved my life. I saved his life too from a huge bug. We've been inseparable ever since. We hunt together, he collects dried-up ferns so I can build a fire, and he shows me what plants are good for eating. I miss him for sure. He was my first friend out here. He'll probably be back soon. He's the one that filled the bowl."

Habbad looked suspiciously at Cole. "You are more special than I thought."

"What do you mean *special?*" Cole asked as he laid himself down on the sleeping mat.

"It seems as if you have bonded with this animal. There are no creatures with that sort of intelligence on Aeneria, unless they are bonded through magic. This relationship sounds like a kind of magic. Are you sure you don't remember any more about how you came to Aeneria?"

Cole yawned. "Definitely not. It may have been by magic, but not from me. I'm as gifted as that chair is. We don't have magic on Terra. My dreams were the only thing out of the ordinary. I guess I could tell you more about them, but that'll have to wait till after I've had some sleep. I'm spent."

"I will hold you to it," Habbad said as he and Lexy joined Cole on the large sleeping mat, which Cole now realized was for an Aenerian.

Cole slept deeply and solidly for the first time since coming to Aeneria. He couldn't remember his dreams however, even when he was woken by something nudging him in the back. He flipped over to see Lexy tossing and turning in what was left of the mushrooms' glow. She was whining and crying softly. Cole reached a hand out to wake her.

"Don't touch her," Habbad whispered from the shadows. "It is much worse if you wake her. She will deal with it in her dreams." Habbad's face suddenly appeared with a soft *thump* as he flicked a mushroom above his head.

"Is she dreaming about…you know…your parents?" Cole asked.

"Yes. I can only imagine what she is seeing." Habbad shifted himself, sitting upright. "I hope to one day learn enough about magic to take the knowledge from her."

"She is strong, especially for a child. Both of you are. I wouldn't be doing so well if I'd been through all of that." Cole felt himself sinking into darker thoughts. He *had* been through something just as horrible.

"With your current self, probably not. You have to change who you are so that traumatic events don't destroy you. I used to be a different person before I met Kreed," Habbad finished, giving Cole a puzzled look.

Cole was on the verge of another fit. Thinking of Habbad's parents being murdered brought him back down into places he tried to forget. Memories of a cobblestone alleyway and the smell of crotch funk brushed against the edge of Cole's mind. He closed his eyes, shoving them deeper where they belonged.

"I see what you're doing," Habbad interrupted.

"Doing what?" Cole's eyes snapped open, realizing he'd been twitching.

"You have a wound." Habbad inclined his head to Cole's. "You're going to have to deal with it sooner or later. It will grow inside you the longer you suppress it. It will consume you."

"Maybe, but I'm not dealing with it now." Cole averted his eyes.

"Hmm." Habbad gave Cole a disappointed look.

"You wanted to know how I came to Aeneria? My dreams?" Cole asked, rubbing his eyes.

"Do you want to sleep more?" Habbad asked.

"Can't sleep. Might as well tell you now." As he had with Kreed, Cole told Habbad everything he remembered from his first disappearances as a toddler. Unlike with Kreed, Cole left out some of the more embarrassing anecdotes. As Cole thought on it, he realized Kreed had probably used magic on him to draw out all those memories he had no recollection of.

"I'm pretty sure my disappearances had something to do with Aeneria. I think I've been coming here my whole life and not realized it." Cole looked to Habbad for his input.

"If you weren't sitting here before me, I would say that would be impossible. How many times did you say you vanished?" Habbad asked, looking up at the stars through the holes in the ceiling.

"Too many to remember. It came and went, but got worse as I got older." Cole's mouth popped open as something clicked into place. "My mother told me it happened when I was three, then I remember being ten when it happened again. Now I'm seventeen. I think Aeneria was next to Earth every time I vanished! Aeneria must come by every seven years or so!"

"Those were my thoughts, though there is no way to know for certain. I'm guessing that our cycle is equal to seven of your, what did you call them?"

"Years." Cole said, running his hand through his hair.

Habbad was silent for a moment, though he looked like he wanted to say something. Finally he spoke: "You are special. You may not know how, and neither do I, but there is some strange magic happening around you."

Cole shook his head, stopping himself from mentioning *Him. He* was there every time, guiding and helping. *He* was the one using magic. For some reason, Cole didn't want to share this knowledge. Not yet anyway. Come to think of it, he hadn't even mentioned it under Kreed's influence. "I'm still not so sure it's me who's special. But who knows, maybe I'm 'Cole the Great Wizard' and just don't know it. You better start showing some respect or I'll turn you into one of those seeds."

For the first time since Cole met him, Habbad laughed. "I think you are being a little too modest. Certainly you would be named 'Cole, the Great Naked One'."

Cole snorted so loud that Lexy woke from her slumber. Fortunately the nightmares had long passed. "What's so funny Habbad?"

Habbad inched closer to her. "Nothing Lexy. Cole and I were just making fun of each other."

"Be nice to Cole, he has sadness in his eyes." Lexy rolled over and snuggled into Cole's leg.

"It's ok, it was nothing serious. And I'm not sad anymore, I've got my new family to look out for me." Cole mussed her curly mess of hair.

A knock at the door broke the silence. Cole and Habbad were on their feet in an instant, knife and sharpened rock in hand.

"Do you normally get visitors?" Habbad whispered.

"Never, it's probably just Goran messing with me," Cole said with more confidence than he felt.

The knock sounded again, slower this time.

Tremors ran up Cole's legs and sweat made him tighten his grip on the stone blade. Steeling himself, he jumped through the door.

A tortured howl ripped through the starlight.

"Colton Carter, *my friend.*"

Chapter 10

Falling

Kreed towered over them grinning ear to ear, looking as if he might cry from hysterical delight. The sourceless white light surrounding him revealed another person as well, though whoever it was stood beyond the edge of its luminance.

"This is just terrific news," Kreed gushed, rapidly clapping his hands together. "I was ever so worried when I discovered you took a night-time stroll. It's much too dangerous to be outside at night, and the woods no less, tut tut. And see who joins him! Habbad, you naughty boy! You of all people ought to know better. Might I guess who else is in there, hmm? Why don't you come on out too, young Lexy."

Lexy pushed herself through the door. She looked as if she might vomit. Cole tightened his grip on the stone, though he knew it would do him no good against a giant capable of unknown magic. A fly landed on his neck and had started biting, but Cole was too scared to swat it.

"Now that we're all gathered, what shall we make of you little troublemakers?" His voice was gentle and pleasant, as if he had merely caught them eating their dessert before their dinner. "Our friend from Terra shall of course be forgiven, as he is not yet acquainted with the rules of Costas. As for you, Habbad and Lexy, correct me if I'm wrong but I do believe the two of you know what comes to those who break the rules, don't you?"

Habbad's lips trembled as his face twisted. The sight unsettled Cole, as he had only ever known Habbad as a tough little rock. Lexy covered her eyes and turned away, mumbling to herself. More of the biting flies swarmed about them. Lexy waved her hands in a panic, attempting to shoo them away.

"That's what I thought." A thin lining of malice embellished Kreed's fatherly tone. "Come forth, Lexy."

"Please! It was my fault. I made them do it. I told them to get me out of there." Cole faltered as Kreed raised an eyebrow. "I...I was locked in the room and... I panicked. I yelled out the window until they heard me."

Kreed's smile deepened as the sourceless light changed from white to blood red. "Oh I can see it in you now. I *adore* liars, and that was a beautiful lie, Colton Carter. Beautiful, but weak. When we're finished you'll be weaving much better lies than that. Don't you fret over little Lexy, I'll not harm her." He crouched, opening his arms in invitation. "Now, Lexy, come to me."

Lexy's face slackened as her eyes went blank. She dropped her hands and took one deliberate step after another. The biting flies covered her face, but she didn't seem to notice or care. Cole pleaded, begging her to stay put, but it seemed she couldn't hear him. She walked willfully and resolutely towards Kreed, her face frozen in stone as tears flowed like rivers into her open mouth. She stopped in between Kreed's arms as he pulled her close, kissing her forehead. There was a hiss of something burning. Kreed released her, his lips smoking into a maniacal grin. A black scar sizzled on Lexy's brow.

The figure at the edge of the light stepped from the shadows. He looked like an ancient man, slightly taller than Cole but enormous around the middle. Instead of wrappings, draping grey rags hung from his bulbous form, hiding his legs. His face was oddly skinny however, and he had the largest mouth Cole had ever seen, which sat atop a neck comprised of countless jiggling folds. As the old man turned, he revealed a large hump in his back that shook with every step.

Still grinning, Kreed extended his arm toward the man. Lexy walked up to him with the look of a person reconciled with death. The rag man stretched lanky arms towards her, revealing long white hands that twitched in anticipation. His fingers were long enough to wrap all the way around her tiny ribs. The air rushed out of her mouth in a tiny squeak. Lexy's feet left the ground as he raised her towards his face.

Frozen with horror, Cole realized the rag man was not about to kiss her, but swallow her. His purple lips separated, connected by a single ropey bridge of yellow saliva. The maw opened to an astonishing gap that could have easily swallowed a larger man. Lexy's curly hair disappeared behind bleeding lips as the man's jaw popped wider, allowing her shoulders and abdomen to enter. He worked her in the rest of the way, throwing his head back and forth, neck folds jiggling with every gulp.

Cole forgot how to use his legs, or even how to breathe. He shouldn't be here, but the voice screaming for him to save himself was buried under miles of cold water. The fear, dripping down his insides and seeping through his flesh, was the only thing that existed. He was at its mercy, fully and willingly.

A cry broke the silence, releasing Cole from his frozen state. Goran descended from the roof of the cabin and landed on the grinning face of Kreed, who was too distracted to see him coming. Blood flew from behind twisting fur as Goran bit and slashed with terrible ferocity. Before Kreed's massive hands could close on him, Goran dashed to the ground, quick as lighting.

"My eyes!" Kreed screamed, covering his face as blood poured out from in between his fingers.

Goran landed on all fours, his wild eyes saying what he could not; *run.*

Without room for another thought, Cole bent down and scooped up Habbad and ran. He couldn't see where he was going, and he didn't care. His limbs needed no conscious direction. The horror of what he had just witnessed fueled and guided his body to flee as fast as he could. It felt as if every hair on his body were rebelling against the fear, every motion bringing him another inch away from the source. By sheer luck he didn't collide with a single tree, fake rock, or any obstacle at all. Cole noticed a small dark figure keeping pace beside him. The figure sprinted ahead, veering left.

"Coo Cha!" Goran cried as he tore through the underbrush. Cole followed, barely able to keep up. As his exhaustion began to set in, his terror subsided enough for Cole to think on what had just happened. He dared not slow. For all he knew Kreed and that thing were right behind them. He hoped their pursuers were too preoccupied to give chase. Cole wondered if Habbad had fainted. His little body hung limp over Cole's shoulders like a bundle of slack rope.

Goran led them into a patch of tall bushes with sharp leaves that thickened with every step. Leafy blades flicked across Cole's face and hands as the foliage grew so dense he was guided only by Goran's insistent barking. The brush slowed Cole, but he could see an opening ahead. Frustrated, he pushed hard through a branch, feeling his stomach drop when he emerged on the other side. Before he had a chance to realize he was falling, he was under water. Fortunately his feet found solid ground and he stood, bringing his head and chest above the surface. As he stood to full height, Habbad woke from his stupor, gasping and writhing. Goran looked like a log floating steadily ahead towards a small island.

"I can't swim!" Habbad squealed, clawing at Cole's back.

"You're good, you're good. Climb on my back. Just don't drown me if we go too deep." Cole spread his hands out, balancing himself.

Cole waded forward slowly and, as he suspected, the water was soon too deep for him to stand. Habbad pushed his head under, not giving him a chance to breathe. Cole had to periodically shove Habbad away to gulp down some air before allowing himself to be pushed back below the surface. It was difficult to follow Goran, but he eventually felt a soft bottom as he approached the island. When he was close enough, he tossed Habbad onto the shore. He fell into the waist deep water and crawled the rest of the way. His breathing came in rasping coughs as he struggled to remain conscious. Once on dry land, he attempted to stand, only to fall flat on his face.

"Cole! Cole get up. We need to hide," Habbad whispered, tugging at Cole's arm.

Cole didn't have the energy to respond. It was all he could do to keep drawing breath. Furry lips scratched his hand as teeth closed around the cloth on his wrist. Slowly he felt himself being dragged through the sand.

Cole opened his eyes, realizing he was on his back. He had passed out, but knew it couldn't have been for long, as he was still soaked and he could hear Habbad gasping. They were inside some kind of structure with a triangular opening that let in enough starlight for him to make out Habbad's and Goran's vague forms.

"Where are we?" Cole asked, sitting himself up.

Steadying his breath, Habbad whispered, "In a tree."

"Oh." Cole chanced a look out into the water, but the starlight was too dim for him to see across to the shore.

They sat in silence, neither daring to say a word. Goran took up sentinel at the mouth of the tree, sitting on his haunches and twitching his ears at the slightest noise.

Cole flinched and whipped his hand as something crawled across it. Eventually he couldn't take the silence anymore. "Habbad, what happened back there? What did I just see?"

Cole expected Habbad to break down into tears again, but it appeared he had regained his robotic composure. "That was a Corpulant, a minion of Decreath. You just witnessed a Corpulant eat my sister."

Cole opened his mouth to speak, but couldn't seem to put the words together.

"We are very fortunate that this animal was there. I assume this is Goran?" Habbad asked. Goran snapped his head around at the mention of his name.

"Y-yes," Cole stuttered.

"Thank you for carrying me. I shudder to think what Kreed would have done to me if you hadn't." He looked at Goran: "Animal, thank you for your help as well."

Goran responded with a quick snort.

"Habbad, I-I can't… She's gone. That thing ate her, it swallowed her. She's gone." Cole paused, waiting for Habbad to provide a better explanation, anything to help him wrap his mind around it. "How are you okay with this? How can you just sit there like you didn't see what I just saw?"

"I saw what you saw, Cole. I'm sure I will have a more fitting reaction soon enough, but right now is a time to act, not to give in to fear as I did back at the cabin." Habbad shifted, rubbing his forehead. "We cannot linger. We must keep moving. Kreed will fix his eyes and the Corpulant is likely on our trail as we speak. I doubt we will get the same treatment as Lexy. Kreed will take his time with us. Even you. As special as you are, you will be punished."

"I can't just yet. I don't think I can stand." Cole tried his legs, but they wobbled and buckled. "I can't get up."

"Then we will have to hope that luck will hide us until you recover." Habbad closed his eyes, turning his ear to the entrance of the tree.

"I just can't believe she's dead." Cole rubbed his face as tears welled. "She didn't deserve that, she was just a kid. No one deserves that."

"She is not dead," Habbad said, his voice as monotonous as ever.

"Wait, what are you talking about? Didn't you see what that thing did to her?" Cole's fingers mushed through the cool sandy floor of their hiding spot.

"Yes, and I also saw what Kreed did before the Corpulant took her," Habbad said, opening his eyes.

"Are you talking about the kiss?" Cole asked.

"Kreed is a master liar, but this time I think he was telling the truth, at least for now. He chose her. You saw the mark on her forehead?"

"Yeah. The burn." Cole winced. He could still hear the skin sizzling.

"That is the mark of the Chosen. Every cycle he picks dozens of Underkin. Usually those who stand out for one reason or another; superior intelligence, an open act of kindness, he even choses us for being too tall. Once Chosen, these people will survive any injury, no matter how grievous." Habbad grimaced, as if he tasted something foul. "It would have been better if he had just killed her."

"But doesn't this mean there's a chance? The Corpulant might not have killed her. We could still save her," Cole's whisper rose along with his hopes.

"I don't know much about the Corpulants or what disgusting magics they follow, but they are mercenaries of Decreath, who isn't bound by Kreed's rules or magic. It is the opposite in fact; Kreed is bound to Decreath. It is possible that she will survive, but she will still feel everything and her body isn't indestructible. Even if she does survive, by the end of this cycle she will be worse than dead," Habbad scowled.

"Why is that, what happens at the end of the cycle?" Cole asked, but he wasn't sure he really wanted to know the answer.

Habbad's face turned to wrinkled stone. "I saw it once. I was young but it was traumatic enough for me to remember every detail. At the end of every cycle Kreed pays tribute to Decreath, Sorronis, and Grotton with the Devotion. They are brought to a tower and strapped to the outside. It was so tall I couldn't see the top. From inside the tower oil is poured out, drenching the Chosen. When The Three arrive the tower is set ablaze from the bottom up. They are very careful with the oil, using just enough to keep the fire going so that the Chosen are not destroyed. They cannot die, but they feel everything. The people at the top felt the worst of it. The screaming was so loud it hurt my ears, but eventually their voices stopped working; either from the smoke or because they screamed them out. The smell is what disturbed me the most I think, because it smelled good. I remember hating myself for enjoying it, but I was so hungry. We all had to watch as the people we once knew lost themselves to the tower. When the fire went out there was nothing left of their minds. Their smoldering bodies were little more than melted flesh, beating and tearing at everything they could reach. To this day you can still taste the hate coming from the tower."

Cole was at a loss for words. The thought of Lexy at the top of that tower filled him with crippling despair, but it also ignited a spark of urgency. "How long does she have?"

"What do you mean? She is already lost!" Habbad blinked, annoyed.

"No, she isn't lost yet. How long until the tower burns again?" Cole was the one annoyed now.

"The tower will burn as we leave the house of Allias, which is the next after Pastori. But you are wrong, she is lost. Kreed has her now." Habbad locked his eyes with Cole's, as if to burn the words in.

"How can you just give up on her?" Cole felt heat return to his cheeks. "We saw her just moments ago and you're already crossing her out like there's no chance. Do you even *want* to save her?"

Habbad's voice was calm, but his eyes told Cole he had just crossed a line: "Of course I want to save her, but *want* is not *reality*. You haven't the dimmest notion of what you're suggesting, or what will happen to us if we are caught. We stand no chance. Even with my limited Wisdom it would be no hard task for me to kill you now, and there wouldn't be a thing you could do about it. Kreed on the other hand has powers I can't even comprehend. And as for The Three, they might as well be gods. What would you have me do anyway? You must have a plan, what with your vast experience on this planet. Please, tell me."

"I certainly wouldn't leave my little sister to rot; that would make me a coward," Cole spat.

Habbad jumped to his feet and stormed towards Cole, his right hand glowing green. Cole knew he had gone too far, even in the darkness he could see murder on Habbad's face.

A tortured howl tore through the night air. Habbad extinguished the light in his hand and dropped to all fours. Goran retreated back into the tree, hiding behind Cole.

"I'm not dying in this tree," Habbad whispered. "Follow me if you choose to not be eaten."

Cole's legs could not yet support his weight, so he crawled after Habbad. The Corpulant wailed again, closer this time.

"It must be just on the other side of the shore. I don't know if they can swim," Habbad hissed, peeking out of the tree.

"Well let's not stick around to find out. Do you have any ideas?" Cole asked.

Habbad squinted up into the canopy. "It's foolish, but it's our only chance. Do you still have your blade? I dropped mine."

Cole tossed the sharpened rock to Habbad, who tucked it under the wrappings behind his back before scaling a nearby fern. Water droplets showered the sandy beach as Habbad disappeared to the canopy. Goran followed Habbad with a look of mingled interest and confusion.

"Move aside, this thing is heavy," Habbad called from above.

Something massive fell to the ground, splattering mud onto Cole's face. Habbad scurried down shortly afterwards.

"What is that?' Cole asked, wiping his eyes.

"This is a sun lily leaf," Habbad said, indicating the large round object. "It is heavy, but it will float. We can use it to escape, but it's too heavy for me to move. Can you stand yet?"

Cole wobbled to his feet, legs cramping. "I don't know how much I can help, but I'll try."

Together they dragged the leaf to the water's edge. Gasping, Cole flung himself onto its waxy face when it was finally on the water. Habbad hopped on, pushing the leaf farther out into the water.

"Wait for Goran!" Cole breathed.

A splash sounded towards the mainland. Cole could make out a large, hump-backed form powering its way through the water. It was close enough that Cole could hear its strangled breathing getting closer.

"Goran let's go!" Cole bellowed. A second later a furry shadow flew through the air, crashing into Cole's stomach and knocking the wind out of him.

"Coo Cha!" Goran barked.

"Habbad help me! We both need to paddle. Why are you just sitting there? That thing is almost on us!" Cole shouted at Habbad, who was sitting cross-legged in the center of the leaf with his hands flat on its surface.

The Corpulant let out a gurgling howl. Cole could hear water sloshing around in its huge mouth. Desperate, he cut both hands into the water and paddled with all his might. To his relief, the leaf began to move, though he realized it was moving much too fast to be powered by his hands alone.

"Habbad, are you…" Cole asked, confused.

"Don't distract me," Habbad hissed.

The leaf was moving steadily now, but the Corpulant was moving faster still. Seeing that it was still gaining, Cole resumed paddling, which didn't seem to make a difference, but he needed to do something. He wanted to tell Habbad to go faster, but it looked as if it was taking all of his concentration to maintain the pace they were already at. Realizing he only had a few more seconds before the Corpulant reached them, he crawled over to Habbad and retrieved the sharpened stone. When Cole turned back around he gasped, dropping the stone.

A white hand gripped the edge of the leaf. Another hand joined the first as solid black eyes and purple lips rose from the water.

The Corpulant let out a gurgling howl. Its saggy neck jiggled and writhed as it pulled its upper body onto the leaf. The outline of a tiny hand stretched the skin from the inside out, causing the Corpulant to cough as it sprayed buckets of water onto the leaf.

As if waiting for a moment of weakness, Goran pounced on one of its hands, slashing with his long canines. Seeing the other hand reaching for Goran, Cole hacked at it with the stone. The hand went for Cole instead, closing around his wrist with fingers longer than his forearm. Cole felt two muffled pops from under the crushing grip as he lost his footing and slipped towards the edge. Goran shrieked, clamping his jaws around one of the spindly fingers, shaking like a dog while Cole stabbed at the hand. A second later Goran spat a severed finger onto the leaf and set himself on another. The pressure lifted from Cole's wrist as the hand released him. With a final whack of the stone the Corpulant slipped off the leaf and sank into the black water.

Without the extra weight Cole could feel the leaf gliding swiftly now, the waxy skin rippling under his knees like a water bed. Growling, Goran took up a defensive posture at the edge of the leaf, scanning the black water. Cole scooted towards the center, crying out in pain after putting weight on his throbbing wrist. When it seemed safe, Goran joined Cole and Habbad, sniffing Cole's injured arm.

Habbad stood from his meditative state, peering over the edge of the leaf. "Is it gone?"

"I don't know, but it's going to have a hard time swimming. We messed up its hands pretty good, though not before it could do *this* to me." Cole raised his tender arm, which was already starting to swell. "Don't suppose you could fix this?"

Habbad placed his fingertips on the swelling skin of Cole's forearm. "Kreed didn't teach me that type of magic. I doubt he knows it anyway. He has no use for healing others. I might be able to immobilize it, but it's taking all my focus to keep us moving." He bent down and picked up the Corpulant's finger, which flapped like a scared fish before Habbad tossed it into the water. "It seems you gave as well as you got. I've never heard of anyone surviving an encounter with one of Decreath's minions. We are very fortunate."

"We're just lucky Corpulants aren't very good swimmers. Goran did most of the work anyway, didn't you?" Goran replied with a snort.

"I don't think I can handle much more of this running and fighting for my life. It's breaking me down."

"This is how things are on Aeneria. You must break and remake yourself if you are to survive. Life on Terra seems much easy from what you described. Here, death and fighting are commonplace. We all experience it." Habbad's eyes fell over Cole's arm.

"I know, but I could still use a break. This is too much. Do you know where we're going anyway? I don't think I can walk right now if we go ashore." Cole lay on his back, holding his wrist.

Habbad scanned the water ahead. "Right now it appears we are headed towards the mouth of a river. I've no idea where it leads, but the current will help take us as far away as possible, which is where we want to be. I've never been this far from Costas before. We are beyond my knowledge of this world."

"Great. The Corpulant's probably not the only thing in this river that wants to eat us." Cole felt the water running under the leaf, wishing it were a bit thicker.

"I would assume so, but nothing could be as dangerous as a Corpulant, which we have escaped twice now." Habbad craned his neck, examining the sky. "It's difficult to tell, but I believe we are traveling towards the Dark Side. If so we must take care not to cross the barrier. From the books I've stolen from Kreed's house, Costas is not far from the Dark Side."

"How will we know if we cross it, and what will happen if we do?" Cole asked.

"I don't know what it looks like, but after the banishing anyone who crossed it would cease to exist somehow. Kreed said that people crossing would die a terrible death, but the books made it seem like people would just vanish," Habbad replied.

Cole inched closer to Habbad. "You learned a lot in Kreed's house, didn't you?"

"Yes. And, like I said, there are a great many things I wish I could unlearn." Habbad sat down quickly, causing a wave in the leaf that made Cole gasp in pain. "Sorry."

"It's getting worse," Cole said through clenched teeth. "I'm pretty sure it's broken, I can barely move my fingers," He waited a moment for the throbbing to subside. When it became apparent that it would not, he looked to Habbad. "So why didn't Kreed choose *you*? You said he chooses people that set themselves apart and using magic isn't common among your people, so wouldn't that set you apart?"

"Kreed told me he wanted me for something else. He was going to make me his apprentice until I refused him. When he killed my parents he left Lexy alive so that he could use her against me should I ever disobey him again. He eventually lost interest in me, focusing instead on other children who were more accepting of his desires." Habbad turned his head, looking away.

"Could you teach me how to use magic? You seem pretty convinced that I've been doing it already." Cole had wanted to ask this question since first learning magic was a real thing here.

Habbad's wrinkles deepened. "You certainly have been taking part in magic, but usually people have conscious control over it. Have you ever done something with magic intentionally?"

"Not that I know of." Air rushed in through Cole's teeth as a fresh spike of pain shot through his arm.

"Then I'm not quite sure how to teach you. I am not even a novice of Wisdom, but it was the only school of magic that I show an aptitude for. Kreed helped to awaken my latent abilities." Habbad leaned over the edge of the leaf and scooped a double handful of water, pouring it in a neat little puddle in front of Cole. "This should be harmless enough. Do you know what this is?"

"Um, water?" Cole said plainly.

Habbad tapped the puddle. "Of course, but do you *know* it? Do you feel a complete understanding of its nature and its properties in this form?"

Cole thought back to everything he'd learned about water. "I know it's a liquid, and what its boiling and freezing points are. We learned about its properties in school. Even the particles that make it up."

Habbad shook his head. "Don't focus on facts and numbers. Instead, shift your focus to the base concepts of the thing. Close your eyes and focus on the very idea of what this puddle is. You need to feel the concept with utmost intimacy." Habbad chuckled quietly as Cole's face strained with effort. "First you must relax, this is not a thing you can achieve through brute force."

"Hey I'm trying!" Cole snapped. "You try focusing with a busted arm."

"My apologies, but I've never seen someone make that face before. Now, empty your mind and focus on the puddle. You need to feel its properties as a whole. Sense them all. Do not attach yourself to a single aspect."

After a moment's strained relaxation, Cole spoke: "All right, I don't know if I'm doing it right but this is as close as I'm going to get." Cole's eyes bored into the puddle as he warded off stray thoughts.

Habbad nodded. "If you truly understand the puddle and all of its properties, pick one now and change the rules. If your conviction is strong enough, the puddle will oblige."

"What do you mean *change the rules*? Like change a property of the water?" Cole asked, feeling slightly stupid.

"Yes, but do not lose sight of its other attributes while you make changes to one," Habbad pointed out.

Cole bit his lip, deep in thought. He felt as if his mind were struggling to juggle the simplest idea. As soon as he got a good rhythm with one property, he would drop the others. After a moment's deliberation, he decided upon changing the freezing temperature of the puddle, though he quickly realized he now needed a concept of what heat was. He tried to imagine all the little molecules vibrating and bouncing off one another, willing them to slow their movement. He swore under his breath as he dropped the other thoughts he was juggling. Concentrating, he tried again. When he felt like he had it, he followed his instincts and extended a finger towards the puddle, not knowing why it felt right to do so. Anticipation prickled up the back of his neck. He could feel something, like an idea twisting and changing its color. He poked the water, which hadn't changed in the slightest.

Cole panted, not realizing he was holding his breath. "Did it change?"

"I haven't a clue. What did you try to do anyway?" Habbad brought his nose down to the puddle, smelling it.

"I tried to make it freeze. I don't know, it feels a bit cool to me." Cole rubbed the moisture in between his thumb and forefinger.

"Perhaps. The only advice I can offer is keep trying, and stick to simple things. Cooling something off is a good start. You could also try to move a small object such as a pebble. Keep in mind you are very tired and injured at the moment, which makes it much harder." Habbad blew a sharp breath and the puddle gave a high-pitched creak. Cole threw out a hand to steady himself as the leaf suddenly slowed. Habbad gave Cole an awkward smile as he tossed the now frozen puddle into the water. "As you can see, I am no master of the Wisdom."

Cole watched in awe as the little disc of ice bobbed and trailed behind them. "I'll keep trying, that's for sure."

"You should sleep. I don't need to be a healer to see that you are at your limit," Habbad said after Cole let out a big yawn.

"You're probably right," Cole yawned again, laying himself down on the leaf. "My body is spent, though my mind is still running all over the place. I don't know if I can sleep. My arm isn't about to let me sleep either." Cole was silent for a moment, enjoying the feeling of the water rippling under the leaf. "We're going to save Lexy you know. I promise, we'll find a way."

Habbad crawled over to Cole, placing a finger on his forehead. "I believe that you believe that. Now sleep."

· · · ·

Cole woke with a start, feeling as if he'd just fallen from a great height. He was disoriented, though Goran's ruby eyes anchored him to the present. Habbad's eyes on the other hand made Cole reach for his stone blade.

"What's wrong, why are you looking at me like that?" Cole asked.

Habbad's eyes sharpened. "Where have you been?"

"What do you mean? Did I go somewhere?" Cole rubbed his eyes, realizing his arm was no longer broken. It was sore, but felt sturdy and he could move his fingers again.

Ignoring Goran's warning growl, Habbad rushed over to Cole, placed his hands on the sides of his head, and looked into each of his eyes, searching for something. He frowned, releasing his grip. "Your body became a ball of light. Green light. Then you shot up into the stars faster than I could follow. You were gone for some time, I woke and slept four times. I thought Goran would leave me too when we stopped to forage for food. Do you remember anything?"

"There were a few dreams, mostly about my home." Cole scratched his cheek, which was soaked. Apparently he had been crying. "I saw my mom with Nana Beth. They were both so sad and I could only watch. I tried to reach out to them, but the harder I tried the worse things got. Nana Beth had to give my mom some pills to calm her down. I felt like I was making it worse, so I left. I felt like a ghost. No one could see me." Cole felt a fresh tear chase after the others.

"Those were no dreams!" Habbad's eyes popped wide. "You Traveled, I saw it myself! And to Terra no less! We are not even in Terra's house. This is important, Cole." Habbad deflated as his eyebrows wrinkled together. "None of this should be possible, the banishing was supposed to be permanent. You are changing the rules. Please, tell me everything you remember."

Cole had a difficult time meeting Habbad's eyes. He knew they weren't just dreams. There was the same feeling of falling into himself and flowing through the river. *He* had been there with him the whole time of course, though for some reason Cole was not ready to tell anyone about *Him*. He could feel *Him* now, watching and observing, though the feeling was quickly fading as he became more alert.

"I think you're right," Cole admitted. "Some of those dreams were so vivid. I still have no idea how I'm doing it though, and I only remember flashes of it. And why is the sky lighter down river, is that the local star?" Cole pointed to the faint glow over the small patch of horizon that the river exposed for them.

Habbad crossed his arms and huffed, looking as though he had been denied a great treat. "We have drifted very far, but not that far. Pastori's star is on the other side of the planet. I'm not sure what that light is but it's been getting brighter." Habbad paused, looking Cole up and down. "I think the next time you fall asleep I will be watching you very closely."

"Go right ahead, but that won't be for a while. I feel like I got the best night's sleep of my life. I feel great, actually, not even sore. Well, my arm is sore, but it doesn't feel broken anymore." Goran cocked his head as Cole's stomach let out a long, low moan. "You wouldn't happen to have any food left?"

"Right behind you," Habbad replied and pointed.

Cole hefted a bundle of leaves with both hands. "Wow, good haul huh? Let's see. Yep, more deka seeds. I'm getting sick of these things. Goran, you and me are going to do some hunting next time we stop. I could really go for a hot meal. Now that we have a spell-caster here we should be able to cook it up in no time."

Goran ignored him as he tickled the surface of the water with his paw. Cole was about to give him a playful nudge with his toe but Goran shot his arm into the water like a spear, and pulled out a fish almost as long as he was, wrestling it onto the leaf. With a few well-placed bites the fish went still. Goran carried the carcass across the leaf and spat it out at Cole's feet.

"I said a *hot* meal." Cole kicked the limp fish back towards Goran, who wasted no time, tearing into the belly as eggs spilled out onto the leaf. Cole dry-swallowed. "Thanks for the deka seeds."

Habbad grimaced as he watched Goran tear at the fish. "Intelligent as he is, he is still an animal. I think I will take a turn to sleep since you're so rested." Habbad curled himself up into a ball on the opposite side of Goran. "Wake me if you see anything unusual."

"Will do." The words were barely out of his mouth when Cole felt the leaf slow with Habbad's breathing.

Cole observed the water and the faraway banks for a while. It was difficult to see anything in the pale starlight, and the river seemed to have gotten much wider since he was last awake. It was hard to tell if the leaf was moving at all in fact. Now that he was rested, he scooped some water out of the river and decided to take another crack at the puddle. It wasn't long before he abandoned the attempt, however. His repeated efforts resulted in nothing but a wet hand and foul temper. Eventually he felt Goran's weight against his side as his friend curled up next to him to sleep. Cole placed a hand over Goran's brindle fur, his rapid heartbeat drumming through the rise and fall of his ribs. Bored, Cole laid himself back onto the leaf and tried to make constellations out of the foreign sky, crafting tales for each one. While in the middle of an epic battle between a dragon and a man wielding a bow, his view of the sky became interrupted by something immense and white as snow. Cole sprung to his feet as Goran barked his annoyance.

"Habbad, Habbad wake up!" Cole jostled his small frame, nearly knocking him into the water. "Get up! Look at this thing."

Habbad's eyes opened slowly at first, then snapped wide, sparkling with white light. He considered the thing for a few seconds, then opened his mouth, his tone morbid: "It's the barrier."

Cole gazed upon the translucent white veil, craning his neck as high as it would go. The gently waving sheet seemed to reach the stars, and expanded as far as he could see into the woods on either side of the river. He felt Habbad plop himself down in the center of the leaf.

"Start paddling," Habbad said, placing his palms flat.

Cole stumbled as they lurched towards the shore. It wasn't until they drew near the ghostly veil that Cole realized how strong the river's current was. He threw himself down on the edge of the leaf and pushed at the water as hard as he could, though it didn't seem to help much.

"Habbad, we're not going to make it!" Cole shouted.

The leaf rippled as Habbad managed to find a small burst of speed, though it wasn't enough.

Seconds away from the barrier, Habbad stood and looked at Cole, his face solemn with defeat. "I'm sorry, Cole."

Instinctively, Habbad and Goran ducked under Cole's larger frame as they readied themselves for the unknown. Cole held his breath and closed his eyes, throwing one arm over his face and the other around his friends. Cole felt a tingling pressure on his back and side. He looked up to see the ethereal sheet of light bending around him, vibrating as it touched his skin. The tingling worsened. It was as if the wall were made out of whatever causes pins and needles. While it was certainly uncomfortable, the sensation did not feel deadly.

They were at a standstill, the barrier holding them in the river's current. Cole pushed his hand into the veil, giving his back a reprieve from the sensation, but now his hand tickled like crazy. Through the prickling in his fingers, he could feel the veil start to give. His fingertips punched through, then his hand and arm. He thrashed and tore at the hole as the veil disintegrated, coming apart like cobwebs. With the aid of the river's current, the leaf passed through the barrier as the hole became larger. Ghostly strands clung to Cole as they moved down the river, unraveling the wall as if it were crafted from woven light. Cole cast off the remaining vestiges as quickly as he could, but the damage was done. The gentle breeze pushed and pulled at the barrier until the tear ran up towards the stars. Cole flinched as the wall flickered once, twice, then was no more. Its absence left the river in a profound darkness.

"I can't see a thing. Did we cross?" Habbad asked.

Cole opened his eyes as wide as he could, trying to coax some light from the darkness. "Yeah we're through. My arm is tingling like hell, but I feel fine. I definitely don't feel like I'm about to die, or stop existing."

"We need to get back to the Light Side. This place is dangerous. Did you happen to see which way the shore was?" Habbad asked, keeping a hand on Cole's shoulder.

"No, but I hear birds over there. Shoot us *that* way..." Cole dropped his arm as he realized Habbad couldn't see where he was pointing.

"Hold on," Habbad said, plopping onto the leaf.

Cole braced himself on all fours as his hair flapped behind his head. A minute later he felt solid ground under the leaf as they skidded up onto the shore.

"Here, give me your eyes. Now that I don't have to move the leaf we might as well be able to see." Habbad walked his fingers up Cole's face.

Cole felt the familiar pressure in his eyes as Habbad's fingers zapped his lids. The shore gradually came into focus with every blink, eventually revealing a pebbly shore lined with what looked like a bamboo forest. Habbad pressed his fingers to his own eyes, blinking wide. Goran's eyes apparently needed no aid as Cole saw him pounce and chew up a winged insect.

Cole kicked the giant leaf. "I'm going to miss this sun lily leaf. That was the most comfortable ride I've ever had."

"It has served its purpose," Habbad said, looking up the river bank. "We should walk upstream. I would rather not tempt whatever lurks in the forest."

"After you then." Cole extended an arm.

They meandered along the river bank, slipping over the loose pebbles. On flat ground Cole was usually faster, but his size was more of a hindrance in this case as he kept stumbling over the larger rocks. Once they reached the river bend where the barrier was, Habbad held out his arm, stopping Cole.

"Do you see those lights?" he whispered.

"No, I'm too busy making sure I don't fall on my face." Cole looked up, scanning the tree line.

Habbad pointed. "On the river up ahead. There are dozens of them. We should retreat into the forest where we can watch from the shadows."

To Cole's great annoyance, the pebbles carpeted the forest floor as well. After walking a few paces into the trees, the trio stowed themselves in a shrub. Goran hid himself completely under a wiry shrub. Flickering orange lights soon painted the bush and surrounding bamboo trunks.

"They just keep coming. Do you think they are boats?" Cole asked, flipping a leaf up so he could see better.

"They are *certainly* boats, but it's their passengers that worry me. Can you see what's on that banner?" Habbad squinted, standing on his toes.

Cole plucked a branch off of the bush and used it to cover his torso as he stood. "It looks like...a set of jaws with a fist inside? Does that mean anything to you?"

"Get down, slowly," Habbad whispered, squeezing Cole's shin. "We need to leave. Crawl as quietly as you can."

When they were a good ways away, Habbad stood and guided Cole to a large boulder. He pulled Cole's head low and whispered into his ear, "They are the Domina, soldiers of Grotton. They must have been sent after us. Cole, I don't know if we can escape them."

"What do you mean?" Cole turned his head to look Habbad in the eyes. "We have a huge head start, can't we just keep running?"

"You don't understand, the Domina are magic users as well. They use Grotton's temptations to bond to animals, and not in the way that you and Goran have bonded. Here, let's take cover behind this boulder for now." Habbad stopped and scanned the ground. "Where *is* Goran?"

Cole searched the canopy, pointing up a tree. "Something's got him spooked, but there's no way they saw us. Can you use magic to check the area?" Cole waited for a response. After a moment of listening to chirping insects, he smacked Habbad's arm. "Habbad, can you check the area? Are you listening to me?"

Habbad's wrinkled face was frozen, his mouth agape and his eyes wide. Without warning, he turned on his heel and sped off into the forest.

Heavy, ragged breathing brought Cole's attention to the boulder, which turned out to be no boulder at all, but a massive animal. As it turned, starlight poured in through the gaps in the canopy, revealing its size. It was the largest creature Cole had ever seen. It looked as if someone had tried to combine a man and a bear, but kept switching their mind throughout the process. A gargantuan paw brushed aside a tree trunk as thick as Cole's leg, the resulting crack echoing throughout the forest. Its other hand, a human hand as large as a trash can lid, held a jagged axe with a blade that curved back down the handle. A ragged howl erupted from the creature's snout, which was full of misshapen human teeth. Cole jumped back. Dropping his sharpened stone, he also darted off into the woods.

His body seemed to react on its own, managing the loose pebbly floor with clumsy footfalls. From the crashing behind him, Cole judged that the creature was too large to fit in between the trees. Daring to look over his shoulder, he could see that he was right, but the trees might as well have been made of paper for all the good they did.

Cole heard a familiar snorting alongside him and saw a small shadow with a white mohawk dart ahead of him and up a hill. He followed Goran up the incline, but a thicket of smaller trees and vines halted him. The smashing and roaring grew louder as Cole squeezed in between the trunks. Hopefully the dense vegetation would slow the beast down. Cole pressed on, cutting his way up the hill. He had to earn every foot as the mass of branches and snagging tried to hook him in place. Seeing Goran waiting at the top, Cole dropped down to the pebbly floor and crawled the rest of the way, finding gaps in the mess. Once at the top, Cole stood and found himself on a dirt path. To the left, the path ran downhill, back towards the beast. To the right, there was a bridge leading to the unknown.

Cole's heart fluttered as the beast snarled and smashed its way up the hill. He needed to make a choice and fast. Fear fueled his creativity, driving Cole towards the bridge as fast as his legs would carry him. Cole's padded feet fell hard on the wooden slats, sending waves down its length. Knowing he couldn't outrun the creature, he threw a leg over the edge of the roped handrail and lowered himself so that he only held on by his fingers. His injured arm ached and creaked, threatening to break again. Goran scrambled down after him. The added weight on his back made him nervous, but Cole's fingers held fast.

A raging bellow and thundering footsteps sounded from up the path. A few seconds later violent waves traveled up and down the bridge, causing Cole's fingers to slip with every ripple. The beast slowed. Cole could feel the wooden slats straining under his fingertips as the thing stopped, sniffing the air. Cole shut his eyes as he heard a grumbling laugh above him. It had found them. He couldn't help but wonder what it would feel like to have that crooked blade drag across his white knuckles.

Cole felt Goran tense on his back, as he barked at the creature. Before Cole could stop him, Goran scaled his back and threw himself at the beast. Goran's menacing growl mixed with the beast's oddly high-pitched screams, making the hairs on the back of Cole's neck stand on end.

"Goran hold on!" Cole hollered, pulling himself up. His head popped up over the slats and his feet kicked uselessly into open air. He couldn't hoist himself up. As his head sank back down, he saw Goran on the creature's face. "Goran look out!"

The thing's massive human hand dropped the ax and snatched Goran with crushing strength, but before he could be snuffed out like an insect, Goran sank his canines into a finger. Howling, the beast whipped Goran onto the bridge, the latter landing on all fours with murder in his crimson eyes. Cole kicked out with his feet again, trying to grab onto something as his head dipped below the bridge, which began to shake worse than ever.

Suddenly, a new roar tore through the night air, startling Cole and hurting his ears. Was there another animal up there now? The creature let out a pitiful wail as the bridge stopped shaking. All was silent, save for the chirping insects and Cole's panting. Summoning the final dregs of strength, Cole pulled himself up. Before his eyes rose above his cramping hands, his sweaty fingertips betrayed him. His stomach lurched and his hair rippled as he saw the bridge get smaller and smaller. The last thing he remembered seeing was a pair of huge ruby eyes watching him fall.

CHAPTER 11

ENLISTING

C ole wove in and out of conscious thought. Snapshots played before his mind's eye; pain, rushing water, choking and fighting for air. Eventually he succumbed to the blackness, unable to maintain the struggle any longer. Dreams of warm waters and soft hands swirled around his head as a whale's song moaned somewhere far off. He woke for a moment, feeling his broken form rise from the water, his gaze drawn into a pair of eyes that held equal parts intelligence and ferocity. He indulged in their beauty before the blackness took him once more.

He rolled over, tightening the blankets around himself as he found a more comfortable position. The smell of breakfast tempted him out of bed, but he was too comfortable to get up just yet. His mom would come get him before it got cold anyway. He buried his head into the pillow and stretched his arm beneath the cool underside. The fog of sleep was quickly lifting, but he was content to lie curled up in his bed forever.

An unfamiliar voice cleared its throat as Cole slowly cracked his eyes. He was in a bed, but it was not his own. He was in a room he did not recognize. Sitting across from him was a very large man with shoulder-length hair the color of clouds, his hands folded on his lap. Cole shut his eyes a little so the stranger might think him asleep. He would wait it out. He hoped the man would get bored and leave. That would be his chance to sneak out.

The man leaned forward, his ancient eyes staring right into Cole's. "I've no doubt your dreams are enticing, but I think you'll find this reality might be more to your liking at the present. It's all I can do to keep from leaving this chair and discovering the source of that delicious smell. Wouldn't you agree?"

Cole thought about continuing the farce, but he didn't appear to be in any immediate danger. He was unrestrained and this man was at least as big as Kreed. The stranger would have hurt him by now if he really wanted to. Cole blinked, pretending to have just woken up.

The man wore plain clothes of drab greens and browns unadorned by pockets or frills. His sat in a relaxed position with one leg crossed over the other, one bare foot bouncing in midair while the other tapped the floor.

"Um, where am I?" Cole shifted under the blankets.

The man gave Cole a smile, deep and warm, as if he were greeting a friend he hadn't seen in a very long time. "You are in a safe place. I could tell you exactly where you are, but I doubt it would mean anything to you. Your kind hasn't stepped foot on this planet in quite some time. Might I ask your name?"

While the man didn't look anything like Kreed, he couldn't help his reservations. Cole wanted to trust him. While his sweeping eyebrows and beak-like nose gave him the appearance of a bird of prey, the man's eyes were soft and kind. "I...I'm Bob," Cole lied.

The man raised an eyebrow. "Is that so? Well Bob, my name is Chiron. You'll be happy to know your Underkin friend is also safe, and is being summoned here as we speak. The Domina that followed you across the barrier, or where the barrier used to be, I should say, have all been dealt with."

Feeling a modicum of bravery, Cole asked, "Are you with the Dark Ones?"

Chiron leaned back in his chair and crossed his arms. "We have other names, but yes, I am with the Dark Ones." Chiron raised his head, looking down at him. Cole noticed a terrible white scar that ran up the man's neck. It was a few inches wide in places and glowed with a throbbing rosy light. What could have caused an injury like that?

Cole looked to the door, and then back to Chiron. "If I try to leave, will you stop me?"

Chiron's expression remained light and pleasant. "No. Is there somewhere you'd like to be?"

"Yes, but I don't think I can go back there." Cole's eyes scanned the room, searching for anything he could use as a weapon.

Chiron crossed his legs, folding his hands atop his knees. "It's funny how we don't fully appreciate a place until we find ourselves in a position where we cannot return to it."

Cole sat up and threw his legs over the edge of the bed. His feet dangled a few feet from the floor. Chiron continued to watch him with polite interest, giving Cole a moment to gather himself. The room was large, though to someone of Chiron's size it would be small. The lack of décor gave Cole the impression that the room may have been some sort of prison or military barracks. There were bladed objects on a nearby table. Their design was elegant but entirely foreign. Cole couldn't decide if they were weapons or tools for torture.

"I imagine you would feel more comfortable if you had something to defend yourself with. Please, take your pick." Chiron waved his hand towards the table. "I see the hesitation in your eyes. With or without a weapon you are no threat to anyone here, but you may take one if you wish."

Cole looked back to Chiron. "My name isn't Bob. It's Cole."

Chiron's mouth stretched into a half smile. "Is it really? That's a shame, I rather liked Bob."

Cole couldn't tell if he was joking or not. "When will Habbad be here?"

"Your Underkin Friend? Not soon I'm afraid. I could tell you the exact amount of time but I don't think you would comprehend it. While I did not inspect your mind without your permission, I could not help but pick up the faintest scent of meddling. Your vocabulary has been tampered with, has it not?"

"A man, big like you, said that he put a cypher in my mind so I could speak your language," Cole said.

"That explains why a human is so fluent in the Aenerian language. Do you remember this man's name?" Chiron asked, tapping his fingers together.

"Kreed." As he said the name, Cole imagined he saw a spark of alarm in Chiron's eyes, but it faded behind his calm demeanor and pleasant smile. "Do you know him?"

"Yes, as a matter of fact I was Kreed's mentor some time ago, but I haven't seen him in many cycles. I would be most saddened if half the rumors about him are true." Chiron leaned back and placed his hands flat on his knees. "Cole, with your permission, I would like to inspect your mind to ensure that Kreed has not done you any harm."

"I…would rather you didn't," Cole said, unsure if his opinion carried any weight. He would have Habbad check him when he got here.

"Very well then." Chiron looked Cole up and down as he drummed his fingers on the armrest. "Our sentries tell me that you are the reason the barrier came down. There are many different factions here on the Dark Side, and this event affects them all. Each one has its own plans as to what should be done with you. While I am by no means in charge of any group, I am listened to by all. Before any hasty choices are made, I would hear your side of the tale."

"All right, where do you want me to start? With the barrier?" Cole asked, feeling as if he had been caught in some wrongdoing.

Chiron looked down at him from his beak-nose. "How about from the beginning."

Cole's eyes fell to the floor. "You might not believe me. I'm not sure I believe it all yet myself."

If Chiron was surprised, his face didn't show it. "You just destroyed Aeneria's most important magical object, an object that eludes the understanding of our most esteemed Wisdom Walkers, including me. You tore it apart as if it were nothing more than tissue paper when it should have killed you and your friends. Before this event I may not have believed you. Now however, I think you will find that I am sincerely open-minded."

Taking a deep breath, Cole told Chiron everything he remembered since his arrival. He still wasn't sure if Chiron could be trusted, but he didn't see the harm in being honest, especially if he could recruit an Aenerian to help save Lexy. His throat was sore by the time he described his encounter with the barrier, but he took special care to emphasize how it was not his fault. Cole expected an interrogation from the grey-maned Aenerian, but Chiron merely drummed his fingers and listened with utmost interest. Cole finished the tale feeling raw yet cathartic. The fate of his friends weighed heavily on him.

Chiron's face finally donned a look of genuine concern. "You have had a rough go of it to say the least. It pains me that your visit has been marred by such tragedy. It is a shame really, Aeneria is a beautiful place. Your Earth has its charms as well, but Aeneria represents the best of all the local planets. We used to bring you humans here for visits."

Cole's mouth popped open. "You've been to Earth?"

Chiron chuckled. "Yes, in my youth, when I was full to the brim with righteousness and cleverness, but back to the matter at hand. You, my brave man, have just arbitrarily destroyed Aeneria's barrier and brought war to our doorstep. You have become something of a big deal among our factions. Some see you as a threat, others as a weapon. I know what everyone else wants to do with you, but no one knows what *you* want to do with you. What paths tempt you now?"

"I haven't thought about it to be honest. I've just been scraping by since I got here, and trying not to get eaten. What I really want is to go back to Earth, but that doesn't seem to be an option anymore. Is it?" Cole added, but he already knew the answer.

"I am afraid you have more experience in this matter than I. You are the only one to have Traveled since the barrier was erected. Perhaps since it was destroyed that means Travel through the aethers is possible again, though I doubt it. In any case, you would have to wait until we were back in Terra's house before you could hope to attempt it."

Cole's eyebrows rose. "I think I Traveled to Earth while I was on the river. I saw my friends and family, but they couldn't see me. Habbad said I Traveled too, that I turned into a ball of light."

"In the spirit of open-mindedness I will have to take you at your word. Travel to a planet out of order is impossible as far as I know. You are quite the anomaly. You may very well vanish and return to Earth any moment now, but in the interim, where would you like to go from here?" Chiron asked, drumming his fingers on his knee.

"I don't have a home or a place to stay, and I can't go anywhere near Costas. I guess I'd like to see if Habbad really is okay. Then I'd want to find Goran. Then, and I don't know if it's even possible, I'd like to save Lexy. Other than that I don't have any idea what I'm going to do here."

Chiron tilted his head in curiosity. "What is it that you would be saving Lexy from? Did you not just say that the Corpulant took her?"

"It did, but Habbad said Kreed put some kind of spell on her so that she won't die. Though if we don't save her before the end of the cycle, she'll be worse than dead because she's going to the tower of Devotion. It's this thing were-"

"There is no need to explain that abomination to me, I am familiar with the tower," Chiron said, halting Cole with his palm. "The Light Side has grown dark indeed. Please, continue."

"That's it really. I want to save Lexy before she goes to the tower," Cole said, biting his lip.

Chiron inspected Cole with such a significant gaze that Cole worried the Aenerian was using magic on him. Chiron finally blinked, relaxing his winged brows. "And how do you plan to accomplish all of this?"

"I don't know. Habbad can do some magic. I guess we'd think of something." The words sounded childish even to his own ears. "Do you know anyone that would help us?"

Chiron nodded, "There are those that would jump at the opportunity to help you, though their aid would come with a price which they would not reveal until they found out how best to use you. We are not the demons that the propaganda of the Light Side has portrayed us as. However, the Dark Side can be a very dangerous place for one in your position. As soon as you leave this room, webs shall weave themselves around you. They already have as a matter of fact. Right now you are adrift in an ocean of politics and everyone is out fishing for you."

The thought of being someone's puppet set a small, riotous fire in Cole. "Is there any way for me to avoid it all? I don't like the idea of being used."

Chiron shook his head. "I am afraid not, though I do have some suggestions if you would hear them."

Cole considered simply taking a weapon off the table and making a run for it. He inched closer to the table. "In the spirit of open-mindedness, I'll hear your suggestions."

"Excellent. Given everything that you just admitted to me, I would suggest that you join up with our local military. Those who demand recompense for the barrier would see this as an act of restitution. It would also take you out of reach of the other groups that would use you for their own gain. There are many roles in the military, and not all of them involve direct combat. Your assignments would never be beyond your honest abilities, unless you seek those yourself. The training and resources you would be exposed to would certainly make you more prepared to rescue Lexy. Would this be agreeable?" Chiron asked, giving Cole a moment to take it all in.

"I feel like I don't have a choice." Cole hugged his arms around his middle, squeezing tightly.

"Of course you do. This is merely a recommendation. Though I suppose you could take to hiding yourself in the woods and just simply wait for this all to pass. No one would stop you." Chiron waved his hand over the weapons on the table.

Cole mulled it over, rocking back and forth. Chiron made it seem like he could come and go as he pleased, and Cole believed him. If this military job wasn't to his liking he would just leave and find something else. "I'll join. At least until Habbad gets here." Nerves bubbled up in Cole's chest. "What will be expected of me?"

Chiron shifted in his seat. "That is for your mentors to decide, though I imagine for now you will be expected to rest and recover. You have been through quite a bit. From what I hear you were clinging on to life by a thread when you washed up on our shores. If not for the magical talents of one of our students, you would likely not be here eyeing that sharp dagger on the table."

Cole brought his gaze back to Chiron. "I wondered how I managed to survive that fall. I'll have to thank him if we ever meet."

Chiron smirked. "You will have a chance to thank *her* soon enough. She is a member of the military as well. She may not be too receptive of your gratitude however."

"Why not? Did she get into trouble for saving me?" Cole asked, confused.

"She will be just fine, and so will you. Now I think it is time we get you up and started down your new path. I am sure that the owner of this room would appreciate it."

Cole hopped down from the bed, sharp pain shooting up his legs when he landed. His body felt as if it had been run through a meat grinder.

"If you would follow me." Chiron rose to his full height, which was taller than even Kreed. He turned and walked out of the room, surprisingly light on his feet. His cloudy grey hair swished, but it was his cloak that drew Cole's attention as it trailed over the ground behind him. It seemed to be made entirely of wood, giving the appearance that the floor continued right up to his lofty shoulders. After Chiron vanished through the door, Cole stood on his toes and snatched a white-bladed dagger from the table. In his hand the knife was more of a small sword. He tucked the blade into the wrappings at his side, taking care not to cut them.

Cole emerged from the room and wondered if he had just walked into a postcard for some tropical vacation spot. His feet sank into cool sand that stretched along the coastline of a lagoon. Lights from other buildings sparkled from across the water. Odd colors glinted off the mirrored surface, drawing Cole's eyes up to the sky, where he saw a moon so large he could count individual craters. The moon was bigger than his outstretched hand, its surface glowing with multichromatic hues, as if someone had painted it with a brush made from rainbows.

"That is Oberon, our moon," Chiron explained.

"I've never seen anything like it." Cole's eyes stretched wide with wonder. "Why couldn't I see it from Costas?"

"You have drifted a long way from Costas," Chiron said, turning away from him.

Chiron set off down the beach and Cole followed, barely able to keep up with the giant's stride. At the water's edge, waves lapped up the gentle slope towards the tree line, which in turn reached out towards the water, as if the branches longed to bathe in it. Cole looked into the darkened huts as they passed. They all appeared vacant, save for the blue lamp over each of the doorframes.

"Does anyone live in those huts?" he asked, trotting along.

Seeing Cole struggling to keep up, Chiron slowed. "Not quite. The occupants are busy patrolling our borders at the moment."

More questions blossomed in Cole's mind as he slogged through the loose sand, but he couldn't quite hold onto one long enough to put words to it. He instead took to watching Chiron's cape, which now looked like he was wearing the sandy beach on his back. Cole held out his hand, catching the tiny grains of sand and shells that rained from the cape.

CHAPTER 12

AMONG GIANTS

A hollow scraping cut through the ocean air as the boat slowed to a halt on the shore of an island. The tall trees and thick vegetation blocked most of the starlight, casting the forest in thick blackness. Cole hopped out of the boat and winced as his feet landed on sharp rocks. This shore that was much less forgiving than the soft sands he and Chiron had just left. Chiron stood inside the boat, the side of his face illuminated by a blue lantern hanging from a vine-covered arch of the vessel. Cole was about to ask him where they were, but paused when he felt a presence coming towards them from the tree line. The presence made itself obvious by the wall of silence it cast. Cole squinted into the darkness, unable to make out a figure.

"Greetings, Rothael." Chiron called into the shadows.

A voice like a mountain's echoing thunder responded, "Greetings, Wisdom Walker."

Cole jumped slightly when the voice came from several feet above where he was expecting. A man emerged from the shadows, leaning trees aside to fit through. He was easily more than twice Cole's height, and built like some freakishly muscular hero from a comic book. Metal plating covered his midsection, but his arms, legs, and parts of his face were shrouded in a material that was several deeper shades of black than the darkest shadows behind him. His wild hair fell back over his shoulders and seemed to be made of the same material, giving it the appearance of a bundle of thin knives that clinked as he walked. The ground shook as the giant approached. In the blue light of the lantern, Cole decided that the strangest thing about the man was his clawed hands and feet, which were freakishly huge and would have looked more at home on a dragon.

"He accepted," Chiron said, shifting his gaze from the moon to Roth.

"Obviously. What was he again? Underkin?" Roth bent down until his nose was an inch from Cole's face, and sniffed deeply. "Smells like one too."

"His name is Cole, and he's a human from Terra," Chiron responded.

Roth stood and gave Chiron a sour look. "Human? If you were anyone else I'd toss you in a tree for lying, but you're you, aren't you." He brought his gaze down to Cole, who almost collapsed under the weight of it. "I don't care how you got here, or where you suckled at your mother's tit. I hear you might be dangerous. I can *use* dangerous. We're going to find out if you're worth more than your weight in shit, even if I have to rip you open to get a peek at it. Now, take that knife tucked behind your back and try to kill me."

Cole looked to Chiron, who was watching with mild interest.

"Why the fuck are you looking at him?" Roth shouted so loudly that Cole's ears stung. "That's a free one, your only free one. Next time you hesitate when I give you a command I'll break one of your arms. Now, try to kill me."

There was no doubt in Cole's mind that Roth was a man of his word. His legs barely had the strength to hold him upright as he reached one shaking hand behind him. The knife slipped in his sweaty grip and he dropped it on the rocks. He bent down to retrieve it, fear chipping away at his heart. Driven by a mixture of instinct and terror, he closed his eyes and slashed blindly up at the giant. His arm wrenched as the blade struck something very solid. With one hand covering his face, he opened his eyes slowly, expecting retaliation.

"That would be armor. Keep your damn eyes open and hit something soft," Roth growled.

Apparently the deep black material covering Roth's legs, arms, hands, and feet were some kind of armor. Cole jabbed the dagger again, aiming for a section of Roth's upper thigh that wasn't shrouded in the dark skin. This time the dagger met a single clawed finger the size of Cole's leg.

"Faster! Like you mean it!" he barked.

Cole swung again and again. He gradually gained speed and confidence as he realized this was more of a sparring session. This wasn't a fight. It was a test. Roth moved with elegance unfitting of his appearance, using only the one finger to block and parry Cole's attacks. They went at it for what felt like an hour, though Cole knew it could have only been a few minutes. His right hand cramped, barely able to hold the blade, but it gave him an idea. Cole dropped the knife in mid-air, catching it in his left, and jabbed at an opening that happened to present itself in the same breath. The knife sank up to the hilt in Roth's upper thigh. Cole froze.

"DO I LOOK DEAD TO YOU?" Roth's voice pummeled the air between them.

Cole barely registered that he'd been struck as he flew backwards through the air. The next thing he knew, water crashed into his back as he sank like a rock. He flopped back up to the surface, unable to breathe even after his head emerged from the water. Panicking, he scrambled back to the shore, trying with all his might to get air back into his lungs. He clawed at the rocks looking for anything that might help, but his lungs were closed. When his vision started to blur, he felt clawed hands grasp his chest, hoisting him up into the air. He was face to face with Roth again. Roth considered him, then pursed his lips and blasted hot air into Cole's gaping mouth, forcing his lungs back open. Cole's chest stretched painfully, but his vision cleared at once. Seeing that Cole was now breathing on his own, Roth dropped him to the sharp rocks.

"I told you to *kill* me. That means you don't stop till I'm dead." Roth turned towards the boat, addressing Chiron. "He's fragile, but trainable. I don't know about dangerous, not unless he can make something of Wisdom."

"And let's not forget Passion. Every school of magic is important here, Rothael. You of all people should remember." Chiron touched the lantern, filling it with blinding blue light.

"Bah! Passion! I don't see how Passion will deal with what's swarming at our borders," Roth paused, pensive, "But I do remember when Rage and Wisdom were not enough. You're right of course, but then again, you're you aren't you?"

"I suppose I am." The boat lurched backwards into the water. "Try not to break him permanently, will you?"

Roth grumbled a chuckle. "I intend to shatter him."

Chiron nodded, as if this were a better option. "Then ensure all his parts are whole when you rebuild him."

"As you wish, Wisdom Walker." Still as a statue, Roth watched Chiron bob away towards the mainland.

Cole watched the boat fade and felt his hope go with it.

"Get up and keep up." Roth stepped towards the tree line.

He was unsure if he could stand, but fear moved his body for him. Cole placed a hand on his knee and brought himself upright. Roth's hulking silhouette was already sinking into the shadows. Cole trotted after him.

"Here." With the talons on his thumb and forefinger, Roth yanked the knife from his thigh.

Cole took the knife, debating whether he should apologize or thank him. Instead he mumbled something inaudible as he whipped the knife back and forth, attempting to fling the blood off.

"What did you just say?" Roth growled.

"I-I said I'm sorry for stabbing you," Cole stammered, suddenly aware of how soft his voice sounded.

Roth's booming laughter thundered through the forest, nearby birds taking flight. "I wanted to see what you'd do when presented with an opening. Think of it as your first test, which you failed. You should have kept attacking. A real enemy won't give you a second chance to finish the dance. Nor will I."

"I've never stabbed anyone before," Cole squeaked, clearing his throat.

Roth held up a single claw. "Inexperience is not the reason for your failure. *Fear* is why you failed. Fear is a magic used by The Three, Decreath to be specific. Remember that. You were pissing yourself with Fear like a scared pup."

The insult stung him. But Roth was right. Cole felt like nothing more than a scared child since his arrival on Aeneria. A question popped to the front of Cole's mind. "A friend of mine told me The Three were Dark Ones. Are they not with you?

"Your friend is either stupid or brainwashed. The Three are the god-generals of the darker magics, and our greatest foes. You'll learn more about them in your lessons." Roth's voice took on a slightly less terrifying tone. "Take heart, human, we'll teach you how to defend yourself. If nothing else, by the time we're through with you you'll have a better understanding of yourself. And if you really do have any tricks up your sleeve we'll find them."

Cole's stomach did a few flips as he wondered exactly how they would try to 'find' his hidden tricks. "What kind of training will I be going through? I don't think I can handle another lesson like that. I'm not built for it."

"If you aren't built for it then we'll forge you into something with a little more hide. Your training has already started. I am the instructor of the Path of Rage, but you will also learn the paths of Passion and Wisdom. Through my training you will become a living weapon, or at least become more deadly than you are now." Roth halted. Even in the near pitch black, Cole had no doubt he was staring right into him. "You have already learned my first rule; never hesitate. My second and final rule is that you will do everything with everything you have. Hold back and I break you. Do you understand?"

"Yes," Cole said in a high whisper, eliciting a rumble from Roth's chest. Cole cleared his throat and took a deep breath. "I mean, YES!"

"Good. You won't be surprised next time my foot sends you for a little ride, eh? Now, let's go find your unit." Roth started off again.

They continued deeper through the woods, eventually finding a path large enough for Roth to walk through without breaking anything. The trees grew so tall that they blocked all light, and Cole had to follow Roth by sound alone. They walked in silence for a while as Cole's curiosity overcame his nerves with every step. He wondered who he might be working with and what type of training he would go through. If Chiron and Roth were fair representatives of their race, he wouldn't stand a chance. Cole had never been the dumbest or the shortest person in the room, but now he felt like a stupid child. Who would take him seriously if he was only waist-high and couldn't do magic? Then again, perhaps his size would make him harder to notice and tempt enemies to underestimate him. Cole wiped his eyes, hoping

Roth wouldn't notice his tears. Memories of home were rising to the fore of his mind. They reminded him of how much he had lost, both on Earth and Aeneria. Looking up from his feet, Cole discovered a faint glow off in the distance. Stepping to the side, he could see lights through the trees ahead of them.

"Behold The Sill, Human. I'd bet you're the first of your kind to lay eyes on its walls." A silhouette of a clawed hand pointed towards the lights, which were evenly spaced and spread as far as he could see in either direction.

Cole didn't say it out loud, but as they drew near there was something familiar about the place, as if he were walking through a forgotten dream. The walls were made of trees thick as buildings which grew so closely together that they appeared airtight. Imbedded in every tree was an oval gem glowing brilliantly, casting hundreds of shadows into the forest. The path led them to a part of the wall that shone a bit more brightly with roots piled above ground. Cole flinched as part of the wall stepped out towards them.

A man greeted them with an airy voice, like ocean waves heard from a distance. "Who approaches so unannounced?"

"It's me, Whind," Roth said, clearly annoyed.

"You did not leave through one of the gates as you know you should have," Whind replied, his outline becoming more solid, revealing a thin, pale man dressed in clothes made from leaves and bark.

Roth grumbled, "Last I checked I didn't need permission to go for a walk."

"Of course. But with events unfolding so rapidly around us, you would do well to communicate such things to the gatekeepers." Whind raised an eyebrow. "You wouldn't want us to attack you by mistake, would you?"

Roth laughed. "I want you to try."

Whind gave Roth a slow blink before bringing his eyes down to Cole. "I am Whind, Gatekeeper of The Sill."

"I'm Cole. I'm the new guy." He wished he had a more impressive title.

"So you are." Whind held Cole's eyes, his face expressionless. "You are a human."

Cole waited for him to continue, but Whind only stared in silence. Cole felt like he was having a staring contest with a tree. "Um, thanks."

Whind maintained his vague eye contact for a moment longer before addressing Roth, "Should I open the gate, or would you prefer to jump back over the wall?"

Cole rubbed his cramping neck as he tried to guess how tall the trees were. He couldn't even see the canopy. There's no way someone could jump that high.

Roth's lip curled, revealing Goran-like canines. "The landing would break the kid's spine. Open the gate, Gatekeeper."

"As you wish." Whind stretched a slender arm towards the roots of one of the trees. His hand glowed a dull olive as vines sprouted from his palm, creeping towards the bark and seeping through the crevices. The tree released a series of earsplitting cracks as it stood up on its roots, creating a neat gap underneath. Whind touched an adjacent tree and it stood up as well, completing a tunnel. The vines receded back into Whind's hand and the green light faded. He stood aside, raising an arm in welcome. "Enter."

Cole followed Roth through the tunnel, which was lit by more glowing gems embedded under the roots. Each gem was the size of Cole's chest, and the trees were so thick it took half a minute to emerge on the other side. As they approached the opening, the air became noticeably warmer and wetter. Cole thought about undoing some of the wrappings which were now soaked in water and sweat. He walked beside Roth, eager to see what lay beyond.

They emerged from the mouth of the tunnel into what Cole first took as another forest. It was far less dense with no underbrush, and the trees seemed to scrape the stars. Hundreds of the glowing gemstones spiraled up the colossal trunks. Cole was awestruck, then movement caught his eye. The trees were not just trees, but structures. What he took as insects were actually people walking up and down staircases that wound up the trunks.

Jogging after Roth, Cole made out windows and doors cut into the tree bark, and bridges connecting branches higher up in countless levels. The architecture looked natural, as if the trees themselves had decided to grow into structures. The city was immense. Cole saw no sign of the opposing wall as they continued on, just more trees that looked like buildings. There were objects gliding and darting far above. As one flew close, Cole recognized it as a sun lily leaf bearing a package. Another had two passengers sitting cross-legged with their hair whipping back over their shoulders.

Cole trotted after Roth, following a path that brought them through a crowded market. Ignoring the stares, Cole gawked at the items displayed. One shop sold clothing and armor, another potions and powders. One shop definitely sold weapons, though Cole could only recognize the most basic of knives and maces. He had hoped that his small size would hide him, but it seemed that every eye was glued to him as he ran by. People offered simple greetings to Roth, bowing slightly or giving salutes. Roth must have been someone of importance, Cole realized. To Cole's dismay, not a single person was under seven feet tall, though none were quite as tall as Roth. Anxiety twisted his guts as he thought about meeting his unit.

Roth led him down a darker path where the trees grew small enough for Cole to see the tops.

Walking a bit more slowly, Roth spoke: "Your unit is just down this path. Should be wrapping up a lesson right now. You'll join them for the remainder, then I'll assign someone to orient you with The Sill properly. You'll have two other teachers, both of which are your superior and have similar rules to mine. You have any problems you come to one of us. Don't even think about asking me for help unless something bit your ass off, or else I will."

Cole took a deep breath and projected his voice: "I understand."

Roth steered them downhill. Cole could hear what sounded like a dozen lumberjacks chopping wood off in the distance. As they neared, the chopping sounds moved up to the canopy, though it was too dark to see what caused the noise.

Cole swallowed, looking up to where he guessed Roth's head was. "Roth?"

"What?" he growled.

"I can't see. I had a friend that put a spell on my eyes so I could see better, but it must have worn off. Can you or somebody here fix my eyes with Wisdom?" Cole knew the answer before he finished.

Roth was silent for a moment, or as silent as he could be with his massive clawed feet tearing at roots and crushing rocks. "No. You'll get no help or special treatment. You'll do everything with your own teeth and blood. And until I say so, you won't tell anyone that you brought the barrier down, or that you're from Terra. If anyone asks, you're an Underkin. Got all that?"

"Yes," Cole responded, grateful he didn't get hit for asking a stupid question. "Do you get a lot of Underkin on the Dark Side?"

Roth shook his head, his bladed hair clinking together. "No. Underkin are the little creatures bred by The Three to fuel their disgusting magics. We've no use for such tricks. You must have seen a few on the Light Side. Stupid things smaller even than you."

"Two of my friends are Underkin. They're not stupid," Cole said, a little more aggressively than he wanted.

Cole saw Roth's teeth flash through the darkness. "You'll make more powerful friends here. Gonna need them too. The Three have grown fat and their armies great. You did us a favor in my opinion, taking down the barrier. It's been too long since we danced with enemies worthy of our Rage. We've grown soft."

Cole swallowed. He had no desire whatsoever to go toe-to-toe with anything Roth considered a worthy opponent. His clawed hands looked like they would make short work of a battle tank.

"There's your unit." Roth halted, pointing at three evergreens. Cole couldn't see anyone, however; he could just hear the chopping noises racing up and down.

"What is it that I'm supposed to do?" Cole asked, feeling a mixture of bemusement and worry.

"This is a physical lesson. They have partnered up and are racing each other up and down the trees." Roth lowered his voice, giving Cole a look that could melt steel. "Get going."

Cole almost asked how, but ran for the trees when a rumbling sounded from Roth's chest. Luckily there were a few of the glowing gems imbedded at the base of the trunks, bathing the area in dull rosy light. His heart raced alongside his nerves. He was sure something was broken in his chest from where Roth had kicked him. Every step and breath sent a hot wire of pain through his sternum. Cole reached the tree, placing a hand on the rough bark. To his dismay, the nearest branch was about ten feet above his head. Heart hammering, he looked to the other trees but there were no better options. Fearing hesitation, he jumped as high as he could. His fingers stretched pathetically into open air about a foot short of the branch. Desperate, he jumped again, a bit higher but still nowhere near the branch. Not sure of what to do, he kept jumping, calves burning before long.

Cole yelped as something huge crashed to the ground beside him. It was a person. Another figure joined the first.

"Hah! Beat you that time!" said a muscular woman dressed in sturdy cloth attire.

"Cheater! You didn't touch the top!" said a man in a similar uniform.

"It's a tad difficult to touch the top of a tree after someone's ripped it off, wouldn't you say?" The woman gave the man a playful slash with a clawed hand. A series of iron bands held a thick rope of auburn hair over one of her shoulders, exposing a squared face of rugged beauty. She snapped into a defensive posture after noticing Cole standing beside the tree. "What the hell is that?"

"Relax, Sitra, that's the Underkin Roth told us about." The man then addressed Cole, looking as though he'd smelled something foul. "Underkin, what is your name?"

Cole looked from the man to Roth, who was watching them intently. He debated whether it would get him another boot if he stopped to talk. "I'm Cole," he replied, then quickly resumed his tree-jumps.

"Well Cole, you know it's rude to ignore your superiors don't you?" The man stepped closer to the light, revealing an adolescent face with a sharp nose and cheekbones. His face curled into a sneer, giving him the appearance of a handsome gargoyle. "That means you look at me while I'm talking to you."

Cole didn't know much about this planet or its inhabitants, but he could recognize a bully when he met one. He stopped jumping and approached the Aenerian, noticing the black claws that adorned his hands and feet. "Who said you're my superior? Last I checked I answered to Roth. I don't even know who you are."

The giant boy's eye twitched. "I've never met an Underkin before. If your intelligence is any indication of the rest of your species, then I see why you make good livestock. Seeing as you are more helpless than even our children, *everyone here* is your superior. You would do well to remember this, or else I may remind you of your place."

Silence fell between them. Cole wrestled with his embarrassment and ire, unsure of how to react. Back home he'd stood up to bullies, but he was not home. This was a world of giants and magic, and so the bully would win this round.

"Oh stop it Valen!" Sitra smacked her male companion on the shoulder with a bladed hand of her own. "He only just got here. You were new here not too long ago. We weren't so mean to you, were we?"

"At least I'm Aenerian. He has no right. He would be more useful digging up-" Valen's sneer melted into mortal terror as a massive clawed hand wrapped around his forearm.

Roth had appeared behind Valen, unheard and unseen. Valen's face paled as Roth squeezed, blood squirting from in-between his bladed fingers. Cole swallowed back vomit as he heard a muffled crunching from Valen's arm. Sitra leapt up the tree, her claws chopping away at the bark and showering them all in wood chips.

"I don't remember idle chatter being a part of this lesson. Get back to it, or else you'll be finishing with no arms." Roth's voice was hushed, though no less dangerous.

Roth released his grip and walked away. Valen's arm now dangled below the elbow like a wilted plant. He cradled his bloody appendage, which looked dangerously close to falling off. Cole had noticed that both his hands and feet had lost their black claws. Without a word, Valen leapt up to the nearest branch and scaled the tree. His speed was unaffected by the loss of an arm and claws.

Cole resumed his attempt at the lowest branch, terrified of what Roth might feel a fitting punishment for him.

Cole felt Roth's massive footsteps draw near. "That's obviously not working. Try a different way." Roth walked past Cole towards the other evergreens.

Shaking with both fright and exhaustion, Cole searched the ground for anything that might help. There were no nearby rocks or sticks he could use as a step. He tried getting a running start before jumping, but he was so tired that he was now a good two feet shy of the branch. The running gave him an idea, however. Stepping back several paces, he ran towards the tree at full speed, continuing up the trunk a few feet before kicking off. To his surprise, his hands wrapped around the branch. Grateful for all the weight he'd lost, he curled his legs up and wrapped them around the branch as well. Cole's elation was short lived however. As he wiggled it became clear that he was quite stuck. The rough bark cut into his palms as they began to slip. Panicking, he adjusted his grip and interlocked his fingers on the top side of the branch. The cloth wrappings stuck to the branch like Velcro, holding him in place. Slowly, he shimmied his body side to side, ratcheting himself around to the topside of the branch. Relief washed over him as he rested his face against the bark. Fortunately the next branch was well within reach. Not wanting to be found resting too long, he continued his way up the tree.

Cole's hands were rubbed raw before long. He had to jump to reach some branches, though the higher he climbed the closer the branches grew together. He couldn't tell how high he was, but Sitra and Valen passed him several times. Eventually the sky opened up above him and he could identify a few of the constellations he'd made up while on the river with Habbad. Winded and soaked, he rested his hand on the broken tree top, sap stinging his raw hands.

For the first time in a very long time Cole felt a sense of accomplishment. He was nowhere near as fast as the others, but he, Cole Carter, had just climbed the tallest thing he had ever laid eyes on. He allowed himself a moment to soak in his victory as he gazed out upon the ocean of life from the city, the lights below mixing with the stars above like mirrored gardens. The air was cooler up at this altitude and a gentle breeze caressed his face, carrying a flowery scent. He took another moment to gawk at the immense moon, which watched him from low on the horizon. He was content to stare at that colorful ball until fate decided to bring him back home. Cole's cheeks and forehead glowed as if he were bathing in the sun itself. Waiting so long, he knew he risked punishment from Roth, but the moment was too tempting. From deep inside his chest Cole felt something stirring in him, something that stood out like a flower in the dead of winter. Budding hope took hold inside him. Hope that he was not as doomed as he once thought. Hope that he could figure out a way to save Lexy and find a way back home. He knew those were tall orders, just far-off dreams, but in the meantime this place didn't seem so bad, at least not in this beautiful moment.

Descending the tree took much longer. Cole was almost thankful for the darkness of the middle layers because he couldn't see how high up he was. Though he tried to avoid it, he found himself facing a branch he'd had to jump from on the way up. The branch was not directly below the one he currently sat on. He would have to swing himself over a couple feet, hoping to land on it. With no other options, he lowered himself until he was holding on by just his hands, which he covered in some of the wrappings that he tore from his arms. His grip held fast as he started a gentle swing back and forth. While he readied himself for the lunge, a crash jarred his hands, loosening his grip. Wood chips pelted him from above.

"How pathetic." A familiar voice chuckled from the shaken branch.

"Hey! Don't do that! I almost fell!" Cole pleaded.

White light flashed into being above him. Cole looked up around the branch to see Valen staring down at him.

"I thought Underkin were better suited for holes in the ground. How did you find yourself in such a lofty place?" Valen's tone was soft, yet dangerous like a wound spring. Through the light, Cole could see that Valen's uninjured hands and feet were wicked black claws once more. A cruel smile played across Valen's face. "Your place is on the ground."

The branch gave an ear-splitting report as it broke from the tree. An odd weightless feeling caused Cole's guts to lurch up into his chest as the light vanished. He knew he was falling, but it was too dark to see how high he was. Nevertheless, he flailed into the darkness, reaching for anything that might slow his fall. His chest hit a branch, hard. Then something else struck him across the back, sending him tumbling. Seeing the distant ground spinning towards him, Cole knew there was no way he would survive the fall. An empty blackness greeted him accompanied by a deafening ringing. Broken, choking, pain dragged him back to consciousness as dulled voices clamored about him.

"Hold him still. I said hold him still!"

"I can't, he's too damn slippery with all this blood. Sitra, get some water and rags if you can find them."

"There's no time, something's broken and bleeding on the inside too, feel it? No, put your fingers here, see?"

"Did anyone see what happened?"

"The Underkin was too small to reach one of the branches. He fell."

"Somebody get Roth! I don't think the kid's going to make it."

"Roth went to get Alvani. Wait, Lileth. What about you?"

"I cannot, I've not the skill."

"What are you talking about? He was all but dead when we found him in the lagoon and you had no problem patching him up. Just do it, we won't tell anyone."

Cole struggled as the unknown voices and hands ministered to him. He could feel broken bones tearing at his insides as he thrashed and tried to breathe. He knew he should lie still, but the blood pooling in his lungs gave him the sensation of drowning and set him into a panic. The pain ebbed and flowed with such intensity that he walked the line between agonizing awareness and blacking out.

"Step aside, all of you. And dismiss your spells, Eliza."

Cole was dimly aware of the hands releasing him, but he was acutely aware of a sudden increase in his senses. The pain shot up tenfold, shocking his vision to white and filling his ears with a deafening roar. He screamed, or at least tried to through a mouth full of frothy blood. The tinkling of wind chimes filled his mind. His vision cleared and he saw a woman looming over him, her raven hair tied in a high bun, save for a few ropes that clung to the sweat on her glistening cheeks. Her hands hovered over Cole's chest, fingers wide and emitting a soft rosy light that poured into him. Cole felt his lungs clearing, and a few things popped and snapped inside his torso, followed by an immediate release from the pain. Her hands traveled over each of his broken limbs, tears leaking from her eyes like a shower of diamonds. Within a minute the pain was entirely gone. Cole sat up, breathing heavily.

"I know you." He breathed.

The woman wiped the tears from her eyes, which looked familiar to Cole, as though he'd seen them in a dream. Her eyes were fierce and burned with intelligence, yet her quivering lips were full and inviting. Without a word she rose and stormed off into the shadows beyond the glow of the tree gems, a short cloak whipping behind her back. Confused, Cole inspected his body. As far as he could tell he had no injuries whatsoever. Even his old surgery scars were gone. His wrappings, however, had suffered such damage that the only function they now served was a meager preservation of his modesty. He tore off the tattered pieces, leaving him almost as naked as when he'd met Habbad and Lexy. Blood rushed to his cheeks as he tore off the final strap. He was surrounded by five Aenerians, all towering over him like the trees above.

"How do you feel, Cole? Your name is Cole right?" asked Sitra, her rugged features softening with concern.

"I, I feel great actually. Hungry, but great." Cole's Gaze traveled up the tree he had just fallen from. "How high was I when I fell?"

"You were more than halfway up, that's for sure." Sitra gave a gruff laugh. "Lucky for you, you hit every branch on the way down. Not so lucky for you, one of those branches landed on you when you hit the ground. Do your legs work okay? Your back was broken."

Cole stood, amazed at the sensation of well-being that permeated his body. "Yeah, everything's working fine. *Better* than fine actually. What was that woman's name? I want to thank her. I don't know what she did but it felt so..." Cole trailed off, still basking in the residual euphoria left by the magic. It was as if she was inside him. "It felt really good. Still does."

The one called Valen hissed with dissent and marched after the cloaked woman.

Sitra scowled after him before turning to Cole. "Her name is Lileth. Do her a favor okay? Don't mention to anyone that she healed you."

Cole frowned, "Why not? Is healing people frowned upon? Somebody healed me not too long ago, and Chiron said that the person who did it wouldn't receive my gratitude or something."

"That was also Lileth. We found you floating belly up in the lagoon. Alvani was certain you were dead, but Lileth felt something. She wouldn't explain it to us. She swam out and got you, then healed you like she did just now." Sitra let out a slow breath as she ran her fingers through her hair. "It's a big deal, her healing you. Where she comes from, Passion is sort of embarrassing. Not only that, but she performed it at a master's level. To her, it's...shameful. This will all make sense to you after a few lessons. But until then, just shut up about it."

"Yeah, no problem. I don't have anyone to tell anyway," Cole admitted, wishing he had Goran by his side. "I'm glad she was there though."

"So how did you fall anyway? Seemed like you were doing all right whenever I passed you." Sitra eyed him suspiciously.

Cole hesitated, remembering Valen looming above him with that gargoyle sneer. Part of him wanted to rat Valen out, but it was his pride that responded instead. "I was too small to reach a branch below me. I tried to swing to it but the branch I was holding onto snapped."

Sitra eyed the large branch next to him. It was thicker than Cole's leg and still smelled of fresh sap. "Hmm. Maybe one of us weakened the branch before you got to it."

"Probably," Cole said, glancing at the rest of the group.

The shortest member of the unit stepped forward, extending a clawed hand. He had a heavy, jutting jaw like a bulldog. "I'm Storn. Roth put me in charge of you -sorry," Storn wiggled his hand as it transformed from jagged black knives to something more human and less dangerous.

Cole grasped a couple of Storn's fingers and shook them awkwardly. "Nice to meet you, Storn."

"You're a lot smaller than I expected." Storn gave Cole an appraising look. "Can you at least do magic?"

"Not at all," Cole said, slightly ashamed. "I wish I could. Definitely would have come in handy."

"Can't be very common for Underkin to use magic, can it? Where are you from anyway?" Storn asked, crossing his bulky arms.

Cole paused, remembering Roth's instruction. "I'm from Costas."

"Never heard of it. But that doesn't matter now. This is your new home, and we're your new family. There's six of us, seven now including you. You've already met Sitra and Valen. And you've sort of met Lileth already." Storn jerked a thumb over his shoulder: "The two behind me are Deekus and Eliza. Deekus is the male. They're our healers, Passion followers."

Two Aenerians smiled warmly as they stepped to either side of Storn. "Greetings, Cole," they said in unison. They each wore a gentle, comforting smile. The claws on their hands and feet faded into smooth flesh as they reached out towards him. Cole shook the fingers of Deekus, who wrapped both his hands around Cole's and held them for a moment.

"You are welcome here, Underkin," Deekus said, patting Cole on the shoulder. He had the gentlest face Cole had seen so far. His eyes seemed to emanate kindness. "Do not fear us, you are amongst friends."

Cole felt every muscle in his body relax. "Thank you Deekus." He realized he was grinning ear to ear. Something about the way Deekus and Eliza looked at him made Cole feel safe and elated.

Cole stuck his arm out to shake Eliza's hand, but she picked him up like a child, squeezing and rocking him in a warm embrace. It was as warm and wholesome as a hug from Nana Beth. Cole laughed and hugged her back.

"I sense that you've been through much, Cole," Eliza said in a motherly tone. Her face was round with soft features, while her honey-blond hair was chopped in a short pixie cut. "Too much, if I'm not mistaken. Don't worry, you are safe now. We will take care of you."

"Thank you, Eliza." Cole wiped happy tears from the corners of his eye. "That means a lot to me. It really does."

Sitra drew their attention as she pointed towards the sky. A heavy flapping echoed off the trees. "And there's our help. Little late now."

Something large blocked the starry canopy above as the flapping slammed louder. If the rest of the group hadn't seemed so calm, Cole would have run to the nearest hole for fear of being eaten.

A golden creature the size of a school bus landed heavily before them, buffeting grass with its wings before tucking them to its sides. Its snout was long and feline and it had tall, wispy ears. Its paws were catlike as well, with curving ebony claws that were almost as long as Cole. Starlight reflected off its shining golden feathers, making the proud creature look like a moving metallic statue.

The beast tucked its wings and lowered its head as a woman in snow white robes dismounted from between its shoulders. She dropped from the beast's wing, alighting on the grass before giving her steed a gentle caress under its chin. She appeared to glide instead of walk, and Cole thought he saw a lavender aura around her, as though someone followed her with a spotlight. Her blonde hair fell straight and smooth to her lower back, held in place by an ornate silver circlet.

Roth, who emerged from the shadows farther down the trail, barked, "Line up! You're still on my time. Don't think I don't see you, Lileth. Grab Valen and fall in."

"That means you too," Sitra whispered to Cole.

The six, now seven, lined up in front of the three evergreens. Bark and branches littered the forest floor around them. The woman in white walked down the line, inspecting each of them. She stopped in front of Valen, eyes sad as she took in his crippled arm.

"Rothael, this is indeed a gruesome injury, but I would think one of the students could handle the likes of this. Was a crippled arm worth the trouble of bringing me here?" She grasped Valen's broken arm with tender fingers.

"No Alvani, no not that one," Roth barked at the woman in white. "The Underkin at the end. The idiot fell from damn near the top. A minute ago he was well beyond our skill to heal." Roth stepped in front of Cole, inspecting his tattered, yet perfectly healthy state with an accusatory glare. "What happened?"

Rising panic bubbled in his gut as his momentary pause bordered on hesitation. He could feel Lileth shift next to him. "I…"

"He was healed, Rothael," Alvani said and smiled, caressing a tear from Lileth's cheek. "By this one. Please Lileth, do not regret it. It is a beautiful thing. If only we could all be so lucky to give the gift of life to another."

Lileth blinked hard. "Of course, Master Alvani."

Alvani nodded, eyes sad. Moving down the line she stopped in front of Cole. She bent down to his height, her smile warm and welcoming like Deekus's and Eliza's. Recognition flared in her eyes as she gripped Cole's face, searching his eyes as though she'd seen something urgent. Flustered, she collected herself, releasing her grip.

"My apologies, Underkin. I must be losing my touch on this reality in my old age." As though nothing had happened, her face resumed its contagious expression of joy. "I am Alvani, it is a pleasure to meet you."

"I'm Cole, and the pleasure is all mine." Cole didn't bother hiding his stupid grin.

"Lileth seems to have done a thorough job on you. How do you feel?" she asked, looking him over.

Cole patted his chest. "I feel great, honestly. Though I'm so hungry I could eat my own hand."

Alvani laughed. "Please, don't do that. I don't think young Lileth has it in her to heal such a wound. Cole, would you let me have a look at you, inside and out? I sense something off-center, though I can't quite put it to words."

Cole was slow to respond. He couldn't stop thinking about Lileth. He could almost feel the anger radiating from her. Why would she regret saving someone's life? Feeling Alvani's gentle gaze still lingering, he shook himself straight.

"Uh, sorry. Yeah, please go ahead." He didn't know what magic Alvani was capable of, but her mere presence felt so warm and wholesome that he trusted her implicitly.

Alvani placed a finger an inch away from his chest. Satisfied, she moved towards his forehead, and a lavender spark flickered in between her finger and his skin. "As I suspected. Someone has been meddling.

A tainted cypher if I'm not mistaken. It doesn't appear to be causing any harm, but you don't feel quite yourself, do you?"

"I feel as normal as I can given the circumstances." He felt Roth's eyes burning into him as he wondered how much he was allowed to say. "Someone did put a cypher in me. I don't remember his name."

"Can you tell me where you are?" Alvani asked, looking pleasantly curious.

"Of course." Cole almost laughed, but just as he went to answer, the thought slipped out of his grasp. "I...I can't remember the name. I know Chiron told me."

She nodded, raising an eyebrow. "How about the name of our moon?"

Cole was at a loss. "Chiron told me that too, but no... I can't remember it. It just keeps slipping away."

Alvani pursed her lips. "Cypher indeed. There is something unwholesome in you, I can feel it. Would you like me to remove the fetters? I promise you won't feel a thing." Alvani placed her hands on her thighs, awaiting his answer.

Cole hesitated. He didn't want someone tinkering around in his head after Kreed, and the only people who ever said 'you won't feel a thing' were doctors, right before they stabbed you with something. Alvani however did not seem like a doctor, or a liar. Cole looked up at her. "Ok."

Alvani situated three of her fingers in certain spots over Cole's scalp. Holding his breath, he waited for something to happen.

"Done." She smiled.

"Really? I didn't feel a thing." Cole rubbed his head.

Alvani gave him a sharp nod. "Of course you didn't. Now if you would be so kind as to tell me where you are, the name of our moon, and what my name is?"

Struck with a sudden case of the giggles, Cole opened his mouth to answer, but realized he still couldn't find the words. It felt as if he were wading in waist deep water, chasing fish too fast to catch. He looked up at the moon with all its scintillating craters and its melting rainbow hues. Something slipped into place.

"This moon is called Oberon." His giggling subsided as more thoughts fell into their rightful place. "We're in The Sill, and your name is Alvani." He could also feel something else inside him, apparent now only because of its sudden absence. He couldn't tell exactly what it was, but he no longer felt as scared and vulnerable as before.

"Right you are Cole." Alvani squeezed her hand over his shoulder before standing up. "Whoever placed the cypher in you intended to keep you in the dark on certain things." She turned to Roth. "I know you still have a little more time with the students, but I think it is a good time to address young Valen's injury. I don't want to know how he sustained it, so I won't ask. However, this *would* be a most useful exercise for the arts of Passion. Is this agreeable? May I start early?" Alvani approached Roth, picking a leaf out of his bladed hair.

"Go ahead," he said, sniffing the air. "I need to hunt anyway. If I stick around much longer I might decide to eat Eliza since she's the slowest of the pack."

Cole heard Eliza shift uncomfortably. He didn't know enough about Roth to know if he was joking. After seeing what he'd done to Valen's arm it was entirely possible.

"Excellent!" Alvani clapped her hands together. "Would you like Gale to fly you to your hunting grounds? Perhaps the two of you could hunt together?" Alvani gestured towards her winged companion.

Roth looked at the giant beast, which paused in its preening and chirped to him. "Nah, I'm too heavy. And I'm faster on foot than that thing is in the sky." He made to walk away, but halted, touching one of his claws to Alvani's hand. "I appreciate your offer all the same."

Roth shot off down the path and out of sight. He moved so fast Cole was barely able to register his movement. How was he supposed to be of use to anyone when everyone here could use magic and climb trees faster than he could run on flat land? Whatever lessons were next, he hoped that they involved something less physical, as well as a meal.

CHAPTER 13

PASSIONS

Alvani opened her arms to the seven, her lavender aura pulsing brighter. "Please, relax. There is no need for such militant formality with me, my dears. Now, to the matter at hand, *your* hand in particular, Valen. I want you all to make an honest attempt at healing poor Valen's arm. Brave Storn will go first. Lileth, you are welcome to go last. I imagine you need some time to recover from helping Cole here."

Huffing, Storn swiped the air with his claws. "All right, but healing's not my thing. I'm more of a fighter, everyone knows that."

Sitra flashed Storn a wild smile. "Warrior huh? Is that what you were when Eliza had you pinned under your own foot?"

Storn waved a clawed hand as though shooing a fly. "She's a female! I couldn't go all out against her, I'd kill her. And besides, she used her Passion to muddle with my brain. I was distracted."

"Careful Storn, or else I may decide to heal you of your hubris once more," Eliza said in her sweet motherly voice.

The entire group laughed, though Valen remained silent. Color drained from him as he started to sway. Storn retorted with a few insults under his breath as he appraised Valen's arm.

Alvani approached Storn from behind, resting her hands on his shoulders. "Admitting to a weakness gives you strength over yourself, brave warrior. Given your limitations with the healing aspects of Passion, is this a wound that you can mend entirely?"

"No, not even close. My job is to *give* the wounds, not *fix* them," Storn grumbled, sounding more annoyed by the second.

"You understand your limits then. That is valuable. You may not be able to fix this arm entirely, but surely you can help your friend but a little? What if it were just the two of you out on patrol and his life were in your hands? Where would you start?" She gave his shoulders an encouraging squeeze.

"Stop the bleeding I guess. Then he won't pass out and he could carry himself back." Storn reached slowly towards Valen's arms with his dagger-like fingers. Cole noticed now that the black shroud did not extend to his hands like the rest of the group. His claws were much smaller than the others'.

"Storn my dear, your munisica," Alvani whispered.

"Right. I was getting to that." Storn closed his eyes and drew a long breath. Air whistled out of his nose and he shrank a few inches as the claws and black skin faded from his fingers and feet. When he opened his eyes, he was noticeably more relaxed. Valen swayed as Storn took his wounded arm into his hands, holding it as one would hold a newborn. Dull rosy light shone from Storn's fingertips, beaming into Valen's open flesh. The steady tapping of blood on the leaves slowed to an intermittent dripping. Valen still looked as if barely awake. Storn's face went from stubborn scowl to genuine worry. "Deekus you're a healer, come take this thing. I...I've done all I can do."

Storn averted his eyes and withdrew to the back of the group. Deekus walked casually over to Valen, humming softly. Cole stood on his tiptoes, eager to see more of the magic.

A hand brushed the back of Cole's head. "Cole, if you would join me, please." He turned around to see Alvani walking towards her flying beast. Reluctantly, he followed close behind. Alvani rummaged through the saddles fastened towards the creature's hindquarters. Cole stopped several paces away, afraid to get much closer to the massive creature. Its lower-canines were as long as his arm, sweeping up its regal snout like swords.

"Do not fear Gale," Alvani called, shuffling through the packs. "He will not harm you, though he is eager to meet you."

Cole stepped towards Gale's head, hand outstretched. The beast's amber eyes glinted with human-like intelligence, blinking slowly as if to encourage him. Gale lowered his massive feline head, allowing Cole to make the first contact. Cole rubbed his fingers on the short velvety feathers above Gale's nose, which was bigger than his two hands put together. Gale rubbed his nose into Cole's bare chest, shooting him with steamy jets of air as he sniffed and chirped. Cole laughed as prickly whiskers tickled his naked arms.

Alvani emerged from around Gale's puffy chest, smiling. "He likes you. He's never met a human before. He finds you intriguing."

"I'm an Underkin, I came from Costas," Cole said, staring into Gale's fiery amber eye.

"Do not worry yourself, you have not broken Roth's orders. I am old enough to remember what humans feel like, so you may speak candidly with me without breaking any oaths. This is for you, dear one." Alvani handed Cole a cloth bundle wrapped in twine. "I'm sorry if it is not to your liking, but I do not partake in the flesh of others, and it is all that I have with me."

"I'm sure I'll love it." Cole unwrapped the elegant knot, unfolding the cloth. He was ready to eat a rock. When he pulled back the last flap he had to swallow so he wouldn't drool all over himself. Inside was a bread-bowl filled with pink cream swimming with tiny seeds. He wanted to thank her for the food, but couldn't resist his primal urges, and dove right in.

Alvani gave Cole a few minutes to indulge. She pulled her snowy robes tight and sat cross-legged on the ground, leaning back into Gale's golden feathers. "You have a special soul."

Cole gulped down a mouthful. "What do you mean?"

"I felt something inside you when I examined your mind. It was ambiguous, yet important. Whatever it was eluded me, yet I felt its power burning in the gaps between your thoughts. It is not mere chance that you are the first human to set foot on Aeneria by your own volition. You flit about as a leaf in the wind, breaking the rules wherever you go." Her tone was chastising, yet playful. "This is not your first trip to Aeneria. We have felt you with us when you Traveled here before, during Terra's last two passings. I sense significance written in between the layers of your soul, though I also feel your crushing doubt and sadness. Aeneria is changing. There is a shifting of the balance and you are pinned at the fulcrum. Do not let your doubts shackle you to what you know, for the life that you once held so dear is but a chapter in your story. Before this is over, you will have to destroy yourself and rise anew, or fade into irrelevance. Magic and cleverness alone will not see us through this storm. We have tried it before and failed. There are dark times ahead for us all, though your own trials will be of a shade darker still. Know this, however; you are not alone."

Cole realized his mouth was hanging open in mid-bite. "I…I don't know what to say. I don't feel special or significant or any of those things. To be honest I feel as if I've been thrown into this world without any say, and now I'm stuck. I don't want to fight in a war, I'd be worse than useless. I can't even go a few hours without something trying to eat or kill me. I'm not made for this world, I'm made for Earth. I'm half the size of you Aenerians and I definitely can't use magic." Cole's voice grew louder as suppressed anger came bubbling up his chest. "How do you know I'm special anyway? Who the hell are you to say that I have to be a fulcrum or whatever? What if I don't want any of this?"

Alvani remained silent. Sadness bloomed in her eyes as if she too felt all of Cole's pain and loss. Embarrassed, Cole wished he hadn't raised his voice. Alvani turned her gaze to the stars, nestling herself deeper into the soft plumage of Gale's flank. She gestured for Cole to join her on the ground.

"I'll stand, thanks." Cole said to the ground.

Alvani let out a sigh, dropping her voice to a gentle whisper: "If it were within my power to send you back to Earth, right this very instant, would you accept?"

"Would I leave? This place is awful! With monsters like Kreed running around, and whatever the hell The Three are supposed to be. Do you even know what they do to people in Costas?" Cole was almost yelling now, picturing Lexy strapped to the tower with hundreds of others. Her woefully defeated face burned in his mind. He felt himself deflate as sadness doused his roaring anger. "No, I wouldn't leave. Not just yet."

Alvani offered the seat again. This time Cole accepted. She wrapped an arm around his shoulders, embracing him. He couldn't tell if it was her magic, or being held by someone who cared, but the weighty sorrow lifted considerably.

"You are quite right. You have been placed here without your consent, and for the moment you are stuck. Another life has been forced upon you." She pulled him closer, burying his wet face in her shoulder, "But you do have a choice. You don't have to do any of this. If you choose to stay with us and continue your training, it will be of your own choice. If you choose to leave The Sill never to return, no one will stop you. Gale will take you wherever you please. There are places on Aeneria that The Three have yet to taint."

Cole pulled back, drying his eyes on what was left of his sleeve. Another feeling rose up inside him, proud and strong. It was a burning desire to act. To save Lexy. He wouldn't let her die like Joshy. "I choose to stay," he said, hefting his white dagger. "Don't think I'll be much use to anyone though. I can't do magic, but I'll learn what I can."

"I wouldn't be so certain of that. You have Traveled. Even before the banishing, such a feat required a mastery of Wisdom. You have also dissolved the barrier, which even our brightest and oldest couldn't hope to do. And when I was inside your mind I felt an empathic bond, which is a powerful and very specific form of Passion."

"What do you mean I am bonded? I'm not in love with anyone." His voice trailed off as his thoughts drifted towards Lileth. He knew he didn't love her, but there was something compelling about her. He flicked his eyes over to the others, noticing her fierce eyes upon him.

Alvani reached out with delicate fingers and ripped off a piece of the bread bowl. "The bond that I am speaking of is similar to the one between Gale and me. You are bonded to another being here on Aeneria. An animal, unless I am mistaken."

Cole swallowed hard, tearing his eyes from Lileth as Goran's ruby eyes and white mohawk came to mind. "How can you tell? How would I even know?"

"With an animal, the empathic bond is initiated when one saves the other's life. It is complete when the other saves the life of the first. There are other requirements, dealing with attunements of the souls, but that happens without your conscious self." Alvani's eyes closed halfway as Gale's chirping turned to a deep rumbling purr.

Cole recalled his adventures with Goran, specifically the battle with the giant tentacle-grub. "It could be Goran. We met my first day here. I saved him from a grub, and he's saved me a few times at least. How can I tell if I'm bonded?"

"It helps if you close your eyes." She waited for Cole's eyelids to meet. "Now picture your friend in your mind's eye. Not only the physical, but the emotional. Think about how this person makes you feel. Allow this feeling to fill you from the inside out."

Cole followed her instructions, but it certainly didn't feel magical. He felt Goran within himself alright, but just in memories. Some were vivid, others vague. He pictured his little saber-tooth fangs, the white tufted mohawk, and the brindle stripes that ran down his flank. He imagined he was out hunting, running through the ferns chasing unwary critters towards his friend. He opened his eyes and found that his teeth were bared. There was something strange happening inside him. He held onto the sensation. "I feel him."

"Very good, now tell me where he is," she whispered.

"I… how would I know? He could be dead for-" Cole's breath caught in his throat as a familiar energy drew his attention, "He's alive! He's alive and…I feel him, that way." Cole pointed off the trail, opposite the others taking turns with Valen's arm.

Alvani's eyebrows met in a neat line below her circlet. "How do you know this?"

"I guess I don't know it, but I feel him," Cole grinned, giddy with excitement. Goran was alive! "I promise you, he's definitely in that direction and he's definitely on his way here. He's moving so fast!"

Alvani waited with a patient smile, allowing Cole to fully enjoy his revelation. When his eyes came back into focus, she gave him a playful rap on the shoulder. "Still think you 'can't do magic'?"

A confused frown straggled against Cole's mirth. "It doesn't feel like I'm casting some strange spell or anything. It feels…natural, like tying my shoes or chewing food."

"That is how it should be. Our magic is felt through the different parts of the soul and brought forth into the physical world." She lowered her head, staring straight into him. "You, my young Cole, have just consciously performed magic from the school of Passion."

Her words left him dumbstruck. "I... I still don't get it. Could you explain more about your magic? Maybe not the finer details, but I feel like I could use a general overview."

Alvani's face lit with gentle surprise. "I give you but a taste and now you want the whole feast! You are more like the other students than you think. Very well, a general overview then." She rubbed her hands together, folding them over her thighs. "At The Sill we concern ourselves with three schools of magic. These schools represent three parts of the soul that resonate with us. There are others, but we will not discuss them yet. First is the school of Passion. Its followers are our healers, artisans, artists, and creators. Passion can also be used to influence the thoughts of others; however, only those with a true moral compass are educated in that field. The cypher that was placed in your mind was not entirely malign, but if he wanted to, Kreed could have caused you great harm. Followers of Passion also connect with other living things. Sometimes this connection is a simple exchange, just a thought. Other times this connection is as severe and intimate as your bond with Goran."

Cole let himself fall back into Gale's fluffy belly as a question tickled him. "Why was it such a big deal that Lileth healed me? They're working on Valen over there and no one is getting upset over that. She saved my life twice. I want to thank her."

"Let's just say that her family is none too fond of anyone who shows an aptitude for magic outside of the school of Wisdom. Some of the older families believe that the other schools are responsible for all of the less savory moments in Aenerian history. They are not entirely wrong, but in my eyes a society governed solely by cold logic seems rather bleak. There would be no fire, no flavor in the world. I am very proud of Lileth. Healing you went against her nature and her upbringing. When we found you washed up in the lagoon, I admit that even I thought you were one with the void. Lileth saw something however, and pulled you from death's clutches without hesitation. In that moment, her proficiency with Passion exceeded even my own. She should be proud and embrace her abilities. Unfortunately, she views her actions through a lens of shame. If you want to show your appreciation, do not speak of it. She may come to you when she is ready."

Cole frowned, casting Lileth a sideways glance. "I still don't see why that's so bad, but I'll take your advice. I need all the friends I can get here, and I definitely don't want to make enemies."

"Very wise. Speaking of Wisdom, shall we move on?" Alvani asked.

"Please!" Cole gushed, imagining himself casting fireballs and shooting lightning from his eyes.

"The followers of Wisdom use their magic to manipulate the physical world around them, changing the properties of mundane material to serve their purpose." She paused, taking in the look on Cole's face. "I see a spark in your eye. Are you familiar with Wisdom?"

"My friend Habbad can do stuff with Wisdom. He changed my eyes so I could see in the dark. He also used it to move a sun lily leaf that we used for a boat. Habbad said that once you understand the true nature of something, you can change the rules if you believe in the new rule hard enough. He tried to teach me to freeze water, but I failed." Cole's hopes rose. Perhaps Alvani would be a better teacher.

Alvani nodded. "Your friend Habbad seems to know what he's doing. He would be most welcome to join us, if he is willing of course."

Alvani plucked a stone from the ground and offered it to Cole. Confused, he accepted it, discovering it had no weight whatsoever. He hefted the rock, but it shot straight up in the air. He snatched clumsily for it, but it was gone.

Alvani watched Cole, amused. "Wisdom has many applications. Masters of Wisdom could Travel to the local planets and interact with the creatures there. Their aim was to quietly observe and learn, while providing gentle nudges to civilizations, guiding them towards advances in technology and society. They would also collect plants and animals doomed to extinction and bring them back to Aeneria, where they could flourish under Oberon's light. I'll not speak further on the subject of Wisdom as I do not wish to interfere with your other lessons. Shall we move on to the path of Rage?"

"Yes please!" Cole blurted, imagining himself with Roth's hulking muscles and huge black claws.

Alvani gave a cautious nod at Cole's fervor. "Rage is perhaps the most dangerous school. The magic itself is but a tool, though its effect on its users can overwhelm if discipline is lacking. By tapping into their Rage, followers of the school are granted increased strength, agility, and reflexes, as well as heightened senses. As they gain mastery, the body covers itself with an indestructible material, protecting from any physical harm. The armor is called the shroud. It starts at the hands and feet, working its way over the rest of the body. It is rare, but when true mastery of Rage is achieved, even the eyes and internal organs become shrouded, granting the user complete immunity to any physical molestation. Mastery of one's self-discipline must go hand in hand with Rage. More than one great Aenerian has fallen victim to their own blood-lust, causing irreparable harm to themselves and others. Take care to not lose yourself to it."

"If I get out of hand I'm sure anyone here could handle me, no sweat," Cole said, feeling very small next to Alvani. "So does everyone focus on just one of the schools or can a person get really good at all of them?"

"If you were to travel the expanse of the Dark Side, a great many tribes would tell you that their school is the right one. In fact, you would be hard pressed to find a city outside of The Sill that would allow other schools of magic within their walls. This line of thinking has produced some of the greatest and most talented Aenerians of our history, but their numbers are few and very far between. For example, a city devoted solely to the arts of Passion would be a beautiful place no doubt. However, they would stifle the talents of their citizens who were born with another disposition. Not to mention they would be at the mercy of anyone adept with Rage or some of the darker arts. Nor would they benefit from the technological and magical advances discovered by followers of Wisdom."

Alvani pulled from her robes what appeared to be a fat jiggly seed, tore off the top with her teeth, and poured its clear contents into her mouth. She then offered the drink to Cole, who gratefully accepted. He was parched from sugary cream and the bread bowl. He hovered his nose over the opening and sniffed a fruity aroma. He tipped the seed back, sipping at first, then gulping. A slight burning succeeded the fruity taste, though not unpleasantly so. He quickly took another gulp, coughing.

"Careful," Alvani chuckled. "The liquor is strong for one of your size. You might not be of sound mind for the rest of the lesson."

Cole set the drink down as a pleasant, fuzzy pressure filled his head. He was relaxed and warm, but still very much interested. "Please, pretty lady, continue."

"You flatter me, human. Very well." She smiled, taking the drink from him. "Here at The Sill, we explore all schools of magic. All ways of life are not only tolerated, but embraced. Many cycles ago, Aeneria played host to its first and only war, which thanks to you, will resume this very hour."

"I'm so sorry." Shame flushed into Cole's cheeks as he thought of all the people who would die on his account. "I had no idea about the barrier. Is there no way to repair it?"

"Do not be sorry." Alvani placed a hand under Cole's chin, lifting his head until he was looking at her again. "The barrier cannot be repaired because we do not know how it was erected in the first place. Even if we could, we would not. We have hidden under Oberon's light for too long. With each passing cycle our power wanes as the Three's waxes. This war must resume."

"But why?" Cole asked. "If you were safe before, why would you want to start it back up?"

Alvani took another long pull from the seed, waiting a moment before answering. "The cause of this war, like most, was a difference of two rights. In this case it was a disagreement over creatures called soul flies. Soul flies are not insects as the name would suggest, but the souls of intelligent creatures from the local planets. Aeneria is fleeting and ethereal. It moves from one reality to another in a repeating cycle, half in and half out. Aeneria is not physically anywhere of course, that is why you humans have never seen it. It is insubstantial, just like the soul, which is exactly what is required to cross the aethers and Travel. When one enters a dream state, the conscious, subconscious, and soul meld together, dancing madly through the halls of the mind. In this state, the soul wanders. The soul is very real, though intangible and not bound by physical barriers. This allows the dreamer to Travel.

On Aeneria the souls manifest as orbs of light, varying in color and size depending on the song of the dream. It is a marvelous sight to behold, and a profound experience to interact with a soul fly." She paused, drinking from the seed again.

"Before the war we saw these orbs as nothing but a resource. They came regularly and the energies emitted by them were potent and easily harvested. There were those among us that saw fit to saturate the soul flies with darker magics, stimulating them until they yielded terrible dark energies. Once ripened they were fed upon, granting immense power to the one feasting. It was an unsavory act, though it went unchallenged because at the time even the wisest of us saw it nothing more than a relationship between predator and prey. We did not know the soul flies were sentient beings from the local planets. It was not until the first Traveling that we discovered what this feeding had wrought. When the Wisdom Walkers returned from their first journey, they recalled tales of ruined creatures whose souls were so mangled and wretched that they were beyond repair. These creatures became the worst of their kind; psychopaths, rapists, torturers, fanatics. They reveled in the pain of others. Wars, genocides, slavery, the most terrible things that intelligent creatures are capable of, all made possible because of us."

Gale's head came around. He gave a mournful chirp as he nudged Alvani's cheek with his nose. A weak smile replaced her sadness and she continued, "Followers of Rage, Passion and Wisdom set themselves against those who abused the soul flies, inciting the war that continues this very day. We were outnumbered before, but now our fate is even more grim. Though the abusers could no longer feed on the soul flies, they have amassed a large population of Underkin from their local planet. Now they feast on the Underkin. Sadly, *our* strength has diminished since the banishing."

Cole couldn't imagine the giants around him losing a fight to anyone. "How have you been getting weaker? You all seem pretty tough to me. Did you think the barrier would protect you so you stopped training or something?"

Alvani gave a single shake of her head. "We have been learning and training every day since, though our education has been limited since we can no longer Travel. Our hearts and minds remain just as strong, but our magic has lost some of its potency. Our strength comes from Oberon, or to be more precise, the soul flies."

"But I thought you said using the soul flies was wrong," Cole said. "Or do you use them in a different way?"

"When the soul flies Travel in between their planet and Aeneria, they emit potent dust that trails off into open space. This dust collects on the surface of Oberon. There are still some remnants of it on the surface now. You can see it now. It is what gives Oberon its ever-changing hues." Alvani pointed to a gap in the trees where Oberon peered through.

"It's the most beautiful thing I've ever seen." Cole searched the sky. Another question popped into his mind. "Does your moon not move across the sky? I swear I haven't seen it move an inch. Ours orbits around Earth. Actually, every moon in our solar system orbits around a planet."

"Oberon does not orbit, or rotate. It trails behind Aeneria, catching the dust from the soul flies. When the dust combines with the light from a star, the reflected light takes on certain magical properties. This light permeates everything on the Dark Side. The plants drink it in, then are eaten by herbivores, which are then eaten by carnivores, who then go back into the soil and insects when they die. Oberon's light is a part of everything, and as it fades, we fade. The soul flies have not visited Aeneria for a long time, and Oberon has dimmed with each passing cycle." Alvani's face drooped with sorrow.

"So we don't stand a chance then?" Cole asked. "You're telling me that you barely survived the last time and now you're even weaker while The Three have grown stronger?"

Alvani waved a finger. "I would not count us out so soon. Though it is against the nature of many, we will adapt and unite. We must remain flexible and universal in our magics and in our minds, lest we fall to pieces as we did before. That is why here at The Sill we study and embrace all forms of magic. In the last war there were a few outcasts like us who could hold their own against The Three. We aim to pick up where they left off, this time with a few thousand capable souls." Alvani took another pull from her seed, sighing as she cast her eyes towards the stars. "Evil tidings plague my dreams. It is possible that our time has simply come and gone, and we are holding on to the light of a setting sun."

"How many other cities and tribes share your views on magic?" Cole asked.

"None. The Sill is unique," Alvani replied.

"But that's stupid!" Cole's cheeks burned. "Why? They know what happened last time. They must know they won't stand a chance if they limit themselves."

Alvani shook her head. "There are few of us old enough to re-member the battle at Oberon Temple. We are ancient, and tired. Some of us don't have the energy for another war. We have tried to enlighten the younger generations, but you cannot force a tree to grow away from the sun. Our people fear change, and for them to embrace another way of magic is to teach a fish to walk on land. Perhaps with the barrier gone they will be a little more open-minded. Even now our envoys are traveling the whole of the Dark Side, spreading our knowledge and recruiting those who will join."

The thought of facing armies of Corpulants and Domina gave Cole's heart an anxious flutter. "Do you think anyone will join?"

"Every town and tribe will have its shunned and unwanted. They usually hide on the outskirts living off scraps. It doesn't take much to convince them to join a life where they would be embraced instead of shirked. Our numbers are slow to grow, but they are growing." Alvani took a deep breath and jumped to her feet with surprising speed. "Enough of this heavy talk, it wears on me. Let us see how Valen's arm has fared."

Cole pushed himself to his feet, stumbling slightly as he followed her. Was he drunk? The world took on a hazy glow, and he had trouble focusing his eyes in the shaded moonlight. They walked back to where the others still ministered to Valen, though to Cole it appeared as if there were twenty or more standing at the base of the evergreens. Even the orbs embedded in the trunks seemed to have multiplied.

"Forgive me, I knew not how the liquor would affect a human. I should not have offered it." Alvani ran a lavender finger through Cole's hair. For a second, his vision flashed white and his skin burned slick with sweat. He cooled immediately as the world came back into focus. His mind still felt pleasantly fuzzy, though not unbearably so.

Valen's arm was much better. It no longer looked like a rotted and crushed stick at least. Valen appeared to be arguing with Lileth.

"This should be no great task for you. Come now Lileth, make an attempt," Valen instructed, anger lacing his tone.

"I told you, I have not the skill." Lileth's eyes fell towards the ground at her feet. "Deekus or Eliza will have to finish you up."

"They are already proficient in Passion." Valen held out his arm to Lileth: "You need practice. Is this not why you are here? Why we are all here? Come, I am injured. Help me."

Lileth affixed Valen with a steely glare. Cole hid slightly behind Alvani in case she brought that look down upon him. "Do I need to give you a child's explanation? I told you, I can't."

Valen's face shifted from polite concern to cold indifference. "*Can't* is quite different from *won't*. I would think a fellow Wisdom-follower would know this. Not once, but twice in a matter of hours you decided that you could heal a groveling Underkin. You are deciding now that you won't lift a finger to help me, your friend. Is it in your nature to be so free with your Passion that you would give it to a complete stranger?"

Lileth's face softened, though her eyes were on fire. She brought her hand to Valen's mottled forearm. Her fingers did not glow with rosy light, however. Instead they darkened and elongated into gnarled claws. Lips curled in a snarl, she clenched her claws down on Valen's arm, cutting through skin and muscle as if it were an overripe fruit. Valen's face twisted in agony as his free hand shone a brilliant jade. The rest of the group stepped back a few paces, taking up defensive postures.

A gust of wind swirled, twirling debris around the two as the air around Valen's glowing hand hummed with energy. The group backed up another few paces as Alvani strode forward. The wind died immediately as she placed a hand on each of their shoulders. Both looked confused at first, then their faces slackened with a look of deep gratification, as if they were having a terrible itch scratched for them.

"If you two are finished, I would like to continue our lesson," Alvani said, patting them both on the back.

They both nodded, faces dreamy.

"Beautiful." She smiled, placing a finger on Valen's freshly hewn arm. A single bead of pink light fell from her fingertip, landing inside one of the gushing wounds. Within a span of two seconds the wounds closed and the whole arm looked as if it had never seen so much as a bug bite.

Beaming, Alvani turned to face the group, clapping her hands together. "Now that you have all had a turn on young Valen's arm, I think it's time we tend to our three ancient friends here. Perhaps it is a good thing I cut Roth's lesson short; had I not, there may not be anything left of these evergreens. Please, pair up and give them back what was taken. Storn, would you be so kind as to show our newest student this particular use of Passion?"

Grunting, Storn took Cole by the shoulder and guided him towards the farthest tree. "Let's go new blood. Don't worry, this part's easy. The tree does most of the work," Storn said, walking with the gait of a strutting horse. "You just need to touch the gratia stone like this-" Storn placed his hand over the glowing gem embedded in the trunk, "-and think happy thoughts about the tree. It helps if you imagine the tree as someone you care about. The gratia stone will draw the healing magic out of you and put it into the tree. Be careful you don't hold on too long. It'll take and take until you're dead as dead."

Storn closed his eyes, stroking the bark of the tree with his other hand. The gratia stone shone like the sun for a few seconds before Storn pulled his hand away. "They don't need much."

A pleasant aroma of pine trees filled the air as the tree swayed excitedly. Thin sprigs budded from the lower branches, sprouting bright green needles. Storn backed away from the tree, motioning for Cole to make his attempt.

Cole approached the trunk, realizing he was at a disadvantage already; he could not reach the gratia stone. Fortunately, Storn seemed to have noticed this already, as a moment later he appeared with the treetop Valen had torn off. "Where would you be without me, huh?" He tossed the thick mass of wood beneath the shining gem.

"Thanks." Taking a step up, Cole was able to get his fingertips to touch the stone, which was surprisingly hot. He flinched at first, but not wanting to appear weak, held his fingers to the stone. It was hot, but not unbearably so. He looked up at the tree and tried to think happy thoughts, whatever that was supposed to mean. In his mind he complimented the tree's girth and strong bark. Nothing. He tried to feel empathy for the damage the others had done to it. Nothing. He found himself more annoyed than empathetic and felt as if he were missing the point.

"Someone you care about," Storn interrupted, jabbing Cole in the rib. "Imagine this person hurt, hurt real bad. Imagine you're helping that person, and the tree will do the rest."

Cole shut his eyes and brought his thoughts back to home. He thought of Nana Beth, but couldn't imagine her getting hurt. She was way too tough. His mind continued to wander. He felt the cold wetness of the puddle on the side of his body. No, he wouldn't go there, he wasn't ready.

He then tried to think about Ashley. One time she came into school wearing a sling from a skiing accident. This was a real memory, which was immediately replaced by real jealousy as he remembered all the attention she got from other boys in class. His mind wandered once more. The smell of chemicals and body odor made his stomach churn. No. Not that place, not that memory.

He forced his thoughts elsewhere, staying far away from home and his neighborhood. Perhaps a character from a movie? Cole focused on a war movie where a friend lay mortally wounded in the lap of his brother-in-arms. Brother. In his arms. His brother.

Joshy lay in his arms, body cold and limp. Cole peeled back his hood, the cloth a damp, dark crimson. There was so much blood, too much for such a small body. He barely recognized Joshy with the side of his head broken in, but the parts that were hardest to recognize were the uninjured parts. Joshy's face was always full of life and laughter. He always had a smile, as if he felt something wonderful that no one else could see. That smile was gone now. His face was as limp and slack as the rest of his body. There was a moment, and infinitely minuscule moment where Cole felt as if he could still help his brother, as if he'd just fallen off his bike and hadn't started crying yet.

"Cole! Dammit Cole let go of the stone! Master Alvani we need you over here now!" Storn cried.

Alvani ran down to the middle tree, sleeves rolled up to her elbows. A look of shock and sorrow fell upon her face as she beheld Cole clutching the gratia stone with both hands. "Do not touch him."

Hands inches from Cole's middle, Storn backed away slowly. His eyes were not on Cole, but the tree. The tree was moving and swaying as if it were being battered by a heavy storm, branches whipping through the air. The tip of each needle blazed with dots of white light.

Cole opened his eyes, taking a deep breath. His fingers were black and smelled of burnt meat. An ear-splitting crack hammered his ears as the gratia stone splintered down the middle, flickering until the light died out completely. He felt a hand on his shoulder.

"Still your heart, Wisdom Walker. You have suffered much." Lileth embraced his hands with her own, joining each of her fingertips with his. Feeling returned to his hands as his charred fingers reverted back to a supple pink.

His breath deep and calm, Cole examined his fingers, flexing and stretching them. "That's three times now."

"So it is," Lileth replied in an offhanded manner, as if Cole had made a comment about the weather. Her eyes locked with his, and suddenly he recognized where he knew her from.

Before Cole could say a word, she turned on the spot and disappeared in the shadows beyond the light of the remaining two gratia stones. Cole shivered. The rest of the group wore looks of mingled confusion and apprehension. Alvani approached him, face somber.

"That is twice now that a student has surpassed my skill with Passion, only a few hours apart no less." Alvani removed a swath of robe from her shoulders, wrapping it around Cole. "I think we have learned enough today," she said, addressing the remaining five as Valen had stormed off after Lileth. "Storn, as Cole's custodian, I'll ask you to take him through the markets on the way back to the barracks. See to it that he is outfitted with the basic-issue."

"You can count on me, Master Alvani." Storn puffed out his chest, casting a sideways glance at the others, as if checking to see if they were watching. "Let's go, new blood. I won't have my newest protégé walking around The Sill half-naked. Your dagger's falling out by the way. No, not that one."

CHAPTER 14

ORIENTATION

H e flexed and smelled his newly healed fingers, checking to make sure they were fully functional as Storn led him away from the trees. He looked to Storn, pulling Alvani's scarf tight around his shoulders. "Did I just use magic?"

Storn gazed down at him, anger flashing over his square face. "Do you think I'm stupid? I'm not you know, even if everyone else says it."

Cole readjusted the dagger tucked at his waist, jogging to keep up. "No, I don't think you're stupid at all. If anything *I* feel like the stupid one around here. What happened with the tree back there? Did I do something wrong?"

Storn slowed for a moment, considering him. "I thought you were making jokes on me. You're not stupid, you're just ignorant, which is lucky for you because stupidity can't be cured. At least that's what Master Roth says. The gratia stone and the tree did most of the work, but you had to get the process started. I told you not to hold on too long."

"I'm sorry. I got caught up in it. I went somewhere else in my head and I sort of lost it." Cole felt like he was caught in one of his middle school pranks. "Am I in trouble for breaking the stone?"

"Probably. I'll talk to Chiron so you don't get into too much trouble. The elders like me. Probably because I'm one of the best students. I'm the most deadly for sure." Storn flexed his fingers as they stretched into black blades longer than Cole's dagger.

Cole noted once again how the shroud didn't seem to cover as much of Storn's hand as it did on the others. "Is it really indestructible? The black stuff on your hands?"

"There's nothing tougher than our munisica, that's what our hands and feet turn into, and the shroud protects us from anything. I could reach my hand into a forge and crush a glowing ingot without feeling a thing," Storn said, sporting a look that reminded Cole of Joshy's cool-guy face.

"I hope I learn how to do that someday." Cole squeezed his hands, imagining them as powerful dragon's claws.

"Worry not, new blood. With me helping you'll grow some munisica in no time." Storn took a swipe at a large boulder, showering the dirt path with sparks and rock chips.

Storn led them back towards the markets. The maze of trees and crisscrossing bridges made Cole's head spin as he tried to remember the circuitous route they took. Left at the weird gadget shop, right at the stand selling wiggling critters in jars, slight right and up the stairs at the bookstore. The markets were less crowded this time, allowing Cole a covetous gaze into each shop. He wouldn't know what to do with any of the items on display, but he would love to have a few unsupervised minutes to poke and prod. It took a herculean amount of self-control not to run his fingers over what looked like a typewriter that shot puffs of colored smoke and jets of light into the air. The last thing he needed was to break something. He had already broken the gratia stone and had no way to pay for it. The thought of money put an abrupt halt to his fantasizing.

"Um, Storn?" Cole asked, feeling very naked in his tattered wrappings.

"What's up, new blood? You didn't break something else did you?" Storn asked, sidestepping a group of women dressed in casual leathers. He puffed out his chest a little, his eyes following the women as he passed.

"No, nothing's broken. I'm not going to be able to buy anything. I don't have any money. Not with me anyway." Cole kept his eyes on the ground. Even here on Aeneria he was poor.

Storn laughed. "I don't know what you Underkin use for money over on the Light Side, but I promise it won't do you any good here. You'll be able to pay for your equipment no problem. The gratia stones aren't just for growing trees. We use them for our currency, or I should say they *hold* our currency, which is energy. You put your own energy into the stone as payment. The shopkeeper can then use this energy to power machinery or fuel spells. Some shops only have specific stones that take a certain type of magic, like how the tree's stones only took Passion."

The thought of going back into the cobblestone alley set Cole's heart fluttering again. "Can we find a shop that will take Rage or Wisdom from me? I don't think I can handle doing the Passion thing again."

"It will have to be Rage then. You aren't ready to give up your Wisdom. Those stones will take your memories from you. Chiron would send me to the back side of Oberon if I let you at a Wisdom stone." Storn shot an annoyed look back at Cole, who still struggled to keep up.

Cole tried to wrap his mind around the strange concepts as they wound their way through the upper levels of the markets. He held out as long as he could, but eventually had to ask Storn to slow his pace when a cramp threatened to split his stomach in half. Cole flat out refused Storn's vehement offering to carry him, the Aenerian insisting that it would be as easy as carrying a child.

Hundreds of feet off the ground, they arrived at a shop near the very top of one of the shorter trees. A single vine-covered walkway led to the entrance of the odd store. The tree's upper branches curved upwards, forming walls before reaching up towards the stars, giving the shop the appearance of a bark-clad pineapple. There was no shopkeeper, merely dozens of shelves that grew out of the walls. The shelves were filled with orbs of viscous gasses, all organized in neat little rows. Each shelf held orbs of differing shades of the same general color, and there was a strange metallic smell in the air, as if the room were charged with static electricity. Cole ran his fingers over the brass labels embedded in the shelves, unable to discern anything from the foreign letters. In the center of the room stood a dark wood pedestal with three gratia stones sunken into its surface. One crimson, one jade, and one soft lavender.

"These are cyphers," Storn said, indicating the rows of gaseous orbs.

"You'll need a couple of the green ones. Just put your payment into one of the gratia stones. The red one in the middle accepts Rage."

Cole tested the middle stone, tapping it gently. Satisfied he wouldn't burn himself, he closed his eyes and tried his best to invoke thoughts of anger and fury, focusing on every fight he had ever been in. Nothing. He thought about times when he had broken bones and had a doctor sentence him to four months in a cast. Still nothing. Frustrated, he grew angry at the stone itself, willing it to break like the last one. The stone remained a cool, dim crimson.

"I don't think it's working for me," Cole said, dejected.

"Definitely not. It's okay though, everyone is born with a different mixture of the three magics. Maybe you just have a more passionate soul, eh?" Storn chided, "There's nothing wrong with that you know, we need healers and artists too. Just leave the fighting to me. You sure you don't want to try the Passion stone?"

"Very sure," Cole said, backing away from the gratia stones.

"Fine, I'll cover you this time." Storn nudged Cole aside, seemingly eager to display his competence with the stones. "You can pay me back when you're brave enough for Passion. There's a set of focusing shards downstairs that I've been saving for. Supposed to help you with Wisdom. You're lucky these cyphers are simple so they're not too expensive."

"I'll find a way to get you those focusing shards. I promise," Cole mumbled, feeling like he was back in grade school asking his friends for lunch money.

Storn grunted as he placed a hand each on the Passion and Rage stones. His face twisted into a comical mixture of compassionate fury. Cole didn't dare laugh however. He had no urge to upset someone nearly twice his height, and he needed all the friends he could get. The stones hummed with light, one a vibrant lilac and the other pulsing crimson. A sheet of light that Cole didn't notice before shimmered in front of the lower shelves.

Storn lifted his hands, looking tired and panting slightly. "All right, new blood, they're unlocked. Start with the bottom right shelf."

Cole walked over to a shelf lined with greenish spheres, settling on the olive one on the bottom right. "Um, do I eat it or something?"

"Sorry. I forgot you don't know anything." Storn averted his eyes, apparently interested in the top shelves. "Yeah, pick one up and eat it."

Not wanting to annoy him further, Cole picked up one of the orbs. Olive clouds swirled lazily through the sphere, and as soon as he put his fingers on it, Cole could hear a sound like wind whispering through the trees. The hairs on his arm stood on end as his skin began to tingle. He brought the orb to his mouth, wondering how he was supposed to eat something as big as his fist and hard as glass. He fumbled for a full minute trying to fit the thing into his mouth, stopping when he heard an odd spitting and hissing sound coming from the other side of the shop.

Storn was bent over, clasping his hands over his mouth as he shook and coughed. Cole ran across the shop, wondering how one was supposed to perform first aid on someone so large.

Panicking, Cole shimmied his way up a shelf for a better look at whatever Storn was choking on. "Storn calm down! Did you swallow one of the cyphers?"

Storn exploded with laughter, placing his hands on his knees. "Maybe you are stupid after all! Eat a cypher, ha! How did it taste? I've never tried one myself."

With a mixture of anger and embarrassment, Cole hopped down from the shelf. He didn't like people making jokes at his expense, but he thought he must have looked ridiculous. "Well how am I supposed to know what to do with these stupid things? You're supposed to be my guide aren't you?"

"That doesn't mean I can't have a little fun." Storn clapped Cole on the shoulder with a de-clawed hand. Cole's knees almost buckled under the force, however. "Hold it up to your eyes and look inside. Really."

Cole decided to play along. If it was another joke he would just have to entertain Storn until the pranks had run their course. He held the ball up to his eye and looked into its cloudy depths. He felt his eyes shift in and out of focus as his breathing slowed. It was as if he were about to fall asleep, though he was intensely transfixed. He couldn't look away if he wanted to. Shapes appeared in the olive clouds, only to vanish a second later. He longed to see what they were. Just as he thought he saw what looked like a spinning wheel, he found himself staring at his empty hand.

"What happened? Did I..." Cole blinked as he felt a disturbance in his thoughts. A profound sensation of deja-vu teased him, tempting him to remember something he felt like he should have known all along. Just when he had the thing in his mind's grip, the feeling slipped away, leaving him yearning for it. "Did it work? I feel like I dropped it before it set in."

"Look at the shelves. The labels." Storn wasn't smiling this time.

"Okay, I'm looking but I don't-" Cole gasped, "There are words! The words on the shelves, I can read them!"

"Of course you can. You have the cypher for our written language now." Storn crossed his arms and leaned against the wall of the shop. "Now do the same thing with the next cypher. Don't try and eat it though, wouldn't want you chipping a tooth."

"Thanks, *Master* Storn," Cole said, injecting as much sarcasm as he could. He side-stepped to the next shelf, which had the word 'TIME' carved into it with choppy letters. The orbs on this shelf were a rich emerald color, and the clouds coalesced in weaving, linear patterns. He held the sphere up to his eye, trying to catch the moment where it vanished, but as before he was struck by a powerful feeling of *deja vu*. Before he could identify the newly forgotten memory, the cypher was gone and his hand was empty. He felt no different.

"That one should give you a better idea of how we measure time on the Dark Side. You Underkin use some backwards way where your days last forever." Storn picked another cypher off a shelf, tossing it in between his hands.

"I don't get it." Cole gripped the sides of his head. "It seems off when I think about it." He thought about time and how it was measured back on Earth, but the concepts were slippery.

"It might take a while to get the hang of it." Storn's voice softened a bit. "I grew up with these ideas so don't ask me how they relate to whatever the hell you use. We've got the second, the minute, the hour, the day, the month, and the Cycle."

As Storn said each unit of time, thoughts and concepts echoed in Cole's mind, new ideas mixing with what he already knew. When the echoing subsided, he had a general idea of how each measure compared with his concepts of Earth-time. Everything was longer to some degree. A cycle felt close to seven Earth years. A month was simply the time Aeneria spent in a local planet's house, which felt like four Earth months. Aenerian weeks, days, hours, and minutes were each several times longer than their Earth counterparts. The concepts were difficult to wrestle and differentiate, but they made sense enough. He rubbed his head, realizing he had developed a throbbing headache.

"You feel up for one more?" Storn asked, tossing another cypher to Cole.

Cole snatched the orb out of the air, afraid of dropping it. "I think so, is the headache normal?"

"Yeah. You just learned a lot real fast. Not everyone's minds can handle it. I could probably take in the lot, but I already know this stuff." Storn motioned towards the moss-colored sphere in Cole's hand. "This last one will give you a mental map of The Sill. Wouldn't want you getting lost. I'd have to go out and hunt you down, though you smell so bad I could probably sniff you out."

Cole resisted the urge to lift his arm and take a whiff. He wasn't offended because he knew it was true; there had been no way for him to clean himself. Cole tried to think of the last time he'd bathed or changed his clothes, but had no idea how long he and Habbad were on the river. He hoped he would reunite with his friends soon. Habbad was like a rock for Cole, always knowing how to react and what step to take next. Though he could feel Goran vaguely through the strange link, he wanted to see him to make sure he was okay.

Cole spun the orb in his hand. "Any chance for me to clean up before the end of the day? I'd rather not go around smelling like swamp muck."

"When we finish up at the markets we'll get you settled into the barracks. There's a shower that will peel that layer of stink off your hide. Hurry up with that last cypher and we'll get you some real clothes." Storn raked his eyes over what was left of Cole's frayed Underkin wrappings.

Cole was reluctant to leave the shop, though his headache now shot spikes of pain into his molars. There were multitudes of cyphers left for him to explore. Dozens of shelves displayed every shade of red, green, white, pink, gold, and even black. He promised himself he would return once he figured out how to safely use the gratia stones. They exited the shop, Cole quickly taking the lead as he was now oriented and knew the quickest route. Storn stopped him however, staring off the bridge as though waiting for something.

Storn held up a finger to the sky, which sparked emerald and let out a high whistle. A few moments passed in awkward silence, but then a massive sun lily leaf shot down from the canopy to greet them. The leaf docked itself at the side of the walkway where the vined handrails split wide to embrace it. They stepped on and the leaf lunged into open air. Cole plopped himself low for fear of falling off. Storn threw his chest out and posed for no one, hair whipping by his ears like a movie star. Cole looked back at the bell-shaped shop, memorizing the name emblazoned in neon vines: 'THE CORDIAL COMPENDIUM'.

Far off in the distance, Cole spied a sprawling cluster of stone buildings emitting captivating music and alluring lights. The cypher suggested he call it the 'Arts District'. Cole added the site to his mental list of places to explore.

The constant breeze of the open leaf had Cole shivering before long. Thankfully, the next shop they stopped in was a clothing store. The shopkeeper dressed like a butler, and his scowl gave him the appearance that he'd rather be anywhere else than at work. He turned his nose up when Storn explained they needed clothes for 'the Underkin'. Cole hoped the look of disgust was because he needed a bath and not because of some sort of prejudice. The man had a reedy appearance of a well-dressed walking stick in Aenerian form. He used only his hands and fingers to measure Cole's body, tapping a clicking silvery gadget worn around his neck after each measurement. When he finished he pulled out a massive set of thick cloth armor, along with matching boots that Cole could have sat in. Just as Cole was about to point out the obvious, the shopkeeper waved his hands as jade light shone onto the sturdy cloth. The clothes shrank until they were the appropriate size. Then the shopkeeper snapped his shining fingers and the fabric shifted from pale brown to a deep jade that matched the rest of Cole's unit.

When it came time for payment, the man heaved from behind the counter a hulking lavender gratia stone. Storn attempted his own offering, making jabs about Cole's bill racking up. The shopkeeper shook the stone, demanding more. Cole stepped forward, and made his payment. It was easier than he thought, but no less painful. He left the shop in tears soon afterwards, though the now jubilant shopkeeper chased after them, offering more clothes and another gratia stone to fill.

Despite Storn's prodding, Cole wouldn't give more than a grunt in response during the rest of their stroll through the markets. His mood only worsened as he had to pay at two more Passion stones. By the time they left he had a leather rucksack full of basic sundries. He stuffed his new clothes as well as Alvani's scarf into the bag, not wanting to wear them until after he had cleaned himself.

Storn invited Cole to join him for a walk around The Sill so he could show him around, but Cole declined. He left Storn at the markets, walking to the barracks by himself. Thanks to the cypher he knew the way, and the day was coming to a close anyway. He could hear music thumping from the arts district as he wound through the towering trees. As morose as he was, he couldn't help but feel a slight lightening of his heart as the sound tickled his ears. He didn't want to be cheered up however, so he trudged on, the heavy straps of the rucksack now digging painfully into his shoulders.

After an hour, Cole arrived at the barracks, which turned out to be a grid of stout trees grouped far away from the rest of The Sill. Evenly spaced doors spiraled up the exterior of the trunks, and bark walkways connected the trees on the upper levels. As Storn had said, there was a glowing mushroom lit for him near the top of his tree. Physically and mentally exhausted, he climbed his way up to his room. The door appeared to be the same flowing-solid variety of his cabin's. He pushed his way in, popping through the other side and dropping his dagger, pommel smashing on his toe. He didn't know any swears in Aenerian yet, but he did hear a few familiar curse words fly from his mouth. The room was absolutely dark. Still hopping, he threw a hand out to balance himself. His fingers bumped into a rubbery mushroom, casting his room in a pale cerulean glow. Once the pain subsided, he picked up his dagger and found a few more blue bells and flicked them on.

The room was bigger than he'd expected. Carved from the interior of the tree, its floors and walls displayed the polished grain of a cherry colored wood that flowed in waving patterns. The furniture looked oddly small compared with the high ceilings. Someone must have shrunk everything for him. He set his rucksack down on a stumpy desk, which seemed to have been shrunk a bit too much. The bed looked to be appropriately sized though, and there was a standing locker for him to store his things in.

After unpacking his meager belongings, he explored a second room cut into the back. It looked as if this was the place for hygiene; there was a squat toilet and a basin with faucets. There was no place for him to shower, however, which was what he really wanted. He tried the faucets but no water came out. He noticed small, clear gratia stones sunken into the knobs. Begrudgingly, he walked back to the main room and found a larger stone embedded into the wall. As he suspected, the room required payment for its appliances to function. Cole bared his teeth and readied himself to watch Joshy die once again. After his sobbing subsided, he returned to the sink. The stones now glowed with soft white light. There was also a shining green ring on the floor, with a matching one on the ceiling directly above. Curious, he stepped inside the circle. A disk of electric-green light descended slowly from the top ring. Even more curious now, Cole stood still and waited for the light to pass over him. He held his breath and shut his eyes tightly as the light touched his head and raked over his face. Green light burned into his eyes as it passed over them. The light felt abrasive, yet satisfying, as if it were lightly scratching every itch he didn't know he had. He laughed involuntarily as the light passed over his stomach and down his legs. When he felt it pass over his toes he looked down to see that he was completely naked. There was a mass of brown muck around his feet. He bent down to inspect the substance, but was immediately assaulted by the worst thing he had ever smelled. The light had somehow taken everything off of his body. He slapped his fingers on his scalp to make sure the light hadn't shaved him too. His hair felt thick and smooth, and the rest of his body felt a bit raw.

Overall he felt cleaner than if he had just run naked through a car wash.

Back in the main room Cole dressed himself in silky undergarments and hopped into bed. Laying himself down, he could feel the tree swaying slightly. He was tired, but every time he closed his eyes he found himself back in the cobblestone alley. He focused instead on everything he'd learned so far. Magic held immense intrigue for him. Rage particularly had a certain seductive appeal to it. He held out his hands, imagining them as munisica capable of tearing through metal and rock like a hammer on eggshells. Wisdom also held a deep interest for him. He envisioned himself as a powerful sorcerer shaping the world around him and flying as he did in his dreams. At the moment, Passion had no temptations for him as he was still nauseated from all the Passion stones. He thought about the other uses for Passion, and Goran popped into his mind. It was easier this time to envelop himself in the mind of his furry friend. He sat up in bed, closing his eyes. Goran was not moving at the moment, but resting far away. He felt different. He was certainly the same Goran Cole knew, but somehow he felt more intense. It was as if there was more of him. Keeping his eyes closed, Cole lay back down and maintained the contact. Goran's dreams of charging through trees and chasing prey flowed into Cole's mind, keeping the cobblestone alley at bay.

CHAPTER 15

CONTRIBUTION

Cole jerked awake as someone kicked his bed. "Get up new blood! Why didn't you set your timekeeper?"

Cole squinted. Storn had a ball of white light hovering above his head. "I forgot," he mumbled.

"Well then I guess I'll forget who I'm supposed to be in charge of when it's time to eat. Get up and put some clothes on. We're all waiting for you outside." Storn popped out the door.

The thought of food made Cole's stomach ache. He hastily flicked on a few blue bells and dressed himself. His duty uniform was very tough and thick, though form-fitting and flexible in all the right places. He strapped on his boots, relieved that they would require no breaking in. He popped out of the door, worrying if his possessions would be fine in an unlocked room. He had to remind himself that he wasn't in the tree streets, and his tiny underwear were probably not a big seller around giants. Looking down the spiral ramp he saw the others waiting in the middle of the barracks grounds. The unit sat in a circle facing outwards. He ran down, nearly tripping over a root as he was not used to his new boots. The others had their eyes closed, apparently meditating. Eliza and Deekus sat comfortably on their sides, resting on their elbows as if they were watching a show. As quietly as he could, Cole sat next to Storn, whose breathing was the loudest sound in the quiet spot.

Unsure of what to do, Cole closed his eyes and tried to meditate. He quickly realized he had no idea what the first step was in meditation. Eventually he gave up, focusing on Goran instead, who was once again tearing through the undergrowth. He found the connection deeply satisfying because it was the only aspect of magic he had conscious control over. After what Cole had guessed to be an hour or two, even the connection with Goran had lost its novelty. He opened his eyes, and out of his peripheral vision he saw a grassy cape glide just out of sight. Chiron circled them, quiet as a shadow, his cape now mimicking the grass that poked out from between his bare toes. The others had a look of strained effort on their faces. Chiron bent down and whispered something in Lileth's ear. Cole watched through squinted eyes as the side of her mouth curled up in a grin.

Chiron circled around and stopped in front of Cole. Cole felt stupid pretending to meditate, so he opened his eyes and gave a polite nod to Chiron, who smiled and beckoned him away from the circle. As quietly as he could, Cole rose and followed, glancing back at the group. Everyone still wore looks of strained effort. Even Lileth's stoic demeanor had broken slightly. Cole followed the sweeping cape, which shifted to black soil and tree roots as Chiron stepped off the grass. Cole had the sudden urge to run up his back, just to see if the cape would hold him. Once out of earshot of the others, Chiron stopped and sat at the base of one of the stocky trees. Cole stretched and twisted. His back was sore from sitting for so long.

Chiron's winged eyebrows knitted together as he surveyed Cole. "I'm happy to see you allowed someone to wash Kreed's taint from your mind. There very well may have been something nasty taking root. Best to remove the weeds before they choke the whole garden. How was your first day playing with Dark Ones?"

Cole shrugged. "Harder than I expected. I fell from a tree and got hurt pretty bad. Lileth saved me again. She seemed really upset about it."

Chiron brought his fingertips together, tapping them in a quick pattern. "Yes, I heard about your little tumble. I hoped that Lileth would have embraced her talent, but Passion is an emotional thing, and defies reason by its very nature. Once one allows an emotion license to burn unchecked, even the wisest become blind with it." Chiron squinted with sudden concentration. Behind them Valen burst into a fit of laughter.

Cole thought about Valen kicking him from the tree, wondering what had prompted the attack. Part of him wanted to tell Chiron about the attempted murder, but another part also felt like this was *his* problem. After dealing with the rude shopkeeper, Cole was curious if this problem was bigger than just between him and Valen. "Chiron, Master Chiron-"

"Chiron is fine, Cole. Titles are unnecessary as long as there is mutual respect between both parties." Chiron's storm grey hair fell over his shoulders as he gave Cole a little bow.

Cole felt himself blush. "Okay then, Chiron. Back on Earth, we have something called racism. Certain groups of humans don't like others because they look different or speak a different language. It's like the color of your skin makes you a lesser being. It gets really ugly. Still is in some places. Is racism a thing here on Aeneria?"

A morose shadow fell over Chiron. "I am familiar with the conventions of racism, bigotry, and prejudice. I'm ashamed to admit they are all very real things on Aeneria. Some like to think we are better than people of the local planets; after all we are the crowning amalgamation of each planet we pass by. We are a mixed breed of every intelligent race, and the best parts of each reside in us. Unfortunately, with the good qualities come the less savory facets. Prejudice is universal and stems from a Fear of the unknown. We are not immune to it. You wear the guise of Underkin. Their very name sets them below all. I assure you it would be no better if we were open about you being human. This will be another challenge for you to face. I suggest you give everyone reason to respect you. Educate them, and show them that you are not as unfamiliar as they Fear."

Cole kicked at a clump of grass. "I'm used to people not liking me for no good reason. I'll deal with it. I'm not sure I'll survive all the training though. The first day almost killed me. What are we supposed to be doing right now anyway?" He waved his hand, indicating the rest of his unit in the circle.

Chiron's eyes remained on Cole. "Before my lessons, we clear our minds of all thoughts and emotions so we can look at the universe with an open and objective perspective. The others are attempting to empty their minds while I assault them with my own. It is a mental dance of Wisdom and Passion."

Cole's jaw swung ajar. He looked from the circle back to Chiron. "Is that what they're doing? I can't clear my mind in a quiet room, let alone while locked in some kind of mental battle. How can you juggle them all at the same time?"

"I've had a very good teacher." Chiron flashed a wink before squinting in deep focus.

Cole looked back to the unit as they rolled in the grass, overcome with laughter. Deekus's hands glowed with lavender light as he howled and beat his fist against the ground. A flowering plant sprouted from the soil with each blow. The laughter stopped abruptly as the group hissed in unison, scolding themselves before settling back into a meditative state.

Cole found himself suddenly elated, as if he caught a whiff of their jubilation. Concern quickly replaced his joy. If overwhelming someone's mind with good things was possible, surely the not-so-good things were also possible.

"Each of us started where you are now," Chiron said in a gentle tone. "You have already shown some aptitude with our magic. Keep an open mind and keep trying. I must admit I am envious of you. You are about to grow in ways you cannot yet comprehend. It has been ages since I have done any growing. Come, it's time for us to leave the barracks and begin the lesson."

Chiron raised a sparkling emerald finger as a fleet of sun lily leaves descended from the canopy. Without a word the unit rose from their circle and mounted the leaves.

A warm breeze whipped through Cole's hair as they floated above the treetops. He sat on a leaf with Storn, enjoying the view over The Sill and the surrounding shoreline. The rest of the unit skimmed ahead, each riding his or her own leaf and chasing each other like birds. Oberon blazed in the starry sky, a chromatic sentinel watching over them all. Following Storn's lead, Cole took off his thick cloth top and undershirt, basking in the warm light. He couldn't help but wonder if he would get a moon-burn from too much exposure. As Chiron had instructed, he took the quiet moment and attempted to clear his mind. He could only hold onto his mental silence for a few seconds before an errant thought distracted him. The fact that he was gliding on a leaf with giant aliens was reason enough to keep his mind racing.

The ocean of greenery gave way to open air as they flew above a bay of clear water dotted with specks of light. The clarity of the water made its depth a mystery. Rocks and plants below were perfectly visible in between passing waves. Cole tried to find the spot where Chiron had dropped him off, but the rocky coast was just a dark blur from such a lofty height. The leaf dropped suddenly as they went over the water. Yelping, Cole threw out his hands, grasping on to Storn's muscled arm.

Storn laughed over the wind. "Watch yourself new blood. The air is cold above the water. Remember that."

Cole's face glowed like a hot pan as he scooted himself away from the edge of the leaf. Cole tried to force his embarrassment out of his head, but his efforts only added frustration to the mix. He gave up on his meditations and decided to enjoy the sights instead, from a safer position this time.

The squadron of leaves scraped to a halt on a winding beach. Unseen creatures squealed from the tree line as they dismounted. Chiron, who apparently didn't need a leaf to fly, alighted upon the sand with fluid ease. Cole scrambled to his feet with the others, who stripped down to their swimwear. Cole followed suit, laughing inwardly as he thought on how many times he'd been nearly naked on Aeneria.

Unabashed envy replaced his amusement as he gawked at the collective physique of the unit. They were all built like Olympic gymnasts crossed with bodybuilders. Moonlight cast flattering shadows over their lithe forms, showcasing lines of hard muscle and bone. Every single one of them looked like a living weapon, exactly what Roth had described. Cole looked down at his own body, which conversely looked like that of an overgrown, shapeless child. He had lost weight since leaving Earth, and perhaps gained a bit of muscle, but next to his unit he felt like the personification of inadequacy.

Storn may not have been the tallest, but he certainly was the widest, giving him the appearance of a walking boulder. Sitra was similarly built, though she still carried herself with feminine grace.

Deekus and Eliza looked like a pair of matching ornate daggers, skinnier than the rest but still quite capable of serving a quick, beautiful death. Valen could have passed for an eight-foot statue of what Greek gods could only aspire to look like. His thin waist was adorned with more abs than Cole could count, and tapered up to broad shoulders lined with striations. He seemed to know how good he looked as he took an unnecessary moment to stretch, twisting and bending in an incredible display of flexibility. To Cole's relief, Valen's showboating held no charm for Lileth, who disrobed and strode barefoot past him towards Chiron. Cole's ears glowed hot as he followed not too closely behind her, taking in her form from his periphery.

Chiron remained fully robed, addressing the group with his hands crossed behind his back. His cape now looked like a sandy waterfall. "Please, gather around. Your lesson today will be a practical one. I have full confidence that you will all provide an exemplary performance; however, I do beg a bit of caution. I'm looking at you, Sitra."

The group laughed as Sitra swiped a clawed fist through the air. "Ha! There's no need to worry about me, Master Chiron. I am the reason for caution! Remember last week's lesson?"

Chiron smiled politely, bowing his head, "Yes my dear, of course you are. That poor orrix will think twice before tangling with you again. Legend of your savagery will be sung throughout the halls of their hooved ancestors for many cycles I'm sure."

Sitra crossed her arms, smiling broadly. The others gave her congratulatory slaps on the back while Cole sidestepped out of the way.

"Violence will almost always yield a result," Chiron continued, silencing the unit. "However, the result may not be what you had intended. Today's lesson will require you to find a non-violent solution. That does not mean there is no risk. On the contrary, an error today may cost you your life."

The unit stiffened, leaning closer to hear Chiron's every word. Cole started sweating despite the breeze that caressed his bare skin. Even Valen looked unnerved.

Chiron paused a moment, setting a clear stage for his words. "The Sill finds itself wanting for more gratia stones. As you all know, the reward for gratia stones is quite high; however, so is the risk. The stones grow in the ventus coral, which lies in the ocean floor off this very coast. As the coral breathes, the stones rise to the surface. A quick witted Aenerian may find herself an opportunity to acquire one of these stones should she catch the current just right."

The atmosphere changed from trepidation to yearning. Even Cole, who had no idea of the value of the stones, felt a longing for treasure. Growing up, he'd never had much to show off, always wearing clothes from the secondhand store. He could almost hear some of those expensive gadgets and nice clothes from the markets calling to him.

"Now, hear my words of caution. The ventus coral is below the sand. The tops of their husks barely reach the ocean floor, which lies at a depth beyond a single breath. You all know what the body requires for nutrient exchange, and the water will obviously pose a certain layer of difficulty. It is up to you to figure out how to navigate the challenge. This will require a constant application of Wisdom. Your focus will be tested by certain distractions. These distractions include some of the larger predatory animals that lurk in the deep, the obvious lack of breathable air, and the currents themselves. Though the reward is of course greater, I advise you not to attempt the omnistones farther offshore. The depth-pressure as well as the coral's breathing are formidable, and you would likely find yourself stuck to the bottom. Your lives will be in your own hands. Trust in each other and maintain your vigilance."

"Master Chiron," Deekus interrupted, "Will you not be joining us? It would give us all much comfort knowing that you will be there should the worst happen."

Chiron gave Deekus a sympathetic, yet calculating look. "I will not be joining you, nor will I be there to catch you should you fall. There is trouble at our borders that requires my attention."

"You mean you'll be tearing a few Domina hides," Sitra said with fire in her eyes. "If you want to give us a practical exercise then take us with you. We should be out fighting, not picking rocks out of the water. We are ready, Master."

The rest of the group nodded and murmured their agreement. Chiron, however, looked sad as he placed a gentle hand on each of her thick shoulders.

"Your thirst for the blood of our enemies is terrifying and admirable, my dear Sitra. However, you do not know what you ask. The full weight of The Three inches ever closer. You will have your blood-lust sated before long, I assure you. In the interim, you will do The Sill an important service and retrieve as many gratia stones as you can." He released her, addressing the rest of the unit: "You will take to this task without me as your safety net. Part of realistic training is making it, well, realistic. In battle you will rarely have someone at your side ready to pull you out of the fire. There is danger and honor to be won in this task. I challenge you all to figure this out on your own."

"We will succeed, Master Chiron," Valen said with a stern nod. "Go tend to your task and we will tend to ours. You will return to a heaping pile of gratia stones and a roaring fire."

"Thank you Valen." Chiron twisted, showering their feet with sand from his cape as he walked towards the tree line. He paused, speaking over his shoulder, "And let's not forget about our newest student. I would be most disappointed if he didn't learn a trick or two while I'm gone."

Cole gulped as all the sand fell from Chiron's cape. The garment took the form of flowing crystal as his feet left the ground and rose above the trees. Within a few heartbeats Chiron was nothing but a shrinking shadow in the eternal night sky.

Eliza was first the break the silence: "Am I wrong to assume that we would be better equipped for this task if we had some food in our bellies?"

Storn slapped his tortoise shell of a stomach. "I'm about two seconds from eating the Underkin. Chiron seems to forget that us mere mortals need food and water. I'm right behind you, Liza."

The group split up into teams, apparently well versed in the on-the-spot feast. Storn and Sitra donned their munisica and charged into the forest. Valen and Lileth sprouted electric green wings from their backs. Wind kicked the sand about them, stretching the ethereal wings taut as they too left the ground and flew into the forest.

"Deekie, would you mind setting the fire? I saw a few hortanials blooming on the way over and they looked perfect for the picking." Eliza stroked a hand over Deekus's bare shoulder.

"Of course." Deekus flashed Eliza a smile, as if telling a joke only they knew. "Will you help me stoke the fire when you return?"

Eliza responded with a wink and a sly grin as she carved off down the beach. Deekus's gaze lingered after her, enthralled. Cole knew that look, it was the same look he gave Lileth when no one was looking.

"It looks like you will be helping me with the fire." Deekus grabbed a smooth rock with his foot and kicked it up into the air, catching it in his hand. "I'll collect some rocks for us. How about you find some wood? The wood is just for flavor, so we won't need much. We're looking for some ria saplings if you can find them. Their leaves look like green hair."

"I think I've seen those before, they smell sweet right?" Cole bounced with excitement, eager to be of some use to the group.

"Right you are. If I'm not mistaken they were-" Deekus stopped himself, "No… it would be best if you found them on your own." Deekus seemed just as excited as Cole. "Sorry, but Chiron wants you to learn what you can. Don't worry, I'll be over in a minute if you can't find them."

Cole ran for the trees, fueled by hunger and a willingness to prove himself to the group, even if he was just collecting a bit of wood. His confidence swelled when he found a whole patch of the ria plants. They always stood out to him, looking like the tufted hair of children playing in the woods. He drew his dagger and set to work. Within ten minutes he had as many of the little plants as he could hold. He returned to Deekus, who now stood over a bed of glowing rocks, throwing his bounty beside the coals.

"Our meal certainly won't be lacking any flavor." Deekus appraised his work. "That will be more than enough for whatever the group brings back. Thank you, Cole, you did very well."

Cole burned with pride. The unit didn't usually call him by name. He threw the bundle of saplings next to the bed of hot stones.

The heat was almost too much for his bare skin. "What's making the stones so hot?"

"I have convinced the heat from the ground to move into the rocks. I pulled heat from the area on the other side of the pit as well, just under the blanket of leaves I set down. That way the others will have a cold spot to put the meat from their kills while we prepare the rest of the meal. Why don't you try?" Deekus threw him two small rocks. "Do you know what heat is?"

Cole was glad to know the answer, but his hopes plummeted as he recalled his failure with the puddle. "Heat is just how fast atoms and molecules vibrate. I've tried to shift the heat in an object before and it didn't work for me. I don't know if I can use Wisdom."

Deekus sat himself cross-legged in front of Cole, holding his palms upwards. "You are more capable than I was when I first came to The Sill. Please sit, I will show you how it's done."

Cole plopped himself in the sand, eager for another chance to learn about magic. Deekus took both of Cole's hands into his, squeezing them and the stones within.

"This is how Chiron first showed me. Please, if you would do your best to clear your mind. I'm going to enter it and start the process using only your body. This will prove without a doubt that you are capable of Wisdom. I will then leave your mind and we'll see how long you can maintain focus." Deekus slapped the underside of Cole's hand, sending one of the stones up into the air, where it floated for a few seconds before smacking Cole's palm. "Relax. I can hear your heart running wild. Just have some fun with me for a moment."

Cole hadn't realized his chest was pounding. He let out a nervous chuckle, hands shaking. "I think this is about as calm as I'm going to get." An anxious laugh escaped his lips again.

"Just have fun with it." Deekus gave Cole's forearms a gentle squeeze with massive fingers pulsing with rosy light. Cole felt a sudden release of stress as his anxiety melted.

A cool breeze stroked the right side of Cole's body as the heat from the stones baked his left side. Suddenly a cold shiver ran down his left side as his right throbbed hot and sweaty. It was odd, the side against the fire feeling cold and the opposite feeling warm, but he felt a balance, a quiet within himself. The sand beneath cradled him perfectly. The stars above sprinkled their light over the gentle waves, crashing like a thousand whispers over the beach. He brought his attention to the objects in his hands. The stone closest to the fire was slightly warmer to the touch. It would make a fine donor. He felt its heat, the essence of excitement within its smooth confines. Hefting the cooler stone in his right hand, he convinced himself that it lacked fervor. A bridge of budding concepts connected the two stones in his mind. The inherent energy in the stone on his left hand would simply exist within the limits of the stone in his right. He beheld the two objects, willing his conceptual bridge into reality with a droplet of thought. There was a shift in the world, unnoticed to anyone but him. The stones traded a modicum of their properties. He sent another thought across the bridge, not a droplet, but a thin stream. The bridge was no longer a concept, but an ironclad idea which he reinforced with every ounce of his conviction. The stones tickled his hands, one cool, one warm. He felt confident and capable as he widened the stream to a torrent. Each stone bit into his palms, their potency opposite yet equal. Until this point his attention had been entirely on the two stones, but now another factor came into play. His hands burned, one hot and one cold.

Cole severed the bridge, leaving him with an empty mind and two injured hands. He yelped, waving his hands through the air as though they were on fire before shoving them into the sand. He looked up to find Deekus standing across the glowing bed of rocks, warming himself.

"How did you do?" Deekus beamed at him, excitement bubbling over every word. He trotted over to Cole and picked up the two rocks, flinching and dropping them both. "Cole this is excellent work! That was a powerful spell!"

Cole stepped to the other side of Deekus, warming his chilled right side. "Don't mess with me. You did all the work."

A broad smile stretched across Deekus's face. "I left your mind long before the stones traded their properties. I only calmed your mind and gave you a little nudge. It took me three attempts to do what you just did. Be proud, Cole!" Deekus clapped each of his giant hands on

Cole's shoulders and the two students jumped up and down in unison. Seeing the pained look in Cole's eyes, Deekus touched a finger to each of his palms and healed them with a quick flash of white light.

"What are you two going on about? That fire better be good and hot by now. I hope you're hungry, new blood," Storn's voice called from the trees.

"Look at them, dancing like fools. Did Deekus just recite one of his epic poems for you, Underkin?" Sitra stomped through the sand, following Storn. Each of them held a large sack on each shoulder.

"I just did magic!" Cole proclaimed, his voice ringing with joy. "Deekus got me going but I just did Wisdom! I made one rock super cold and another super hot! Touch them, they'll burn your hands!" Cole kicked one of the rocks towards Storn.

Sitra and Storn heaved their loads, which turned out to be the carcasses of their kills, onto the cold leaf pile.

Storn bent low and scooped up one of the rocks with a black clawed hand, pinching it between two wicked knives. "Nothing burns my hands, new blood." He tossed the rock into the water, where a wave swallowed it in a cloud of steam. "Not bad though. Don't get too caught up in the Wisdom stuff, Rage is the muscle behind this war."

"And Passion is the soothing waters that cleanse the fires of war." Eliza's voice swam from the shadows as she emerged, dragging a large basket full of fruits. Cole recognized some of them, including a few handfuls of deka seeds. The basket was intricately woven from a green plant with long thin leaves. It even had sleds running along its bottom, making it easier to drag. Eliza touched the knot at the top with a shining violet finger. The leaves unbound themselves as the fruits spilled out into the sand. The basket plant continued to unravel, shuffling in the sand as it rooted itself beside them. Eliza saw Cole eyeing the plant. "I would love to show you how to work plants with Passion. Perhaps in our free time between lessons?"

"Yes please! You should have been here, Deekus just showed me how to use Wisdom." Cole's cheeks were starting to ache from smiling so hard. "I've never seen magic before coming here, and now I'm casting spells! I can't wait to learn how to use all the schools."

"Rage is the only school that matters in a fight," Storn scoffed. "But enough learning, let's get some food in us."

The group set to preparing the meal. Deekus and Eliza readied the fruits, peeling shells and shucking husks. Cole helped shell the deka seeds, which were much larger than any Cole had ever seen. He thought Eliza might have used her Passion on the plant to alter them. Sitra and Storn set to cleaning their kills, burying the viscera under the roots of the basket plant. Valen and Lileth returned a moment later, alighting on the sandy beach without a sound. Valen carried a dead bird larger than Cole and Lileth produced half a dozen eggs of equal proportion. Cole watched with hungry eyes as the group used Wisdom in various ways to prep the food. Within minutes there were four plucked and skinned carcasses floating over the coals as if on an invisible spit. Some of the hot rocks were placed inside the cavities to cook them faster. The fruits were done first, and while they were delicious, it was the meat that Cole longed for. The roasts sizzled and crisped over the bed of embers. Cole asked if they could just use magic to cook the meat faster, but Sitra took great offense, stating that any meat worth eating deserved the proper flavor and touch of a good smoky fire.

After they had their fill of tender fillets and juicy steaks, Valen opened the discussion to strategy. Each had his or her own ideas on how to tackle Chiron's challenge. Cole was keen on the underwater breathing, but the methods they described didn't sound pleasant or easy.

"Depending on how deep the coral is, we may need to use the internal exchange method," Lileth said through a mouthful of fried eggs. "It's uncomfortable, but if your lungs are full of air at great depth, the weight of the water will make it impossible to breathe. It would be better to fill them with water."

Sitra chimed in, "Well that's a great idea Lil, but none of us besides you knows how to make all those itty bitty pockets in our lungs run on water. Can you maintain the spell on all of us?"

Lileth swallowed, wiping her mouth with her arm. "I can alter myself and perhaps one other, but I would not be able to do much else, lest I lost focus."

"So that's a no." Sitra turned to the others. "Anyone else? Or are we going with the old bubble-head exchange?"

"A bubble of air would be harder to maintain at greater depths for the same reasons Lileth mentioned," Deekus stated, rising to his feet. "Pushing the bubble against the weight of the water would take immense focus, and we still have the carnivorous sea creatures to defend against. I was thinking we could maintain a magical field within our throats. It would be much smaller and more resistant to the crushing forces of the water."

"Would the surface area be great enough to allow enough gas exchange?" Eliza asked, taking a sip from a hollow fruit.

Deekus nodded hopefully. "With Valen and Lileth maintaining the spells I think the field should be efficient enough. They are fairly adept with Wisdom. Would you agree, Valen?"

"Absolutely," said Valen, tearing a hunt of dark meat off a bone. "I could do it myself, so long as the rest of you can handle a few fish. Has anyone given thought to how to mitigate the blurriness of the water? Eliza, you are most familiar with anatomy, what are your thoughts?"

Eliza's brow wrinkled. "The problem is within our eyes. I think our sight is blurred underwater because of how the light enters after bending through a different medium, but I haven't the slightest idea as to how we are to manipulate light."

The group fell silent, dejected but not defeated. They bounced around a few ideas but they ran into the same problem; the spell to bend light would be too mentally taxing to allow them the mental acuity for anything else. Eventually the group agreed that they would have to just deal with the blurry vision. Cole sat in silence the whole time, enjoying the smoked meat. He came up with a simple answer to their quandary, but ate in silence for fear of saying something stupid. After all, what could he possibly contribute to a conversation about magic and spells?

Valen noticed Cole on the outskirts of the circle. Sneering, he cocked his head and called out to him. "Underkin, you've been as quiet as a stump over there. Surely you must have come up with at least one idea. Please share your Wisdom with us, just one little nugget."

Cole blushed the same color as the glowing embers. Storn and Sitra laughed as the others averted their eyes from the uncomfortable silence. Valen sneered triumphantly. Cole longed to jump up and punch him right in his handsome face, but kept himself firmly planted in the sand. He hated bullies. Every fight he had ever been in was from either standing up for himself or someone else. The laughter subsided eventually, Valen enjoying every second to drink in Cole's shame.

"I have an idea." The words were out of Cole's mouth before he had a chance to pull them back in. He was committed now, either to stumble over his own foolishness or to possibly build his social platform a little higher. Every eye was on him now. "Back where I come from, we don't have magic, but we can see easily underwater. We use a device that traps air behind a flat glass lens, making the water as clear as the fire is now."

"It seems I misjudged you, Underkin." Valen took on a tone of mock sincerity, as if talking to a child. "Clearly you were not listening, or perhaps you were not able to follow our conversation. Do you remember when Deekus was talking about air? Air under deep water gets crushed you know." Valen exemplified his point by summoning a ball of green light between his hands, compressing it to a smaller size.

Storn laughed again, but he was the only one. Sitra punched him in the shoulder with a deep thud.

"I didn't say anything about using air," Cole murmured in a voice barely heard over the waves. His tone was much softer and higher than he would have liked. Taking a deep breath, he continued, projecting his voice, "We don't need to use air. I think the trick is the flat lenses. If one of you could change the shape of our eyes to make the surface flatter, then I think we could see clearly underwater."

Deekus slowly turned his head towards Cole, giving him a look of surprised appraisal. "Well done, Cole. Sometimes the most beautiful solution is the simplest one."

CHAPTER 16

DESCENT

C ole waded into the warm water, waves crashing over his bare legs. He blinked rapidly. His newly flattened eyes did a poor job seeing out of water. The others were ahead of him, holding their hands up to their throats, jade light flashing in between their fingers before diving into the water.

"Are you ready?" Lileth asked, her form silhouetted in front of Oberon as she looked down at him.

Cole panted in anticipation. This was the part he was most scared of. "Yes."

Lileth crouched, wrapping her soft yet powerful hands around his ribcage. Under the riot of Fear and apprehension, he felt a sudden comfort and pleasure at her touch. An emerald glow lit the sharp features of her face as he felt the Wisdom shock its way through him. Cole felt in his lungs an annoying burning that soon throbbed into unbearable pain. He coughed, clapping his hands to his throat. He couldn't breathe. His chest was heaving, filling his lungs over and over but he still felt as if he were drowning. Lileth's eyes drew him out of his panic, steadying him for what must be done. She readjusted her hands, wrapping one firmly around Cole's thigh and the other around his head. In one smooth motion she flipped him downside up and held him under the water. Cole struggled, fighting with all his might as he choked to death. He pulled at her fingers, trying to break one free, but her grip was as steel. He coughed again, swallowing salty water as his free leg kicked at Lileth like a wild animal trapped in a snare. His lungs burned for oxygen, his instincts overrode his focus. He inhaled. A mouthful of water rushed into his lungs, quenching the fire. Seizing a temporary moment of clarity, he threw his primal urges against his

Fear, sucking a bigger breath this time. The relief was immediate. He inhaled fully, dousing the fire entirely. It was awkward and very uncomfortable, but he forced himself to keep breathing as soothing seawater replaced the air in his chest.

Sensing that he was no longer struggling, Lileth released him. Cole floated below the surface, watching with crystal clear vision as Lileth flashed a green palm to her throat and dove in. She locked eyes with Cole, relief softening her features. The same part of him that enjoyed her touch hummed with satisfaction as he beheld the worry on her face. Cole nodded, giving her a casual thumbs-up.

Cole followed, wiggling his way through the shallows, amazed at the clarity of the rippling sand and darting fish. Deekus alone was able to flatten the surface of all of their eyes, showering Cole with praise all the while. Cole felt a swell of pride as he navigated the water. He'd actually contributed something to the group! No longer was he the useless pretend-Underkin. He may be half their size and unable to do magic, but now he was worth something. His ideas were valuable and they would be listened to from now on. He replayed the moment over in his mind, savoring the sour look on Valen's face and reveling in how very impressed the rest of the group looked.

There was a surprising number of fish in the shallows. Each was a different color and none were shy. A few brave cichlids swiped by, taking an investigatory peck at Cole's feet and belly. He reached out slowly, stroking the flank of one that looked like a zebra-striped football. As they swam into the deep, a light crunching and cracking filled the water, as if someone were chewing rock candy right next to him. The din grew louder, but he couldn't identify the source as it sounded as if it came from all directions. Deeper they went, the sandy floor now darkening beyond the reach of Oberon's rainbow shower. Cole's limbs ached from the constant paddling. His chest muscles pained him as well. Water was much harder to breathe than air.

The sand dropped, giving way to a vibrant reef curated with towering spires and sweeping fins with tasseled arms. Fish surged about in droves, as if rushing through their morning commute. Cole allowed himself a moment to imagine he was simply on a tropical vacation, like a normal person. He was just scuba diving with some friends.

The others were still far ahead. Cole could just barely make out four little figures floating in the distance with streams of bubbles trailing from their heads.

Lileth looked back and Cole gave her another thumbs-up. She gave him a bargaining expression, holding out a foot and pointing to it. Cole begrudgingly took hold of her ankle. He didn't want her assistance, but he knew he was slowing everyone down. He paddled along with his legs, imagining how stupid he must look. With her arms alone, Lileth powered them through the water like a racing falcon. Cole had to remind himself that he was not useless, that there was still an important job that only he could do. She led them deeper, gliding over the shoals of fish cutting in and out of the coral city. Cole watched as a yellow spear-shaped object shot at a cluster of coral, producing a small *click* on impact. Realization struck him as Cole saw dozens of other fish doing the same thing. The fish pecking at the coral was the source of all that clicking and crunching. The sound carried much farther than he would have thought.

They left the city of coral behind, making for the deep cold where they could no longer hear the reef's chorus. Cole detached from Lileth when they neared the rest of the group, paddling through the last stretch by himself.

Dense silence permeated the chilly water. Oberon's light was a mere ghostly pallor, its silky shafts fading into the void below. Cole's resolve felt like a card castle before a steady breeze. The surface felt like a mile away, and he didn't want to guess how far down the floor was. Following Valen's lead, they descended into the empty murk. Chilled Fear tickled over Cole's heart like an eager spider. Soon he would be alone in the crushing darkness.

Their descent took them to nowhere, surrounded by nothing but empty silence. Cole squinted, barely able to make out the shadows of the others. Someone stopped and pointing to their throat. The others nodded in confirmation; they had gone as far as they could. While Cole's lungs were full of water, the rest of the group's were full of air and they could go no deeper. They formed a circle, six thin streams of bubbles trailing towards the surface. Valen's shadow went to the middle and addressed each of them, running his glowing hands over their bodies. He didn't seem to put as much effort in when it was

Cole's turn. When Valen completed his circuit, he closed his eyes, face slackening. As he popped his eyes open, soft white light engulfed each member of the unit. Cole couldn't help but notice that his light didn't seem as bright as the rest.

Eliza approached Cole, kissing the tips of her first two fingers. The water around her fingertips thickened and warped with magic. She brought the magic to Cole's chest, transferring the Passion into his skin. He didn't feel anything, but her confident smile told him the spell had been successful. The predators of the deep would not trouble him.

The unit dispersed as planned. Everyone had their job. Lileth, Deekus, and Eliza hovered pensively as they maintained the various spells needed to keep the group alive at such depth. Valen, Sitra and Storn shot off like clawed torpedoes, running laps around the others, ready to defend against any of the predators of the deep. Eliza assured Cole that since she only had to maintain her single spell on him, he would have no trouble from any creature. Cole steeled himself for his part. It was time.

Cole flipped upside-down and made for the bottom. If it weren't for the lights of the others he wouldn't know which way was down in the weightless, featureless void. He descended one stroke at a time as his imagination assaulted him with sea monsters and giant sharks. He felt supremely vulnerable and helplessly small with nothing around but miles of unknown. With every stroke he wanted to turn back. Back to the safety and security of his giant spell-casting friends. Back to dry land, never to step foot in the ocean again.

Just as he began to wonder if he would ever see the bottom, he realized he had been looking at it for some time now. The grey sandy floor only made itself visible by the shining circles that peppered the bottom, as well as the shadows cast by two large animals. Cole froze. The creatures glided along the floor, appearing as large and thick as pickup trucks. They looked and moved like sharks, though their heads would be more at home on a crocodile. The largest one turned to face him. Its entire eye was solid black but there was no doubt it was looking directly at him. It shot for him with a swish of its tail, the smaller one following. Sickening dread blossomed in Cole's chest, setting his heart fluttering its final beats. Before he could so much as raise a hand in defense, the shark was upon him, its jagged maw wide and ravenous. The creature halted abruptly, turning as it surveyed him with its empty, lifeless eyes. It snapped its elongated jaws, which were easily big enough for a man to lie comfortably inside. Cole flinched, chest shaking and heart hammering. The creature paused a moment longer as though thinking him over, then slunk off into the shadows with its fellow trailing behind.

Eliza's spell had worked. Though the crippling Fear still shook his limbs, he wished the sharks had stayed within sight. He didn't want to be surprised by them. Gathering himself, he made for the ocean floor. Even though he could see the bottom now it took him minutes to reach it. He stopped a moment, looking back to the surface. The lights from the others were nowhere to be seen. Cole hoped that it was only because his unit was so far away, though he began to wonder what he would do if they abandoned him.

His feet ploughed into the pillow-soft bottom, silt mushing between his toes as he half-walked, half-paddled his way over to the crest of the ventus coral. The opening was about a foot wide, its rough-cut rim barely visibly above the silt. As he neared the ventus coral, the current wrestled him as little motes floated in and out of its opening. He had to time this perfectly, or risk having an arm sucked into the hole. He waited. The particles eventually slowed, then reversed direction. This was his chance. He set himself over the hole, fingers outstretched, ready to grasp the gratia stone and kick off before the current changed. Deep within the tube he saw something rising, glinting in his dim ambient light. The gratia stone shot up, slowing to a halt just below the rim. Desperately, Cole lunged and wrapped his fingers around its smooth surface, unable to get a good grip. As soon as the current hinted at a change in direction, he released the gratia stone, kicking madly away. Water rushed back in and the stone shot back down the coral tube.

Heart hammering, he looked around for the sharks. There was nothing in the immediate area, save for a spindly crustacean scuttling by. He hoped to see a single light above from his unit, but there was nothing. He would give the stone a few more tries, but he was fully prepared to return and accept their disappointment. The oppressive darkness of the featureless bottom gave him an unsettling sort of claustrophobia.

The current shifted, warmer water rushing up from the ventus coral. Cole settled himself above the hole again, pushing his hands inside. The gratia stone rushed up again, this time into Cole's waiting fingers. Grip sure, he planted his feet and kicked off with everything he had. The stone resisted with some unseen force, but broke free as soon as it breached the rim. Cradling his prize in one arm, he kicked at the water, paddling for the surface. He had a strange feeling he wasn't moving, however. Looking down, Cole gasped as the floating specks rushed back into the hole. Before he knew it, he was floating inexorably downwards, faster with every heartbeat. He thrashed, trying to move himself anywhere but down. The sharks returned, taking interest in his flailing. The coral had him now. Mind racing, he allowed the current to pull him, spreading his legs into a wide squatting stance. His feet met the silt-laden bed on either side of the hole, striking soundlessly yet firmly. The current yanked him down, nearly sucking the stone out of his arms. It was all he could do to maintain balance and hold onto his prize. The sharks circled faster now.

When the coral finished its breath, Cole kicked off again, moving painfully slowly as the sharks raced about. One of the predators shot so close that Cole could feel the swish of its tail. In a flash of movement, it was level with him, black eye staring right through. Had Eliza's spell worn off already? Faster than Cole could blink, the shark dove down to the floor and clamped the same spindle-legged crustacean in its terrible jaws. A hard cracking interrupted the empty silence as the beast fed.

After paddling for far too long, Cole was back with his unit. He offered the stone to Eliza, but she pulled Cole into a tight hug, conveying all of her comfort and affections through the contact. The Fear that coated Cole's insides melted away. Welcoming the Passion, he wrapped his free arm around her muscled back, squeezing tightly. She leaned away, placing a hand over his heart, her smile as warm as their fire on the beach. Cole pressed the stone into her arms. His courage restored, he returned to the blackness for another stone.

He made the trip twice more, the last stone so heavy that he almost had to leave it on the bottom. The sharks were there every time, waiting for his light to draw in more of the crunchy crustaceans. Cole actually looked forward to seeing them on his final trip, but they shot off into the darkness soon after his appearance. Confused by the sudden change in their behavior, Cole twisted around in the darkness. His eyes scanned the void, snapping wide when something the size of an office building floated near. If he could have screamed he would have, but the only sound to emit was a dull rushing of water. The thing was somehow darker than the water around it, and so vast that Cole had mistaken it for the void around him.

Cole held his breath and tucked his limbs into his chest, wishing himself invisible until the leviathan passed, leaving him alone once more. He decided he'd had enough. He had recovered three gratia stones to repay his broken one. The debt was paid. Cole set his mind for the surface and swished his way back to his unit.

Eliza signaled to the others with a rapid pulsing from her hand. One by one the unit returned, forming their circle of lanterns. Lileth's face sagged with exhaustion. Valen waved his hands defensively as the unit started for the surface. He jabbed a finger at Cole, then back towards the bottom. Cole shook his head slowly, donning a look of pleading as he attempted to convey the severity of his weariness.

Valen's lips curled, disgusted. He faced Deekus, inclining his head with a look of challenge. Deekus cocked his head, lips pouted in contemplation. He locked eyes with Valen, smiling with a quick nod. Deekus brought his hands to his ribs, emerald light beaming from in between his fingers. His face went slack in forced calm as he expelled a geyser of air from his mouth, with hollow chugging sounds. He breathed rapidly, clearing the rest of the air from his lungs. Deekus now seemed less focused, appearing almost drunk as he smiled and swayed. He bowed to the circle before shooting off into the darkness below.

Cole wasn't sure what made him do it, but he tore after Deekus, following his soft glow into the darkness. They didn't go to the place where Cole had found his stones, however. They went farther from shore, towards the omnistones Chiron had warned them about.

Deekus slowed his pace when he recognized Cole swimming after him, offering an ankle as Lileth had.

The ocean floor came into view, but it ended abruptly with a rocky cliff. They alighted on the edge, gazing down into a void so profoundly empty that Cole felt as though he'd lose himself if he stared too long. Deekus placed a hand on Cole's shoulder, shrugging towards the surface. Cole knew what that look meant; he could turn back now without shame. Cole frowned and shook his head, clasping Deekus's arm. Deekus gave him a drunken smile, bowing his head in thanks. He then tilted his head and plunged over the cliff, moving without paddling. Cole grabbed his ankle and the two sank like an iron spear into the abyss.

Cole was terrified, but knew it couldn't be worse than doing it alone with sharks. This time he had a spell-casting giant with him. The descent didn't take as long as he expected, thanks to Deekus's magic propelling them along. Cole recognized the ventus coral and gratia stones nearby, though they were several times larger. The floor was a bit softer and squishier than the shelf above, and the ventus coral breathed with such force that it was audible. Cole paddled away from the opening, keeping far outside the reach of its current. Deekus, on the other hand, swam closer without hesitation. A small part of Cole worried at the slightly vacant, drunken look on his friend's face. He hoped Deekus wasn't exerting himself too much maintaining his spells. Cole dismissed his doubts, however. He knew nothing about magic and Deekus was one of the most adept in his unit.

Deekus approached the hole a little too soon in Cole's opinion, as the current was still inhaling. It pulled Deekus violently off balance. Deekus corrected himself, laughing silently as the current halted. As Cole had done on the shelf above, Deekus planted himself above the coral, waiting to snatch the gratia stone when it reached the crest. The exhaling coral was powerful enough to lift Deekus's giant frame off the floor, making him look like some absurd parade float. Deekus righted himself as the current slowed, eyes lit with recognition. He reached down into the coral and without any apparent effort, pulled out a large milky omnistone.

Deekus held the stone out for Cole to see, which was unnecessary because the thing was larger than Cole himself. Cole smiled and nodded, congratulating Deekus, but an anxious fire was spreading rapidly in Cole's heart. The current would change direction any second, and while Deekus was undoubtedly very strong, so was the current. When he finished appraising his treasure, Deekus kicked off of the floor, cradling the stone under one arm. He was too slow, however, as the coral had already begun inhaling the water around him. An annoyed grin spread across Deekus's face, as if the coral were nothing more than a minor inconvenience. He kicked powerfully with his legs, shooting himself up several feet with every stroke. He was losing ground, however. For every foot he gained he lost a few more in between strokes. He no longer looked annoyed, but desperate as he kicked and pulled himself away from the hole. Cole inched forward to help, but felt as if he himself stood on the edge of the coral's singularity. Deekus continued to fight, dropping the stone and knifing his hands through the water, moving faster than Cole thought possible. The omnistone sank back to the coral as if dropped through air.

Realizing he had been overpowered, Deekus set his eyes for the coral, allowing it to pull him down. Just as Cole had done, he squatted over the rim, landing with a poof of silt. Cole watched helplessly at the edge of the coral's pull as Deekus fought the invisible force, muscles bulging and veins popping. Deekus's legs wobbled and buckled as he slammed into a seating position over the coral. His shorts ripped and disappeared in a flash. Surprised, Deekus looked to Cole and laughed at his own nakedness.

Relieved, Cole laughed as well. Thankfully this would make for a funny story to tell the others back on the beach. He'd been convinced that Deekus was about to sink right down like the omnistone. Now they would have to just wait for the coral to exhale.

There was a sudden change in Deekus's demeanor as his face went from amused embarrassment to grim confusion. His eyes snapped open as all color vanished from his cheeks. Deekus bared his teeth, electric green webbing appearing in between his fingers and toes as he forced himself up from the hole, paddling faster than ever. He broke free from the current, but something odd caught Cole's eye. A wriggling fleshy rope now connected the ventus coral to Deekus's backside. It looked eerily like the tentacles of the grubs that had almost eaten him and Goran. Deekus kicked and pulled as if he were on fire, the thing behind him rippling like a ribbon, Deekus gulping like a fish out of water in between strides. Without warning, a cloud of blood erupted from his rear and Deekus stopped paddling. The tentacle broke free and shot back down the hole, carrying a crimson hunk of something with it. Deekus's face went peacefully blank as the Wisdom webbing flickered and vanished from his hands and feet. Cole watched in silent horror as his friend drifted like a ragdoll through the bloody cloud, disappearing headfirst into the coral.

Cole waited for the coral to exhale and release his friend, but it seemed to be stuck on a vacuum setting. He was alone again. Alone in the dark listening to the low hum of rushing water. He waited, unsure what to do. He was too scared to move, too scared to return alone to the crushing void above him.

Cole's ambient light flashed three times. That was the signal to return to the surface. He only had a few minutes before it flashed again and the group would return without him. Something about being so far away from the rest of the unit changed his hopelessness into fresh terror. He would not die down here.

Valen's light flashed again, faster this time and much sooner than it should have. The others were gone, leaving for the shore, leaving him. How long would it be before Eliza's and Lileth's spells wore off? Would they just cut the flow of magic, assuming him dead? Cole launched himself from the floor, creating a cloud of silt that flowed into the hole. He ascended into the empty blackness, hoping desperately that Eliza's magic would still keep the monsters at bay. Cole's heart sank as his own ambient light began to fade. Within a few strokes it was gone entirely, leaving him flailing in absolute darkness. A crushing vertigo now blended with his ripening fear, powering his limbs as he propelled himself towards what he hoped was the surface. Any second now his hand might swipe through the darkness, only to be caught by the stabbing teeth of some unseen horror.

As he swam, Cole felt a familiar presence beside him. It had been watching all along from the shadows. *He* was there, gliding smoothly next to him, watching him flail in the void. Cole had no interest in his imaginary friend at the moment, though it was slightly comforting to have someone next to him that was definitely not a shark. His comfort was soon replaced by hot ire. Why would *He* show himself now? He could have used *His* help countless times since his arrival on this death-planet. Maybe *He* wasn't there to help, maybe *He* just liked to watch Cole struggle. That must have been it, Cole thought. Here *He* was now, gloating and gliding along without even needing to paddle.

An idea crossed the bridge between them. Cole couldn't discern the source of the thought. It very well may have come from his own mind. It was a concept so simple that Cole chastised himself for not having thought of it before. Together, they cleared Cole's mind, just as Deekus had done for him hours before. Unbidden images of Deekus's lifeless form folding into the coral waded to the fore of his thoughts. In that moment he realized with horrifying acceptance that the tentacle had not come from the coral. It had come from Deekus's bowels.

He pressed the idea again, drawing Cole out of his grim trance. Cole shivered and nodded. *He* was right, they had a job to do, and very little time in which to do it. Clearing his mind once more, they set their focus to the water around Cole. He understood the water well enough, and it was time to change a rule or two. Inspired by the breathing of the coral, a current fueled by Cole's own conviction swirled around him, pulling and pushing him upwards. He cupped his hands and flattened his feet, granting the current more purchase over his body.

He was not moving terribly fast, at times losing his focus as he thought he saw a body ahead of him, but he was certainly making progress. Even with the magic helping him, it took much longer than he expected to see the first shafts of Oberon's light. He checked around him as he ascended into warmer waters. There was no sign of the others. He continued, returning to the surface feeling as if he'd just come from another planet.

Cole paused just below the rolling waves. He wouldn't be able to breathe the air above the water. Shaking his head at the absurdity of what he was about to do, he held his breath before bobbing his head up into the chilled ocean air. His vision blurred from his flattened eyes, preventing him from seeing the shore. Plunging himself under, he took another breath and tried again. Nothing. He circled around twice and saw nothing but blurry waves a few feet in front of him. Panic mixed with frustration as he went under again. He saw a flash of movement below him, though luckily it was one of the smaller fish from the shallow reef. Seeing the fish made him aware of the faint crackling, which could only be heard from the reef. Cole spun, trying to find the source. He shoved a finger into his right ear and spun around again. Logic and reason eased a modicum of his hopelessness as he considered the facts. The reef was definitely in between him and the shore, and he now knew where the reef was. As if to affirm his judgment, the fish below flew ahead of him towards the source of the clicking and crackling. Cole surged after the fish without paddling.

Mired in his exhaustion, Cole barely registered another fact; he was casting a spell. Cole might have needed *His* help to get it started, but he was certainly maintaining it by himself now. His excitement would have to wait, however. He was a long way from shore. With the aid of his magical current, the reef soon came into view. His spell was much harder to maintain with the litany of colorful fish darting below and nipping at his toes. Cole popped his head out of the water once more, finding a dark mass far ahead that looked to be the tree line.

Exhausted but finally safe, Cole released his spell. He allowed himself a moment of relief as he floated in waist-deep water. He didn't know if he could stand anyway. A violent swishing neared him, but he was too tired to even open his eyes. Something grabbed his ankle, lifting him completely out of the water. He had enough sense left to hold his throat closed, holding a half-lungful of the life-giving water.

"Open your throat, Cole," said a familiar voice as a soft hand pressed into his ribs.

His face became a waterfall as salty water and mucus poured from him. He coughed, choking on the water which just a minute ago was essential and comfortable. It was painful, but within a few breaths he had expelled almost all of the water. The hand became shockingly cold, magic chilling his lungs as the remainder of the water was turned into brackish vapor that streamed from his mouth and nose. Finally catching his breath, Cole wiped his eyes as he was flipped upright and placed on solid ground. He swayed, falling into the sand. He felt several times heavier and had no sense of balance. Huge fingers pressed over his eyelids, tickling magic shaping his eyes back to normal. Cole opened them, seeing Lileth crouched beside him wearing a look of utmost urgency.

"Why is Deekus not with you?" she demanded, pulling a clump of seaweed from his hair.

Cole's voice scraped and cracked as he tried to speak, though the sad look on his face said what he could not. Lileth closed her eyes as her expression twisted with sorrow.

Her voice softened. "Can you run?"

Cole shook his head. He felt ready to vomit.

She put her hands on him again, warm and strong. "Then I must carry you. Forgive me."

Lileth scooped Cole up into her arms as if he were a child, his head resting on her shoulder. He didn't resist, though he worried the jostling may be too much for his stomach. After a minute he mumbled his apologies as he wiped his salty vomit from Lileth's arm. Her only response was a quickening of her pace, which Cole judged to be the lower end of highway speeds. He closed his eyes, resting his head against her chest as he fought back another wave of nausea.

Lileth slowed as Cole heard the worried voices of the others. He recognized Storn's boorish voice above the rest. "Whatever it is we're ready for it. We need it! You all got to do something useful down there, I just swam around waiting for enemies that Eliza kept charming away."

"We're fresh, Valen, let's go. Fly above us if you can keep up," Sitra teased, pulling Valen towards the tree line. "Once Deekus gets back, he and Eliza can heal whatever wounds we might pick up along the way."

"Master Chiron would not have signaled us unless it was serious, so we will take it seriously." Valen's voice was of forced calm, though his pacing said otherwise. "It would be wise for us to keep unit integrity and wait for his return. We are stronger together. Ah, Lileth. I hoped you would return soon. You nearly started a riot with your sudden departure. You ought to explain yourself next time before running off. I had not the chance to tell you that Master Chiron contacted me with Passion. He did not elaborate, however it sounded urgent." Valen paused, noticing the bundle in Lileth's arms. "Is that the Underkin? Where is Deekus?"

Lileth set Cole gently on his feet. Cole stumbled over to a tree, using it to keep himself upright. Lileth made sure he was all right before addressing Valen. "I sensed my magic returning from the depths and found Cole a ways up the shore, alone. Can you sense your spells on Deekus?"

"No, I assumed he dissolved my magic and cast his own once he got to the omnistones. It's what I would have done." Valen then approached Cole. "Underkin, why did you abandon Deekus? Did he manage to secure an omnistone?"

Unable to stand any longer, Cole plopped himself into the sand and cleared his throat. "Deekus is dead," he whispered.

"Your tongue is running ahead of your mind," Valen dismissed. "Tell me exactly what happened before I pull your memories myself. Do not test me, Underkin. I am in no mood to tolerate your ambiguities."

Cole spat out a wad of salty phlegm before speaking: "He got pulled into the coral. Trust me, he's gone. Deekus is dead."

Valen's tone shifted to quiet venom as he reached a glowing emerald hand for Cole's head. "Forgive me, wise one, but we cannot afford the word of livestock at the moment."

Lileth stepped in front of Valen, her own eyes glistening with fresh tears. "It is true, Valen. You need not pan through his thoughts to know the truth. Set aside your prejudice and analyze the facts."

Valen smirked. "War is upon us, Lileth. It is not prudent to allow emotions to fetter your judgment. What would your parents say?"

Lileth's tears seemed to dry immediately as her face resumed its usual stony frown. A loud silence fell between them, embellished by the cries of the nearby insects and birds. Lileth's eyes sparked with jade light. Valen drew a sharp breath as his feet left the ground, causing him to look like a puppet on invisible strings.

"Release him Lil," Eliza said, her voice lacking its usual cheerful song. "Valen, Cole speaks the truth. If you don't trust him then trust me. He should never have gone for the omnistones. He lacked the focus to maintain so many complex spells." Her voice dropped to a quivering whisper. "I can no longer feel him in my heart."

Sitra trudged through the sand and took Eliza into her arms, soothing her with soft words. Valen regained his composure as Lileth released whatever spell she had on him. Disheveled, Valen ran his fingers through his hair, and resumed his pacing.

"Clothe yourselves!" Valen spat. "We need to be ready for anything. Master Chiron should be back any time now. He'll know what to do."

Storn tossed Cole his clothes, which landed in a heap at his feet. They were still warm from the fire. Cole embraced the warm garments. Sadness tugged at his heart as he realized that the momentary warmth would be the last time he felt Deekus.

"Hurry, all of you. Chiron approaches." Valen crossed his arms and faced the tree line. A violent snapping of trunks and branches grew steadily louder.

Storn turned his ear to the trees, giving the forest a skeptical look. "Valen, buddy. I don't think that's Chiron."

CHAPTER 17

TRIALS

C ole dressed himself, fingers stumbling over the buckles and straps of his cloth armor. He braced himself for the inevitable chafing that would result from his wet, sandy skin. Deep in the wood line, the crashing noise grew steadily louder, sounding like an approaching tornado. With a jolt, Cole recognized the noise, apprehension gripping him by the throat. He hopped away from the trees, lacing his boots behind the others.

"What do you think it is?" Sitra whispered, shuffling and peering through the trunks. "Chiron definitely wouldn't do that to a tree."

"It could be animals, but there's nothing big enough around here to make that much noise. And from the sound of it there's a whole herd coming right for us." Storn closed his eyes, listening as he flexed his claws.

"Should we make for the water?" Eliza proposed, stepping behind Valen. "We could hide and observe from a distance, then decide what action to take. Stars, they sound like a landslide-" She squeaked as a mad bellowing echoed through the trees.

Cole had heard that cry before. Part man, part beast. One of the Domina was charging full speed towards them. It would be on them soon. "We need to leave!" Cole croaked, standing on shaky legs. "That's a Domina! It will rip us apart if we don't get out of here now!"

With a grim fire in his eyes, Valen pulled off his boots, black knives exploding from where his feet and hands were. "We will not flee. It is time we test ourselves."

Storn and Sitra needed no encouragement. They joined Valen's side with claws of their own, bloodthirsty grins on their faces.

"Finally!" Storn shouted, "A real enemy! I've been waiting my whole life for this."

Cole backed away several paces. Even if they were a match for the Domina, there was no place for him in a fight of this scale. He was more likely to be crushed or gored than of any actual use. Even so, he drew his dagger from behind his cloth-armor coat. Lileth donned her green wings, wind rushing about her as she hovered above the unit. Eliza fell back with Cole, shaking with terror. The snapping trees went silent. For a moment there was no noise other than the flowing air holding Lileth aloft. Sitra whipped her banded braid over her shoulders and loosed a thundering roar, a death-challenge to any creature foolish enough to face her Rage.

As impressive as her battle cry was, it was a candle before a furnace compared to the roar that boomed in response. Cole flinched, covering his ears. Trees thick and strong bent and snapped in front of them, revealing not one, but three Domina. They were much larger than the one that had chased Cole to the bridge; they made even Valen look as small as an Underkin. The monsters also appeared more beast than man, possibly a crude mixture of several creatures. The beasts sported hooves and gigantic rolling horns, though their snouts were more wolf-like. One had enormous leathery hands of a man, dragging a granite mace the size of a small car. The other two had shovel-shaped claws that looked capable of digging through solid metal. The only things remotely human about them were their upright posture and eyes burning with sinister Hunger. Storn and Sitra dug their bladed feet into the sand, ready to pounce, but were clearly surprised at the scale of their foes. Valen placed a claw on each of their shoulders, steadying them.

Seemingly unperturbed, Valen raised his chin and addressed the beasts: "You are not welcome here. Return to the Light Side now, or suffer us."

Cole despised Valen, but he couldn't help but feel impressed by how calm he was, as if he were merely giving strangers directions.

The club-wielding Domina sucked in a deep, wet breath, licking its jowls in anticipation for the blood about to wet its throat. It appeared to have understood Valen, responding with an almost cocky grin. It opened its wolfish maw, releasing the whole volume of air from its barreled chest. Cole expected words to come out, but instead gravelly laughter poured from its bared teeth as the massive club came whistling through the air.

Valen took flight as Sitra and Storn darted to either side. The mace ploughed into the beach, sand exploding in a great wave. Cole and Eliza covered their eyes, temporarily blinded. Before the last bit of sand fell to the ground, the three beasts charged with speed unfitting for creatures so large.

"Focus on the largest one!" Valen called from above the bellowing Domina.

Sitra and Storn set upon the biggest creature before it could retrieve its weapon. The hairy behemoth faltered as the two warriors collided with its chest like a pair of battering rams. They didn't wait for it to recover from the blow, but hacked and slashed with their munisica. They moved faster than Cole could see by moonlight, but they seemed to have the upper hand. The beast howled as they carved at its flesh, showering the sand with blood and hunks of hide. The other two Domina ran around their wailing comrade, ignoring its human-like squeals, charging with single-minded determination. They appeared hell-bent on reaching Cole.

"Flash!" Lileth's voice rang clear through the chaos. The unit responded by covering their eyes as Lileth landed in front of the Domina, arms outstretched.

Eliza clapped her hands around Cole's eyes and ears. A painful ringing pierced his ears as harsh white light stabbed through Eliza's fingers. When Eliza released him, he saw the three beasts bent over, covering their faces and moaning in agony. Valen shot a beam of emerald light from his hands, forming a pool of muddy, flowing sand around the two smaller Domina. He flipped his palms upwards, sending torrent of sand pummeled the two, burying them entirely within a few seconds. Lileth alighted atop the pile, smacking her hands against the side with cold murder in her eyes. Cole felt a chill in his feet as the ground beneath him started icing over, stinging his soles. Steam rose from the pile of sand beneath Lileth, accompanied by muffled cries of pain.

The largest Domina stumbled drunkenly, one leathery hand rubbing its eyes and the other blindly searching the sand for its weapon. Seizing the opportunity, Storn jumped for its neck, but the beast's horn caught him under the arm, stopping him in mid-air. The Domina gave a curious jerk of its thick neck, confirming what the whims of battle had gifted him. A grating laughter rumbled from its chest as the beast abandoned its search, shaking its head like a dog with a rat between its jaws. Storn loosed an agonizing wail before silence took him.

Enraged, Sitra roared. She ran straight up the beast's leg, leaving deep gouges with every step. The Domina shot a hand out, catching her around the middle, crushing and squeezing. Her face screamed in pain, though her mouth made no noise.

The Domina's belly shook with laughter as it gripped tighter still, ignoring Sitra's munisica, which were raking deep into its hands and forearms. A series of muffled pops sounded from her torso, and Sitra went limp.

Storn still dangled like a wet towel. A spiral of crimson blood formed in the sand at his swaying feet. The Domina slammed Sitra's lifeless body against the ground twice before heaving her into the now glowing sand pile. It then set its eyes on Storn, nostrils flaring at the smell of his blood. It cocked its head so that the hot blood flowing from Storn's armpit poured into its mouth. Storn awoke suddenly, flailing and searching with his feet for anything that would take some weight off the sharp horn. His bladed foot found the Domina's face and stabbed indiscriminately. For a moment it seemed he would be free, but the beast snatched Storn's foot, holding it in place as its own blood joined Storn's in its maw. Pain, which seemed to be of no concern for the Domina, finally overwhelmed Storn. He sagged limply as the Domina yanked his foot, working its horn deeper with every tug. A grunting laugh shook the creature's belly.

Cole could no longer stand by and watch. Abandoning all reason, he tightly gripped his dagger and ran for the Domina. He didn't care what might happen to him, he couldn't stand by and watch the monster butcher his friend. He faltered and fell as a jade disc screamed over his shoulder, missing his head by inches. Spitting out a mouthful of sand, Cole looked up to find Storn suddenly on the ground with the

Domina's severed horn. Cole glanced behind him to see Valen standing with his hands together as in prayer, another jade disc crackling to life between his palms. The momentary distraction gave Lileth time to pull Sitra from the burning sand, Passion glowing over her fingers as she tended to Sitra's wounds. The Domina loosed a mournful bellow as its fingers searched the smooth stump of its severed horn.

"Eliza! Snap out of it!" Lileth yelled. "We need you!"

Eliza stood at the edge of the water, her face matching the Fear that Cole felt. She blinked, her eyes darting about as if she had just been woken from a daydream. She twisted, vanishing in a splash of sand before reappearing next to Sitra. Rosy light poured from her hands into Sitra, who thankfully arched her back in a deep breath.

The Domina shook its head, confusion boiling over to fury. Its Aenerian eyes snapped wide as it found the one responsible. Valen flicked one of his hands out, sending another jade disc towards the Domina. Cole dove out of the way as the disc buzzed through the space he had just occupied. The Domina snatched Storn's squirming form off the ground, using him as a shield. Shock fell over Valen's face. He grimaced in concentration, throwing his arms wide. The jade disc shattered into harmless flecks that trickled over Storn and the Domina.

Changing direction, the Domina thundered its way towards Cole, raising Storn over its head like a club. Cole scrambled to his feet, dropping his knife. He wasn't going to make it, the thing was way too fast. He barely took a step before something struck him across the back. He winced, opening his eyes to see the ground shrinking below him. He twisted and found Lileth's arms wrapped around his middle, rushing wind filling his ears. They flew higher, away from the fight. The smoldering pile of sand exploded as the two smaller Domina emerged looking entirely unharmed.

"Stay in the water," Lileth called over the wind.

"What?" Cole cried out, or at least tried to before his stomach lurched up into his throat.

He was falling, then he was under the water again. He didn't want to hide in the water, he wanted to help. His head bobbed above the surface and he immediately set for the shore, all weariness forgotten. Cole paused in waist-deep water, taking in the battle before him.

His unit fought with such savagery that he quickly realized why Lileth had wanted him out of the way. Storn and Sitra were back on their feet dashing about like a pair of dervishes made of Rage and claws. Lileth and Valen attacked from the sky, diving on the heads of the beasts with their immaterial wings. Besides the missing horn, none of the Domina appeared any worse. They didn't even seem tired. The largest had recovered its mace and was swinging it in great sweeping arcs, the air humming with each miss. It was terrifyingly nimble for such a massive creature, dancing with the mace as if swinging a pillow. The unit worked in unison, never focusing on one enemy or staying in one spot for more than the blink of an eye. Valen sprayed a gout of fire directly into one of their faces while Lileth assaulted another with a volley of snapping lightning bolts. The magic surged with deadly force, but only seemed to slow the Domina momentarily. They were simply too massive.

Cole watched with bated breath, wincing whenever the Domina landed a blow, which became more frequent as the fight wore on. Eliza was now fully active in the fight, playing her role as healer. Each time someone was struck by horn or claw, she would appear from nowhere, healing light pouring from her hands before she vanished in a splash of sand. Lileth and Valen landed on the shoulders of the one-horned Domina, driving their claws as deep as they would go into the creature's head. Their munisica had little effect, other than anchoring them to the beast's shoulders. Unable to detach themselves, they each felt a full blow of the colossal mace. Eliza appeared in a flash, tending to their broken bodies.

After a few minutes the battle had shifted entirely. The group was no longer landing any hits, and the Domina had somehow healed from the ones they had landed. Sitra and Storn rolled and dove in an attempt to create space. Each time they dodged a mace or claw, they found their backs facing another attack. The unit was trapped in a circle of hooves and teeth. The wicked mace whistled through the air, finding a new victim with every blow. Eliza could no longer keep up with the wounded, having to focus on defending herself instead.

The Domina slowed their attacks, ceasing them altogether as the unit wilted before them. They knew their prey was both crippled and exhausted. Now it was time to savor their meal.

Time seemed to slow for Cole as the sound of his heart throbbed in his ears. He swayed on the spot, his mind wandering. He knew where he was, but something about the scene before him was blending with a previous memory. Here he was, a mass murder about to take place before his very eyes, but part of him was no longer on the beach. He was lying in a cold puddle, watching his brother's final moment. Joshy was so sure of himself, holding out his stupid hat as he gazed into Cole's eyes with a knowing grin, as if he knew a secret that would make everything better.

"I know."

"No Joshy!" Cole screamed, tearing himself from the memory. He was back on the beach, but something terrible and powerful began to thaw the Fear that chilled his limbs.

The largest Domina paused, curiosity bringing its murderous glare to Cole. The Domina lowered its mace and spoke in a language that sounded more like a hacking cough than words. One of the smaller Domina grunted in response, stalking over to Cole. As the beast drew near, Cole felt the odd power surge from somewhere deep. The Fear shrank back as something else rose to the surface, anticipating and eager. Without conscious thought, Cole found himself stepping towards the Domina. The beast paused, bemused by Cole's change of behavior. The Domina's fleeting confusion turned to savage pleasure as it tore into a run, bearing down on Cole with Hunger in its eyes. Cole didn't blink or change his course. It pleased him to see the beast charging. They would meet all the sooner and would have an outlet for whatever roiled up inside him. The Domina seemed to take ages to cross the gap. Cole felt as if he were going to explode, like he was a spring coiled to its limit. To his fury, the Domina never made it to him.

Just a few paces away, the beast smashed into an invisible wall, a sickening crack sending it bouncing back on its haunches. Its limp body rose into the air, encased in a sphere of shimmering green light. The remaining Domina were similarly affected, thrashing and slipping inside their frictionless prisons. The three orbs came together, joining to form a larger sphere with all three Domina inside. It was then that Cole noticed a tall figure descending from the sky, silhouetted by Oberon's chromatic hues.

Chiron landed softly on the beach, ignoring the three monsters' roars of protest. He swept over towards Cole, who was now shaking in silent fury, barely able to contain himself. The power was still rising.

"Release it, Cole," Chiron said in a voice as calm as a summer breeze.

Cole couldn't respond. He could barely hear Chiron at all. An overwhelming destructive desire was taking hold, searing him from head to toe. He needed an outlet, to unmake, to kill.

Chiron's voice sounded as if it were a mile away. "Release it, or it will destroy you."

He could hold it no longer. The old Aenerian would have to do. Vision flashing red and black, he lunged at Chiron, seething fury pounding through his veins.

Cole suddenly found himself lying on his back with no memory of how he got there. Chiron leaned over him, a hand on his chest. Cole's skin was boiling hot, as if he were just pulled from a fire. Steam rose from his clothes as he gasped for air.

Chiron smiled, taking his hand off Cole. "That's better I think."

Cole sat up, tearing his cloth armor off. His skin was cherry red and painful to the touch. He dove headfirst into the water, the relief immediate. He could almost hear himself sizzling under the water. Climbing back onto the beach, he saw Chiron helping the others to their feet. Cole walked around the imprisoned Domina, not daring to get too close as they wailed and thrashed against each other.

"Thank you, Master Chiron." Storn rose to his feet, his crippled leg having just been restored.

"Think nothing of it, my dear Storn. I hope you managed to land a few hits before your leg was taken out of the fight." Chiron then turned to an unconscious Valen, running a hand along his body, amber light beaming into the open wounds.

Valen's eyes popped open. He sprung drunkenly to his feet and assessed the scene before him. "Wise One…" He bowed his head low.

Chiron set a steadying hand on Valen shoulder. "If I had been a bit wiser your unit would not have met such misfortune. Speaking of, you are one short by my count. Where is young Deekus?"

"Ask the Underkin." Valen jabbed his chin at Cole.

Cole hid behind Eliza, who graciously stepped aside to reveal him. All eyes were upon him.

"What has befallen Deekus?" Chiron asked.

Cole paused as guilt coated his heart. He felt somehow responsible for Deekus's death. "I only got three gratia stones from the sea bed, so Deekus went to the deeper waters to try for an omnistone." He faltered, stomach churning with horror as he pictured what he thought was a tentacle coming out of the coral. "He...he got sucked into the coral. He's gone. He's dead." Cole pulled at his hair, wringing salty water down over his eyes. "I should have gotten more gratia stones. I was too tired and scared to go down again. It's my fault Deekus is dead."

Chiron shut his eyes, turning his head as the grief stung him. Cole noticed once more the thick ropey scar that ran up Chiron's neck. "Cole, I assure you, not one of us here would blame you for Deekus's death. He was one of the most capable of our students, but he was young and in this case, foolhardy. This was an extreme situation, and not even I imagined that you would be the one to go for the gratia stones, let alone the omnistones. There was nothing you could have done to save him. I will ask something of the unit, however. Why was young Cole the one to go to the bottom? He is the least experienced of you and posed the greatest risk."

Everyone dropped their eyes to the sand.

Valen stepped forth, holding his head high. "The spells required to keep one alive at such a depth were too taxing for one of us to maintain while also retrieving a stone. The Underkin is inept with all forms of magic, though his smaller frame was easier to enchant. After three stones he refused to go back for another. Deekus claimed that he could reach the omnistones by his own power, though we originally decided against it as the risk was too great. Both Deekus and the Underkin knew the risks and agreed to everything before we started.

It was a good plan, and it worked well enough until the Underkin deviated from it."

"And now, do you think that your plan was the best course of action?" Chiron asked.

"At the time it was the best we could come up with," Valen replied, holding Chiron's piercing gaze. "Our plan was sound. The Underkin's actions were not."

Chiron's eyes sharpened, holding Valen's for a moment longer. "I think it's time we return to The Sill. Gather your things, and let's not forget the gratia stones that you worked so hard for. Grieve on flight, for when we return we will discuss these events in detail." Chiron paused as a drawn-out, whining moan came from the Domina behind him. "Ah, I almost forgot our friends here."

Sandy cape flapping behind him, Chiron twirled and approached the imprisoned Domina. The beasts groaned in their orb, but appeared to have finally tired themselves out. Chiron opened his palms, closing his eyes as a pacified smile spread across his face. The spherical prison filled with an occlusive white smoke. Bursts of snowy lightning outlined horns and hooves, as well as the unmistakable figures of Aenerians.

"Grotton's promises are not so sweet now, are they?" Chiron then lowered his head and clapped his palms to the sphere. "I release you."

Cole stepped back a few paces, snatching his dagger from the sand. Surely Chiron wasn't about to set those monsters free? Cole watched in awe as a playful barking came from the cloudy sphere, followed by what looked like three wolves that dropped to the ground below. Each was the size of a horse and their coats were made from moss instead of fur.

"I hope next time your pride is not so easily purchased." Chiron warned them, "Off with you now, before the others come out."

The wolves scampered down the beach, nipping at each other's tails. A moment later the sphere flashed as a trio of massive creatures crashed into the sand. They had horns that twisted around their stony skulls before jabbing out in front of their wrinkled snouts. Leathery skin hung loosely over bulging muscle. Their front arms were short with curved, spade-like claws. Broad hooves on their rear legs looked perfect for pushing them through any terrain. These creatures were not happy or playful like the wolves. They had a murderous air about them, arching their spiny backs as they made a line for Chiron.

"You are livid of course," Chiron said, still smiling. "If you wait but a moment, the ones who betrayed you will be at your mercy."

The creatures stopped, looking to one another before the largest one snorted and sat back on its hind quarters. The two smaller ones followed suit. The smoke cleared in the green orb, revealing three naked Aenerians, one man and two women. Fear painted each of their faces as they struggled to remain upright in their slippery prison. Chiron dropped his arms and the sphere vanished as they fell to the sand.

"I hoped that we would have progressed beyond Grotton's temptations, but you three are shining examples of our darker impulses." Chiron measured the three Aenerians with a sour look. "You disgust me."

"Please don't kill us!" said one of the females, dropping to her knees. The others seemed too scared to talk.

Chiron replied, "I have my flaws just like any other, but I do pride myself to say I don't make a habit of murder, even when a situation warrants it."

Relief flooded the woman's face. "Thank you, Wisdom Walker. Thank you!"

Chiron ignored her. "But I cannot speak for your recently freed slaves. I wonder, do you think it murder if a creature is merely hungry? Carnivores need to kill in order to survive, it's only natural. But I suppose one could argue that by walking away, I could be held accountable to some degree, for these hungry orrix will surely do you in." Chiron bit his lip, shaking his head. "Ah, this moral conundrum is too twisted for my weary mind. What I will do is strip you of Grotton's gifts and let things sort themselves out. What do you think?" Chiron asked the horned beasts beside him.

The three orrix stood, stalking with deadly determination towards the three naked Aenerians.

"Well there you have it." Chiron clapped his hands together. "Valen, when your unit is ready, take them back to The Sill. Do not delay however. The area is safe for now but our borders are tenuous at best. Wait for me at the necropolis."

"Yes, Master Chiron," Valen said with a solemn nod.

The group gathered their things and made for the sun lily leaves. As they flew from the beach, Cole looked over his shoulder to see the three orrix circling around the naked Aenerians. Morbid curiosity held his gaze as he watched. One of the women made for the water. Cole had to look away as one of the creatures caught her with its horns, making quick work of her bare flesh with its claws. Cole winced, shutting his eyes as her screams tore into silence.

Giving into exhaustion, Cole fell asleep for the majority of the trip back to The Sill. Woken by a turbulent shudder, he inched closer to Storn. "Where do you think Chiron went?" Cole asked as their leaf skimmed over the treetops of The Sill.

"He flew out over the reef where we were. I'd say he went to get more gratia stones," Storn called over the wind, putting a protective arm around Cole.

"We're meeting him at the necropolis, you dumb animal!" Sitra called from her leaf, gliding up beside them. "He's gone to get Deekus's body."

"That was my next guess," Storn said, shooting an angry glare at Sitra.

"But that's dangerous," Cole yelled over the tearing wind. "Chiron might get sucked into the coral just like Deekus did. He shouldn't have gone alone."

Storn shook his head dismissively. "Nah, it's Chiron. He'll be fine."

The shock of battle began to fade, leaving Cole drained like a wrung-out rag. He felt numb, yet deeply disturbed. He spent the rest of the trip trying to empty his mind, but thoughts of his last moments with Deekus kept swimming to the fore of his mind. A burning question kindled within him as well. What was that odd power he almost loosed on Chiron?

The sun lily leaves slid to a halt in a grove that lay in one of the farthest corners of The Sill. The spot was the highest point within the towering walls, though a pond somehow rested at its center. The Necropolis didn't look like any graveyard Cole had ever seen.

The shallow pond glowed a vibrant cerulean, seemingly from the water itself. Lavender flowers blanketed the surface in island clusters, swirling around in little eddies. Bearded moss hung from the arms of willow trees that dotted the pond, glowing with the same cool hue as the water below.

Following Storn, Cole stepped off the leaf and hopped into the water. The lavender flowers swam away as they sloshed through the chilly pond. As they approached the center, two figures appeared from behind curtains of glowing moss.

"Greetings, Masters Roth and Alvani," Valen said, pushing his way towards the fore of their group. "I assume you heard of our loss?"

Roth scanned the unit, counting them with his eyes. "Chiron just said one of you had been hurt, and told us to meet here. I knew one of you must have gone for the omnistones. Which one was it?"

"Deekus. The Underkin claims to have seen his demise." Valen sighed, interlocking his fingers behind his back.

"Deekus huh? Thought he was one of the smart ones of your group. Damned fool," Roth growled.

Valen nodded in agreement. "He was confident, perhaps too much so in this case. He was also our best healer. Our unit is diminished without him." Cole couldn't help but sense that Valen was more concerned with the efficacy of their group than the loss of his friend.

Roth crossed his thick arms. "You'll adapt. I've seen units take a hit before. Someone else will pull up the slack, they always do. You all should be proficient with Passion anyway. That's the whole point of what we do at The Sill. You're supposed to do what we couldn't during the last war. Isn't that right, Master Alvani?"

Alvani cut past Roth without responding. She continued through the rest of the unit to a spot several yards behind them, where Eliza sulked in quiet tears. White robes billowing in the water, Alvani wrapped her arms around Eliza in a motherly embrace. Up until this moment Eliza had appeared to be holding it together, but as Alvani embraced her she came apart at the seams, sobs taking and shaking her whole body. Alvani dropped into the water with her and whispered something into her ear.

Roth, who appeared entirely unaffected by the display, kicked at a flower that got too close. "At least the girl wasn't bonded to him. She'd have a scar like Chiron's. That's if she even survived the ordeal. Speaking of, where is the Wise One?"

"We believe he is retrieving Deekus's body," Valen said, frowning with a question. "Master Roth, are you aware that there are Domina not far from The Sill? Our unit encountered three of them not an hour ago, each with two thralls."

Roth erupted with savage laughter, flecks of blood dropping from his bladed hair into the water below. "I am intimately aware. The unit I was training out by the barrens happened upon a pack of Domina that were triple-thralled. I tried to give the whelps a fair crack at them, but their Fear swallowed their Rage. I had to step in after one of them lost an eye. Felt good though. Hadn't killed a real enemy in far too long. Almost thought I'd forgotten how to, but the motions came back soon enough." Roth examined his munisica, seemingly admiring how the light glinted off the shiny surface. "Turns out, with enough force anything made of flesh comes right apart." His thundering laugh hammered their ears. "How did your unit fare? You better have felled at least one of them, seeing as they were only double-thralled."

Valen swallowed, raising his chin a little higher and looking past Roth. "We fought with munisica and magic, but in the end we were outmatched. Deekus's absence was painfully apparent after a few minutes. Chiron saved all our lives, then stripped the Domina of their thralls."

Roth bent down, washing his munisica in the water. "Sounds like you did better than the whelps I had. What did Chiron do with the Aenerians and their thralls? I suppose he held a fancy dinner and told them all to play nice from now on?"

"Master Chiron stripped the Aenerians of their magic. The thralls were then left to do as they pleased with their former masters." Valen gave Roth a grim look, implying the fate of their foes.

"Now that's the Chiron I remember!" Roth growled. "He wasn't always so diplomatic. It sets a hearty fire in my blood to see he still remembers the finer points of well-placed violence. Still, I would have killed the whole lot, thralls and all. Weakens the herd you know, to release those animals back into the wild. If they were stupid enough to fall for Grotton's filth then they'll do it again."

"Of course, Master Roth," Valen said, bowing his head in agreement.

Roth approached Valen, bending down so that their eyes were almost touching. Valen shrank back, averting his eyes. Roth's lips twitched to a toothy smile before he stepped forward, pushing Valen aside with his bulk. He then interviewed each member of the unit, asking questions regarding tactics and techniques used during their skirmish. He awarded little praise and his criticisms cut to the core. He passed over Eliza, who was now staring glassy-eyed at the sky as Alvani cradled her, singing softly. Roth stopped in front of Cole, who looked up into the giant's face.

"Your dagger." Roth held out a claw.

Cole drew his dagger and placed it handle first into Roth's black hand. The hilt clinked as it struck.

"Still unused," Roth said, smelling the blade. "We'll find you something to stick it in soon enough."

"Thank you, Master Roth," Cole said, though he had no desire to do any such thing.

Roth's face softened almost imperceptibly. "You saw Deekus at the end?"

"Yes," Cole replied, bringing his head to the side.

"First time you've seen someone take their last?" Roth asked.

Cole paused, anchoring his mind away from the cobblestone alley. "No."

Roth splashed to a knee and dropped his voice to a rough whisper: "I'd like to tell you it gets easier, but it doesn't. We're at war. Deekus won't be the only friend you see take his last. My advice? Stop making friends." Roth stood and walked away from the group, eyes to Oberon.

Cole swayed. He was exhausted in more ways than he knew. He felt a hand on his shoulder. Lileth held out a water skin. He accepted, thankful that the container was made for someone much larger than him, as he was able to drink his fill without draining it. The liquid wasn't water, but it was refreshing. When he filled his stomach to bursting, the bag still had plenty and his limbs no longer shook. She gave him a comforting squeeze on his arm, nodding towards the sky behind them.

The unmistakable silhouette of Chiron appeared in front of Oberon, clear cape flowing like liquid glass. In his arms was a body, which could only be Deekus. The glow of the pond illuminated them as they descended past the bearded willows. Deekus was fully clothed and looked as if he were merely sleeping. Eliza stood abruptly, no longer crying. She donned a look of calm acceptance as she left Alvani's embrace and made for Chiron. The floating lavenders swirled about the Wisdom Walker, following him like eager sailboats. The petals flowed up his cape, giving him the appearance of wearing a garden on his back. He stopped, offering Deekus to Eliza.

"Thank you, Master Chiron," she breathed.

Chiron deposited Deekus's body into her arms, placing his own arms around her shoulders. He kissed her twice upon the brow before she waded out into a spot devoid of trees. Cole followed the group as they circled around her. Eliza knelt and dipped Deekus gently into the water. She gripped his shirt to hold him afloat, fist trembling as fresh tears fell to his chest. Breath shaking, she steadied herself before letting him go. Eliza retreated, careful not to disturb the floating lavenders. The group circled close as the lavenders sailed in between their legs. Eager to reach Deekus, they bustled over him, blanketing his body from his serene face to his bare toes.

Cole expected someone to say something, but the only eulogy was from the distant song birds whooping in the eternal night. Unsure of what to do, Cole watched the flowery heap before him. It seemed appropriate, so he perused his memories of Deekus, which didn't take long since he'd barely known him. What little memories he had were good ones though. From the first moment they'd met he had shown him nothing but kindness, and thanks to him Cole had a better understanding of Wisdom. He made a silent promise to Deekus that he would heat up some rocks all on his own.

"What is that? In the sky, something's wrong." Valen pointed his hand up towards the stars. Pulsing orbs of every color dropped from the stars, pouring down in shoals through the bearded willows. They appeared to dance and chase each other, but there was no doubt they were headed towards their group.

"Nothing is wrong, my dear Valen." Chiron said, his face lit with adoration at the approaching orbs.

"Then what is it?" Valen asked, unconvinced.

Alvani responded, a smile audible through her words, "Something that has not occurred for an age."

Even from a distance Cole knew what they were. He had seen them in his dreams back on Earth. He had led them through the river, upwards and onwards to Aeneria. Seeing them now was almost like seeing old friends.

Alvani turned to Cole, giving him a knowing smile before addressing the group. "Open your eyes and your hearts. You are all in for a quite the treat. The soul flies have returned."

The flowers covering Deekus had begun to flap slowly, giving them the appearance of a carpet made of butterflies. Everyone peered through the branches, craning their necks to get a better look. Roth, Alvani, and Chiron sat themselves in the water. A single ball of light tinkled down the nearest tree, bouncing off every branch as if on purpose. It rapidly flashed through several colors, seemingly unable to make up its mind. Plopping atop the water, it rolled towards Deekus's mound of flowers. The petals quickened their pace as the soul fly hovered itself inches above the mound, settling on a royal blue and shrinking slightly. Without warning the orb shot straight up, disappearing in the river of lights that had collected in the sky above. Eliza let out a disappointed sigh, then drew a sharp breath as teeming hundreds of soul flies rained down around them. They were all the same shade of royal blue.

Most swam with the flowers, rolling and weaving under tree roots and over the water. Others floated about Cole and the others, coalescing around them as if they were inside a freshly shaken snow globe.

One of the flies stopped before Cole, presenting itself before his eyes. Cole felt profound grief rise up from deep within him, grief he had been actively suppressing nearly every moment since his arrival. The pain was crushing, his breath coming thin and weak. It was too much. All at once he felt the weight of his sorrow from losing Joshy, as well as how much he missed his mother and Nana Beth. He mourned too for Lexy, and his heart ached for Habbad and everything the Underkin had been through. He didn't realize until now how much Deekus really had meant to him. The sorrow stacked up and threatened to break him under its weight. Cole wished for a release. Even death must be better than such infinite sadness.

As if in response, the soul fly nudged Cole's nose. He rested his forehead against the orb, which hummed softly, soothing him as it pulled his sadness from him. Where each puddle of grief stood in his mind, warm comfort quickly replaced it. Cole felt guilty for giving the soul fly so much misery and tried to pull it back, but the soul fly beamed a deeper shade of blue and willingly took the rest. Cole wiped his tears on his sleeve before reaching out and caressing the orb, conveying every ounce of his gratitude through the touch. The soul fly bobbed away from him, joining the others that swam over Deekus's body. Cole looked around. The rest of his group appeared to be having a similar experience.

Eliza interacted with her own soul fly. She leaned forward, kissing the azure ball as a tear rolled off her cheek, smacking into the water. The soul fly bumped her on the chin before scooting down towards Deekus, who was now accompanied by dozens of the rolling orbs.

The petals danced faster, as if they longed to take flight. The soul flies swirled around, touching each flower and soaking them with a dab of liquid blue light. When each flower had been saturated, the orbs rolled off, forming a circle around the unit. The lavender flowers ceased their flapping and started flickering, each a slightly different shade of blue. Thin, wiry roots spread from their bellies, wrapping and crawling over Deekus. One by one the group backed away from their friend, giving the flowers more space as they continued their work. The flowers rose above the water, pushed by their roots, which were now forming a solid trunk. Deekus was no longer visible as a tree took shape above his body. The tree grew until it was larger than any in the pond. Soul flies jumped up its branches, chasing each other as they abandoned their sad blues and adopted happier colors.

Alvani's voice broke the silence: "Storn, would you be so kind as to hand me that gratia stone in your bag?"

Broken from his trance, Storn shook his head. "Yes, of course Master Alvani." He handed her the stone with a solemn bow.

Alvani took the clear stone in her hands. "Master Chiron, I think Deekus's tree a fine place for this stone, don't you?"

"I couldn't agree more, Master Alvani," Chiron replied, smiling through the grief that tugged at his features.

Alvani approached the tree, stroking the base of the trunk as a gap appeared in the bark. She placed the stone inside, the bark closing around it, leaving a portion exposed. She then touched the gratia stone with her fingertips, depositing pink Passion into it. She stepped aside as Chiron gifted his own golden Passion, mixing it with the pink. Roth approached next, thudding an un-bladed fist against the gratia stone. His white Passion swirled with the gold and pink.

Each of the unit took a turn giving Deekus their final gifts. The tree acquired new growth with each deposit. Branches thickened, roots crawled, and newborn lavender flowers fell to the water, chased by the soul flies. Cole approached the tree last. He wasn't eager to revisit the cobblestone alley, but for Deekus he would. It was the least he could do. Cole knew he couldn't reach the stone, but Lileth was there in an instant.

"Be careful," she said, lifting Cole from the water.

He placed both hands flat against the warm stone. He searched his mind, stepping into the cobblestone alley. It was easy to put himself there, as all he really had to do was stop actively suppressing the memories. This time was different, however. He no longer felt the crushing agony of loss, or the twisting guilt. He only felt his love for Joshy. He immersed himself in it, bathing in its fraternal glow. The love he felt for his brother was not exclusive, this was the same part of him that loved his mother and Nana Beth. He measured his relationship with Deekus and found that he could give this part to his friend as well. He focused his love, his Passion, willing it into the stone.

"Not so much, Cole. You'll overload the stone," Lileth whispered into his ear. She set him back down into the water. "I think the soul flies like you."

Cole backed away, eyes squinting at the sight before him. Every soul fly in the necropolis was upon Deekus's tree, which now stood head and shoulders above any other. Hundreds of soul flies rested in the branches, or floated after the falling lavender petals.

"Masters, what do you make of all this?" Storn asked, directing the question to all three elders. "The soul flies returned, the barrier gone, The Three crossing over to our side. These are big changes."

"Big changes indeed, Storn." Alvani caught a falling flower in her delicate fingers. "We don't believe these events are merely coincidence. Dark times are fated for us all. We must stand united so that we do not fall into the same traps as before."

"Even we elders will have to bend our nature to adapt," Roth growled. Flowers landed in his bladed hair, giving him a terrifyingly beautiful wreath on his bloody head. "It does no good to have the strength of a mountain if you fall prey to Hunger and Fear. All three fires must burn within each of us. When one is snuffed out, the others must burn all the brighter." Roth sneezed, scaring a few nearby soul flies with the concussing boom. "I say this, but I must admit that I revel at the chance to use my Rage against our enemies. As should all of you."

"Rage certainly has its place, Rothael," Chiron agreed, gazing at a few garnet soul flies looping around his head.

Cole suppressed a shameful feeling that cropped up from somewhere behind his curiosity. How much was he to blame for all of the evil that now plagued Aeneria? He destroyed the barrier, which allowed the Domina to cross over. If Chiron hadn't been distracted by the Domina by the lagoon, he would have been able to watch over Deekus and save him. He even felt he was somehow responsible for the return of the soul flies, which were probably even now being tortured and fed upon elsewhere.

His curious guilt was interrupted by a sudden change in the soul flies. All at once, the glinting orbs fell from Deekus's tree. Hundreds of them swirled around the base, rising gradually back towards the stars like a tornado made of rainbows. The river formed again. Cole could see the dust drifting from them as they shot up into the sky. The glittering substance formed a hazy cloud high above, drifting slowly and steadily towards Oberon, which was blazing anew with fresh hues.

CHAPTER 18

REUNITED

Deekus's death left Cole diminished and withdrawn over the next few weeks. His guilt mingled with his longing for home, sinking him into a quagmire of his own dark thoughts. After lessons he would retreat to his room and sleep in hopes of waking up back on Earth. Not only did he wake up in his tree every time, but he didn't even dream about Earth anymore. The demanding lessons consumed his waking hours and spilled over into his sleeping thoughts. Cole made infrequent progress, though it never seemed to amount to anything besides the occasional happy accident.

With Chiron's guidance he developed a tenuous level of control over his Wisdom, though the lessons never got any easier. Chiron assaulted his mind so often that Cole eventually stopped resisting altogether, which left him mentally raw and drained for the rest of the day. The hard part was determining when Chiron was inside his head. The elder had a way of disguising his presence as one of Cole's own thoughts, tantalizing and distracting Cole while stealing memories or taking control of his limbs. Cole would have given up on the school if not for one aspect that worked with increasing reliability. He kept two stones on his bedside table. Most nights, if he wasn't too tired, he was able to shift a bit of heat from one to the other.

Roth's lessons increased in brutality as Cole proved himself little by little. Roth had them fight each other, hunt wild animals, move immense objects, and even fight him. Each lesson only served to remind Cole that if he were ever confronted by an actual threat, he had best run away or have a few friendly spell-casting giants nearby. Despite his relative physical handicaps, Roth never give him an inch of tolerance for his small size. He would hit Cole with the same force he used on everyone else. If it crippled him or broke his internal organs, then it gave someone else a chance to use their Passion to heal him. Though the physical training hardened him into better shape, Cole was unable to summon any form of Rage. He remained just as delicate as the day he arrived. But he would definitely make first cut in basketball tryouts at the very least.

Alvani's lessons always followed Roth's, the reason being that the students often nursed terrible injuries that required her expertise. Her lessons were most welcome after Roth's, and Cole took to Passion a little easier than the other schools. He may not have been able to heal so much as a scratch, but he was bonded with Goran, something no one else had achieved save for Alvani and her Gale.

In the evenings when alone in his room, Cole was not entirely alone. He spent a good amount of time experimenting with his bond with Goran. He found he was able to communicate certain things with his friend, such as brief thoughts and feelings. Goran even initiated the communication sometimes, presenting Cole with a kill he was proud of. Cole didn't recognize the creature, but it seemed much larger than something a twenty-pound animal should be able to take down. Goran was different somehow, as if there were more of him.

Eventually the novelty of a magical city full of aliens wore off entirely. To break up the monotony of his routine, Cole stopped by the markets on the way back from his lessons. Most of the merchandise was unidentifiable, and the locals scoffed at him at every turn. Cole had never known what it was like to be the target of bigotry. It didn't bother him overmuch as the prejudice was founded on the premise of him being an Underkin, though it did make things inconvenient. He was denied entrance to certain places and completely ignored when he asked for directions or information. He went to bed hungry on more than one occasion after being physically removed from various establishments. Storn was helpful during lessons, but after hours he was usually too busy to accompany him.

Cole was able to persuade one shopkeeper to sell to him, however. The rude man at the clothing store had him duck in after-hours so Cole could pick up food and supplies, to include a straight razor and a mirror that could stretch to almost any size. He could feel scraggly patches of stubble running wild over his cheeks, and could only imagine how foolish he looked.

One evening after shaving his face he set his mirror against the wall and stretched it as tall as he could, examining the rest of his body. Unexpected pride shocked him from his usual melancholy. His belly no longer hung over his belt line. His stomach was quite flat, though he lacked any sort of definition. Overall he thought he looked shapeless. Even Eliza had more muscle than he did, though he conceded that skinny was better than chubby. He twisted, running his fingers over his ribs and protruding hip bones. Had his head always been so large? He thought of Valen and how he looked in his swim-wear. Cole promised himself he would start eating more. Perhaps Storn knew some exercises that would bulk him up.

Along with the clothing store, another place he could frequent without issue was the library. There was no check-out system, but Cole always returned the books he borrowed. He'd never been a big reader back at home, but he found reading through the Aenerian language cypher immensely satisfying. There were dozens of volumes on Aenerian history, but even on an alien planet with all its magic and wonder, the subject bored him into a stupor. Cole mainly focused on the books that depicted tales of ancient heroes and their adventures. One night while curled up over an epic about a Wisdom Walker who single-handedly ended a local planet's war, a soft knocking at his door interrupted him.

Cole shot out of his chair, nearly drawing his dagger before forcing himself into a calm. Roth's lessons had him on edge. If a visitor meant him harm they likely wouldn't announce their presence first.

"Um, Come in?" Cole said to the door.

The door stretched slightly as Lileth's massive head popped through. Her raven hair was freed from its usual bonds and fell in smooth curtains beside her face. She had a broad smile on her face.

"Lileth!" Cole blurted, hastily tossing his dirty clothes into his closet. "What are you doing here?"

"You've lived at The Sill for most of the month, yet every night you shut yourself away," she said, eyeing his personal effects with interest. "I thought I might convince you to see a part of The Sill other than the library and your bedroom."

Cole took a step towards her, smashing his bare foot against his bedpost. With an effort he kept the pain off his face. "That sounds great, really. Do you want to come in and sit?" He pulled out his chair, which might have been big enough to hold her foot.

Lileth eyed the tiny chair, "It is a bit too…cramped in here for me. I shall wait outside for you."

"Right, okay." Cole blushed, pushing the chair with a bit too much force and sending it crashing under his desk. He strode away, attempting to make his blunder appear intentional. "I'll be right out."

"Cole," she said, still smiling.

"Yeah?"

"Be sure to change that shirt before you come outside." The door popped as her head disappeared.

He pulled at the hem of his torn shirt. It was still stained with blood from Roth's lesson earlier that the day. After a quick wash in his laser-shower he pulled out his meager selection from his wardrobe. Unsure of the rules of Aenerian fashion, he decided upon an outfit he had yet to accumulate any stains on.

When Cole emerged from his room Lileth was nowhere to be found. Had she grown tired of waiting for him?

"Up here." She laughed from above.

Cole looked up to see a sun lily leaf descending smoothly from the canopy. Lileth perched herself cross-legged in the center. She wore a flowing dress of chestnut brown, with a silvery chain coiled tight around her arms and waist. Her appearance was a stark contrast to her usual cloth armor and shoulder-cape, especially with the sprig of pine needles she'd fastened behind her ear.

"Where are we going?" Cole asked, jumping out onto the leaf. He wished he knew how to make objects fly. He would like to carry someone else for a change.

"I've seen the look of longing on your face whenever we pass the Arts District. I thought you might enjoy a tour." Her hair whipped behind her as the leaf surged forward. "Also, it is the eve of the house of Allias. We are leaving the house of Pastori tonight and I want to show you our sunrise. It is quite breathtaking, especially now that the soul flies have returned."

Cole was taken aback. Until now no one other than the elders had shown much interest in him. "Thank you Lileth, this means a lot. I don't socialize much outside of lessons. People don't like Underkin around here."

Lileth placed a glowing finger over his boot. Cool relief replaced the throbbing pain of his stubbed toes. "That is true, but they are blinded by their bigotry. Most have never seen an Underkin before. If they looked but a little closer they would realize they have still yet to see one."

"What do you mean?" Cole asked, averting his eyes.

"I've seen you before. Or part of you I should say. You are no Underkin." She gave him a serious look.

"I'm not supposed to tell anyone!" Cole pleaded. He'd be in serious trouble if that secret slipped out. "Roth said he'd break my arms if I said anything!"

"Roth would not want you to reveal your secret," she said, lifting her gaze up to the sky, which Cole only now noticed was slightly brighter. "Since I already know your secret, you are revealing nothing."

"It was the meadow, right? That was you?" Cole asked, remembering his dream back on Earth.

"Yes. I had my suspicions, but after healing you so many times I recognized your essence. You brought the soul flies to that meadow. It was the most wondrous thing I had ever seen, and it came at a time when I needed it the most. I was in a very dark place and my heart was sick. I went into the forest to lose myself forever. Then you came from the sky. You found me in that meadow and gave me a candle to find my way." She locked eyes with Cole, giving him a warm smile.

"I remember you," he said, inching closer. "I remember your eyes mostly. I could feel pain inside them. I wanted to help."

"You certainly did, and for that you have my gratitude. I would not be here today if not for you." Her tone was light, but Cole knew the sentiment was serious.

Silence fell between them. Cole decided now was as good a time as any to breach the subject. "Is that why you keep saving my life? Are you trying to pay me back?"

Lileth's face hardened to an emotionless mask. "I owe nothing to anyone other than myself. I healed you because it was the right thing to do. Any decent person would have done it."

"I don't know much about your magic, but I do know what you did to me was serious. Alvani herself said she couldn't have healed me, and she's a master of Passion. Where I come from, saving a life is a good thing no matter how you look at it. I know it's a touchy subject for you, but I just want you to know I appreciate it." He swallowed and chanced another question: "Why were you able to save my life but unable to heal Valen's arm? I was hurt way worse than he was when I fell from the tree."

"Could you explain how you were able to heal me in that meadow?" she asked.

Cole, thought about it, then shook his head. "No way. I just sort of felt my way through it."

"I thought as much. The arts of Passion are as foreign to me as they are to you. I, too, am trying to feel my way through it." She cast a sideways glance at Cole.

Cole thought she knew more than she was saying. He held his tongue though. He appreciated her company and didn't want to push her away with his prying.

"Do not worry yourself over it," she said, giving him a playful elbow. "Tonight is not a night for learning and heavy talk. Tonight is a night for enjoying yourself. So find some joy, won't you?"

The leaf hissed to a stop on the wet grass outside the Arts district. Fast-paced music thumped under the pale sunrise, instilling Cole with an energy he couldn't explain. The district itself was a maze of tall stone buildings that stood out from the surrounding trees. The variety of colors on display was a welcome change compared to the earthy tones he was accustomed to. Ribbons hung between windows, and paper statues dangled on wires set between the buildings, each lit by tiny gratia stones in their centers. Fat beetles hummed overhead, bombing from tree to tree and blinking acid-green with the music. The people were noticeably friendlier, some even giving him a smile or a nod.

He followed Lileth to an open square where crowds were gathering around two women carrying heavy baskets. Lileth guided him up a set of stairs where they watched from a balcony. Each woman opened her basket and pulled out a long ribbon made of what looked like liquid metal. They walked in a circle opposite each other, their ribbons billowing far behind them, seemingly unaffected by gravity. Without a word they clapped their hands above their heads and their ribbons exploded with magic. One ignited with violent orange flames and the other shimmered into a glinting snake of pale-blue ice. The crowd took a collective step back, not wanting to touch either ribbon. The two women began a dance, still clutching their ribbons. From the balcony Cole thought they looked like a pair of serpents fighting each other. They twisted and jumped to incredible heights, using the entire square as their stage. They ran up the handrail of Lileth's and Cole's balcony, leaving a helix of orange and white dust in their wake.

Lileth tugged at Cole's sleeve. "Come, there is much to see."

Begrudgingly, Cole tore his eyes from the dueling women, admiring their athleticism. "Could we get some food soon?" he asked, remembering his promise to eat more.

"Of course. There are vendors throughout the district. I'm sure we'll find something to your liking," she said before descending the stairs.

They walked through an arched alleyway of flowering vines, passing by a group playing wind instruments. They sang a mournful melody about swimming with your lover under Oberon's glow. Cole was suddenly reminded of Lileth's hands on his bare chest back in the lagoon. The incident was purely professional of course, but he couldn't deny the part of him that had enjoyed the touch. He looked up at her, reveling at how the passing lanterns played across the angles of her face.

They stopped by a few vendors, each selling tasty wares from a cart. Cole didn't recognize any of it and in some cases couldn't tell if it was plant or animal. He experimented with some fried deka seeds, gradually broadening his selections as each treat left him wanting more.

With their appetites sated and thirsts quenched, they wound deeper into the Arts district. Everywhere they went people were creating something. There were Aenerians with charred faces and heavy aprons working with molten glass and metal. They passed a set of podiums on which people stood and took turns speaking in rhymes.

They couldn't go more than a few minutes without finding someone slouched over a tree branch or leaning against a building, rolls of parchment scattered around them as they put quill to paper. In another square towered an ornate ruby obelisk. Passersby would stop on a whim to pick up a leftover tool and climb up to a naked spot and start carving.

"People may stop to work on the obelisk for a few minutes or a few months, depending on what they are feeling," Lileth said, seeing the questions burning in Cole's eyes. "There is one woman near the top who has been there my whole life. No one knows her name, though it has become customary to bring her food and clothes."

Just as with the duelists dancing with fire and ice, Lileth had to pull Cole away from the sight when he picked up a chisel. Half dragging him from the square, she meandered onto a rooftop walkway, leading them towards a source of peculiar lights and sounds. The rooftop path brought them to the edge of an amphitheater which sat below them in descending concentric circles. In the middle was a stage filled with actors in plain white robes, working through their scenes. There were people scattered about, sitting on pillows and gazing not at the actors, but every which way, as if they saw things Cole couldn't. The entire theater was covered in a thick amber cloud. Voices and lights exploded from the haze at various spots, though they seemed muffled and distant. The spectators were enthralled, gasping, laughing, or crying out in unison. Cole couldn't figure out what was so interesting. The actors seemed like they were doing a decent enough job, though no one was looking at them and they didn't say a word.

Lileth walked over to a rack set on the edge of the theater. She pulled off a pair of beaded necklaces, offering one to Cole. "Here, put this on."

"What are they even doing down there?" he asked, clasping the necklace behind his head. "That's the most boring play I've ever seen. You can't even hear the actors."

Lileth raised an eyebrow and gave him a wry smile. "Let's see how you feel after the show." Without warning, she hopped sideways off the ledge.

Cole swore, looking for a safer way down. The drop was about twice as tall as he was. During Roth's training he sometimes jumped from greater heights, though with varying success. Steeling himself, he lowered himself with his hands before dropping. He landed roughly, rolling into a complete stranger.

"I'm so sorry!" Cole blurted, scrambling to his feet.

The woman appeared not to have noticed, however. She ignored him, looking at the air in front of her, groping at nothing.

"This way, fumble feet," Lileth chided, leading him to a set of pillows close to the stage.

Cole plopped himself onto the pillow, looking up at the actors. The sporadic lights and noises around him were interesting enough, but at this point he had seen enough magic that he knew this would not entertain him for long. He still couldn't hear the actors, despite them being close enough to touch. He didn't want to be rude however, so he sat politely in mock interest and tried to mimic the reactions of the people around him.

"Does this not interest you? Should we retire back to our rooms and shut ourselves away for the night?" Lileth asked with a look of suppressed amusement. There was something she wasn't telling him.

"No! Please, this is great. I've never seen a show like this before." Cole chose his next words carefully, dropping his voice to a gentle whisper: "I'm just not sure what exactly the show is supposed to be. I might be missing a cypher or something, I still can't understand a word these guys are saying."

Unable to contain herself any longer, Lileth buckled over with a belly laugh. Cole's cheeks burned with embarrassment. Seeing the chagrin painted over his face only seemed to make her laugh even harder. Cole felt himself suddenly captivated by her genuine, unrestrained joy. He didn't mind being the butt of the joke as long as he made her happy.

Her mirth settled to a simmer as she reached behind Cole's neck and unhooked the necklace. As soon as he heard the clasp click open, he knew something was wrong. His stomach dropped as if he were falling from a great height. He was no longer in the theater, but on a ship in the middle of a rolling ocean. He squinted as a blazing sun warmed his bare chest.

"Captain, the Galdebrean dogs are nearly on us!" Cole shouted to Captain Rustin from the crow's nest.

"Right you are Master Borneo!" Rustin hollered across the deck as he pocketed his looking glass. "All right boys, just like we planned. Limp the lines and let some slack in the sails. Prepare to surrender yourselves to the mercy and grace of our Queen's navy. Don't you fret now! They'd be as generous a bunch as I ever saw!"

Laughter echoed across the deck as the crew set themselves to sabotaging their own ship. Borneo cut a few guide lines, leaving only a sliver of the rope intact. His heart quickened with anticipation. He loved a good bucket-shuffle.

Cole shut his eyes and held his breath, just as he did when trying to wake himself from a dream. He felt the pillow under him as his wandering hand found Lileth's. When he opened his eyes he was back on the ship, seeing the world through the eyes of a man called Borneo. He closed his eyes again, gripping Lileth's fingers. She squeezed his hand, letting him know he was safe. He opened his eyes again, joining his crew upon the Painted Star.

It was as if Cole were at the movies, though he was living the experience instead of watching it. He guessed they were on Aeneria, though the magic they used was unrefined and crude. They didn't have the traditional three schools, though Cole did recognize when someone used Wisdom to age and weaken the lines for the rudder. Another crew member was clearly adept with Rage, displaying strength and tenacity that Roth would be proud of. Holding tightly to Lileth, Cole immersed himself in Borneo's vision.

The Galdebrean navy approached their ship in a marvelous triple-masted leviathan. There was no way they could outstrip a ship of this caliber, but that was the whole point of the bucket-shuffle. After a feigned heist at the Brineport Trading Company, the crew of the Painted Star fled on their tired old vessel, leaving a breadcrumb trail of jettisoned cargo. The leviathan docked alongside the Painted Star and Rustin's crew surrendered to the Galdebrean navy. Once safely below deck in the brig, Rustin's crew broke their bonds with magic, which the citizens of Galdebreah were not yet privy to.

The majority of the Galdebrean crew was now on the Painted Star, taking inventory of the stolen cargo. They were exemplary sailors. They didn't pocket a single trinket or bauble, even when no one was looking. With only a few lumps and tossed sailors, Captain Rustin's crew commandeered the leviathan. Without the aid of magic, the Galdebrean sailors didn't stand a chance. Captain Rustin was an honest man, especially when it came to dishonest work. Their would-be captors were generally unharmed and left with the crippled remnants of the Painted Star, which was stocked with a week's worth of provisions. The navy would have no trouble limping back to the Galdebrean shore.

With their newly acquired and immensely expensive vessel, the pirates made for Gambit Cove. With such a treasure they would be welcomed as royalty, and partake in wanton debauchery for the rest of the cycle at the very least.

After a hot meal from the galley, Borneo took his spot in the tallest crow's nest, which to his delight was outfitted with a padded floor. Angling away from the sun, the leviathan aimed for the inky skies and eternal night of Aeneria's Dark Side.

An odd feeling roused Cole from Borneo's tale. He felt a pressure on his arm that didn't correlate with what he was doing in the crow's nest. He closed his eyes and felt Lileth's hand on him.

"This is a good stopping point. We should go," she said, snapping Cole's necklace on for him.

"But we're just getting to the good part!" Cole exclaimed. "I want to see what Gambit Cove is like. The boys made it sound so…alive…" His voice trailed off. By 'alive' he of course was talking about the gratuitous revelry, wine, and women.

Lileth's eyebrows disappeared in the locks of her raven hair. "Alive you say? Stay here if you like and see what Gambit's Cove has to offer, or come with me and see what else The Sill has to offer. We've been here for several hours already and Pastori's sun will be rising soon. A sunrise is quite a sight to behold on Aeneria, especially with the return of the soul flies."

"Several hours!" Cole gasped. As if to accentuate her point, Cole's stomach roared with hunger. "Lead the way then, so long as the way brings us by a few more of those vendors."

"Of course." She rose from her pillow with a fluid motion and leapt the height of the wall in a single bound.

Cole stood at the bottom of the wall, judging the height. It seemed much taller from down here. Refusing to ask for help, Cole decided to try using magic to make the leap. He was still hopeless with Rage, so there would be no help there. There was certainly no way to Passion himself up a wall. It would have to be Wisdom. He toyed with the idea of using air to push him, just as he'd created a current of water about him in the lagoon, but he didn't trust the air to hold him. His recent weight loss gave him another idea, however. The idea was simple and he could trust it. Imagining the planet's gravity pulling him not just towards the ground, but to every speck of matter about him, he committed his focus to those connections. He willed gravity itself to ignore him, creating a rule for the universe to follow. Cradling his rule with every ounce of his conviction, Cole jumped.

The speed at which he ascended surprised him. When the ledge flew past his chest he dropped his focus and felt gravity's grip once more. He grappled his way onto the platform, realizing with giddy pride he had just consciously used Wisdom for the first time.

"I worried you were on your way to Gambit's Cove." Lileth's wry smile greeted him as he finished scaling the ledge.

"Did you see? I just used Wisdom to get up that wall!" Cole beamed, peeking over the edge. "No one helped me this time!"

She gave him an appraising nod. "I saw. It was…cute. Before long we'll be shooing you off the tallest of tables."

"Don't laugh! This is a big deal for me! I swear once I figure this stuff out I'll have you flying up in the trees," Cole jabbed in mock-offense. He elbowed her and ran ahead, though he had no idea where they were going.

"Why wait? Let's see what you've learned so far," she jeered, catching up to him within a few strides.

"Ha! That would be hilarious. I don't even want to know what you'd do to me if we squared off. I saw how you fought the Domina.

You were terrifying." He slowed, looking up at her with open adoration. "Who were you in the show? Were you Seive?"

"I was the captain of the Galdebrean ship." Lileth grinned sheepishly, turning away. "You don't get to choose your role in the show."

Cole laughed. "Sorry for cracking you over the head. But in all fairness your crew should have given up by then. Half of you were in the water at that point."

Lileth shrugged. "What can I say, Captain Harmoy was a stubborn man."

His curiosity quickened with his stride. "So what exactly did we experience back there? The arts district is supposed to be full of people who use Passion, but that felt like it was more than just Passion. I was really there, like someone was messing with my mind."

Lileth took his hand and wove them through a crowd, taking them farther from the district's center. "We have our three schools of magic as you well know, but there are ways of combining them. What we just experienced was a blending of Wisdom and Passion. The visions were real memories from real people. The actors on stage orchestrate and refine the temporal impressions of those involved in the event. Their magic crafts a dreamscape for us to see and feel in our minds and in our hearts. Followers of Wisdom perfected the art long ago, but it was the Followers of Passion that saw the potential beauty in it."

"That stuff really happened?" Cole fell silent for a moment, mouth agape as he took it all in. "I… I miss them. My friends on the Painted Star. Are these people still alive?"

"No, they are from a different age," Lileth said.

Cole deflated somewhat, feeling as if his crew had just died. "Then how did their memories get to the stage? Were they passed down through storytellers or something?"

"Pirates care little for others, including their children." Lileth flicked at a paper statue, spinning it on its string. "No, the memories were passed down through books infused with Wisdom. The books in your room have memories and magic embedded in their pages. Not only through the ink but within the words themselves. I could show you how to feel through them, but it is one of those things that are best discovered on one's own."

Cole resisted the urge to run back to his room and peruse his books with magic. "I thought I felt a little something while reading them. Now that I know what it's like, I'll watch out for it. I can't wait to dive back into them."

Lileth smirked sideways at him. "I thought you were enjoying our time together. We can turn in if you are ready to retire."

"I'm sorry. I didn't mean-" Cole sighed as her wolfish grin cut him short. "I need to do a better job of recognizing your humor. You're so serious all the time it's almost impossible to tell when you're joking."

"Me, serious?" she said, a hint of sarcasm apparent this time. "Come to think of it I may have been told that before. Don't go spoiling my reputation." She slapped Cole's shoulder with the back of her fingers. It hurt, but he didn't let her see it. "Do you feel up for a little run? Assuming you can keep up with me, that is."

"Please, I can keep up with you giants no problem. Humans are quick little creatures." He averted his eyes, remembering he was supposed to be an Underkin.

"Human you say? We Aenerians have some human in us as well you know," she said offhandedly.

"That can't be right, can it? I mean you generally look like us but no human has ever come close to your size- hey wait for me!" Cole cried out as Lileth took off at a full sprint.

Cole ran as fast as he could, but Lileth disappeared almost immediately. It felt good to stretch his legs, however. His muscles may not have been augmented with Rage, but his training with Roth had improved his flexibility and strength. Running for his life from time to time had also paid dividends. Between the pounding steps of his feet he tried to encourage his Wisdom to lessen the effect of gravity on his body. It worked only sporadically, however, and threw him off balance more than anything. But the sense of accomplishment was too satisfying to pass up. He flew around a corner and approached the edge of the Arts District, but Lileth was nowhere to be found. Cole wilted, wondering if she really expected him to keep up.

"Don't stop now!" Lileth cried as she somehow came from behind him, passing him with a gust of wind. She slowed her pace enough for him to run just behind her.

She led him up a solitary tree, sprinting up a spiral ramp to the top. Lileth graciously slowed to a walk as Cole's dizzied panting nearly caused a return of his fried deka seeds. The tree swayed excitedly despite the windless evening. The walkway narrowed as they climbed, forcing them to walk slower and closer. The branches thinned as the tree's architecture yielded to a more hand-crafted look. Carvings of tiny moons and stars embellished a polished handrail that led to a structure very similar to a crow's nest at the very top.

"Is this to your liking, Master Borneo?" Lileth asked.

"Very much so, Captain Harmoy. Help me up will you?" Cole raised his hands up like a child as Lileth's strong hands wrapped around his chest, gently lifting him up into the center opening of the crow's nest.

The view was breathtaking. Their tree was tall enough to grant them views of the toothy mountains and shimmering oceans beyond the walls of The Sill. Oberon was radiant as ever, throwing its ever-changing hues over the land like passing clouds. A pinkish glow tinged half of the horizon, teasing the imminent arrival of a rising star. On the darker horizon loomed a sliver of a greenish planet swirled with snow-white clouds. Cole could make out individual rivers of soul flies returning to the local planet, their dust trailing off to Oberon.

"Pastori?" Cole asked.

"The one and only," Lileth said, her voice soft and dreamy.

"It's so green." Cole turned his head, looking from the impending sunrise to the local planet, trying to wrap his mind around the sheer concept of what he was seeing. Something dark below the moon caught his eye. "What's that below Oberon?"

"I'll show you." Lileth brought her fingers together, faint emerald sparks jumping between them and solidifying into a crystalline cylinder. She handed the device to Cole. "Look through the smaller end, and be gentle so you do not bend the light overmuch."

Cole brought the weightless object to his eyes. He squinted and focused until he saw what looked like a tiered wedding cake as dark as space.

"That is Oberon Temple," Lileth explained, twisting and adjusting the tip of the telescope. "The leaders of our race live there. They are called the Celestial Council. One Wisdom Walker for each of the local planets. It is where our knowledge is collected and combed through. The Celestial Council holds court and deliberates over the greater issues that plague Aeneria. All of the Aeneria's sovereignties heed the word of the Council. From what I've heard, your arrival has roused the Council into contention."

"Because I broke the barrier," Cole said, voice darkening.

"That, as well as a couple other flouted rules. Your arrival brought the return of the soul flies, granting strength to Oberon as well as our enemies. You Traveled when it has been, and still remains, impossible for others." She held Cole's eyes with an iron gaze. "You are an anomaly, Cole. I felt it in you when I woke you from death's slumber. There is something very different about you, and I've yet to figure out if it is for good or something else."

Cole pulled his eyes away, looking out to the rivers of soul flies. "All of that stuff was accidental. I had no idea what I was doing. Things just happen around me and I have no say in it. But sometimes I have help," he added, wishing he hadn't said the last sentence.

"What do you mean by that? Who has been helping you?" Her hand pressed on his back.

"I'd rather not talk about it," Cole said, shying away.

Lileth's face softened, however it was clear that she was worried. "Very well then. Should you ever need someone to speak to, I am here."

Silence fell heavy between them, leaving Cole feeling very much alone once again. Even with all the magic and fantastic things happening on Aeneria, he wished he was back home. Back in his ghetto-trash, Tree Street apartment with what was left of his family. Lileth pointed over the wooden railing, drawing his attention to the sunrise.

"It is starting." Lileth whispered, "Look close and see how the light falls upon the peak of Oberon Temple. When that happens we will leave the house of Pastori and enter Allias."

"Will we feel anything?" Cole asked, putting the looking-crystal up to his eye again. He felt a sudden sadness, as though the passing of Pastori brought him one step farther from Earth.

"Not a thing. We are not truly here in the first place, and neither will we physically enter Allias's realm." Her eyes snapped wide as she pointed once more. "There, the temple. Do you see the light?"

With the aid of Lileth's magic lens, Cole saw a faint beam of light fall from Pastori's rising star. Cole held his breath as the beam fell steadily towards the peak of Oberon Temple. Lileth took the lens from his hand just as the beam touched, which was a good thing. As the beam struck the temple, a brilliant light exploded from the summit, outshining Oberon and even the rising star. As quickly as the light flared, it was gone, leaving the world in supreme darkness. Every single star had vanished, as well as lights from The Sill below. Oberon was a dim ghost, barely visible against the impossible void. Cole couldn't see his own nose. It was darkness as he had never experienced.

"Watch the sky," Lileth said, her voice seemingly magnified in his blindness.

One by one, little specks of light appeared in the void, forming an entirely new starscape across the ebony blanket above them. Oberon woke above them, shining with newborn rainbow hues.

"Welcome to the house of Allias," Lileth said, tossing her crystal lens over the edge where it fell to pieces, clinking down the branches below.

For a moment they held each other with their eyes. Cole suddenly felt not so alone. Perhaps him being here was not the worst thing that could happen. Cole felt other urges as he swam through Lileth's eyes. He placed a hand over hers.

"Lileth...I-" Cole flinched in fright as if someone had slammed a door, though he was certain there was no sound. Lileth reacted as well, though not as severely as he.

"*Lileth, Cole, please come to the Lurkwood Gate as soon as you can.*"

If Cole hadn't been already accustomed to Chiron's presence in his mind, he would have thought he was going insane. The sensation was still unsettling, however.

"We are on our way now, Master Chiron," Lileth said aloud. "What might we expect to find at the gates of Lurkwood?"

Chiron's voice echoed in their minds: *There is someone here who is very interested in seeing our newest initiate. I must beg some haste from both of you. Our guest is most irascible at the moment.*

An abrupt emptiness filled Cole's mind as Chiron left it. His sense of self filled the void like a waterfall pouring into a teacup.

"Goran!" Cole cried out before closing his eyes, his face strained as he focused his Passion. "It's definitely him, he's real close." Cole paused, concern washing over his face. "Why would Chiron get involved with this? Goran's just a little guy, only about knee-high to me. He can be fierce for sure, but I don't see why an elder would find him interesting."

"There's only one way to find out." Lileth said, tightening the bands on her dress.

"Follow me!" Cole said as he readied to drop down to the ramp below. He couldn't wait to see his friend again.

"Chiron's message was urgent. We will fly there instead." Jade wings sparked from her shoulders as the wind kicked up about them.

"Right." Cole turned his back to her, lifting his arms. Nothing made him feel more like a child than being carried like one.

Lileth's grip was gentle yet unyielding. Without warning she planted a foot on the railing, launching the two of them into open air. Cole's stomach lurched up into his chest as they dropped several feet before wind filled Lileth's wings. The Arts District was soon far behind as they darted under and over the branches of passing trees. Though Oberon and the stars had reignited, the lights from The Sill's gratia stones had not, and that left the ground below bathed in shadow. Sooner than Cole expected, they alighted in a whirlwind of dried leaves and dirt. They were at the Lurkwood Gate, the same one Cole had first entered with Roth. The tunnel was already open. Chiron strode barefoot towards them, an ambient white light illuminating the ground about him.

"Haste indeed. If the both of you would follow me." Chiron's voice had no trace of its usual polite cheer. Worry blossomed in Cole's thoughts.

They walked with purpose, guided through the dark tunnel by Chiron's light, empty gratia stones gleaming as they passed. Cole had to jog to keep up, but he didn't care. He checked his bond with Goran, ensuring he was okay. Goran was close, and to Cole's relief merely felt bored.

They emerged from the tunnel to find a train of wagons lined up towards the gate. Sourceless light ran down the trail, illuminating the entire area. A dozen Aenerians bustled in a group near the middle of the convoy. Cole looked down the line. There was no sign of Goran.

"Your arrival is most welcome human, or should I call you Underkin?" Whind's form melted from the nearest tree. He knew Cole's secret as well, it seemed. "As I have been told, your friend has given the caravan endless trouble since placed in their custody. They have restrained him both physically and magically, so that he does not bring harm upon himself or others."

"What are you talking about?" Cole scoffed. "He doesn't need restraining! He's tiny. And I'm pretty sure he was doing just fine on his own." Cole pushed past Whind, ignoring his rebuttal.

He ran down the line to where most of the Aenerians were gathered. They laughed at him as he drew near, joking at his size.

"Get out of my way," Cole barked, elbowing them in the knees.

The Aenerians laughed even harder, though a few moved just enough to let him through. Cole squeezed his way close to the nearest wagon. Sitting in a cage plain as Oberon, was Habbad.

CHAPTER 19

ANGELS AND BURDENS

"Habbad!" Cole jumped up into the wagon, both hands wrapped around the bars of his friend's cage. He found Habbad sitting cross-legged with his feet bound to his hands. "Are you ok? We'll get you out of there in a second," Cole said, his mouth pushed between the bars.

"Oh no we won't! And he can't hear you anyway," said a stout man from the crowd. His sleeves were rolled up over hairy forearms and he wore a black eye patch. He looked thoroughly travel-worn. "That one's been nothing but trouble since your sentries dumped him in our laps. Gave me this," he said, jabbing a thumb towards his eye patch, "and that was after we restrained him for attacking Wendel." He gestured to a chubby boy sporting a thick crown of bandages. "We've blinded his eyes and plugged his ears, but every time we relax some, the mongoose wriggles out of our bonds. Don't matter if we tie him up with magic or with steel. Which one of your lot is taking him? I warn you, you close an eye and he turns to a flaming weasel."

"I'll take him, he's my friend," Cole explained, hopping down from the wagon. "He'll listen to me I promise, just let him out of there."

"Not a chance, Underkin. You'll forgive me if I'm a little less trusting of your kind than I was before this push. Be gone now before I take it out of your hide." He shooed Cole away, hollering back towards the Lurkwood Gate. "Oi! Who's taking the rat? And if you got a healer in your bunch send him our way!"

"How can I assist?" Chiron seemed to appear from thin air, rolling up his own sleeves. "Your eye, sir? And the boy's head I assume?"

"Master Chiron." The man shrank with a stumbling bow. "No-no, please. Trivialities such as ours are not worthy of your attentions. We'll find a healer inside, please don't trouble yourself."

"To help another is a privilege, not a burden," Chiron said, cupping his hand over the man's wounded eye. "No trouble at all my good man."

"Thank you! The honor…Wait till my kids hear about this." The man ripped off the eye patch, blinking and grinning. He looked as if he wanted to say more, but Chiron was already ministering to Wendel's injury.

"Chiron, can you tell them to release Habbad?" Cole interrupted. He ignored the offended looks of the group about him. In Cole's opinion their injuries were less than minor. He himself received much worse during Roth's lessons.

"You may release the Underkin," Chiron addressed the group as he finished with the boy's hand.

The stout man gripped Habbad's cage, shaking it violently and startling Habbad. "It may be wiser to leave well enough alone. Maybe place him inside a proper jail before you undo the magic at least-" The man faltered as Chiron gave him a gentle, yet expectant look, "-but I'm no man of Wisdom so what would I know. Glendail, remove your trickeries from the Underkin."

A tired, aged woman stepped into the light. She shut her eyes and tickled her glowing fingers through the air as though playing a piano. Hands dimming, she opened her eyes, appearing wide awake and years younger. "It is done."

Habbad opened his eyes with steady caution. His face was equal parts Fear and ferocity. Recognition flashed when he found Cole.

"Habbad it's me!" Cole jumped back up onto the wagon, yanking at the bars. "You're safe now, it's okay."

Habbad squinted at his jailers, but otherwise didn't say a word.

The stout man climbed atop the wagon, rocking it back and forth with his girth. "All right you little blighter, I'm going to let you out. Your friends assure me you won't be any trouble. Our orders were to get you here safe, which we've done. The contract's complete. Now, if you so much as make a queer look my way I'll break those nimble little hands of yours. And I'll still get paid," he added in a deadly cheerful voice.

Habbad remained quiet as the lock snapped open and the cage unfolded around him. Apparently he didn't need help with bonds as he twisted his hands, unraveling the cords before throwing them aside.

"Good for you then," the man spat, kicking the rest of the cage flat and knocking it to the deck of the wagon with a clang. "Off you get. May you stub your toes on every rock from here to the Light Side."

Habbad jumped off the side of the wagon, his wrappings tattered and torn, exposing parts of his skin. He was shorter than Cole remembered. "Goran is in the wagon behind me," he said to Cole, jerking his head over his shoulder.

"If you're talking about the mirak, he's ours. Caught him fair and right we did. Biggest one I've ever seen." The stout man hopped down from the wagon, his rotund belly dancing from the impact. "He'll be worth a fortune."

"He *let* himself get caught, you lumbering simpleton," Habbad snapped. "He's only in there because he *wants* to be."

"In where?" Cole asked while running to the next wagon. "Goran!"

There was a loud snort and the wagon rocked. Cole backed away a few paces. In the dim light he saw another cage, much larger than Habbad's. The wagon rocked again and Cole made out a pair of red eyes in the shadows between the bars.

"I told you he's ours." The man stepped forth, illuminating the wagon with a gratia stone lantern.

Thick leathery paws reached from the inside of the cage, wrapping their black claws around the bars. Cole covered his ears as the metal screeched and squealed, snapping and breaking apart. The cage splintered apart with a hammering report. A massive, brindle-patterned form erupted from the wagon, landing with a thud that nearly buckled Cole's knees.

Goran was enormous. Once fierce but somewhat adorable because of his size, he now carried the wild majesty of a tiger mixed with rolling muscles of a gorilla. On all fours he was two feet taller than Cole, but there was no mistaking those sweeping, saber canines or his tufted white mohawk. Roth-sized muscles flexed under his brindle fur, which had receded into his shoulders and forearms, giving way to a stone-like armor. The stout man ran back behind the wagon, reappearing with a bladed pike.

"I don't think that stick will be necessary, or very effective," Chiron said as he approached, illuminating the whole with a flick of his hand. "We will work out the details later, but I will personally pay for the mirak, or as he should be called, Goran."

The man looked from Goran to Chiron several times before relaxing his stance, though he still held onto the pike. "Of course, Wisdom Walker."

Goran ignored everyone else and stared unblinkingly into Cole's eyes. Hulking shoulders bulged as he sauntered close to Cole. He leaned down until their noses touched, Goran snorting hot breath over Cole's face.

"So you're a mirak huh? I always thought you were some kind of weasel," Cole laughed as he waved Goran's breath from his face. "Ugh, smells like you've been mowing on fish again."

"Coo-cha." Goran's voice rumbled like falling boulders. He nudged his velvety nose into Cole's, pushing him back a step.

"It's good to see you again too, Bud." He knew Goran had changed somehow, though he hadn't expected to find his friend transformed into a ginormous monster. Still, Cole was happy to be reunited. He leaned around and inspected the remnants of Goran's cage, which was covered in mounds of peeled fruits and animal bone. Cole smacked Goran on the arm. "I see why you stayed in the cage. All the food you can eat and you don't even have to hunt for it."

Goran nudged him again and grunted, "Coo Cha."

Chiron clapped his hands together and addressed the caravan's leader, "Well then, it looks like everything is in order, with your payment still outstanding of course. The day is late and there are soft beds to be filled. Might I tempt your outfit to stay for a while? We've only just begun to celebrate the arrival of Allias."

Using his pike as a walking stick, the stout man came out from behind the wagon. "Please, Master Chiron. Take no offense but my men and I would rather set up camp along the beach. We've had enough dealings with The Sill to know that we're better off as far away from it as possible."

"No offense taken, my dear man. You'll be wanting your payment now then?" Chiron asked politely.

"The day is late like you said. No need to trouble yourself now. We can square up tomorrow," the man said to the ground.

"Nonsense." Chiron looked down the line of wagons. "Are the omnistones at the head of your carriages acceptable?"

"That's what they're there for," he said, pulling a blanket off the front of the carriage Goran had just vacated. "This one will be just fine, thank you."

Whipping his brick wall cape around his back, Chiron raised a glowing hand. A blinding emerald light grew from each omnistone until the air was thick with energy. The entire caravan erupted with cries of disbelief and gratitude.

"You are most generous, Wisdom Walker!" the man exclaimed.

"That should cover the damage to your cage as well," Chiron said, dropping his hand. "Thank you for delivering our friends safely to our doors. Now, if you'll excuse us."

Chiron walked back towards the Lurkwood Gate. Cole jogged after him with Goran in tow. Habbad trailed reluctantly, scowling at everyone. Both Lileth and Whind stared wide-eyed at Goran's imposing size. Cole stopped before the dark tunnel, noticing that Habbad had stopped several paces behind.

"What's up?" Cole asked in a gentle tone. He didn't like the look on Habbad's face.

"I'm not going in there," Habbad said.

"Why not? This place is great. The Dark Ones are not the monsters they've been made out to be. They've been nothing but great to me since I arrived. Lileth here saved my life twice." The rest of their group stopped now, watching the two of them with reserved interest.

"Well that's funny, because the Dark Ones have been nothing but terrible to me since my capture, in case you couldn't tell by my accommodations on the wagon." Habbad pointed over his shoulder.

"You shouldn't have fought them, they were only trying to help. They were under orders to bring you here where it's safe." Cole could see his words had no effect. "Habbad, this place is amazing. They can teach you all about magic, not just Wisdom but Rage and Passion too.

You'll get your own bed and regular meals, and I've only just started exploring the rest of the city. There's the markets, the Arts District, the dancing gardens. It's the only place I ever felt safe in since coming to this planet. Not everyone is trying to kill you out here, you know."

"And what do they want in return? They extend a sweetened hand of friendship, but there must be a cost. I'll hear it before I enter that gate." Habbad's expression darkened. "I'll not be used or made a fool."

"Well, I'm a student here now, and when my unit is ready I'll be a member of the military," Cole said, pride bolstering him. "The Dark Side aren't working for The Three, they are united against them. We're learning how to fight them and their minions."

Habbad crossed his arms. "What if I don't like how I'm being used? What if I'm assigned to attack a village of Underkin because they're perceived as a resource or merely in the way? My entire race has been taught since birth that the Dark Ones are the true demons of this world. Surely *these* Dark Ones will face my kind sooner or later now that the barrier is down. If I disagree with their tactics would they simply let me pack up my bags and return home?"

Cole struggled to find the words. Habbad made a good point. Chiron stepped forward, hands open. The size difference between Habbad and Chiron was astounding. Habbad only came up to Cole's belly button, and Cole was equally small compared with Chiron.

Chiron squatted low, his cape a carpet of mossy dirt running down his back, merging seamlessly with the ground. "Hello Habbad. My name is Chiron." His voice was kind, but held no hint of tolerance for disrespect. "You stand at the gate of The Sill, an independent city I am proud to call my home. Every person within these walls is of utmost importance to me, and should you enter I would count you as one of them. But before I allow you to enter, we will come to an understanding. I will tell you no lies, nor lay any traps for you to later fall into, but I expect an equal level of honesty from you. Does this sound reasonable to you thus far?"

"Make your case, Dark One." Even though Chiron was crouched as low as he could, Habbad had to crane his neck up in order to maintain eye contact.

"Firstly, I apologize for the rough treatment you received during your travels here. Had I not been so preoccupied with the Domina I would have retrieved you myself. Given the circumstances this caravan was the best we could do to ensure your safe delivery to us."

"I needed no retrieval or saving," Habbad spat. "I was forcibly taken and held without my consent. Where I'm from we call that *kidnapping*."

Chiron donned a pensive look as he brought the tips of his fingers together. "By the trouble you caused the convoy, I can surmise you are resourceful and have some skill with Wisdom. However, I assure you, had you escaped both our sentries and a division of Domina, you would have fallen victim to the wild beasts or environment sooner or later. This is not the Light Side you are accustomed to. We have dangers across our lands that even our most experienced warriors must pay heed to. Your skills, however formidable, would not have been enough to save you from a painful death. That is why I had you brought here with all haste. Now that you are here and safe, we will go over your options."

Habbad turned his head away. "Already I am limited to options."

"Your doom is not as grim as you think. If you choose, you can turn around right now and brave both the elements and the war on your own. From here I could even provide you with quick transport back to your home, where you would be safe, for now…" Chiron stood, setting a hand on Cole's shoulder. "Another option is for you to do as Cole has done and enlist in our military. You will receive training in various schools of magic. You will be roomed, fed, clothed, and your free time is yours to do with as you please. Eventually, when you are ready, you shall be given missions to accomplish with your unit. Yes, these missions will likely be dangerous. We will do what we can to ensure that you are not given a task too difficult; however, war is utter chaos by its very nature. No one is your master here, and should you at any point decide this option is not right for you, no one will stop you from leaving. You may consider the education you receive as a parting gift. I only ask that you use your power to help others from time to time."

Habbad's eyebrows curled with suspicion. "There is no such thing as a free meal. Someone somewhere is paying for it sooner or later. I have a funny feeling that someone will be me, though you won't admit to it now." Habbad pulled a piece of his tattered wrappings off, tossing it aside.

"Feel free to look for the viper in the grass, but I assure you there is none. Unless your morals are vastly different from our common law, then I foresee no issue. Cole is an upstanding and trustworthy person and he vouches for you, so I trust you to act decent and trustworthy as well. Be warned however. Should you leave here and ally yourself with The Three, or cause harm to anyone in my charge, you will answer directly and decisively to me." Standing at his full height, Chiron brought his gaze down upon Habbad, giving him a moment of silence to ponder his words.

Habbad didn't blink or back down, but stared right back into Chiron, who loomed over him like an ancient tree.

Placing a hand on Habbad's shoulder, Cole broke the silence. "Think about it, it all makes sense. Costas is a miserable place and there's nothing there for you. Kreed's after you anyway. I'm growing stronger every day, and if the two of us train as hard as we can I know we can save Lexy before the Devotion. We'll bring her back here and they'll remove Kreed's spells from her. Then if we want, the three of us can go make a new life for ourselves." Goran snorted and punched one of his cinder block fists into the soil. "Sorry, I mean the four of us. We can make it here in The Sill or go out and help fight The Three, but it will be our choice."

Habbad faltered at the mention of his sister. For a split second his wrinkled face twisted as his eyes searched the ground, crazed and pleading. He opened his mouth to speak, but closed it and shook his head. He took a steadying breath and became robotic once again, as if he were never capable of anything other than cold logic. He glared at Chiron. "I can leave whenever I want? You said it, give me your word."

"I have made my intentions crystal clear, my friend. I will not repeat them. Do with my words what you will." Chiron spoke with a firm finality that settled the matter.

"I trust Cole. I will go with him," Habbad said.

"Very well then. Cole, as Storn was your guide you will be Habbad's. I hold you responsible for both his well-being and his actions. Now, I must be off. We have spent too much time with heavy talk. I suggest you both get some rest, I hear Roth has a particularly savage day for you tomorrow." Chiron set off through the gate, gratia stones blazing to life as he passed them.

Cole said his farewell to Lileth, who remained behind to talk with Whind. Though elated to have his friends back, his thoughts wandered amongst the Arts District, reliving the time he spent with Lileth.

The trio arrived at the barracks and entered his room. An additional bed even smaller than his own had somehow appeared in a newly carved-out section. After a broken table and shattered window it became apparent that Goran was entirely too large for the dorm. Goran snagged some food off the table before squeezing himself through the door.

"Where's he going?" Habbad asked.

Cole's eyes followed the cracking noises traveling up the tree. "Judging by the tree's shaking, I'm guessing he's gone to find a nice spot up top to sleep in." Cole closed his eyes and checked his connection with Goran just to be sure.

"Are you finished with your adolescence?" Habbad asked, giving Cole a suspicious look.

Cole paused, his hand halfway to hanging his jacket in the dresser. "That's the strangest question I've been asked in a while, and that's saying something. I'm just about done with it now that you mention it, fully grown and everything. Would you like to have my adolescence when I'm through with it? You'll love the pimples and mood swings." Cole finished hanging his jacket and undressing himself.

"You're taller," Habbad said. He looked Cole over one more time before climbing into his bed. He was asleep before Cole could question him.

Cole woke the next day to find Habbad reading one of his books by mushroom light. Checking his time piece, Cole decided they had enough time to shoot down to the markets and replace Habbad's worn-out clothes before Roth's lesson.

The gratia stones baffled Habbad, and Cole still didn't have a good enough grasp on the concept to explain them properly. With an audible sigh, the tailor, with whom Cole had built a good rapport, stowed his Passion stone and pulled out a dusty Wisdom stone for Habbad. Habbad took to the green stone with confidence. Ignoring Cole's protests about giving up his memories, Habbad filled the gratia stone to the brim. The tailor looked as if his birthday had come early, and he wrapped his burning hot treasure in cloth before stowing it in a safe behind the counter.

"Don't worry," Habbad said to Cole in an undertone. "There are some memories I am better off without." Habbad then turned to the tailor. "That has to be worth more than what I'm getting today. I trust I will have credit with your shop in the future." Habbad gave the tailor a shrewd look, and the man nodded dismissively and started taking his measurements. "That won't be necessary. I'll just take a few rolls of wrappings."

The tailor looked as if Habbad had just insulted his mother. "Then why the blazes would you come to my shop if you are just going to walk out looking the same as when you walked in?"

"Why would a shopkeeper give a well-paying customer a hard time with such a simple order?" Habbad raised a glowing hand and four rolls of dark earthy colors flew from the shelf into his bag.

"I suppose you'll be wrapping yourself then?" the tailor asked, lip curling.

"Very astute," Habbad said, walking out of the shop

"Don't forget a few extra loops around the neck!" the tailor called out as they left the shop, ignoring Cole's apologies. "Wouldn't want that puffed-up head of yours to fall off!"

"Did you have to be so rude?" Cole asked, running to catch up. "It helps to have a few friends around here."

"I'm not here to make friends," Habbad replied, hefting his bag higher on his shoulders.

Cole huffed, "Yeah, I can see that."

They took a quick loop around the rest of the markets, enduring snide remarks and sour looks from passersby. Habbad flat out refused the cyphers, saying he had enough of other people meddling with his mind. After assembling the rest of Habbad's basic supplies they returned to their tree, where Goran had finally woken up. The mirak dangled from a lower branch, yanking it to the ground as eggs fell into his waiting jaws.

Cole showed Habbad how to use the shower, and waited outside with Goran while he cleaned and dressed himself. Habbad emerged, wearing fresh layers of colored wrappings that made for good camouflage. The brown and greens blended well enough with the general foliage of the area and looked to provide a decent layer of armor.

Since Cole was the only one with the cartography cypher, he led the three of them towards the training grounds Roth had specified at the end of his last lesson. The walk was longer than Cole had expected, reaching deep into parts of The Sill that he only knew from the cypher. After half an hour Cole spied the distant figures of Eliza's spiked honey blond hair, and Storn's heroic stance.

"Either the new one is small for an Underkin or Cole's a giant amongst his people," Storn said, and greeted Cole with a bladed fist. "And what's that thing supposed to be?" He regarded Goran, sizing him up.

Unconcerned, Goran sniffed the air for food before slumping back on his haunches.

"That's a mirak!" Sitra jogged up to Goran, her banded braid waggling between her shoulder blades. She placed her hand palm upwards so he could smell her. Since she had no food to offer, Goran didn't show much interest. However, he certainly didn't object to her scratching under his jaw. "He's beautiful. I didn't know they could get this big."

"They don't," Eliza said, joining Sitra in scratching Goran's brindle fur. Goran released an indulgent groan as his back leg started kicking on its own. "He and Cole have a Passion bond, which is responsible for his growth. Mirak are usually a tenth this size." She gave a Cole a suspicious grin. "The bond is reciprocal. If the Mirak has grown this much, then our Cole has grown proportionately. I'd wager he is not the same person he was before he met his friend here."

Feeling Lileth's eyes upon him, Cole dropped his gaze to the ground. "I don't know about all that. Goran's bigger but he's definitely the same crazy bundle of fur and teeth. He might be a bit lazier though." Cole walked up and kicked Goran in the hindquarters. "I don't believe it, he's actually asleep. *Definitely* lazier." He could still feel Lileth's eyes scouring him.

"Who's your other friend?" Eliza asked, giving Goran one final pat on the belly.

"This is Habbad. He and I grew up together in Costas." Cole gave Habbad a serious look, though he didn't really seem to care. "Habbad already has some skill with Wisdom and saved my life a few times. He can be trusted."

He then introduced each of his unit to Habbad. They were polite except for Valen, but that was to be expected. Eliza actually bent down and hugged him with her hands, as he was too small to hug with her arms. Cole could tell that she put every ounce of Passion into the gesture, though Habbad looked as if he'd just been presented with a gift-wrapped pile of steaming manure.

"If you're all through gushing over monkeys and cattle, I suggest you prepare for the task at hand," Valen interjected. "Has anyone heard more on what Roth has in store for us today?"

"I believe the words that Master Chiron used were 'particularly savage'," Lileth sighed as she removed her boots and rolled her sleeves. "I'm sure it will be dreadful."

"It can't be any worse than the time Sitra drew some of his blood," Storn said, drawing munisica from his hands and feet. "It's a good thing Alvani showed up early that day. I don't think my left buttock has been the same since."

Cole remembered the incident all too well, running his hands over his recently healed shoulder bones. They were supposed to be fighting Roth as a unit that day. Lileth had created a phantom image of Sitra, while Valen had made the real Sitra invisible. While Roth was explaining the rules of their impending skirmish, Sitra had dropped from the branch above and struck a fierce blow to Roth's unarmored neck. Cole couldn't remember the rest of the lesson, other than it being short and terrifying. He'd woken up to Alvani's glowing hands and crushing pain in his shoulder.

Sitra laughed with brutal pleasure. "If he were actually angry I don't think any of us would be here to talk about it. If anything I'd say he's never been more proud of us. Too bad I forgot how sharp his hair is. Might have gotten more than a scratch on the old mountain if his hair didn't gut me right from the start."

"You'd be dead before you knew it." Roth's voice thundered from down the trail, startling Cole. He wondered how Roth could hear their conversation from such a distance. Cole thought the Rage must sharpen his ears as much as it did his hair.

"Indeed," Sitra said, swallowing hard.

As Roth approached, the nearby gratia stones illuminated a heavy chain that he dragged over his shoulder. The chain ran straight back towards a sturdy wagon not unlike the ones that had delivered Goran and Habbad, except this one was as large as a building. Sitting atop the wagon was a heavy metal shipping container with barred windows running along the sides. Apprehension infused Cole's imagination as he heard the feral cries of several large animals from the container. The wagon came to a creaking halt as Roth dropped the chain, shaking the ground at their feet.

Without a word Roth stomped over to Habbad, scooping him up in one massive claw and bringing him nose to nose. Habbad looked shaken, but did not struggle. He forced a look of disinterest, pursing his lips and peering off in the distance as if Roth bored him.

"Look at me," Roth growled.

Habbad moved his gaze into Roth's eyes.

"Are you dangerous?" Roth demanded.

"Anyone can be dangerous if properly motivated," Habbad replied. In a flash of movement, Habbad snatched a lock of Roth's hair, placing the point under his chin.

A half-grin pulled across Roth's face as he gave Habbad a squeeze in warning. The air squeaked out from Habbad's little lungs as he dropped the blade of hair and squirmed against Roth's munisica.

Roth licked his teeth, as if tasting the words before he spoke them. "Not bad, Underkin." He released Habbad, who who fell into a half-crumpled heap from twice his height. "Were you briefed on what's expected of you here?"

Habbad rose, unable to hide his grimace. "I am to train and learn your ways so that one day I can aid in the war."

"In a broad stroke, yes. To put a finer point to it, during my lessons I expect nothing less than everything you have. Every bone, every drop of blood and sweat, all of it. Don't hesitate or relent, or I'll take something from you that you'll sorely miss. Easy enough to understand?" Roth's grin stretched to reveal more teeth, as if challenging Habbad to say something churlish.

Habbad straightened his back. "Yes."

Roth considered him for a moment longer before returning to the wagon and pulling something out of a side compartment. "Gather 'round."

The unit formed a circle around him, moving with a bit more haste than usual. No one wanted to be made an example of in front of their newest member. He planted the device between his legs. The thing appeared to be a bronze barrel lined with buttons and knobs. It started buzzing softly after Roth twisted the top off. "Hold out your arms and roll your sleeves unless you want me to ruin your pretty fineries."

Those who had not yet done so rolled their sleeves up to their elbows and held their arms out. A small wave of nausea crashed against Cole's stomach as he remembered the last time Roth had touched Valen's arm. To his relief, Roth walked around the circle and used a separate bladed finger to make a quick dash across each of their naked arms. Concern woke Goran as the mirak shot to his feet and stalked closer.

"Is that thing going to be a problem?" Roth demanded, giving Cole an annoyed look.

Cole opened his link with Goran, impressing upon his friend that they were in no real danger.

"No, I don't think so. He's just curious," Cole lied.

"If he gets a *too* curious I'll make sure he and I come to an understanding," Roth said offhandedly as he approached the wagon.

Worry gripped Cole. He wasn't sure who was more deadly, but he didn't want to find out. "Master Roth, please don't hurt him. He's my friend and doesn't know any better," Cole pleaded.

"I had a mirak as a pet growing up," Roth said without looking at him. One at a time, he placed each of his seven blood-stained claws through the gaps in the bars. The things behind the bars snapped and thrashed, as if fighting to be the first to clean the blood off. "Your mirak is a tad bigger than mine was, but lucky for you I know how to humble him without hurting him."

Cole still wasn't convinced. He held his arm out as Eliza did a quick loop around the unit, healing everyone's cuts with a rosy finger. She looked sullen, and Cole's scratch did not fully heal as he expected. It was very much unlike Eliza to make a mistake with such a simple task. Deekus's death must have hindered her Passion.

Roth came back to the humming barrel, picking it up and passing it to Storn. "Dump a mouthful down your gullet and pass it around."

Without hesitation, Storn tipped the barrel back and handed it off. He smacked his lips, doing a poor job of hiding his confusion and worry. Cole cupped his hands and took his share. It tasted like warm metal. When everyone had their dose Roth took a seat next to Goran, who backed away, snorting as if offended.

Roth tossed a rock at the metal container, causing the beasts within to writhe and snarl. "There are seven bog angels in the wagon. Your task is to evade them for as long as you can. Each one has tasted the blood of one of you. They will track you down and attempt to kill you. Something funny Storn?"

Storn's chest rose and fell with a haughty laugh. "The day a bog angel catches me is the day I become a dancer for the Arts District. They're so slow I could run away with two broken legs."

"That's enough, Storn!" Valen shot him a warning glare, looking cautiously back to Roth as though afraid Storn had just submitted a great idea for the lesson.

"The thought crossed my mind, but for the sake of magical diversity I thought I'd ask Chiron to craft this device for me," Roth said, kicking the humming barrel before him. "By now the elixir should be in every tissue of your bodies. Just as you are each bound to an angel, you are also bound to this thing. When we start I'll make adjustments to the machine which will..." Roth paused, thinking for a moment before shaking his head dismissively. "You'll find out soon enough what the machine does."

Amused faces turned to grim acceptance as a silence fell over the unit. Habbad looked to Cole, blatant dismay painted on his wrinkled face. Cole wished he had something encouraging to say, but felt as if he might vomit if he opened his mouth.

"You've got your task. I've even identified most of the challenges you're about to tackle, which is more than any enemy would do for you. I'll flatter myself and say that makes me a damn nice guy. Now get going." Roth flicked a claw, sending a green bolt of light to the back of the container. A heavy iron door banged to the ground as the beasts came shuffling out.

Even with everything he'd seen on Aeneria so far, every beauty and horror, none of it gave Cole a hint as to why anyone would name these creatures angels. They looked as if someone had mated a frog with a deep-sea fish and fed it steroids and rotting meat until it was the size of a horse. Their stumpy legs could barely lift their girth from the ground, giving them a whale-out-of-water sort of wobble. They had two sets of eyes perched atop bobbing growths that stuck out at asymmetrical angles from their bulbous heads. Their skin was covered in weeping pimples that oozed a little more with each wobble. One particularly disheveled specimen tripped over its own legs, the pressure bursting several of the sores on its back, the resulting pus covering its flank in a fresh glean.

It was like watching a dumpster fire or a gruesome car wreck; Cole simply couldn't tear his eyes away. The more he looked, the more the revolting, pained creatures tempted his morbid curiosity. Cole decided that the worst part had to be their mouths. Dozens of thin needles protruded from jaundiced lips that bled freely and skewered rotten clumps of their own puffy gums. Apparently whoever had designed these horrible things had forgotten to give them a place for their teeth to rest when they closed their mouths.

The bog angels shuffled on, snapping at the open air as their misshapen jaws produced a sickening, squishing sound, as ropes of blood and drool fell from the fresh wounds in their gums. The bog angels were the most repulsive things Cole had ever seen, and they were wobbling slowly and steadily for him.

Goran jumped to the ready, preparing to lunge at the new threat. Moving faster than Cole could see, Roth appeared in front of Goran, rocks cracking under his black-clawed feet. Goran puffed his chest and released a marvelous bellow, that Cole recognized from when he fell from the bridge. Roth slammed his forehead into Goran's with a loud crack. The mirak set his shoulders lower and planted his feet, pushing with all his formidable strength. Roth deftly placed one foot behind him and Goran gained no ground as he pushed the earth away from under his paws. After a few seconds of struggling, Roth took a step forward, and then another, driving Goran's head lower and lower until it was on the ground.

"You'll stay right there," Roth whispered to Goran, whose proud ruby eyes sagged with defeat.

Roth gave him one final shove and stood upright, walking over towards the barrel. He bent over and began mussing with the delicate controls. He paused, looking around at his enthralled audience. "What the hell are you all still doing here?" Without looking down he twisted something on the base of the barrel.

Cole felt the effects immediately. He dropped to one knee to support himself, feeling as though a sack of bricks had just dropped across his back. So that was the catch. A shuffling sound drew his eyes towards the wagon and to his horror the angels were within spitting distance, which he could tell by the flecks of mucus flying from their eager jaws. He righted himself and began a heavy run in the opposite direction. The rest of the unit was far ahead of him, appearing less affected by the increased gravity. Cole found his rhythm and made a good pace away from the hungry jaws. He ran until he felt his lungs might tear, then stopped and hid behind a cluster of ferns, listening between gasps for air. He was alone, though he didn't remember separating from the others. As his panting relented he heard it. The shuffling, the dragging.

Calming his mind, he found his established ideas for reducing the pull of gravity on his body. He ignored the imminent threat as he willed his concepts into reality. The weight lifted slightly from his body, but increased tenfold on his mind as he started at a jog. He was running at his normal speed, but soon fell skidding to the forest floor, unable to focus on moving his legs and maintaining the spell. Severing the Wisdom, Fear pricked at his legs as the shuffling had grown alarmingly close. Spitting dirt from his mouth, he stood and set off into the darkness.

Roth did not wait long to test them further. Another layer of gravity piled atop the first, tugging his cheeks toward the ground. He scanned for an escape, wishing for anything that might help. He found one; a perfectly good climbing tree with branches that he didn't have to jump for. He made for the tree, ignoring the wet dragging sound that came from the spot he was just lying in. He wrapped his hands around the lowest branch and heaved, stomach and arms screaming and tearing in protest. Months ago he wouldn't have been able to hoist himself up even under normal gravity. It was a testament to Roth's training that he was able to achieve the feat now. Cole straddled the branch and took a moment to catch his breath, regretting it immediately when he felt a fire in his right leg.

The bleeding jaws had snapped shut over his calf as something inside the beast's mouth worked his boot loose. Two teeth pierced his leg, poking through the armor on the other side. Cole drew his dagger and drove it into the bog angel's weeping gums. The blade found flesh easily enough, but did no more damage than the rest of the pale teeth. The bog angel tugged rapidly at his leg with greedy grunts, nearly unseating him. One tooth struck a nerve and sent a bolt of lightning up Cole's leg. A hair's breadth from falling, Cole made another attempt with the dagger, striking instead at the teeth themselves. One tooth shattered, leaving the length buried through Cole's leg. The bog angel released his leg.

The angel fell back in an explosion of popping sores. A bubbling came from the paunch between its front legs as the jaw opened wide, hissing and exposing an ivory tongue that looked like a winged woman wearing a dress.

Cole waited to pull the tooth from his leg until he was a few branches higher, throwing it down at the bog angel as hard as he could. Frustration pulled just as hard as the gravity when he saw the hungry creature plop its girth upon the trunk and start to wobble its way up. How could it climb anything with such small, useless limbs? Passing branches tore at the growths on its skin releasing fresh, stinky pus over its hide. Cole wished he could summon fire like the others. If he could he would burn this tree to the ground along with this forsaken creature. Now was not the time to experiment, however. He climbed, hoping he could go high enough where the angel's bulk couldn't reach. He neared the top and was pleased to see the angel struggling as the branches grew closer together, blocking its path.

Cole climbed a bit higher just to be safe, but he was confident that the angel would eventually reach branches too slender for its weight. When he reached for the final limb, his feet fell from under him as the branch he stood on snapped off. He had miscalculated. The silvery potion made him far too heavy for the thin branches of the tree top. Hanging by one hand, he lunged with the other but it was too late. Cole hit every branch as he fell, before his head jarred against the ground. He pushed himself upright without assessing his injuries. The angel shuffled its way down the tree without hesitation, spit and broken pimples raining down over him.

Cole rose shakily to his feet, the variety of pain blending into one coherent sensation. He knew there was no way he would last much longer. He could feel himself bleeding on the inside as well as out. There was only one option at this point. He trudged off in the direction he'd come from, following the damp drag marks left by the angel. Just as he found a steady pace he could barely maintain, yet another layer of gravity broke across his back.

Before he knew it he was tasting the sweet froth left behind by the angel's leaky sores. He pushed the ground away from him, but his arms buckled as the tainted mud splattered in his eyes. He lay there, choking in the wet soil. He was defeated now. He weighed so much that even the effort it took to breathe caused him to lose his breath. He resigned himself to the warped maw of his bonded angel. Through his weariness, thoughts of zoology class swam to the fore of his foggy mind. He remembered a video of a bison warding off a pack of grey wolves. The bison was massive and fought for hours, but eventually it just gave up. It probably had more fight left in it, but it just lay there on the tundra moss. The wolves just got on with it, starting at the bison's hindquarters while the proud beast looked out onto the rolling mountains.

As Cole thought on it, the idea of him being eaten by such a failure of an animal became increasingly unacceptable. He'd imagined he might die in battle, but not like this. Not to such a revolting animal.

Ironclad defiance sharpened his senses, dulling his pain. He flat out refused to be laid low by something that should not exist in the first place. In the quiet of his mind, he felt it. He'd felt it before, when Mark Sullivan had thrown the banana at Joshy's face, and once more when he'd nearly attacked Chiron on the beach.

Rage flared to life, its roaring torrent consuming him with every thump of his heart. Power he had never known surged through his limbs, fueling them with a need for action.

With single-minded determination, Cole found himself on his feet walking steadily towards Roth. The shuffling behind him grew louder, but that was of no concern to him now. He would deal with the angel if it was necessary. He found Roth still bent over the barrel, peering into its open lid. The Rage quieted all other thoughts in Cole's mind, making it easy for him to levitate the smoking barrel towards him with Wisdom. Roth raised a clawed hand ready to snatch it back, but seemed to decide against it. Metallic liquid spilled into the soil as the barrel fell and rolled towards Cole. With a roar that came from his toes, Cole wound up and swung at the barrel, smashing it with an ebony dragon's claw.

CHAPTER 20

LORE

The weight fell from his limbs, freeing him. Cole turned to face the bog angel, which was nearly upon him. It was now necessary to deal with the horrible creature, its lolling eyes and wheezing mouth begging to be put down. Cole planted an ebony bladed foot behind him, yearning for violence, but before he could unleash his need a blur of brindle thundered past him. Goran was upon the angel within a heartbeat. Within another heartbeat, the angel was broken, parts of it falling off as Goran's boulder-like fists wove through its pulpy flesh. Cole watched in awe as the mirak displayed strength akin to a landslide, his assault unrelenting even after the angel stopped moving. A queasiness replaced Cole's Rage. He watched his munisica fade back into his normal hands and feet. Tattered vestiges of his boots clung to his ankles.

"Didn't take you long, did it?" Roth's voice grated behind him. "Be proud. Never in all my cycles have I seen munisica sprout so soon from a student. Or a human."

Cole would have appreciated the compliment, but with his Rage waning, his pain and weariness took over. Nausea bubbled in his gut as Goran chewed on something he pulled from the bog angel's carcass.

Roth swept over to the body and slipped one of his bladed fingers along the remains. He held his hand out, offering a thin slice of pale flesh to Cole. "Your mirak has the right idea. Feast on the flesh of your enemy."

There was a momentary pause in Cole's movement that thankfully he passed off as exhaustion. He knew better than to hesitate. He took the hunk of stinky meat from Roth's claw and tore a piece off with his teeth. He cut the roof of his mouth on a sharp, bony bit, mixing blood with the rubbery texture of the flesh, which was thankfully tasteless. He forced a swallow. The blood coated his mouth and made it easier.

Roth sharpened his claws against one another, a look of hard pride flashing momentarily. "I better tend to the rest of the herd. Might need to cut your friend out of the belly of his angel. His beast was twice the size of the others. Funny, ain't it? The smallest one got the biggest angel, Ha!" Roth glanced down at Cole's pierced calf, which could barely hold his weight. "If you can walk, get yourself to a healer, then turn in for the day. If you can't, well then just wait here and I'll carry your poisoned carcass over myself. The venom isn't deadly, but it's no stroll in the garden."

Cole nodded as Roth pounded off towards the sound of a struggle from a nearby tree. Thankfully Goran sensed his need, hoisting him up on his broad shoulders and setting off at a trot.

Cole woke in his bed with no memory of how he got there. After the bout with his bog angel he could only recall a severe headache and overwhelming fit of disorienting panic. He checked his leg. Someone had mended it. The rest of his body seemed in good working order, though he had some lingering soreness throughout. Habbad was fast asleep across the room. Cole snatched his time piece and flicked on a mushroom. He still had several hours before the day ended. Part of him wanted to find Lileth and explore more of the Arts District, though a louder part wanted to simply lie in his bed and delve into a book. After a moment's deliberation, he attempted to summon a book from his shelf with Wisdom. The book wobbled and fell to the floor.

After a couple hours Habbad finally stirred, tossing his blankets violently. When his thrashing subsided, he woke fully, taking a full minute to orient himself. "What happened to you? Roth wouldn't tell us."

Cole finished the page he was on before responding. "I had enough of Roth's lesson, so I ended it."

"What do you mean you ended it?" Habbad's face screwed up in confusion as he hopped to the floor. "The weight of the spell had us all crawling about like infants. But then it just…vanished. Was that you?"

Cole snapped the book shut. "When you've had as much training as I have, certain things just come naturally." Cole climbed out of his bed and replaced his book on the shelf. "I tricked the bog angel and made my way back to where we started. Then I ventured down the path of Rage for the first time and smashed that stupid machine with my claws."

"You had munisica?" Habbad asked, his wrinkles widening with incredulity.

"Yep." Cole went to his closet and pulled out the cleanest set of clothes he owned. "Put something decent on. We're going out."

Cole led Habbad out of the tree and towards the lights and music that had been tugging at his mind ever since his last visit. As they stepped off the ramp Cole shut his eyes and found Goran, who was busy feasting with someone. Upon closer inspection, he saw through Goran's eyes a figure that could only be Roth. Together they had felled a large flying creature and were enjoying the spoils of their hunt. Confident that his friend would be happily occupied a while, he broke into a run. Habbad kept pace, even when Cole sporadically focused his Wisdom into lengthening his stride.

The silent walk made for a long trip. Cole attempted conversation, but Habbad never gave him more than a word or two in response. When they arrived they sought a few vendors peddling meats and stuffed fruits. With their bellies full, they wandered through the crowds and squares. Habbad's stature made him almost invisible amongst the towering Aenerians. Cole had previously discounted the idea, but he thought he may have been a bit taller since their parting alongside the river. Either that, or Habbad was shrinking.

"Is this place dedicated to nothing but nonsense and revelry? I thought we were supposed to be training to fight in the war?" Habbad asked.

"This district is dedicated to the followers of Passion. The Three are going to use every type of dark magic against us, so we need to know every type of good magic to use against them. At least that's what we've been told." Cole stuck a finger in his mouth, working a strand of meat from between his teeth. "The Arts District is just a fun place you know? I feel alive in here, and I think it's important to throw some *revelry* into the mix every now and then. I can't wring myself out every day without soaking up something nice every once in a while."

"I think I see what you mean. You require balance in your daily schedule. This place is an outlet for some of your other desires." Habbad ducked in between the legs of a dancing couple, shooting through unnoticed.

"Generally, yeah." Cole suppressed a laugh. Habbad's skin was visibly crawling with discomfort. He was not enjoying himself. "There's a spot where they mix some Wisdom with the Passion. You might like that a bit better than this noise."

"I have to admit, this is not *entirely* unpleasant. The music is…palpable." Habbad's face lifted slightly, for a moment looking as if he were not marching to the gallows. "I have no fondness for these throngs of giants, but the melody has a way of lifting the spirit. I have heard music before, but it was during my imprisonment within Kreed's home. It was not like this, however. I feel more…aware. More present. More alive, as you said."

Cole admired his friend for a moment. "That's a good start. Wait till you see the theater, you'll feel something for sure."

Cole led Habbad past the ruby obelisk and up the walkway towards the amphitheater. Cole felt a pang of disappointment when they arrived. There was no shimmering golden haze or muffled sounds of other worlds, and the actors were nowhere to be found. Oddly enough, however, the seats were full of people waiting in hushed whispers for something to start.

Walking up to a couple sitting on the edge of the wall, Cole dropped his voice and whispered to a red-haired woman, "What's going on here? What kind of show is this?"

The woman flinched as if a spider had crawled up next to her. Her partner gave her a stern look and an elbow. She shook her head, donning a polite smile. "Hello there. Please, pardon my rudeness. I was not expecting to see a pair of Underkin."

"Really it's fine," Cole assured her. "It's better than the looks we get at the markets. So what's up with the show tonight?"

"The exalted orator Ka Reine is performing this evening."

"Sorry, but who is Ka Reine?" Cole winced. Fortunately they were not offended.

"She is our Master orator and keeper of knowledge. She is revered throughout the Dark Side for her contributions to our history. It is a great privilege to host her this evening."

"What does she do though? Sorry, I'm not too familiar with the Dark Side," Cole added, worried he might offend the woman.

"Ka Reine is a speaker. I have had the pleasure of seeing her once before in my home village, where she told stories of her adventures on every single one of the local planets. She is very old. Older even than Chiron." She patted Cole on the stomach. "I hope you had a decent meal before you came. You might be here a while."

"We just ate, thanks." Cole spoke to Habbad in an undertone: "This isn't the show I thought it was. Do you want to go somewhere else?"

Habbad shook his head. "No. I am interested to hear stories other than the filtered drivel from Costas. I will stay."

They took a seat on the upper wall, setting themselves a respectable distance away from the couple.

"Hey, Underkin!" cried the man next to the red-haired woman.

A set of small pillows flew through the air, Cole and Habbad each catching one.

The man called over again, smiling. "Might as well make yourselves comfortable."

Cole thanked him as he and Habbad sat themselves on the embroidered seats. He leaned in, speaking quietly into Habbad's ear. "I told you they're not all bad."

Habbad looked as if he were about to rebut the statement, but a loud silence fell over the theater. Lights dimmed, leaving only the stage in spotlight. Stepping out of the shadows, a hunched woman with silvery hair hobbled to the center. She was the first Aenerian Cole had ever seen who showed signs of age. The cycles had rounded her back and crippled her gait, though she held her bony chin high and moved with sure steps towards the center. Her charcoal robes had twinkling embellishments throughout, giving her clothes the appearance of the night sky. In each of her hands she carried a bouquet of flowers, though Cole thought her crooked fingers would have been better served resting on a cane. She stopped in the middle of the stage, releasing the flowers. Unseen currents carried arrangements away from the stage, scattering the petals and stems throughout the circular theater where they began to kindle and smolder. Winding ribbons of smoke wafted throughout the theater. Following the others around him, Cole inhaled. The fruity scent was pleasant and invoked a sense of calm. He sank into his padded chair, thoroughly content. Cole didn't realize she had already begun to speak.

"It has been some time since I last visited The Sill." Though age had taken her body, her polished voice was that of a powerful and confident matriarch in the height of her prime. "I see many familiar faces. Many young faces too. In your eyes I see hope and burning vitality. I myself feel an age younger just walking amongst you. I have Travelled the expanses of Aeneria and the local planets more than any other, and still I feel my heart rests here at The Sill. I can say with open honesty that your lot has the right of it. I remember an age when we were new to this planet, our magics unrefined and wild. The three schools were wholly divided, but we liked it that way. Segregated, each tribe shunned all schools of thought that did not coincide with what their ancestors deemed appropriate. This line of reasoning worked just fine when left well alone, but when contention arose our downfall ignited. As I stand within your Sill now, I recall a very special group of Aenerians who veered from this established tradition. This group is the very reason that you are all here today, and two still walk among you. With Aeneria's first and only war rekindled and crashing upon your borders, I tell you now the story of your heritage."

Ka Reine pointed a hand towards the shale stage at her feet, swirling her bedraggled finger in tight circles. The stone below her melted, rising up to greet her as she sat herself cross-legged upon her newly formed seat. She pulled a pipe from the folds of her robes and lit it with a spark from the same finger. Taking a deep pull, she released a billowing snowy cloud into the air.

"Some of us call ourselves *true* or *native* Aenerians, but that is utter nonsense repeated by those too proud to listen to reason. The truth is that not even the oldest and most regal families can trace their lineage back indefinitely. Just like every other life form on this planet, we were brought here by the same cosmic tides that carry Aeneria through the aethers. Before recorded time, our planet was a barren rock. Then, whether by their own volition or under the guidance of some higher power, the soul flies visited our rock. Some of these soul flies carried with them the makings of life, and under the radiance of Oberon and the local stars, a verdant biosphere was hewn from the rock and soil. When the time was right, the soul flies brought sentient beings from each of the local planets. These beings mated and melded together, forming the mutts that sit before me now. This mixed breed represented the best of the dominant life forms of each local planet, eventually becoming something similar to an Aenerian. With Oberon's warmth laden with magic, every plant and animal, every rock and pinch of soil became saturated with latent energies. The early tribes evolved rapidly, and with each passing generation they discovered more about their magic. While they were not acutely aware of the varying parts of the soul, they were able to wield their powers with wild success. After a time, the tribes began to expand and explore. Their numbers swelled and they flourished into societies, eventually blending into the established governance that we are familiar with today. They became enamored with their own brilliance and success. Technology and magic mated and leapt faster than their understanding of it. They were so concerned with their discoveries that almost all traces of their ancestry were forgotten."

Cole shifted on his pillow. One of his legs had fallen asleep. He looked to Habbad, who sat utterly enthralled and frozen like a statue. In Cole's brief moment of distraction, he noticed a sudden pause in Ka Reine's speech. He returned his gaze to her. There was no doubt she was staring right at him. To his immense relief, she continued, though after giving him an almost imperceptible wink.

"Somewhere among the wildfires of their genius, it was discovered that the soul flies contained vast amounts of untapped energies. The simple floating lights were used as a resource to fuel massive projects, Oberon Temple and its surrounding shrines chief among them. During this period of revelation, various parts of the soul were discovered and refined into the schools of thought that we know today. They are Rage, Passion, Wisdom, Hunger, Fear, and the twins Despair and Hatred. Societies blossomed under separate banners of magic.

Rare was the individual who shied from tradition and embraced another school. Those who did were shunned and ridiculed as fanatics."

Ka Reine took a long pull from her pipe, thickening the fog around her. "Though each group held fast to their different beliefs, peace and prosperity ruled Aeneria for hundreds of cycles. The factions left well enough alone, only interacting with others when all parties could benefit. There seemed no end to the harmony, but when the first Wisdom Walkers returned from the local planet they discovered something that would change Aeneria forever. It was clear that the soul flies were the actual essence, the very minds and hearts of the creatures born from the local planets. It was also plain to see that certain factions of magic had damaged the soul flies beyond repair. Fear, Hunger, Despair and Hatred were found guilty of nightmarish crimes against nature. Their victims returned to their homes to become rapists and murderers, socio and psychopaths, and the defilers of children. Entire wars and genocides had come and gone before we became aware of the abuse of the soul flies. Those responsible claimed that there was no crime, stating that their relationship with the soul flies was nothing more than that of predator and prey. Thus a rift began. The followers of Rage, Passion, and Wisdom set themselves against those who practiced the arts of Fear, Hunger, Despair and Hatred."

Ka Reine paused to indulge in her pipe once more, flashing Cole another significant look. "The followers of Rage deemed the crimes profoundly dishonorable, as they took far more than necessary for any predator. The followers of Passion labeled the accused as evil, claiming they took gratuitous pleasure in the suffering of others. The followers of Wisdom concluded that the crimes were a violation of basic vital rights that every creature was entitled to. The issue sparked such heated contention that leaders from Passion, Rage, and Wisdom formed Aeneria's first centralized government, which we know of course as the Celestial Council. With overwhelming support, the Council commandeered Oberon Temple and within its walls held the first of many meetings. Though Passion and Rage had their place, it was not in the halls of Oberon Temple. Though they took advice from the other schools, only the Wisdom Walkers held seats in the council, one for each local planet. The twenty-one Wisdom Walkers brought consensus to how they would all proceed. It was with long talks and heavy hearts that they decided the accused must be cleansed, lest the chaos and suffering spread like a plague. The council then cast the first stone in the war that continues to this day."

Ka Reine paused. Cole worried that she wouldn't continue, but after wiping something from her cheek she drew a series of short puffs from her pipe, speaking through the smoke in her throat.

"The followers of the darker schools were not prepared for the initial onslaught and suffered heavy losses. During the first skirmishes, three individuals stood out amongst the accused: Decreath the Feared, Grotton the Hungry, and Sorronis the Hated and Despaired. You know them now as The Three. They were perhaps the best and brightest of our kind, and together they joined their powers into a cohesive and dynamic force that none could withstand. The Three soon recovered from their initial losses and brought the full measure of their might against the Council's forces. Unfettered by ethics or morals, The Three swelled their masses to uncontrollable swarms, devouring entire cities as they marched for Oberon Temple. The Celestial Council and their followers were tested all too soon in the fires of battle."

"In the heat of the war, ever increasing pressure was placed upon the Wisdom Walkers. Not only were they responsible for mending the local planets, but they were also charged with discovering new uses for magic to aid in the war effort. With the influx of knowledge, the colleges at Oberon Temple made leaps and bounds, propelling their magics and technologies forward dozens of cycles. Few became renowned enough to earn the title of Elite, achieving complete mastery a school of magic. The Elites changed how the game was played; masters of Rage wielding the strength of mountains, masters of Wisdom bending reality to the breaking point, and masters of Passion commanding the power of life itself. They made their own rules and everyone else fell in line, or fell behind. Some said they had too much power."

"The Three didn't care for rules or power, however. In fact, that is exactly what they used against the Council and their Elites. The Elites were still bound by the limits of their segregated magics, and fell victim to the ever-flexible minds of The Three. Grotton the Hungry was the perfect temptation to Rage. Decreath the Feared was the mirror poison to Wisdom. Sorronis the Despaired and Hated was the bane of Passion. Once beacons of hope, the Elites became nothing more than another meal for The Three."

"The followers of Rage, Wisdom, and Passion were losing the war, and so the Celestial Council began to explore the most desperate of options. A plan was devised to salvage what could be saved. Those who could would join with the soul flies for one final journey and leave Aeneria forever, while the Wisdom Walkers remained behind to see to the complete annihilation of Aeneria. Before the Wisdom Walkers could initiate this plan, however, a very young and very talented Aenerian changed the world forever." Ka Reine stared back at Cole again, squinting.

"Varka was born into a well-respected family of Wisdom Walkers. He showed promise in the school; however, his interests wandered beyond just one school of magic. It became apparent at an early age that within him also burned the fires of Rage and Passion, an embarrassment for any respectable parent in a Wisdom clan. These emotions were usually stifled at an early age, merely weeds to be plucked before they infested the garden of the mind. His parents steered him with a firm hand down the path of Wisdom, but Varka was found all too often fighting other children or bonding with the simplest of animals. He was shunned, a shame on his family as if he had been born with some deformity of the mind."

"The war had left no part of Aeneria unscathed. The arm of the Dark Three eventually cast its shadow over Varka's village. Decreath's swarm flooded the town with a Fear designed to undermine the crystalline laws of logic and reason. Before long the town had been overrun, and Aeneria lost some of the best and most revered Wisdom Walkers of the time. Varka fared well in the battle, better even than the elders. While Fear consumed the rest of the village, Varka's Rage kept the sickening magic at bay."

Cole swallowed, relaxing his cramped hands and taking a much-needed breath. He felt like he was really there. Hoping that no one saw, he stilled the Rage, shrinking his munisica back into his normal hands and feet. The Rage felt good. He marveled at the angles of his black blades before they vanished.

Ka Reine went on, "The battle was all but lost until Varka did something that could never be forgiven, though it was his actions that saved the town. After laying eyes upon the corpses of his family, part of Varka's soul had come undone. His Rage had awoken fully and completely. Without the established trials or formal training, Varka acquired complete mastery of the Rage within himself. The atrocities committed by Decreath's hordes were terrifying to the hardest of spirits, though they were candles before the sun compared to what Varka wrought. His munisica exploded from his hands as his entire physical form became shrouded in the black armor of fury. His chaos was swift and necessary. Within minutes Decreath's minions lay strewn throughout the streets, hundreds of their tortured forms dashed to pieces. Once recovered, the few surviving elders were left with no choice but to cast Varka into exile. He was no Wisdom Walker, and in their eyes never would be."

"While Varka had mastered Rage, he was also wise enough to accept his banishment and seek his fortune elsewhere. There was nothing left for him in the town anyway. Throughout his subsequent adventures he fell in with other outcasts. Together they shared ideas and concepts previously deemed taboo. Wisdom, Rage, and Passion were appreciated and studied equally. Varka was the first to achieve mastery of a school, but soon others had their minds unleashed and they achieved Elite status as well. To his own chagrin, Varka fell in love and mastered Passion. To master one school was rare and unheard of for one so young, but to achieve full mastery of two was unprecedented."

"The group called themselves the Unbound and chose Varka as their leader. The Unbound were not only dynamic and powerful, but steadfast companions. During their adventures and experimental practices, new concepts were born to Aeneria. They Traveled to each of the local planets, sampling the varieties of life as they went. The Celestial Council were left dumbstruck as the Unbound solved immense problems in a fraction of the time that it would have taken the old Wisdom Walkers. For the betterment of all, the Unbound worked tirelessly to improve their skills and increase their knowledge of the universe around them. With each passing moment they grew stronger; however, so did their enemies. While the Unbound were away on the local planets, The Three had spread to every corner of Aeneria, leaving a wake of festering death behind them. Eventually the Unbound had no choice but to face The Three in open combat."

"The last of Aeneria's traditional Elites had fallen, either beguiled into temptation or killed personally by The Three. The tides of war crashed against the walls of Oberon Temple, where the survivors of Rage, Passion, and Wisdom dug in for the final stand. Varka and the Unbound returned from a Traveling to find the temple ablaze. The entire population of their allies had sought refuge within the walls of the temple, fighting tooth and nail against the plagues that besieged it. The Unbound rushed to the aid of the Celestial Council, bringing their full might to bear. Rage, Wisdom, and Passion worked in unison, ever flexible and adaptive to the onslaught of The Three. With their dynamic powers they stole through the temple and found that they could hold the line indefinitely, though they could gain no ground themselves. The swarms of The Three had grown beyond comprehension, drowning out even Oberon's light. During the stalemate, Varka sought answers deep within Oberon Temple. He had mastered both Rage and Passion, but they were not enough. The Unbound faced impossible odds, so he decided to do the impossible and attempt to master the final part of himself. During their final hour, Varka entered the Vault of Wisdom, never to return."

"The Unbound trusted Varka. After all he had already achieved the unfathomable and brought them thus far. Varka remained in the vault for the rest of the month with no results. When he had spent more time inside than any other before him, they knew that he would never return. The Hope of the Unbound wilted. This was the chance that Sorronis had been waiting for. The chink in the armor, however slight, was enough for him to seep through and work his craft. Despair creeping, the Unbound faltered and their barriers faded. The swarms broke upon the temple and the battle recommenced. Those adept in Passion were the first to fall to the Despair. Without their master healers the rest stood little chance. When only two of the Unbound remained, they used the last of their strength to call out to Varka in the depths of the Vault of Wisdom."

"As if in answer to their plea, Oberon blazed through the sickly clouds of The Three. Brighter than a rising star, it expelled its latent energy directly into the temple. The finer details of what happened next were never fully understood, but the consequences were thus: First, Decreath, Sorronis, and Grotton were banished to the Light Side as the barrier appeared around Aeneria's Dark Side. Second, Travel became impossible, preventing all passage to the local planets. Third, and most sad, the soul flies never returned to visit us again."

"There are several theories as to what happened to Varka. He may very well still be inside the Vault of Wisdom. Or he may have left with the soul flies. Some say he simply disappeared into the aethers. Or perhaps he was destroyed when he wielded Oberon's power. There are those that still search for him, but since that day there hasn't been so much as an echoed whisper of the Master of the Unbound."

"The Three may have been banished, but they were still very much alive and spent every moment working against their bonds. Without the soul flies they were denied their most valuable resource; however, they had already amassed a sizeable population of Underkin, which made for a potent substitute. Their strength continues to grow to this day."

Ka Reine fell silent, indulging in her pipe as the memories of ages swam in her eyes. The crowd waited in quiet patience as the minutes dragged on. Her head sank to her chest and she appeared to have stopped breathing. Cole wondered if she had perhaps fallen asleep, and they would have to wait in respectful repose for her to wake up.

Eventually Ka Reine stirred, pulling her head up towards the sky and releasing a cloud of smoke. She continued as if nothing had happened. "I tell you this not just as an old woman's lament of the past; this tale is also a warning. War is creeping for your door, and when it comes calling it may not wear the face of an honest enemy. It may present itself as a deceitful ally or perhaps some sinister part of your very own souls. The Three are ever changing and evolve their arts in ways we cannot possibly comprehend. To be blunt, we are weaker than we were before the banishing, and they have only grown stronger. The Unbound, they had the right idea. These old eyes of mine have seen it first-hand. To limit yourself to a single way of thinking is a death-sentence gilded with pride."

Ka Reine looked around the amphitheater, taking several minutes to plant her eyes on every spectator. Cole suspected her ancient gaze lingered on him a little longer than the others. Satisfied, Ka Reine up-ended her pipe and tapped it on the floor of the stage, emptying the ashes. Storing the pipe back up her sleeve, she brought her rickety body back to its feet.

"Keep your fires warm, your waters flowing, and your skies clear." Without another word, Ka Reine hobbled off the stage.

Slowly, people began stirring and talking again as they made their way out of the theater. Habbad remained sitting, his face locked in a vacant stare as if his entire world had been turned upside-down.

Cole attempted to break him from his reverie. "I had no idea The Sill was so important. And to think we're in worse shape than the last time. Kind of makes me wonder if we should bother trying so hard when we're the only ones on the planet willing to learn all three schools." Cole leaned back, stretching out on his pillow. "What do you want to do next? I know I'm starving after all that."

Habbad was slow to wake from his daydream. "So much has been revealed to me. I need some time to think on Ka Reine's words. Thank you for bringing me here, but I would like to return to the room now."

Cole wasn't quite ready to turn in yet, but he understood. Habbad's whole life had been a lie. He had lost his entire family and had his world shaken. Thinking of Habbad's losses reminded Cole of his own. "All right, let's head back then."

"I'll take myself back. I know the way," Habbad said, standing up.

"Are you sure?" Cole asked, secretly glad for the excuse to stay a bit longer.

Habbad nodded without hesitation. "Quite. I need some time alone."

"I'll see you later then," Cole replied, thinking on a few places he had yet to visit.

CHAPTER 21

WARRIOR

"Where the hell is Master Chiron? My mind is about as relaxed as it's going to get. I'll fall asleep if he takes any longer." Storn rose from the circle, rubbing his back. "Why don't we get started on our own? Someone attack me."

"Storn, for once in your life why don't you sit down and try some patience." Sitra chucked a rock at Storn, which he caught in midair with the power of his Wisdom alone. Since Deekus's death, Storn had taken a greater interest in the other schools.

Valen rose from the circle as well. "Storn is right. Chiron has never been this late. Something is amiss, or else he would have at least sent a message to me."

While Cole was inclined to disagree with Valen out of sheer spite, he was admittedly waiting for a chance to stretch his cramping legs. The rest of the group rose as well. They started an exercise that Chiron would normally have them do on their own. They picked an object, which this time happened to be Cole's dagger, and took turns changing one physical property while the rest of the group guessed what the change was. Cole was limited to a few simple alterations which no one had any trouble guessing, such as weight and temperature.

Habbad surprised the group by winning a round. When the dagger made its way back to him he hefted it with a triumphant look. "The dagger is a cycle older than it was before we started the game," Habbad confessed, passing it to Eliza.

"How clever!" Eliza gushed. "Very subtle of you, Habbad. I never would have guessed, even if I had a whole cycle to myself."

Storn kicked a clump of grass. "Cheater! There's no way to prove it. The little rat's probably making it up. I couldn't sense a damn thing different about the knife."

"That is because you did not look at it properly," Lileth interjected. "None of us did. Well done, Habbad."

Habbad wore a look of unrestrained pride, but otherwise did not respond. Cole knew he was not actually proud of his work, rather he was pleased that he had fooled the Dark Ones. *They* were the cattle for once.

"If you're all through messing with my things, I think our Master is finally here." Cole reached out with tenuous strands of Wisdom and levitated the dagger slowly towards himself. The dagger wobbled and plopped into the grass at his feet. Fortunately everyone was looking the other way as he bent down and picked up his weapon, which was now older, sharper, duller, and shocking shade of pink. He knew he had an arduous project ahead, trying to restore it to its original state.

"Whind? Good morning, honored elder. Are you here in Master Chiron's stead?" Valen greeted the gatekeeper with a solemn bow.

Whind returned Valen's greeting with one of his own, spreading his arms as a few leaves fell from his torso. His robes seemed crafted from the surrounding flora, giving him the appearance of a walking tree. "Greetings Valen and company. I come bearing a message from your masters, and it is thus; all future lessons have been cancelled indefinitely. Return to your barracks, pack your things, and await further instructions." Whind turned his head towards Cole and Habbad: "Except for you two. You will accompany me, now."

"Right now?" Cole asked, casting Habbad a sideways glance. He couldn't help but feel as though he were in some kind of trouble.

"Right now," Whind repeated.

Cole and Habbad followed Whind away from the group. Feeling eyes on his back, Cole glanced over his shoulder and saw Lileth, concern lining her face. Habbad looked as if he could not care less as to how the day proceeded. "Where are we going?" Cole asked, trotting to keep up.

"To speak to your masters," Whind replied, locking his hands behind his back as he walked.

Worry gripping him, Cole asked, "About what? Did we do something wrong?"

"I believe not," Whind said in a voice as slow and indifferent as a tree swaying in a gentle breeze. "They merely wish to speak with you."

While he was not entirely relieved, Cole's anxiety lifted considerably. He was sure he himself hadn't done anything wrong, but he couldn't speak for Habbad, who'd rubbed everyone the wrong way since his arrival. Still, the events were significant. Never before had a lesson been cancelled, and never had one of the elders asked for him specifically.

They followed Whind to the center of The Sill, an area Cole was only vaguely aware of thanks to the cypher, a knot of apprehension growing in his stomach all the while. Goran's thoughts suddenly pressed on his own. Cole's vision flashed with a snapshot of Goran descending quickly from a tree, intent on joining him and Habbad. He impressed upon the mirak to stay where he was. This was likely not to be a good time to have a giant furry bodyguard snorting over his shoulder. He knew Goran received his message, but wasn't sure if he would comply. He followed Goran's thoughts back up the tree, where he trailed after them from The Sill's canopy.

They arrived at a wide, seamless door at the base of the fattest tree Cole had ever seen. It looked too wide to have been made entirely by nature's whims. Two silent figures wearing midnight-plum robes stood sentinel at the entrance, giving no notice to them other than a quick glance at Whind.

Whind stopped before the door, stabbing his shimmering hand into the center. He twisted his wrist and the door rippled like a puddle. "Please, follow me."

Cole pushed himself through the door, which felt considerably thicker than any liquid stone door he had gone through before. He took three awkward steps before emerging on the other side, slightly out of breath. The air was much colder inside. He and Habbad followed Whind up a set of stairs that climbed up the wall of the tree. Bowls of flames lined the walls, somehow leaving the wood unharmed as the tongues of fire lapped about. The stairs were not designed for anyone shorter than the Aenerians, and Cole quickly fell behind.

He noticed Habbad had no trouble keeping up as he shot himself from step to step with bursts of Wisdom. Catching on, Cole summoned magic to aid him along.

They arrived at the top, pushing their way through another thick door. On the other side they found Alvani, Chiron, Roth, and Ka Reine sitting around a table in the center of a room with no roof. Dim constellations of the house of Allias watched over the congregation as thick clouds began to roll in over The Sill. A warm breeze poured over the walls, carrying a fragrant scent of flowers. Looking for the source of the delightful smell, Cole jumped, noticing a pair of massive yellow eyes looking down from directly above the door. Alvani's winged friend Gale chirped as he took in the new arrivals before resuming the preening of his wings.

They followed Whind towards the elders, Roth's booming voice echoing throughout the room as he argued with a face inside a large glass jar set upon the table.

"You have our demands," said the sneering face in the jar. "What you do with them is up to you. We have been patient with your eccentricities up until now, but our tolerance wanes. The Three press upon *all* of the Dark Side. It would not be in the best interest of The Sill to fight this war on two fronts."

"Threats from cowards are akin to a toothless bite. Be gone, snake." Roth slammed a bladed fist on the table, rattling the jar as the liquid inside evaporated into the open ceiling. "The Celestial Council has grown as bold as they have stale. That they would even dare challenge us at a time like this shows their weakness. I could cripple them myself if I had the time."

"They will likely not attack us outright, though I'm sure they could cause no end to our troubles." Chiron brought his spindly fingers together in a heap on the table. "All things considered, it is a tad foolhardy for them to conspire against The Sill. They too can ill afford a war on two fronts."

Alvani shook her head, her tone both tired and pleading. "It shouldn't have to come to this. We are all on the same side. We all have just as much to lose to The Three's hordes. A compromise must be made."

"A compromise? Bah!" Ka Reine blew a gust of smoke from her lips, tapping her pipe on the table. "You were but a child during the last war, Alvi. You wouldn't recall the bureaucratic swindling that cost us lives and time. I'm with Rothael on this one. The Celestial Council can go chew bark. We'll tend to the hordes and pull their pompous heads out of the fire when the times comes. Should the Council follow through on their threats then they won't have long to regret it."

Alvani deflated slightly. "You are right of course, oldest one. Even I forget that my school is not the only one that matters. Though it pains my soul to see the suffering of others, catering to the Council's strictures will likely cause greater suffering for us all."

A silence fell over the table as Alvani's words hung in the air. Roth broke himself from a daydream and brought his eyes down upon Cole and Habbad. "Come forward, we've business with the two of you. We'll take them from here, Whind. Go back to your gate."

Whind gave the table an expressionless nod before disappearing through the door. Chiron opened his mouth to speak, but twisted and stared curiously at a thumping, crunching noise coming from outside the tree. Cole winced as Goran landed with a crash, leaving deep gouges in the polished hard wood.

"I suppose your mirak is welcome to join the discussion," Chiron said as he regarded Goran, who sauntered over to Cole's side. Chiron returned his eyes to Cole and Habbad. "We have summoned you to discuss your futures. As I told both of you, you are each free to do as you please. No one will have hold over you, though some factions seem to think they do. The war moves apace and The Sill can no longer sit idle. We are activating all of our forces and will soon bring the full measure of our efforts against The Three. As of this very moment, the two of you are no longer students. You are soldiers of your own fortunes. You are of course still in the infancy of your training, and considerations must be made. I hold true to my word when I told you that you could leave whenever you please, and after I've had my say, you may very well do so. That being said I will also hold true to everything else I said." Chiron's eye lingered on Habbad. "The end of Allias's house is nearly upon us, which means that the Devotion in Costas will take place shortly. Your unit will disrupt the ceremony before The Three can use the tower to further swell their strength." Chiron's tone shifted as Habbad's uncomfortable demeanor became the loudest thing in the room. "I see a question burning in your eyes, young Habbad. Please, put words to it."

"What of the Underkin?" Habbad said. "What will happen to them? Every child has grown up thinking you are all demons, and they will fight you to the death. Will you strike them down just because they are in your way?"

"You have much pain in your heart, young one." Alvani's voice was soft and soothing. "Sheath your worry. Violence is not the only tool in our arsenal. If you devoted a bit more of your efforts to the school of Passion you would understand this."

Habbad twitched as though shaking off a retort. "I have spent enough time among you all to know you can be trusted. You say you won't hurt my people. I will hold you to it, Dark Ones."

Roth interrupted with derisive laughter. "You couldn't hold us if you tried, whelp. Chiron wanted to do you the kindness of giving you options. Either stay with your unit and join the assault on Costas, or we'll reassign you to supporting roles where you'll be safe and remain untested. This is how we see it. If you have a better idea then spit it out. Time is burning."

Cole knew his own choice already. Panic tickled him as he imagined Lexy strapped to the outside of the tower. While there was breath in his lungs he would do whatever he could to save her from such a grisly fate. He looked over at Habbad, who appeared more ambiguous with his intentions. A flicker of distant light caught Cole's eye. He looked skyward to see the heralds of the impending storm falling from the clouds above. He watched the droplets of rain curve away from the opening, as though it was shielded by an invisible umbrella.

"Events move swiftly young ones, we need your answers," Alvani said as lightning streaked across the sky.

Thunder rattled Cole's teeth. He took a deep breath. "I will go with my unit to Costas."

Alvani gave him a sad nod before turning to Habbad. "And you?"

Habbad brought his stony gaze up to the table. It amazed Cole that even though he was only knee-high to the Aenerians, he wasn't intimidated in the slightest by their size or powers. "I will also remain with the unit. I may be of some use in Costas."

"You trust us not to eat your kin?" Roth sneered, licking his teeth. "Believe me whelp, there is no challenge or honor in conquering your kind. In war there will always be collateral casualties, but your kin will be safe, from us at least. Most of them won't even know we're there. As long as they don't cause us too much trouble, and you don't flip a turncoat on us, there should be no need to interact with them."

Habbad regarded Roth for a moment, his eyes calculating as they darted about the room. Cole knew he was figuring out different ways to kill Roth given every resource he had in front of him. After coming to a decision, his wrinkled face relaxed. "As I said, I will hold you to your word. I will remain with the unit and go to Costas."

Roth leaned back in his chair, indifference pooling in his features.

"It's settled then," said Chiron, slapping a hand down on the table. "Please return to your barracks and pack your things. You have the rest of the day to collect any provisions you may need for your journey. Please, go now."

Cole fiddled with the straps on his cloth armor. "Master Chiron?"

"What is it Cole?" Chiron shuffled a stack of papers on the table, stuffing them into a fat, dusty book.

"What about Goran? Can he come with us?" Cole asked. At the sound of his name, Goran stood and strutted in front of the table, as though displaying himself as a show horse.

Chiron surveyed Goran for a moment. "From what I've heard, this mirak is horrifying in battle. I don't think it possible to separate you two, seeing as he recently crossed a good portion of Aeneria just to be at your side. I think he would make an excellent addition to the unit. What say you, Rothael? Alvani?"

"I've rolled with the mirak a few times. He's deadly enough. Physically he'd be the strongest fighter in the unit, as long as the human can keep him from chasing rodents up trees." From his seat, Roth gave Goran a playful punch in the ribs as he trotted by.

Alvani looked from Goran to Cole with open admiration. Gale hopped from his perch with a gust of feathers and landed behind her, resting his feline head on her shoulder. Alvani inclined her head and offered, "Speaking for the arts of Passion, I can only see the benefits of Goran joining the unit. Such a bond is rare and not to be wasted. As Cole learns and grows, so will Goran. The opposite of course is just as relevant. I am interested to see how these two will evolve in the coming months." She gave Cole a seated bow of affirmation. "Goran will stay with you. You must go now, however. The three of you must ready yourselves for the journey ahead."

Relief washed over Cole's face. Even though he considered the rest of his unit reliable friends, having Goran by his side made diving into the unknown a much less daunting affair. Goran had been as resolute as Oberon's constant presence. The mirak had been there for him since he'd first arrived. Even after he fell from the bridge and all was lost, Goran had spent every waking moment trying to return to him. Without words, Goran's presence had always told him that everything was going to be fine in the end. Now that he had his furry friend back, he loathed the thought of being apart again. Eyes shining, he thanked Alvani and the rest of the elders before making for the door.

"Wait a moment, young ones," Ka Reine's regal voice halted Cole and Habbad in their tracks. "I'll have a look at you before you depart. Might not see you again after this."

Cole turned on the spot to see the ancient woman hobbling from her chair to meet them. The other elders looked to one another, exchanging silent messages of concern. Chiron flicked his hand, which seemed to have settled the matter as the three of them watched Ka Reine with mild interest.

"Don't make me walk all the way around, these old bones don't have many more steps left in them," she snapped, her arms continually reaching for things to aid in her shuffling gait. "Goran, be a gentleman and come hither."

To Cole's surprise, Goran's eyes and ears perked up as if he had picked up the scent of prey. He made a beeline for Ka Reine and stopped directly in front of her, resting on his knuckles. With a knobbly hand she grasped the brindle fur on Goran's arm, holding him for support. With the other hand she touched and inspected every inch of Goran's form. Crooked fingers pulled at his jowls, flicked each of his canines, caressed his eyelids and finally mussed his snowy mohawk.

Even Cole wouldn't have taken such liberties with his friend for fear of being bitten, or given Goran's recent growth spurt, tossed from the tree.

"The finest specimen of a mirak these eyes have ever seen. Unusually solitary, but all the stronger for it." She clapped Goran on his hulking arm. "May you find your mountain."

Goran gave a jerking snort, blowing hot breath over Ka Reine's face.

"All right Habbad, bring your angry little ass over. Hop up on the table so I don't have to slouch." Ka Reine hobbled a step to the table and rested a hand upon it. Habbad rushed to the table, jumping the height with a twist of Wisdom. The look on his face clearly showed his impatience to be done with the whole ordeal.

Ka Reine looked down her bent nose with her head tilted to the side, a hand on her hip. She waited a moment for Habbad to make eye contact. Eventually Habbad broke under the weight of her perception. She did not touch him as she had with Goran, though she seemed to not need her hands to see what she needed. Cole couldn't see her face, but Habbad's stony mask seemed to crack, breaking into profound anguish. With her gaze alone, she held him for a moment longer before letting out a sigh and running a hand along her jaw. Habbad's eyes remained lost in a waking dream, lines of tears rolling over his wrinkles. Ka Reine leaned in and whispered something into his ear. Habbad nodded, unblinking.

"Off you go then." Ka Reine jerked her head to the side, dismissing him.

Habbad dropped from the table, landing with a muffled thump on the polished wooden floor. Ka Reine looked to Cole expectantly. He shot a quick glance into Goran's red eyes. The familiar ferocity of his gaze steadied Cole's legs and relaxed the muscles in his shoulders. There was still a slight fluttering in his chest, but at least he no longer felt as if he might fall over as he walked over to the oldest Aenerian. He considered using Wisdom to jump up onto the table as Habbad did, but decided not to risk messing it up and looking a fool in front of everyone.

"I have seen many humans in my life, and I have to admit I don't much care for your kind. Too greedy. Too easily swayed." Her pipe slid out from the depths of her sleeve, already lit. She took a few quick puffs, clamping the stem between her teeth and beckoning him with both hands. "Get over here then."

Cole stepped between her arms, the pleasant aroma of fruits and spices filling his nostrils. Her hands wrapped around his head, her thumbs under his eyes. She closed her own. Cole tried not to, but found himself taking in every detail of her aged face. She was old, no doubt, but she was still attractive in a handsome and intimidating way. When he came to her drooping eyelids, they snapped open, revealing glassy orbs that swirled with ever changing hues, like two miniature Oberons. Cole felt as if he were back in the river, floating upwards and onwards away from his body, away from the mundane. He was lost, falling into himself. Memories flew by, their ghosts calling to him. He settled just long enough to feel parts of himself emerge from his subconscious, curious as to who had intruded upon their homes so uninvited. Before he could identify or communicate with them, he drifted down another level. Some parts of himself he recognized, but others felt so foreign and strange that he recoiled in worry that they might do him harm. As he drifted and fell through the chambers and halls of his mind, *He* followed, watching and observing quietly. Cole wondered if *He* was just another part of himself, or something else entirely. Cole felt Ka Reine there with him as well. She poked and prodded each part that flew by, as if checking fruits at the market for bruises. She felt everything, was everything, sifting through thoughts and memories that even Cole didn't understand. She didn't seem to notice *Him,* even though *He* was right there beside her, standing over her shoulder. When she was through, she pulled herself out, dragging Cole's conscious self with her. They rose to the surface and just before they breached the veil to the corporeal, *He* grabbed them both, holding them fast with an iron grip. For the first time, Cole looked into *His* eyes, taking in every detail. Cole didn't bother struggling; he knew there was no release until *He* allowed it. Ka Reine on the other hand fought like a wolf caught in a snare. Cole felt a painful throbbing throughout his mind with the force of her thrashing. *He* released Cole, pushing him beyond the veil while pulling Ka Reine into a tight embrace.

Cole opened his eyes, unable to move. Ka Reine's eyes flashed rapidly through every color. She wasn't breathing and the pipe had fallen from her teeth, smoldering on the floor. Suddenly she took a breath and the swirling colors faded from her glassy orbs. Cole then felt weight return to his body as he resumed full control of it. He knew he was fine, but he was unsure if Ka Reine had escaped unharmed.

"Are you okay?" he asked.

"I am fine, child." She blinked slowly and picked her pipe up off the floor. "More than fine. That little exchange explains quite a bit as a matter of fact."

"What does that explain?" Cole dropped his voice to just under a whisper, noticing the others staring at him with looks of supreme interest. "Who the hell is *He*? *He's* been in there as long as I can remember."

Ka Reine re-lit her pipe and took another pull, blowing white smoke up into the rain. "You are thoroughly you, my dear Cole. It is not my place to show you who you are, not a single part. My heart weeps for your losses, though it also leaps at your arrival on our planet. You will play no small role in coming events, of that I am sure."

Cole scowled. He was getting tired of the vague answers and secrets. He wanted to know more, but he was confident that the ancient Aenerian would reveal nothing she didn't want to. "May we leave now? We have packing to do."

Ka Reine nodded, sucking on the inside of her cheek. Cole lowered himself from the table and followed Habbad and Goran through the door to brave the deluge outside.

CHAPTER 22

RISE AND ENTER

"Did you accept?" Lileth asked in a brittle tone.

"Yes, we both did," Cole replied as he and Habbad approached the base of their apartment. Butterflies took flight in his chest as her expression changed from concern to elation.

Lileth's hands relaxed as she uncrossed her arms. "Good. You are a part of this unit after all. Both of you."

Cole and Habbad jumped down from Goran's back. Cole scanned the empty barracks grounds. Darkened windows peered back from the tree apartments. "Where are the others?"

"They are packing and saying their goodbyes. You should hurry and do the same. We leave within the hour. Gather your things and meet us outside the Lurkwood Gate." Her raven hair whipped over her shoulder as she ran off.

He knew it was probably nothing, but Cole was glad she had waited for him. The way her eyes lit up at the sight of him played through his mind as he walked up the ramp to their apartment.

"You have feelings for that one," Habbad interjected, breaking Cole from his daydream. "I see the way your gaze lingers and your thoughts wander. I may not be as adept as you with the arts of Passion, but even I can see it plain as starlight. You have emotional ties to that female."

"You can call her *Lileth* you know. And so what if I do? Is that a crime here?" Cole thrust himself through their liquid stone door before Habbad could respond.

"We are going to war, Cole," Habbad stated, popping through the door. "The Dark Ones say our mission won't involve combat, but I'm certain we will once again be fighting for our lives. Your mind ought to be on the task at hand, not swooning over someone who isn't even the same species as you."

Cole turned around and made sure Habbad's eyes were locked on his before responding, "Right now the most important thing to me is saving Lexy. You do remember Lexy don't you? Your sister?"

Habbad deflated, dropping his gaze.

"I care about your sister, just like I care about you. Since I've been at The Sill I've started caring about other people as well. I can't help how I feel about Lileth, but I promise nothing is going to interfere with us saving Lexy." Cole threw open his closet and began tossing things onto his bed.

"I am scared, Cole." Habbad said in a weak voice.

"Yeah me too," Cole replied in a harsh tone as he shoved clothes into his bag. "We only made it here by dumb luck. If we met another Corpulant or Domina there's no way we'd be alive today. And let's not forget the spell-casting giants. Our enemies have those too."

Habbad rubbed the back of his neck. "That is not the reason I am scared. I feel something that I have not felt in a long time." His eyes met Cole's once more. "I feel hope."

"Why the hell are you afraid of hope?" Cole asked.

"The last time I felt hope, Kreed used it against me. I hoped he would give my parents a swift death. Sensing my hope, he did not. Then I hoped he would kill Lexy. Sensing my hope, he did not. Then I hoped he would never let me out of that box. He took my hope and turned it on me. I feel it now, blooming like a little flower. Your confidence has planted a seed of hope within me. I will go with you to Costas and I will try to save Lexy." Habbad's face and voice became flat. "If we fail and she suffers the tower... I will never forgive you."

Cole deflated this time, but he held onto Habbad's eyes. "Then we had better save her. You're the last person on this planet I would want for an enemy. You might not be the biggest, but you are definitely the most dangerous." Cole gave a weak smile, intending to lighten the mood, though the words were true. There was something about Habbad that seemed more deadly than even Roth.

They finished packing and made for the Lurkwood Gate, full rucksacks bouncing heavy over their shoulders. Anxiety fluttered in

Cole's chest as Habbad's demeanor hardened back to his stony determination.

"New bloods! Welcome to the war!" Storn shouted as they emerged from the Lurkwood Gate. "Couldn't resist the chance to spill the blood of our enemies?"

Sitra punched Storn with a clawed hand, drawing blood from his side. "Spill your *own* blood, meat brain! Storn the thorn indeed."

"What was *that* for?" Storn gasped, holding a shining pink hand over his fresh wound. Blood ran back into the center of the wound as the skin knitted back together.

"Think about where we are going, and then think about who you are talking to." Sitra jabbed at him again.

"All right, all right!" Storn said as he dodged her punches. "I know we're not to hurt the Underkin, but if we happen upon a few Domina along the way…" His hands elongated into munisica and he swiped at a nearby boulder, scooping out a clean hunk of granite.

"I am of the same mind as you, brother." The light of the Gratia stones lit Eliza's short spiked hair, making it look like a torch. Her munisica were a good measure larger than Cole had ever seen them, the shroud now covering a portion of her forearms. "I would have pity for our enemies, but I find the Rage comforting. And the Wisdom within me tells me that creatures such as the Domina deserve no pity. They are a blight upon our land, and must be cleansed along with The Three. I thirst for their blood as well."

Eliza's change of behavior was alarming, but understandable. If not for the Domina, Chiron would have been present when Deekus made for the omnistones. Eliza had spent every moment of her free time at Deekus's tree, meditating and contributing to his gratia stone. Cole had visited her once, but she was aloof and gave only a word or two in response.

"It's good to see a follower of Passion take up arms. I'm sure you will be just as skilled a fighter as a lover," Valen said. "This is what we are here for. We mustn't get too attached to one school or another."

"We also must not attach ourselves to old prejudices." Lileth carved into Valen with a glare. The others muttered in agreement. Valen's snide comments and harsh treatment of Cole and Habbad had been blatant from their first days. When Valen's cold indifference made it clear he wasn't about to respond, Lileth took a step closer to him. "We are on the brink of our first real mission. Let us be open with each other."

"I agree," Sitra said, crossing her arms.

Storn and Eliza nodded their approval, while Goran rolled onto his back and promptly fell asleep.

Valen glowered at everyone. "I have been open to all of you since the inception of this unit. I know not what you accuse me of, but I will hear it." Venom lined his words, daring anyone to challenge his morality.

Lileth stood a little taller. "Since Cole's arrival I have seen a change in you, Valen the wise. You have spurned both him and Habbad at every turn. I know what happened in the tree on Cole's first day, and I also know of your family history with the Underkin and Sorronis. You have suffered much and my own heart weeps for you, but know this; should you again cause undue harm to a member of this unit, you will suffer me."

An awkward silence fell between them as Valen's stony face crumbled into shameful resignation. Seeing the disgrace in Valen's face reminded Cole of when he was ganged up on by a group of bullies in school. While there were many parts of him that despised Valen, he couldn't help but feel a modicum of pity for him.

"I know I'm the weakest one in the unit," Cole started, his own cheeks flushing as he felt everyone's eyes upon him, "but I'm here for you too. You can count on me to play my part in the mission, and if I see you in trouble I'll do everything I can to help. And I'm not completely helpless anymore, I've got some muscle now." He slapped Goran on his round belly, who gave an amenable snore. "As long as there's food to keep him awake that is."

After searching the ground for the words, Valen looked Cole square in the eye. "I never thought I'd be taught a lesson in Wisdom by an Underkin. Thank you, Cole. Your assistance will be most welcome. You as well, Habbad."

Habbad inspected Valen for a second. "Your approval is not necessary. I will contribute to the unit regardless."

Cole knew that was as close to a peace treaty as Habbad was likely to offer. Nevertheless, Valen seemed satisfied.

Sitra thankfully interrupted the awkward silence that clung to the air. "Hurry up and get your hugs and kisses in now because our ride is here." She leapt and ran up the side of the nearest tree, chopping her way up into the canopy.

Without hesitation the rest of the group unsheathed their munisica and followed her, leaving Cole with Habbad and Goran.

"I still don't quite have the hang of this," Cole said, flexing his fingers. He brought his mind back to the bog angel, remembering the awful taste of its slime in his mouth. His neck prickled as Rage clicked into its rightful place. His fingers and toes creaked with satisfying pain as they transformed into jagged black claws. He allowed himself a few seconds to admire their savage beauty, proud of his new weapons. They were not nearly as impressive as the first time, but they would get him up the tree. The magic roused Goran, who rolled upright, eyes wide and nostrils flaring.

Habbad watched Cole's struggle, unimpressed. "Helpful, but unnecessary." His face relaxed as he drew upon his Wisdom and shot up alongside the tree, unaided by physical means.

Goran snorted, twitching in response to Cole's Rage. There was controlled fire in his red eyes.

"Try to keep up, eh?" Cole said, scratching Goran's chin before leaping up the side of the tree. Rage fueled his muscles as his munisica hammered into the tree bark. After the lesson with the bog angel, he'd spent a portion of every evening working on his control of the new magic, astounded by the power and dexterity it provided. Even with his rucksack weighed down with his new boots and a week's worth of provisions, he scaled the tree with ease, jumping from branch to branch without the aid of Wisdom. As fast as he was, he was still much slower than the rest of the group, and Goran certainly didn't have any trouble keeping up.

Cole arrived at the top of the tree, landing roughly on a platform someone had persuaded the upper branches to grow into. He marveled at the display the stars had put on for them. The local starscape was littered with comets, visible even with Oberon's blaring luminance.

Something was wrong, however. A good portion of the sky was blacked out, seemingly missing. Cole searched the void, eyes darting. He jumped as a keening whale's moan pierced the night. The void swam closer to them, revealing a gargantuan whale adorned with shining gems along its eyes and fins. The whale cried again, beautiful and sad. On its back standing erect in the moonlight, was Roth.

Cole had fully expected a squadron of sun lily leaves to fly them to Costas. The rest of the group looked as if flying whales were an everyday occurrence, however, joining Roth on the creature's back when it swam close enough. Habbad looked just as shocked as Cole felt, and Goran inched towards the edge of the platform, ready to bolt.

"Move your asses!" Roth roared.

Unwilling to be caught hesitating, Cole stowed his concern and sheathed his Rage, invoking his Wisdom instead to assist him with the jump onto the Whale's back. Closing his eyes, he took a few long breaths to soothe the Rage, which submitted reluctantly. He poured himself into the concept of gravity, feeling every part of his body being pulled towards everything around him. It took only a minor tweak of thought to lessen the pull enough to make the gap. He and Habbad landed softly on the whale's rubbery skin. With a bit of coaxing, and a marvelously detailed and specific threat from Roth, Goran begrudgingly joined them on the whale. As formidable as Goran was, he was terrified of the flying leviathan.

"What is this thing?" Cole asked Lileth. He had a vague memory of encountering one of these creatures in a dream.

"This is a baileen. They are one of The Sill's most ancient allies." She ran her hand over the bumpy skin on the baileen's back. "During long voyages, they can be persuaded to transport us much faster than we could move on our own."

Roth shouted towards the baileen's head, "To Costas now, and stay as high as you can. The Domina are crawling and would love to take a shot at you."

The baileen released a trumpet blast in acknowledgment. Cole threw out a leg as the baileen lurched forward, rising swiftly towards the stars.

"Take a seat, Cole," Roth said, eyeing Cole's ungainly wobble. "Wouldn't want you going overboard until we are well above Costas. Actually, all of you take a seat, we've got a couple hours before you drop in, and I've got to get your thick skulls caught up to speed." The wind howled as the baileen accelerated higher above The Sill. Roth took a deep breath, shouting over the gusts, "Valen, tend to the air will you? Don't need the whole lagoon listening in."

Valen's fingers flowed over one another. Beaded emerald lines of Wisdom flowed between his hands as the roaring wind stilled to a calm eddy around them. Cole peeked over the edge. He had grown accustomed to heights, his Fear dulling somewhat after climbing and falling a few times from the behemoth trees of The Sill. This was different, however. From this height even The Sill's walls seemed miniscule. He was also not eager to discover what Roth meant by 'dropping in'. Goran cowered in the middle of the baileen's back. Lying flat on his stomach, he grasped a short fin with one hand and covered his eyes with his other hand.

Roth kicked at Goran's haunches. "Don't worry you furry coward, you won't be dropping in. This is a discreet operation, and you aren't exactly a shining example of discreetness."

"So Goran won't be coming with us?" Cole asked, putting a hand on Goran's shoulder.

"Goran and I will hang back on the baileen as your quick reaction force," Roth explained. "Your priority is subterfuge, though if you get made and things get too hot we'll drop in to pull your asses out of the fire."

"Master Roth, what exactly do you mean by *dropping in*?" Storn asked, addressing the question they were all thinking.

"I thought I told you all to take a seat!" Roth barked, whipping their legs out with a flash of Wisdom from his munisica. "We might not be training at the moment but don't think I won't take it out of your hide."

In unison the group scooted over to Cole and Goran on the leathery floor. Roth circled around them. Cole winced as his master's claws dug mercilessly into the baileen's back, leaving gouges in their wake. The gargantuan whale took no notice however, releasing a cheerful keen that echoed throughout the lagoon below.

"Enough of that!" Roth barked, stomping his foot.

The baileen rumbled beneath them in what was unmistakable laughter.

Roth halted at the rear of the baileen. Oberon loomed several feet above his head, silhouetting him like a bladed mountain peak. "This is it. This is the moment you are no longer students. You have a job, and you're going to do it or die in the attempt. I suspect some of you will suffer the latter. Though if you remember your training, keep each other in check, and stay flexible in your magic, then we may avoid another mess like Deekus."

Cole chanced a sideways glance over at Eliza. Her face was cold and still, though her munisica flexed threateningly.

"The dangers on the Light Side are very real, and so are the consequences for failure. I've no idea what demons The Three have cooked up since the banishing, though if it's anything like the last time, your little unit won't have a snowflake's chance in hell no matter how adaptive you are. That is why your mission is not that of open combat, but of stealth and thievery."

The group stirred with dissent. While no one dared voice their disapproval, it was clear this was not the assignment they had hoped for. Cole on the other hand was grateful. He may be a touch stronger and have a few shoddy tricks in his magical repertoire, but he knew he would be more of a hindrance than a help in a real fight.

A rough smile broke across Roth's face. "There are many battles in war, especially a war of this scale. Not all of them involve tearing throats and crushing limbs. As you all know the Devotion is about to take place in Costas, and this cycle's tower is rumored to be large enough to tip the scales further from our favor. We suspect they are doubling their efforts in anticipation of a massive maneuver. So far their attacks have been probing strikes meant to measure our reactions. Something big is coming, that much we know, and this Devotion will be a keystone for their success."

Roth resumed circling around the group. "Your mission is to disrupt the Devotion before it has a chance to start. The Three will arrive within the next day. By that time your asses had better be dust in the wind or you'll suffer something worse than death. How you disrupt the Devotion is up to you." Roth dragged his claws under his chin where they screeched against the black armor that stubbled his neck. "I was going to let you figure out the targets for yourselves, but I think I'll give you a few clues. Must be Alvi making me soft. I don't give out hints for free, especially ones that cost us lives, so if one of you whelps gets yourself killed without completing your mission, I swear I'll find you in the aethers and tear my payment off your soul."

Cole swallowed the threat, casting glances at the others. He had never heard of any magic enabling a person to follow another through death, but he had no doubt that Roth could do it.

"From what the Council's intelligence teams have gathered, there are a few crucial items that, if removed, would cripple the entire ceremony." He held out his munisica, clinking off the targets as he counted them on his claws: "There's the vats of odium oil. Burn these before the ceremony and they won't be available to burn the hosen. Then there's Sorronis's Priests. Kill them of course. And obviously there's the tower itself. Bring the structure down on their heads if you must. Lastly there's the Chosen themselves. Free them if you can, eliminate them if you can't. As Chosen they are immortal, so be sure there's no pieces large enough for The Three to harvest."

Cole's back straightened. "I thought we weren't supposed to harm the Underkin. Master Roth," Cole added.

Roth grunted in affirmation. "Right you are, Cole. The Underkin are not to be harmed. You are to use what you have learned at The Sill to trick them into thinking you were never there. The Chosen, be they Underkin or Aenerian, are a resource you will deny the enemy through whatever means possible. If the only possibility is to destroy them, then that's what you're going to do. If The Three add their tortured souls to their pools, then they will amass a sizeable amount of fresh power to maim and torture others." Roth paused behind Cole, donning the softest tone that his avalanche of a voice could manage. "An agonizing death is better than what The Three will do to them. Either of you have a problem with this? Answer me honestly and fully." He pointed the question to Cole and Habbad.

Habbad answered first. "Absolutely not. There is nothing preventing us from removing the lot of them. I've seen a Devotion, I know of what you speak. The Chosen may as well be named the damned. They all begged for death long before it was over, and none of them died."

Roth grunted his approval, shifting his blazing eyes to Cole.

"No, Master," Cole said.

"Outstanding. This is war, kids. You'll kill some bad ones if you're lucky, but sometimes you have to kill some good ones. You won't fully appreciate why until you've seen what your enemies do to the innocent. Now, what are your questions? I've told you the majority of what we know."

Valen spoke without pause, as if he'd been waiting on the chance: "Master, while your hints are greatly appreciated and will no doubt be of great assistance, we know not the location of the targets. Can you elaborate any further as to where we can find them? None of us has set foot in the city. You are rightly hesitant to hand out clues but our time is limited."

Cole worried Valen had stepped out of line, but to his surprise Roth started chuckling, "You know, Valen, despite coming from such a regal line of Wisdom Walkers, you're as dull as a cobb snail sometimes."

Valen let the insult stand as he pressed on. "I do not doubt you Master, but please, enlighten us. We can mend my error in intellect later. For now my concern is for the safety and efficacy of the unit."

Valen must have been genuinely concerned if he was speaking in such a forward manner with Roth. Cole had seen him punished for far less.

Roth considered Valen for a second before responding, "You express concern for your unit, but had you taken the time to properly know each and every one of them, you would know that two of your number have already been to Costas. Cole and Habbad would be happy to enlighten you, wouldn't you whelps?"

Cole blushed, feeling every eye upon him. Habbad would of course have to do most if not all of the enlightening.

Roth let Valen's shame sink in before continuing. "There you have it. Your unit has not one but two tour guides for this mission!

That's more than I've ever had, though my assignments were never as delicate as this one. I know it's not much, but if I had more intel for you I'd give it. Damn me if I haven't grown somewhat attached to your unit. I would be chafed indeed if you all didn't make it back alive for another lesson. We haven't even done a condensing yet." Roth walked towards the head of the baileen, beckoning to Valen with a jerk of his head. Valen followed and the two exchanged a few moments of unheard discussion.

Cole grabbed Habbad by the collar and yanked him close. "We're not killing Lexy."

Habbad's eyes were blank and his face expressionless. "We may not have to, but if it comes to it there's no one who will stop me."

Cole felt the Rage tingle up his neck as his fingers began to elongate and darken. He looked at his budding claws to make sure they weren't cutting Habbad, only to realize he was grasping nothing but the night air.

"You least of all," Habbad said, not bothering to look him in the eye.

"All right warriors," Roth called out to the group. "We've got some time before we're over Costas. Let's take a quick review. Nothing too deep in the weeds, just want to make sure there's no rusty surprises in the chain."

While Roth was no master with Wisdom or Passion, he was magnitudes beyond anyone in the unit. As for Rage, he was second to none. He first had each member of the unit dawn their munisica, poking and prodding with provocative insults to encourage full release. All but Habbad were able to bring forth their ebony dragon claws, with Sitra and Storn even spreading their shrouded armor up to their elbows. He then tested their Passion. Valen volunteered to receive a series of calculated injuries from Roth, after which each member attempted to heal the injury. Everyone except for Cole, Habbad and Lileth were able to completely heal the collapsed lung, broken ribs or torn skin. After an all too brief respite Roth then individually assaulted each of their minds. Unlike Chiron, Roth's presence in Cole's mind was blaringly apparent. It felt as if he were an ant standing upon the rail of a train track, watching and waiting for the locomotive to crash into him. Time and again, Cole found himself paralyzed by the sheer force, as Roth swept through his memories as if skimming a book with a chainsaw. Try as he may, his efforts yielded nothing except the knowledge that should his mind ever be attacked, he'd better have a friend nearby to save him.

"That'll do, that'll do," Roth said as Cole regained use of his limbs. "Pick yourselves up and gather round. We're going to review one more thing before I release you all to devise your own battle plan."

Cole stood, swaying slightly. He rubbed his temples in an attempt to clear the foggy pain that remained. He felt a warm hand at the base of his skull. His eyes met Lileth's as ringing clarity replaced the weariness. She pulled her lavender hand away, though she stepped closer to him. Cole silently indulged in the feeling of her arm against his shoulder.

Roth stood in the center of their group now, scrutinizing each of them in turn as if he were inspecting meat at the markets. "Individually you've each got some gaping holes in your training. Some worse than others of course. No surprises though, which is good. You know whom you can rely on, and for what." A grim shadow fell over Roth's face, his ferocity fading somewhat. "There is a chance you may face some of the more elite minions of The Three. I'm not talking about Domina or other monsters that you can simply break with fire and claw. I'm talking about fellow Aenerians skilled in dark magics. Hell, you may even find yourselves standing before The Three themselves. In that case you'd better kill each other before they notice, but let's just focus on your run-of-the-mill expert-level enemy for now. I know you've all been taught the basics of their magic, but I need to hear you say it. What is the enemy of Rage?"

Cole's knees almost gave out at the weight of Roth's stare. He took a deep breath and made sure he spoke loudly enough: "Master, Grotton the Hungry is the enemy of Rage."

"Right you are. Don't be fooled by the whispered temptations of Hunger. Grotton knows what makes you powerful, and his minions will offer you all you want, for a price." Roth turned to Habbad. "What is the enemy of Wisdom?"

Habbad raised his chin and threw his shoulders back. "If Wisdom were one side of a coin, then Decreath the Feared would be on the other. Fear is the antithesis of Wisdom."

"And don't forget it. Nothing will do more to take away a warrior's ability to think than a stomach full of cold fear. Decreath knows your shame and his minions will soak you in it." He twisted around, this time facing Eliza. "What is the enemy of Passion?"

"Master, Sorronis the Lord of Despair and Hatred is the enemy of Passion," Eliza replied, her munisica flexing in the moonlight.

"He is indeed. Sorronis may as well be called Sorronis the Patient. He sits quietly on the edges of your thoughts, waiting and watching for a moment of doubt. When the smallest crack presents itself he will seep in like a poison and flood you with Despair until you have nothing but your own Hatred to keep afloat. Sorronis is perhaps the most dangerous of The Three. Elites and empires alike have crumbled from the inside out by his magic."

Roth went to his bag and pulled out a large object wrapped in burlap. "It is one thing to talk about dark magics. It is another beast entirely when a skilled enemy turns the worst parts of your own soul against you. The only defense is to be flexible and dynamic in your hearts and in your minds. Were you not trained at The Sill, your unit would quickly find itself at the mercy of a skilled enemy who played your weaknesses like a lock and key. But you *are* from The Sill, and therein lies your advantage. Your enemies are powerful, but rigid. Find the narrow bridge they walk on and kick them off."

With a flourish, Roth yanked the burlap cloth free, tossing it into the wind. In his clawed hand was the largest and brightest gratia stone any of them had ever seen. Had he not known better, Cole would have assumed Roth was holding a barrel of molten lava. "This is my gift to you. Should you find an enemy who can be broken, this will aid you. Take as much as you can without killing yourselves, and use it only if you need it. Should you not use it the Rage will eventually dissolve into your bodies, granting you a permanent increase in your physical abilities. It is best to not gain power this way. It's too fast, and you won't have earned it, but I'd rather see you fumble about like strong idiots than dead scholars."

Following the lead of the others, Cole and Habbad each placed a hand on the stone. Seeing munisica sprout from their hands, Cole tapped into his Rage. His own claws sprouted much more quickly than usual, and the shroud covered his entire hand. His vision flickered and vanished until he was only aware of what felt like a massive storm bearing down on him. The thunderhead poured all of its lightning and Rage into him. His skin hardened, his bones hummed, and his muscles swelled painfully. Above all else he felt an insatiable desire to direct this power at something. He wanted to tear through rock and metal, jump to Oberon, run faster than the wind. He needed a release. His muscles continued to swell until he felt they might literally explode. He knew he was dangerously close to the 'killing yourself' part, but it felt too good. He took a little more before yanking his hand from the stone. His vision cleared and his mental acuity returned, though he could barely move his arms and legs. Looking down he could see steam rising from skin stretched over veiny bulges. Muscles he didn't even know he had were ballooned to cartoonish proportions. Just as he began to worry how this new growth would affect his ability to walk and fight, the muscles shrank gently back to their original size. The burning transferred to his bones instead, settling deep in the marrow, waiting for the right moment to be called for release.

After everyone had taken their fill, what little scarlet light remained faded as Roth touched the stone to an unshrouded portion of his abdomen. The gratia stone cracked and crumbled as he cast it off the side of the baileen.

"Master Roth?" Valen asked, visibly struggling with his Rage.

"What is it, Valen?" Roth picked a bloody shard from the skin on his stomach.

"I am curious as to how we became entrusted with this mission. Surely one as experienced as you would be better suited than an untested group such as ourselves. We are all grateful for the chance to prove ourselves, but the risk… I have to ask, why are you not joining us on this mission?"

"You're too clever for your own good." Roth ran his munisica through his bladed hair. "Some people smarter than us decided that you were the right unit for the job. We'll just leave it at that for now." He frowned, shaking his head dismissively as if churning over some internal debate. "To hell with it. You are not the only unit working this mission right now. You are merely a finger in the fist. You weren't supposed to know that, but you've got the right. I'll be up here monitoring each unit and relaying your progress back to The Sill. But like I said, should things get too hot down there I'll drop in and throw some oil on the fire before I pull your asses out." He nudged Goran's ribs with a less pointy part of his foot. "I'll bring this one too."

Valen cocked his head thoughtfully. "I have full confidence in our unit; however it is comforting to know that we are not the only means of success for this mission. Thank you, Master. If you are finished I would like to spend the duration of the flight discussing strategy with the others."

"Have at it. You've some time. When you see lights on the horizon that would be Costas. I'll be up front if you have any questions."

After an hour of the unit's deliberating, the nervous pit in Cole's stomach had hardened into a sickening bundle of frozen snakes. He imagined scenarios of facing these skilled enemies alone, and he couldn't imagine what it would be like to face The Three. What scared him the most, however, was that he was pretty sure of what Roth meant by 'dropping in'. Even now the others discussed strategy without a care in the world about falling miles through open air. They had their own Wisdom to trust in for the descent. Cole interrupted the strategizing to make it abundantly clear that there was no way he could maintain any sort of spell whilst freefalling. Thankfully Lileth assured him that she would catch him, one way or another.

"Line up along the flank. Not too close to the tail," Roth bellowed above the wind. Valen had released his spell in preparation for their drop.

Cole shuffled his feet up to the edge, careful to avoid the bumps along the baileen's back so he would have sure footing. His legs shook with debilitating jolts of anxiety. He reached out for something to hold on to, as if that would somehow make things easier.

He leaned his eyes over the edge, feeling as if the open air below were trying to yank him over. Cole's legs wobbled as his lungs couldn't seem to breathe fast enough. His heart slammed against his chest, as if trying to escape so it wouldn't have to join the rest of his body in the fall. His fingers searched for something familiar as he glued his eyes to the baileen's back. A warm hand found his, solid and safe. Cole looked up at Lileth. Her warm smile alleviated all his worry, though only for a moment. To his horror, he noticed they were the only ones left on the baileen, save for Roth and Goran. He expected some sort of count-down or signal, anything to ready him for the leap. Lileth dropped her gaze and tightened her grip on his hand. Her expression was grave. She had him now. With a slight nod, she stepped out into open air.

CHAPTER 23

FINAL RENDEZVOUS

Cole's instincts took hold of his limbs, replacing his shaking Fear with primal defiance. He would not go off the edge. He was simply not ready. But there he was, tipping over into open air. He gnashed his teeth as his munisica flared, sinking his claws as deep as he could into the baileen's hide. For a split second, he held both himself and Lileth with a single claw gripping with the power of mortal terror. He made to readjust for better leverage, but a sense of weightlessness took him, and he and Lileth began to float from the baileen. Then before he knew it, he was falling. His stomach lurched up into his mouth as he flailed like a cat forced into water. Lileth pulled him into her, wrapping her arms and legs around him and trapping his limbs. Cole fought with everything he had, but her grip was unyielding. Helplessness smothered him as he succumbed to the crippling sensations. He released a long guttural moan as his unruly organs forced the air out of his lungs. He tried to take a breath but his abdominal muscles were clamped tight. He was in wild freefall and there was nothing he could do about it.

Lileth pressed her lips to his ear, speaking through the tearing wind: "You are safe, Cole. I have you."

Cole's body continued to revolt, though the sensations relented as they approached terminal velocity. His munisica receded and his guts untangled themselves. It now felt as if he were being held aloft by the air, not falling through it. Pragmatic clarity replaced his primal Fears as he realized he was not about to die.

"I have you," she said again. "I won't let go."

Cole looked below them, taking in the lights of Costas, still miles away. Below them Cole made out an emerald light which flashed twice.

Lileth released one hand from Cole and returned the signal with her own flash. She tightened her embrace on Cole and aimed towards where the light was. They accelerated again, cutting through the air like a javelin. Cole's intestines squirmed, though not overwhelmingly so. The light flashed again, this time Cole finding five black specks floating in the air below them. As they approached, he noticed their arms and legs were spread wide, directing them through the air.

"I am going to release you now. Move yourself to my side to complete the circle," she said, giving him a reassuring hug.

"All right!" Cole attempted to shout, but the wind ripped the words from his mouth.

Lileth released him and gently guided him to her right. Cole wobbled, fighting to steady himself. After a few ungainly tremors he became somewhat accustomed to the torrent of wind and joined the circle. As they had planned, they joined hands, forming a ring of rippling cloth and sprawling legs. Valen squinted, checking with each of them before starting his part. He closed his eyes as the muscles in his face relaxed. A scintillating liquid-like substance spread down his face, neck, and body, leaving open sky in its wake. After a few seconds, Valen was entirely invisible. When the glittery liquid reached his hands it spread to Sitra and Habbad, dousing them as well before spreading to Storn and Eliza, and then to Lileth and Cole. The entire unit was invisible now.

Falling without even his own body as a point of reference, Cole felt as if he were nothing but a ghost. He squeezed Eliza and Lileth's hands, just to be sure he was not alone. They continued to fall, but they were now moving laterally as Habbad used Wisdom to guide the group towards the spot where they would land. Without Oberon's glow, he could just barely make out the grassy fields in the starlight. Deciding he was now relaxed enough to attempt the magic, Cole recalled a lesson with Chiron about the anatomy of the eye. The ideas tried to wriggle loose in his mind like a fish in his hands, but his will clamped down on the concepts and forced them to his liking. He closed his eyes and felt the parts of his orbs stretch and grow. When he opened them again he saw the ground below them as if illuminated on a cloudy day. He could even make out the colors of the trees and houses below. Above him he saw clusters of stars and even little swirls of distant galaxies in the constellations.

They were now directly above the grassy field. Cole could make out individual waves as the breeze raced through the grass. As Habbad had mentioned, the vegetation offered ample concealment even for the giant Aenerians. He'd also said the locals avoided it for Fear of venomous critters that called the grassy pond home.

The ground revealed more detail as they neared it. Soon they could no longer see the entire city, just the fields and some of the outlying buildings of Habbad's district. Before Cole had a chance to worry about hitting the ground, he felt a comforting resistance throughout his body as Lileth's magic took hold of him once more, slowing him to a creeping fall. Cole kicked out his bare feet, trying to feel the tops of the grass with his invisible toes. The dried blades tickled the soles of his feet as the unit slid down, unseen and unheard over the stalks whispering in the breeze. With steadying relief, Cole felt his naked feet land on solid ground below, cool soil filling the gaps between his toes. They were in Costas.

"Don't let go yet," Lileth whispered as Cole tried to wriggle his hand free to scratch his nose.

Through the blades of grass, Cole saw the members of his unit, flickering with crackling white light before appearing in full. The grass between them began to fall away as Sitra walked in loops around them, gusts of air bursting from her outward-facing palms. As the air hit the grass, the blades shrank rapidly back into the soil. They were now enclosed in a dome of tall stalks carved out by Sitra's magic. Both Lileth and Valen swayed slightly, recovering from the mental exertions of their respective spells.

Valen regained his composure first, his dreamy countenance hardening back into cold reason. He turned to Habbad. "I hope you have something by now. Where should we start our search for the targets?"

"Just head towards the City. Can you render us invisible again?" Habbad asked.

"Not for some time, but I do not think we should wait for me to recover. We must be gone from here as soon as possible. I shudder to think how we would fare against The Three." Valen motioned towards Sitra. "If you would lead the way."

"Of course," Sitra replied, blasting the grass in front of them with more gusts of air, clearing a wide path. The group stepped forward, following closely behind her.

"If one of you could change the color of your garments to all white, we may be as good as invisible. Make Valen's red. With some luck we may pass as a group of priests with Cole and me as your servants." Habbad gave Cole a shifty look, dropping his voice into an undertone. "Your stature can no longer pass for an Underkin, so try to stay in the middle of the group.

"What do you mean?" Cole then dropped his voice so only Habbad could hear. "I'm a full grown. I was when I first met you."

"He means you're getting taller," Storn said, clapping Cole on the shoulders. "Thicker in the limbs too. Maybe it's all the market food and exercise. You're not the same starved rat that washed up in the tide. I swear you weren't even up to my belt line. Now you're up to my belly button at least, and that's with bare feet. You keep growing like a vine and you might actually put up a decent fight in Roth's lessons." Storn chuckled, mussing Cole's hair.

"You guys are out of it." Cole jerked his head away, dodging Storn's claw. He knew he was putting on some size, but he still wasn't sure about getting taller. Maybe he was going through some late adolescent growth spurt.

"It is true. You are taller than when I met you," Eliza said, following with a hand on Storn's shoulder. Her eyes were closed and her face twisted with concentration. "There are no critters from here to the city, venomous or not." She relaxed, bringing a warm smile down on Cole. "And you are no Underkin."

"I...well of course I am. Didn't Roth tell you I came from Costas?" Cole faltered. Eliza continued to smile through his lies.

"That's an invasion of my privacy you know!" Cole blurted. "Inspecting me with your Passion like that! Roth told me not to tell anyone. When he finds out he'll break my arms and toss me into the lagoon."

"Calm down jitter brains," Sitra called from over her shoulder. "We don't need Passion to see you aren't made of the same stuff as Habbad. It's like looking at two different species of plants. You're the same shape but you two are no more alike than he is to me. And don't worry about Roth. I made him bleed once, I'll do it again if he punishes you for being a bad liar."

Cole laughed nervously. Here he was on a real mission with real life or death consequences, but he was more afraid of Roth's reprisal than real enemies. "To hell with it. If we make it through this alive then I'll give you guys the real story."

"I for one would enjoy that immensely." Valen flashed an inquisitive look at Cole. "We are family. Secrets do nothing but divide us when we should be working as a cohesive whole. If we are successful in our mission, I will tell you and Habbad the story of how I came to hold such strong feelings against the Underkin, until recently that is." The last words were spoken gently and directed at Habbad.

Habbad turned his nose from Valen. "And I will explain my abhorrence for all of you Dark Ones, but right now we ought to keep our discussion to the task at hand. Your clothes, can you change them or not?"

"We can," Valen replied.

"Then do it now before we enter the city. Once inside, Valen stays to the rear where I will walk beside him. The rest of you walk in a group in front of him. Avoid any other Aenerians, and if an Underkin talks to you, you strike them down on the spot, no magic. Walk uphill, towards the center of the city. Hopefully we will find some targets along the way."

Storn interjected, "What do you mean *hopefully*? Are we tackling this tower with our hopes and dreams? I thought you grew up here. Don't you have a plan?"

Habbad sighed. "If nothing else, Kreed is effective. Ignorance is but one finger on the hand of tyranny. I have never seen anything outside of my little district and some of the surrounding forest. The general population knows nothing outside of their world. Kreed has taken a liking to me so I know a bit more than most, but he's never shared the intricacies involved in the Devotion."

"Then what are we supposed to do, walk around town until we bump into one of our targets? Or should we just sit and wait for The Three to come find us?" Storn's tone was accusatory, though it carried hints of suppressed dread.

"More or less, yes," Habbad replied, unconcerned. "With the rest of you wearing the colors of the priests, we can explore Costas unmolested and possibly draw the attention of other priests that we can dispatch at our discretion. I do not think the priests will be a valid target though. There are hundreds of them wandering around the city. The majority of them will be congregating in Kreed's estate, which we should avoid. Should we kill even a score of them, there will be others to see to the Devotion. That leaves the vats of odium oil, the Chosen, and the tower itself. I don't know where the oil is stored, or if it's all in one place, but without the flames from the odium they can't burn the souls of the Chosen. The tower should be easy enough to find, however."

"I'd say so." Sitra paused in her pruning and let out a low whistle. "That wouldn't be the tower right there, would it?"

"Not likely. We are too far away from the center of the city." Habbad frowned as he used Wisdom to float up over their heads, emitting dull jade light from under his hands and feet. He swore, cutting the light off and dropping back to the soil. "No!"

Habbad pulled at his hair, eyes glassing over, "Last Devotion had the largest tower anyone had ever seen and this one is easily twice that height." He paused, regaining his composure somewhat. "And there are three of them."

"What is the significance of two extra towers? As tall as they are we can topple any structure, no matter the size," Valen said with unrestrained pride.

A grim shadow deepened Habbad's wrinkles. "The Chosen from last cycle dwindled our numbers to an almost unrecoverable point. Should these towers burn, this will be the end of the Underkin."

"I see." Valen scrunched his brow. "Then we will ensure that these towers never see the light of flame."

Lileth and Valen changed the colors of everyone's clothes, and at Habbad's direction, altered their armor to look more like ceremonial robes. They dropped their packs and donned their boots before eating a quick meal. When their bellies were full and they looked their parts, they emerged from the grass in a somber formation.

"Are the streets usually this empty?" Valen asked without looking at anyone.

"This is unusually barren, though we are only on the outskirts," Habbad replied, eyes darting from empty doors to alleys.

The lanterns outside each of the ramshackle homes emitted a glow barely visible. Carts full of rotting food littered the streets as though abandoned in a hurry. Cole stepped on something soft. Looking down he saw a doll made from cloth and bits of grass. With each step they took, an eerie silence grew louder, wrapping around them. It felt as if the district had been waiting for them.

"Eliza, can you sense anyone nearby?" Lileth asked, keeping her head and eyes forward.

"For some reason my Passion can't feel anyone outside our unit." She closed her eyes while maintaining her stride. "Either the city has been abandoned or the entire populace has been Chosen. Kreed's taint may very well be hiding them from the eyes of Passion."

"It is likely, judging by the volume of the towers." Habbad voice was devoid of emotion, as if he had already accepted the doom of his people. "Let us see what there is to find farther in. I suggest you release whatever spells you have active. If there are any Corpulants skulking about they will sense your Wisdom."

A collective sigh of annoyance spread through the group as they dissolved their spells to sharpen sight and hearing, slowing their pace commensurately. They drove on into the depths of Costas, checking inside empty rooms and alleys along the way. After a half hour of wandering they passed through a polished marble threshold carved in the likeness of two Aenerians. With one arm they formed the arch, hands meeting in a gentle embrace. With the other hand they each wielded a knife buried into their own ribs. While one face was twisted with agony, the other beamed with elation. As the team walked under the arms, Cole averted his eyes from the grisly scene. The sculptor had obviously spent an indulgent amount of time on the wounds and faces.

"We are now leaving the Underkin's quarter." Habbad leaned his head around the legs in front of him, casting furtive glances down the road. "Underkin are not permitted to walk these streets without Aenerian escort. I have only done so a few times, and Kreed made me wear a mask so I couldn't see where I was going. I'm afraid we have reached the limit of my knowledge of the area. I suggest we split the group to cover more ground. What say you, Valen?"

Valen checked the surrounding area before dropping his gaze to Habbad. "That would obviously be more efficient, but I am concerned with our combat strength. We would have no way of knowing if one group was in danger, and we may need the strength of the entire unit to respond to whatever troubles await. We will stay together."

"Then we must move quickly," Habbad replied.

"Wait a second," Cole interrupted. "Eliza, you used to link up with Deekus and talk with your minds. Chiron once talked to me with his mind too. Couldn't we do that now?"

Eliza twitched at the mention of her mate. "Deekus and I had a fraternal link, which is no small feat of Passion. Even if I could maintain the link to another heart, the information exchanged would be limited, and one-way, and seeing as no one else has bothered with that aspect of Passion..." She trailed off, as her tone sharpened to accusation.

"Try it," Cole said, ignoring her glare.

"Try what, exactly?" she said with an impatient hiss.

"The link. Try the fraternal link with me. I know I'm the worst with magic, but I am bonded with Goran. Even now I can feel how afraid and uncomfortable he is, and he's miles away. I'm not asking you to give your heart to me, just try the link." Cole reached out and took one of her large hands, wrapping his around two of her fingers.

She brought her other hand over his, covering them both. Tears threatened to roll from her eyes. "You don't understand. The link requires certain parts of yourself. I cannot give those parts to anyone else, they are broken and raw. I may damage you through the process."

Cole adopted a consoling tone: "I've lost someone I loved too. I know what it feels like." He winced as the memories flared up to the fore of his mind. He pushed them back like he had done countless times before. "Try the link with me. If it's too much we'll just stick together and search as a group."

Eliza regarded him for a moment, then clasped her hands over his face and crouched down to meet him. "We haven't much time, relax your mind and open your heart to me. Think about how I make you feel. Don't hold anything back or it won't work." Her eyebrows joined as she pierced him with her gaze.

"Ok," Cole said, regret pooling in his chest. He relaxed and stared into her eyes.

He thought about what he knew of Eliza, which was embarrassingly little. He had known and worked with her every day for months. Would it have killed him to ask a question or two about how she was feeling one day, or something about her past? He focused instead on how she made him feel. He remembered feeling comforted and welcomed by her on their first meeting. He recalled seeing her in her swimwear, and how good she looked. He immediately shifted his focus to more innocent thoughts.

Eliza shook her head, the urgency in her eyes clearly reminding him not to hold back.

He delved into the feelings again, arousal now mixing with the other sensations. She nodded, encouraging him to continue. Cole brought his thoughts to the subject he was avoiding. He could feel the weight of it behind a thin gap in between where he stored his nightmares. He thought of Deekus.

This is what she had been waiting for. Their mutual relationship, however slight, was enough for her to create the link. It was a thin strand of empathy at first, but then she widened it, pouring her love and agony into him. The force of it almost overwhelmed him at first, but he too had suffered such loss. His emotional scars were strong enough to carry the weight. Cole accepted the burden, sharing it with her, offering his own grief and love for Joshy. Even though she didn't know his brother, she was able to understand what he had been through. The link was strong enough now. Relief flowed over both their faces. Her eyes softened and offered Cole a look of deepest gratitude.

"I had no idea you suffered so much. You are a resilient one, Cole Carter." Her voice echoed into his mind.

"You are strong as well. We both lost something. I used to think I was pretty tough, but the truth is I had never been tested. I'm still not

strong enough to face my demons though. Maybe someday," he replied, thinking the words directly to her. *"Is the link strong enough?"*

"Oh it's strong enough. We can communicate as clearly as we are now from any distance." Eliza released Cole's face, turning towards the rest of the unit. "It is done."

"Are you sure? There can be no doubt." Valen gave her a skeptical look.

"There is no doubt. Split the unit as you see fit," Eliza said.

Valen rattled off the names without hesitation. "Storn, Eliza, and I will go left here. Lileth, take Habbad, Cole, and Sitra to the right. We'll loop around the towers from opposite directions and relay our findings along the way."

Sitra cut in, "You mean to tell me my group's going to be without a competent healer?"

"Each of your number is competent to some degree," Valen offered.

"You know what I mean. Lileth can only seem to heal Cole, and he and Habbad haven't been able to heal as much as a bruise yet."

Eliza shook her head. "I wouldn't be so sure about Cole. He just hasn't had the proper motivation to use that aspect of Passion. He is most adept with other areas."

"Hmph." Sitra crossed her arms. "Until he shows a bit of aptitude, I think we'll just have him take the lead. That way if he gets mangled Lil can patch him up."

"Do what you must, but do it quickly." Valen straightened his red robes. "Storn, Eliza, let's get moving."

Valen's group set off at a brisk pace, leaving the rest of them in thick silence.

"Shall we?" Lileth brushed her fingers over her robed armor, turning it blood red with each stroke.

Habbad walked beside Lileth in the rear, but he led the group with whispered instructions. With his guidance, they wove their way through thoroughfares, each street and alley more elegant than the last, but still eerily deserted. They passed through residential and commercial areas, peering sideways through each darkened window. There was no sign of life, though the area didn't have the abandoned look of the Underkin's district. After a while they rounded a corner, looping back towards the tower.

"Anything yet?" Cole asked through the link.

Eliza did not respond immediately. Cole asked again, widening the link and pressing his urgency into the message. Eliza replied with a soothing tone. *"There is no need to shout. I can feel you as if you were riding on my shoulders."*

"Then what's with the delay?" Cole demanded.

Her tone was that of violent calm: *"While inspecting a warehouse we were questioned by two priests. I was…distracted."*

Cole didn't like some of the images that joined her words. *"What happened, is everything all right?"* he asked.

"We are perfectly safe. The warehouse held linens, not odium as we'd hoped." She pressed upon him images of Valen and Storn, who were busy cleaning something that looked like blood from their robes.

"And what about the priests? Did they question you?" Cole was absolutely terrified of the possibility of hostile magic users. He had seen the things his unit was capable of, and heard stories of what the minions of The Three could do.

"They didn't get the chance to ask us anything. Just know that there are two fewer priests for us to worry about." She flooded his mind with reassuring images, putting an end to his questioning.

Cole stopped walking, jittery shock setting in. The gravity of the mission hit him with a morbid sense of reality.

"What's wrong, Cole? Are they ok?" Sitra gripped his arm painfully.

"They're fine. They just killed two priests." The words tasted like sawdust in his mouth.

"Dammit, I bet Storn I would get the first kill. Now I have to buy him a cypher from the erotic section," Sitra said through clenched teeth.

Cole stared at her, incredulous. How could she be more concerned about losing a bet than about an imminent fight for their lives?

Sensing his discomfort, Eliza chimed into their link. *"The priests seem more accustomed to torturing Underkin and groveling to Sorronis than any real fighting. They are easy to kill. Steel your heart, Cole. I felt their souls as they left for the aethers. They were evil priestesses and not to be mourned. Do not hesitate."* She repeated Roth's first rule, which hardened his heart considerably.

Eliza withdrew from the connection, leaving a thin yet unbreakable strand. Cole shook off his worry. If Eliza said these were bad people, then he wouldn't feel sorry or scared of killing them.

"You are too engrossed in Passion." Lileth pulled his eyes into hers. "Do not forget your Wisdom and Rage. You may well have need of them all too soon." She turned towards the others. "As Roth said, this is a mission of stealth and thievery. We will kill if necessary, but our primary concern is for the targets. Keep moving."

Lileth was right. Cole felt so full of Passion that his other parts faded to the back of his mind. Valen's team likely had no choice but to kill the priests, and they would have done so with maximum efficiency and minimal suffering. The mere thought of someone threatening his unit almost brought his munisica through his new boots. It was with an effort that he didn't pounce when they rounded a corner and came face to face with a group of Underkin.

Habbad put a hand on Sitra and Cole, stilling them. He moved to the front of the group. "How dare you stand in the path of an agent of Sorronis? And you've no escort in the Valley District! Explain yourselves while you still draw breath."

The four Underkin cowered together, attempting to appear as small as possible. A man in front gripped his large water skin as if it were a life vest on a sinking ship. His lips trembled as he spoke. "Our deepest apologies sirs and ma'ams. We meant no offense. Our dull ears can't hear graceful footsteps such as yours from around the corner."

"Tell them that they can avoid punishment if they can pass my test," Lileth said, her voice as calm as it was deadly.

Habbad locked a raised eye with Lileth, patting his dagger as though letting her know the cost. He turned back to the four trembling figures, relaying her message. The Underkin deliberated for a moment before nodding their approval, eager to please.

Lileth raised her chin and spoke in a regal tone. "The test is thus; they are to explain to me everything they know about the Devotion, and of its importance. If their answer satisfies me, then they shall not be punished."

Habbad cocked his head, visibly pleased. He repeated her words, even though the Underkin had clearly understood what Lileth said. They apparently had no right to talk directly to an agent of Sorronis.

Relief washed over the man in front as he relaxed his grip on his water skin. "Ah, but of course we are not to speak of the Devotion. Father Kreed told us what we needed to know, and his words were for our ears only. It is forbidden, sirs and ma'ams. Does this answer please the ma'am?" A smug grin spread across his face as his comrades clapped him on the back.

"Very…good. Very good indeed. You may go now." Lileth's confidence faltered, but the Underkin seemed not to notice as they bolted towards the towers, showering praise upon the one who'd passed the test.

"That could have gone a lot worse," Cole remarked.

Habbad kept his murderous glare on the Underkin as they disappeared around a bend in the alley. "That was clever, but next time we ought to kill them. Our gamble yielded nothing except for a very proud man who is itching to tell his friends how he passed a test for Sorronis. If a real priest gets wind of his deeds then there will be questions. Questions that will likely lead back to us."

They agreed to be more careful and continued their search around the edge of the city. Twice, Sitra spotted a group of Underkin and took the team on a more circuitous route.

"There shouldn't be any Underkin without escort in these parts. Did my eyes deceive me or were they all headed for the towers?" Habbad asked.

"I think you're right. Do you think the Devotion's already started?" Cole asked.

"It is possible. I was very young during the last one. The only part that stuck in my memory was the burning of the tower. That and the celebrations beforehand." Habbad scowled, "Men and women alike giving into their most primal desires. The fact that they were Chosen gave them license to do terrible things that they would never dare on a normal day. Fights and murdering, lusting in the streets, thievery and overindulgence. The Aenerians encouraged it." Habbad nodded with grim realization. "It must have made for better harvesting when they went to the towers."

"From what I know of the darker magics, that makes sense," Lileth said, peering through the window of a large empty building. "Debauchery fattens certain parts of the soul, a much better meal for those willing to feed. Something doesn't make sense to me, however." She turned to Habbad: "Do Underkin dehydrate easily in Costas?"

"Those of us working hard labor do. It is not uncommon for someone to drop dead during the daylight months. Usually the very old or very young." He stopped. "Why do you ask?"

"We've seen over a dozen of your kind so far. Each one was carrying a water skin so large and full that they were sweating from the exertions, though the skins were all full to bursting, untouched."

Habbad rubbed his chin. "I noticed that as well. Perhaps they are bringing liquors to the Chosen."

Cole gasped, slapping his forehead. "Or they're carrying bags of odium to the Chosen at the towers!"

"That is my conclusion." Lileth's face darkened. "Only I believe that they *are* the Chosen. Each one is carrying his own supply of odium for the burning."

"What makes you think that?" Cole asked, his eyebrows joined in concern as the implications fell into place. "That means the odium's no good! There must be thousands of bags crawling all over the city! We're running out of targets."

"I tried probing those Underkin with Passion," Lileth said, her face drooping with sadness. "Their hearts and minds were nothing but dank voids resonating Despair. Also, each one of them had a blackened scar on his face or neck. They must be the Chosen." Lileth slowed, turning to Cole: "And I believe you to be right, the odium is no longer a valid target."

Sitra's munisica sprang from her hands, tearing her boots completely off. "That leaves the towers. *That* we can do." Fire blazed in her eyes as she flexed her black claws. "We'll bring them down on their heads."

"Are you sure?" Cole asked, his heart skipping double time. "There has to be another way. The towers are probably guarded."

"There are no other viable targets," Lileth said. Her face was grave. "The priests' numbers are too great, and scattered. The Chosen and odium even more so. The towers are our only option. We will bring them down." She put a hand on Cole's shoulder, squeezing him gently. "Tell the others to make for the center of the city."

"All right," Cole said, voice cracking. Taking the towers would surely mean a fight. A real one. He had been in life-threatening situations before, but he'd never had time to think about it beforehand. He swallowed, trying to wet his throat before speaking to Eliza with his mind. He closed his eyes, reaching for the thread. He couldn't find it. Worried, he reached again. Nothing. The familiar link was nowhere to be found. There was something else there, however, something serious. He found another strand. He tuned his empathy to a pitch that better suited this link.

"*Cole!*" Eliza's voice echoed with panic and urgency.

Cole enveloped her: "*I'm here. Is everything all right?*"

Her panic and tears were palpable through the link: "*There are Domina within the city. They came out of nowhere. Dammit they're fast. Storn's down, wounded. They opened him right up. Something is preventing my Passion from healing him, some kind of poison. Valen is doing what he can to stop the bleeding, but I don't think Storn's going to make it.*"

Cole could feel the eyes of his team on him. "*Where are you? We'll come help!*"

Eliza's tone steadied to resigned sorrow. "*No, see to the targets. There's nothing to be done for him now. Perhaps Alvani could heal him, but that's not an option. Have you found the odium?*"

Cole rubbed his thumbs on his temples. His head was starting to hurt. "*The Chosen are each carrying their own bags of odium. There's too many of them. The towers are the only good targets now. Have you seen any of the other units that Roth was talking about? It seems like it's just us out here.*"

"*No, but the city is large.*" There was a pause. Cole could feel the wheels spinning in her mind. "*We're close to the towers now. Meet us on the roof of the dark stone building. It's the one next to the belltower.*"

"What about Storn?" Even as he asked, images of Storn's limp form swam in front of his mind's eye.

"We'll bring him with us. Maybe Lileth can do something for him. Whether he survives or not, we are not leaving his body for some wretched Corpulant to find. Hurry Cole." She withdrew from the link.

"We're on our way." Cole opened his eyes, coming back to reality.

Lileth hands clamped down on his shoulders, fingers bruising his flesh. "What happened?"

Cole flinched, attempting to shake her off. "There's Domina in the city. One of them got Storn and he's hurt pretty bad. Eliza can't heal him. We're going to meet up by the towers."

Lileth released his arm, spinning towards the towers. "Move your asses then."

Her boots split and tore as the black daggers sprouted. She jumped most of the way up a three-story building before digging her claws in and showering the team with bits of brick and mortar. Sitra flew right behind her. Cole hesitated for a moment as he dug into his Rage and summoned his munisica. The stretching and hardening of his flesh still pained him, but it felt good in a way, as though fulfilling his need for violence. He felt Roth's Rage boiling up from his bones, but he was careful not to use it. This was clearly not the time. He kicked off the remains of his boots and looked to Habbad, who was already floating up the side of the building, little eddies of jade light trailing under his hands and feet. Cole leapt as high as he could, reaching the top of the first window before slamming his claws into the brick. He felt like a cat as he scooted up the wall, catching up to Habbad. He wished he had Goran with him now.

Lileth and Sitra waited for them on the roof. They had a clear view of the towers from here. Habbad took the lead as they ran for the towers, hopping from roof to roof. Luckily the gaps weren't too wide, though on more than one occasion Cole had to stretch his jump with Wisdom to make the distance. Hopefully there weren't any Corpulants nearby to smell his Wisdom.

As they neared the towers more and more people could be seen in the streets below, both Underkin and Aenerians. They had to sheath their munisica. Their claws made entirely too much noise as they tore through the various materials of the rooftops.

Cole skidded to a stop, scraping his bare feet on a rooftop patio as he bumped into Sitra. Habbad ducked, motioning for them to go back, but it was too late. A door opened. Out came several Aenerians, including two priests wearing red robes.

At first the Aenerians looked pleasantly bemused, sipping their drinks and laughing merrily. A woman hanging off the arm of one of the priests was first to speak.

"Are these friends of yours, Rebuno?" she asked, sloshing her drink down the priest's robes. "A haggard-looking bunch, but they'll make a nice addition to our little party." She paused, leaning down to better look at Habbad and Cole. "Shouldn't the Underkin be down in the square?" She gasped, bubbling with excitement, "Oh Rebuno, they aren't for us are they? I've been waiting for you to teach me how to feed!"

The priest on her arm cast a wary glance around the patio. "Still your tongue, woman." He threw her off, sending her giggling and sprawling into the arms of another. "Who are you and what are you doing in my home? Answer me!"

Lileth raised her chin, fixing herself in a regal posture to match the priests. "These two," she said, indicating Cole and Habbad, "wandered away from the festivities below. My associate and I followed them up here to ensure they weren't trying to escape. As a fellow priest I'm sure-"

"That's enough!" Rebuno spat, rolling his sleeves. The other priest took a step forward. Something dark began dripping from his fingertips. "Close your mouth before any more of that excrement falls out. You are no priest." His lip curled as he regarded their bare feet. "It is of no consequence, however. After I've torn your secrets from you we'll see what Father Kreed feels a fitting punishment. The towers could always use a few more souls."

Lileth opened her palms to show she was no threat, taking a slow step towards the priest. "Please, inspect me first. I'm sure you'll find nothing worth bothering Father Kreed over."

"I told you shut your mouth, you lying harlot!" Rebuno slapped Lileth, splitting the skin under her eye. It was nothing compared to

Roth's training, but the insult sent tingles of Rage pounding up Cole's spine. "Give me the Underkin first. I am most curious as to how..." his voice trailed off. Recognition flashed in his eyes. "That one, that's the one Father Kreed is looking for. Habbad, that's his name. And this one must be the hum-"

Rebuno's words were cut short. Sitra was suddenly standing in front of him, as though she'd teleported there magically. She pulled her hand from his throat, her munisica scraping against the bones in his jaw on the way out. Blood gushed from the wound as Rebuno's body heaved with an agonal hack, spraying the entire patio. Munisica flashing, Sitra and Lileth dove for the other Aenerians, dispatching them just as quickly. The other priest stumbled back, grabbing and tossing one of his friends into the whirling butchery before him. Lileth and Sitra finished the group within a few breaths before turning towards the remaining priest, whose hands were now dripping with what looked like purple mud.

The priest flung his hands out at Lileth and Sitra, the dark liquid spackling over fresh blood. As if struck by a sudden seizure, Lileth's and Sitra's legs crumpled beneath them. They trembled, vomit bubbling from their mouths as smoke rose from each of the dark droplets that peppered their faces. The priest pulled a wicked dagger from the folds of his robes, setting upon them with gruesome intent etched into his face. Sitra's munisica receded as she moaned.

Still standing on shaky legs, Lileth raised a glowing hand. A flaming lance shot from her palm, sailing harmlessly over the priest's shoulder and splashing over the brick wall behind him. She fired another. Her aim was true this time, striking him in the stomach, but the flames lacked conviction and withered before doing any real damage.

"So much fire! So much life!" the priest gushed. "It would be an appalling waste to kill you as quickly as you've done my comrades here. I do think I'll indulge myself, just a tad." One hand twitched longingly, dripping with foul magic. His other clutched the dagger, holding it like a dinner knife. Lileth moaned, choking on frothy vomit as she collapsed beside Sitra.

Cole felt tingling shoot up the back of his neck as a hammering began in his eardrums. He didn't recall feeling them, but his munisica were out, larger than ever. He didn't recall taking a step towards the priest, but he was moving faster than ever. He didn't recall making the decision to kill the man, but his claws were whistling through the air, fueled by an insatiable need for the man's blood. There was no shred of Passion or modicum of Wisdom within him, there was simply no room. He was Rage. He landed beside the priest, the claws on his back foot digging into the tiled patio for better leverage. He flattened his right hand into a single blade, driving it through the priest's thigh, tearing through every major vessel, nerve, and bone on its way up to the base of his spine. He opened his bladed hand as wide as he could before jumping away, yanking out precious innards before the priest had even noticed.

Cole watched the priest's face, savoring every detail. The fool's eyes were still upon Lileth, intent on having her. He had yet to realize he was dying. As he began to fall, his face shifted from sickening glee to annoyed befuddlement. He scowled, confused as to why he was crumpling like a card castle. He hit the tiled patio in front of Lileth, smashing his face on the hard tile. Cole took savage pleasure in his clumsiness, his weakness. The priest picked his head up, blood and teeth spilling from broken lips pulled back in cold fury. He looked to his lifeless legs, then to Cole, who was already upon him, munisica raised for the final blow.

"Wait!" Habbad cried out.

Cole turned his ear, but not his eyes to Habbad. "Why?" He emptied his lungs on the single word, saturating it with his restrained Rage.

An invisible force yanked the priest's dagger from his hand, sending it skittering across the tile. The priest didn't notice, however. He fumbled over his flowing wound as he gave his legs a shake, as though trying to figure out why they weren't working. Habbad stormed over to the priest and promptly kicked him in the jaw, knocking him out cold.

"I need to see what he hit them with." Habbad pointed towards a writhing Lileth and Sitra. In his bloodlust Cole had forgotten they were even there. Habbad placed both his hands on the priest's head, running his fingers under sheets of smooth hair. Habbad's fingers shone a dull purple as he blinked rapidly. With a look of disgust, he pulled his hands free, wiping them on the priest's robes.

"What is it?" Cole asked, hiding his suspicion. Whatever purple magic Habbad used certainly wasn't taught at The Sill. He sheathed his munisica.

Habbad turned his head dry heaved. "You don't want to know. Turn them on their backs. Don't touch the dark stuff."

Cole flipped Lileth and Sitra onto their backs, turning their heads so they wouldn't choke on their frothing vomit. Habbad straddled Lileth, sitting on her stomach. He touched each drop of the dark substance, the tip of his finger a shimmering emerald orb. The oily liquid evaporated as he passed over every drop. Deep holes remained where the fluid had touched her skin, exposing a thin layer of fat and glistening ruby muscle beneath. When the final glob had been cleaned off, Lileth coughed, shooting upright and throwing Habbad off her. She cleared her throat, wiping her face with her sleeve. Habbad wasted no time tending to Sitra.

"See if you can heal her wounds," Habbad said as he worked. "I lack the Passion to do such things."

Cole approached Lileth with caution. She was upright and breathing, but she looked as if she was not entirely there. When her eyes met his, she reached for him, pulling him into an embrace, shivering. Cole had never been able to heal so much as a scratch, but seeing Lileth in such a state had clicked something into place. It felt right. He hugged her tighter, feeling the healing energies fill his heart. His Passion was made for her and her alone, crafted by his emotions and memories. He now understood why she hadn't been able to heal Valen or anyone else. The healing Passion required love for the injured person to work. Enamored, Cole poured his Passion into her. He savored the physical contact before focusing his power on the wounds. The sunken holes filled with a dim snowy glow as flesh mended, knitting itself back together.

"That's twice now," Lileth said, happy tears filling her eyes.

"So it is," Cole said, with mock indifference. "How do you feel?"

She dropped her eyes. "Unwholesome and sick, but I will recover." She snapped her head towards Sitra, hair whipping Cole in the face. Sitra had just woken. "Will you be able to heal her as well?"

Cole considered his feelings for Sitra. He was fond of her and cared for her as a friend, but it might not be enough. "I'll have to try won't I?"

Still humming with the lingering effects of healing Lileth, Cole approached Sitra. She wrestled a vicious cough as she clutched her stomach. She held an arm up, keeping Cole at bay. Cole brushed her arms aside and pulled her into a tight hug. Sitra didn't have the strength to resist. Cole searched his emotions, trying to find anything that would connect him to her. It took longer, but their relationship was strong enough to reveal a wholesome love of friendship. A few moments passed and he released her.

"Thanks Cole." Sitra rubbed her belly, groaning. "We should have killed the priests first. Their magic is so…crippling. My Rage wasn't strong enough to fight it off. Whoa…" Her eyebrows went up as she beheld the remains of the priest Cole had maimed. "Someone did a good job on that one. Must have been you, Cole. Your arm's still covered in guts. Here, let me fix that for you. You must have cut yourself on a bone."

She twisted his arm gently, exposing a fresh wound on his wrist where the black shroud didn't reach. With a flick of rosy light the wound vanished.

"There, now we're even," Sitra said with a smirk, standing up. "I feel like hot garbage, but I'm ready. Lil, you ready?"

"Yes. Hopefully we can avoid another encounter like this. If we had more time I would say we should hide the bodies." Lileth stood as well, checking herself over for injuries.

Habbad walked over and placed both his hands flat on the door, closing it. The door flickered green as it groaned and creaked, swelling into the frame. "It's not ideal, but it's better than nothing. Let us be off."

They moved more slowly, inspecting each roof before they jumped to it. They were close to the Devotion towers now. Each was almost as tall as the walls of The Sill. Before Valen's team came into view, two slouched figures and one prone waited for them on the roof of the dark stone building next to a belfry. Eliza and Valen flinched as Cole's team landed among them.

"I felt something amiss through our link," Eliza said. She sat with Storn's head in her lap, stroking his hair. "I'm glad to see you fared better than we did. Domina?" She pointed her chin at the bloody stains on Cole's team.

"Two priests and their concubines," Lileth replied, crouching down and inspecting Storn's injuries. "They were easy enough to kill, but we were ill prepared to deal with their magic. Habbad, Cole, are these wounds similar to what you mended on Sitra and me?" She pointed to Storn's prone form, slapping a bug on her outstretched arm.

Habbad's nose scrunched at the acrid smell coming from the still smoking holes in Storn's neck and face. "The chest no, but the poison I can neutralize. Before the priest died I ripped the knowledge from him. Feel free to inspect my thoughts as I do it. We will likely see this again, and the more of us that can deal with it, the better."

The faces of the others slackened as they reached for Habbad's mind. Cole didn't bother. He had always failed miserably at tinkering with the thoughts and memories of others. The unit let out a collective hiss as Habbad worked each of the smoking holes littered over Storn.

"That is truly atrocious." Eliza shook her head. "Why would anyone pursue such magic?"

"Because it is effective," Valen remarked. He swatted at an insect buzzing around his face. "Are you through, Habbad? Can he be healed now?

Habbad nodded, stepping back, but Eliza was already at work. Her fingers became lavender embers as she waved them over the wounds. His rib snapped and pulled itself back into his chest as the sucking-hole shrank away.

Through his emotional link with her, Cole could sense Eliza's love for Storn. The fraternal affection fed into Cole, and he was positive that if need be he could heal Storn as well. Pride filled Cole's chest as he reflected on how far he'd come. He was no longer a helpless liability to the unit. He was a contributing member, a warrior, and now a healer. There was some guilt in between the layers of pride, however.

He'd taken entirely too much pleasure in killing the priest. He could have been quicker and cleaner about it, but he'd enjoyed the idea of crippling him first. He felt ashamed of his Rage bringing this part out of him. He flexed his hands, bringing his munisica forth far too easily. He admired the way the starlight tinkled off his claws. He loved how menacing they looked, and to think they were indestructible! He dismissed the Rage before his urge for violence grew any stronger. He felt eyes upon him. Looking up, Cole saw approval written on Valen's face.

"There, good as new. How do you feel?" Eliza brushed off a few biting flies from Storn's forehead, leaving trails of blood across his face. She healed the tiny bites as well.

"Sick. Like I just ate a bowl of bog angel soup." He tapped the newly healed wound on his chest, producing a healthy thump. "I'm whole though. Not too bad considering."

"You better feel good." Sitra kicked at him. Storn jumped to his feet. "You've missed all of the action. You probably got yourself knocked out on purpose so you wouldn't have to do any of the real work."

"Bah, the Domina got a lucky shot on me," he said, clutching his chest. A belch gurgled up from deep within. "The Domina seem to choose different animals every time we see one. These were some brew of reptile and insect. You should have seen them, Sitra, they were fast. Real fast. Easy enough to break apart once you got ahold of them though."

"Looks like *you* were easy enough to break apart too," Cole said, tapping Storn's chest through the hole in his armor. "I've never seen a lung before. Thanks for the visual."

"Like I said, they were fast," Storn shot back. "I killed a few of them before a priest flung that stuff on me. I only got this after his magic started working. *You* wouldn't have lasted *ten seconds*."

"Cole is more adept than you give him credit for," Habbad interjected. "If not for his quick application of Rage, a priest would have killed Lileth, and likely the rest of our group. It was…impressive to say the least."

Cole was completely taken aback. Habbad had never complimented anyone before.

"'Bout' time you got yourself a kill. And a priest too!" He tapped Cole's shoulder with the back of his hand. "All those slimy bastards could use a good 'application of Rage'. Valen killed two with a fancy bit of Wisdom while Eliza lulled them with Passion. Just goes to show how useful our magics are against these freaks. It warms my warrior's heart to see that violence is a perfectly good answer sometimes. How'd you kill the other one?"

"In a similar manner," Lileth answered. "Though if we were more careful we wouldn't have to kill anyone." Her hand went up to her neck, smothering another biting insect. She peered over the edge, taking in the crowds below.

"We could all do with a little more caution," Valen said. "This mission was supposed to be one of stealth. I think at this point we'd better take up our usual faculties of Wisdom and Passion. We'll risk the Corpulants. Our presence will be apparent when we assault the towers anyway."

"What about the other targets?" Storn asked, stepping to the edge of the roof. "Wow they're really going at it down there."

"They are no longer viable." Valen moved next to Storn, inspecting the scene below. "You'll be glad to know that this is a problem which requires violence to answer. Lots of violence. We will bring the towers down. Keep your other magics at the fore of your mind as we work. We are likely to rouse the interest of every priest in the city."

Cole joined them at the edge of the roof. Habbad's description of the celebrations did them no justice. Throngs of Underkin crawled about the base of the towers like a colony of ants. There were thousands of them. Most were unclothed, throwing their sweaty bodies at one another with wanton lust or squabbling viciously. Peppered throughout were crippled bodies dragging themselves through the mud. Kreed's magic prevented them from dying, even the ones who were maimed beyond recognition. Carts of food and liquors rolled in from capillary alleyways, only to be overturned as the Underkin fought tooth and nail over their contents.

There was a smell in the air, a rancid stench that reminded Cole of a public bathroom that had seen heavy abuse in the summer months.

Judging by the pungent aroma, the Underkin had been at it for days, not leaving to defecate or bathe. The sight was the most desperate and repulsive thing Cole had ever seen. Having had enough, he turned away to find Habbad far away from the ledge, eyes clamped shut.

"I guess that's something you only need to see once, huh? And the smell." Cole buried his nose in his undershirt.

Habbad didn't answer.

With a sudden jolt, Cole realized why Habbad didn't look over the edge like everyone else. He wrapped an arm around him, giving him a brotherly shake. "We're going to find her."

Habbad opened his eyes, Fear painted over his little wrinkled face. He grabbed Cole and pulled him close, burying his head in Cole's chest. He murmured something, but the words were lost in the thick cloth armor.

"What did you say, Bud?" Cole gave him another gentle shake.

Habbad's head came back up, gazing into Cole's eyes. He smiled, parting his lips to speak, but his face shifted to a pale shade of horror as his mouth fell open. One of the biting flies landed on the tip of his nose.

"Habbad, what's wr-" Cole's knees buckled as a deafening sound crashed into him. It was the bell tower. The bell gonged again, the sound bringing him to his knees. He turned. A figure cast in bloody torchlight stood at a platform atop the bell tower.

Kreed flicked a finger against the bell again, hammering the air. "Cole Carter, *my friend!*"

Chapter 24

The End of Habbad

K reed flicked the bell once more, grinning from ear to ear. The air vibrated with such force that Cole felt as if his bones might shatter. He tried to stand, but his limbs seemed to have forgotten how. His instincts told him he was in danger, that he must do something, but something else was growing louder by the second: Fear. With each heartbeat, his terror intensified, its chilled talons pinning him to the rooftop like a rabbit in a hawk's embrace. Kreed's face twisted with mania, ecstatic with deadly intent, his thin lips stretched over his perfect teeth. Cole looked to his unit expecting to see the flashing of munisica and palms blazing with magic, but they too seemed paralyzed by Fear. The same trepidation that crippled him painted each of their faces. They were lost. The game was already over. There was something about the way Kreed moved; his careless gait, the lazy kick that sent a coil of rope down, and the playful way he swung down the rope, jumping from side to side. There was no sense of urgency, no worry in the world. He already had them. They were his. There would be no chance to fight back. In the quiet of the moment the biting insects swarmed thicker, though no one moved to swat them.

Kreed fell the last few feet, landing clumsily on the roof of the dark stone building. He inspected his hands, frowning slightly as he brushed them against each other, picking off specks of dirt. He then meticulously readjusted his suit, careful to put each ivory strap back in its proper place. Satisfied, he gave his lapels a little tug and took a step forward. His foot plopped immediately into a puddle of blood from Storn's newly healed wound. Kreed's eyes went wide as his lips twitched between disgust and fury. He wiped the leather shoe on a clean part of Storn's armor. He took a deep breath as if praying for patience before stepping around the puddle and directly to Cole.

"You've been a naughty little shit you know." Kreed's tone was light, as if he were merely scolding a child who'd stayed up past his bedtime. "Running off with no proper goodbye, traipsing through forbidden jungles, destroying an ancient magical barrier, and worst of all," he bent down, lifting Eliza's trembling chin with his little finger, "cavorting about with *Dark Ones*," he spat, taking out a cloth from his jacket and wiping his finger. "I've been worried something awful about you, Cole Carter. So far from home, so far from everything you know, all while gorging on a gruel of lies from my enemies. Who knows what tales they've spun up for you, or worse yet, how they plan to use you for their own gain? I'd wager they didn't even bother to tell you what you are, or why you're so important to this war. No matter, you're safe now. *You* are at least. You didn't know any better."

Kreed strolled around the group, weaving in between them, looking each of them in the eye for a moment. "So many new faces. I can't tell you how pleasing that is. I have somewhat of an affinity for new faces. Ah, but here's an old face. Young Habbad. So angry, so smart, and so…rebellious." He said the final word through clenched teeth.

Habbad worked his jaw as if he wanted to say something, but the words fell from his quivering lips. He looked how the rest of the unit looked, how Cole felt.

Kreed bent low and fixed a twisted piece of Habbad's wrappings. "My heart is broken, Habbad. You made a fool of me. While you've been out working against me, I've been here looking after Lexy for you. I've even kept her from the decadence in the streets below. She's far too young for that sort of nonsense anyway. Not that anything down there would be the most *graphic* thing she's ever seen…" He laughed, gazing at the stars for a moment before shaking his head. "No, not by a long stretch. Wouldn't you say?" He cupped his hand around the side of Habbad's head, which was covered in flies.

Habbad worked his mouth again, but nothing came out. The insects were unbearable now, stinging and biting every exposed bit of flesh. Cole could feel them, but he couldn't bring himself to swat them. What was the point? Kreed had them now. It was over. Soon they'd be climbing the tower, or dead if they were lucky.

"I will admit," Kreed patted Habbad on the cheek, turning towards the rest of the group, "Your band of misfits made the greatest impact so far. There were others, little teams of seven or so. I don't recall the exact number, I don't trouble myself with those who aren't worth killing myself. They were incredibly useful, however. They're up on the towers now, at the very tops. Go on, behold them."

Some of them looked up, though most didn't bother. Their last bit of hope had shriveled and withered away. They were utterly alone now. Cole could barely make out the figures strapped to the top of the towers. There were dozens of them. He dropped his head, silent tears running down to the flies on his cheeks. Lexy would surely be punished now, and it would be his fault. He had failed to save her, just as he'd failed to save Joshy. It had all been for nothing. Kreed had turned Cole's own hope against him, just as he had with Habbad. There was no hope now. No chance at all.

"What I find most disturbing is that your elders thought it appropriate to throw away so many young lives while they hide behind their trees." Kreed rubbed his chin as he approached Storn from behind, careful to avoid the puddle this time. "The elders would have been far better suited to disrupt the Devotion, possibly successful even. I know I certainly wouldn't have stood a chance against their combined might." Surveying Storn, he removed his jacket and hung it on a loose nail on the wall of the bell tower. The manic look spread like fire on his face, giving him an appearance of an insane clown. He crouched behind Storn, wrapping his arms lovingly around his front, caressing the skin through the tear in his armor. "I'll make a promise to you all, right here and now. None of your lives will go to waste." He brought his lips to Storn's ear, running his tongue up the length. "Especially yours. Come warrior, show me how you want to bleed tonight."

Storn shuddered awake. Rage flaring at last, he exhaled through bared teeth as his hands slowly became the black knives of his munisica. He had found the will to fight. Storn kicked and pulled at Kreed's arms.

Storn's mumbling steadied into clear words: "Disgusting… traitor…kill…break you…"

Kreed pulled him closer, hugging him tight. "What a hot soul you have! Yes, bring out that fire. Give yourself to Rage, let it fill your warrior's heart. Don't hold back now."

Storn's struggling became coherent thrashing as he gained clarity and strength. He kicked out with both feet, sending Kreed sailing into the wall of the bell tower. Rage burned in Storn's eyes as he rose to his feet. Kreed rose to his feet as well, his teeth bared in a jester's grin as blood oozed from the claw marks on his arms.

A tortured howl shattered the air between them. From the ledge beside Kreed arose a bulky, robed figure scuttling its way onto the dark stone roof. Another ragged figure joined the first. Then three more. The tallest Corpulant opened its maw wide enough to swallow a man. Its purple lips cracked with thin wires of blood as it bellowed with the voice of a dozen old men begging for death.

Storn's resolve wavered. He took a step back, his munisica receding slightly. Shaking his head, he threw his shoulders back and roared, sending shivers running up the back of Cole's scalp. Perhaps the fight wasn't over. Maybe they would have a chance to fight.

The Corpulant closed its mouth, scabbed purple lips meeting in a bullfrog's frown. Its head snapped up as it brought a bundle of spindly fingers to a clasp on its chest. With a powerful jerk it tore its robes off, revealing a body crafted in the dank cellars of nightmares. Its skin was pruny and crinkled, as if stolen from a much larger corpse that had been at sea for days. The hairless skull travelled down the back of a long crested neck, settling between spired shoulder blades. Great flaps of spider-vein skin hung over the protruding ribs of its torso. Between winged hip bones dangled a wrinkled bag of skin larger than its whole body. Its legs were thick and muscular with knees that bent backwards like a grasshopper's. The Corpulant shuffled forward, its solid black eyes on Storn as the sack of skin snagged and scraped over the tiled roof.

Storn's munisica stretched bigger than ever as he threw his shoulders back and roared, his voice amplified with Rage. Cole stirred, emboldened by Storn's fury. Warmth returned to his limbs as his own munisica inched their way out.

The Corpulant's mouth twitched with contempt as it brought its thin fingers to the flaps on its chest. It pinched one, tenderly pulling it up and revealing ruby red flesh like a fish's gill. An odor of fetid meat wafted over the roof. Insects writhed in the wound, teeming thousands taking flight as the Corpulant gave the flap a rattling shake. The cloud hung in the air before gathering and swarming over Storn.

Storn held his breath and shut his eyes, swiping at the insects with a tornado of claws, but to no effect. The bugs were on him, covering his face like a grey mask. His munisica disappeared entirely as he fell. Kreed appeared behind him in a flash, catching and cradling Storn's head as he laid him down gently.

"That will do, that will do." He waved a hand, shooing the flies away. "Not too much now. The boy needs to know what he's about to do." He set Storn's head in his lap, running one hand through his hair as the other fingered the hole in his armor. "There warrior, that's where the Domina got you, isn't it?"

He pinched Storn's chin, bringing his eyes up. Storn gave a solemn nod, his face welted from the insects. He gazed up at Kreed with the same defeated acceptance that Lexy displayed when she walked willingly to the Corpulant.

"That's what I thought." Kreed's smile slackened into a snarl of pleasure as his eyes rolled back. He circled his finger over the exposed skin, dousing it with inky stains. His finger snapped erect as he tapped it over Storn's mottled ribs. The blackened flesh rippled as if made of jelly. Kreed's mouth opened, releasing a little squeal as he pushed his finger into Storn's ribs. Storn groaned, unable to muster the strength for a proper scream. The skin and muscle beneath gave with the slightest prodding, as if the flesh had been rotting for weeks. Kreed worked a rib loose, snapping it off as it clattered to the tiled roof. Storn writhed, hands and eyes reaching out to nothing as he gasped for air.

"That's good warrior, very good," Kreed cooed into Storn's ear. "But they went a little deeper than that, did they not?"

Storn paused in his writhing and hissed, "Yesss."

There was a pop and a rush of air as Kreed's finger worked a hole through Storn's lung. He moaned with visceral pleasure as his hand wriggled deeper in search of profound agony. Kreed's head turned, listening carefully to Storn's labored breathing. With a smile, he found it.

Storn's eyes snapped wide as he screamed at the stars. The sedative effects of the Fear would not deny him the intimacy of Kreed's greedy fingers. Storn was alive and very aware. He bucked, smashing his fist on the roof, shattering the tiles.

Kreed's eyes went wide, his face blank. "Fight it warrior, fight it! Rage against it. Don't go willingly to the void. Burn for me."

Kreed's free hand locked into a crooked talon as he hovered it over Storn's face. As Storn thrashed and screamed, a fiery light erupted from his mouth and eyes. His screams hung in the air even after his body went limp. The light shone brighter, beaming and blinding as it rushed out of his face and coalesced into Kreed's waiting hand. The scream yielded to silence as the fire ceased flowing. Kreed removed his other hand from its fleshy glove and stood. Storn's lifeless head clopped against the hard tile, his face no more than a torn paper mask.

Kreed shut his eyes and spread his arms wide as he greeted the stars. His right hand clutched a molten ball of Storn's life force, flames licking up through his fingers. He slapped his gore-covered hand against his face, wiping the blood over his mouth and neck. Another squeak escaped his lips as he brought his glowing prize up to his mouth. He twirled the bloody fingers of his left hand over his right, summoning a long violet needle in midair. With a flick, he lanced the blazing orb. Liquid flames shot from between his fingers and into his open mouth. Kreed sucked it down, drawing the power into himself. The flaming orb collapsed, coating his hand in the dim light.

Kreed's lips returned to their manic grin as he considered the rest of his guests. "Exquisite. He tasted better than I imagined. And the power, so raw and pure…I had almost forgotten what proper Rage felt like." He held out his hands absentmindedly as a Corpulant went to each, lapping the gore and residual energy from his fingers. "Oh I'd love to see how the rest of you would taste, but I mustn't get greedy. The Three won't begrudge me one meal, but the rest of you will go to the towers. Except for you, Cole. You are special."

Cole sat frozen, mired in the wake of his Fear. He couldn't peel his eyes from what was left of Storn's face. He was no stranger to death, but this was entirely different. This was malicious gluttony, the piggish gorging on the suffering of another. This was evil.

Cole sank into himself, unaware of the biting flies or the clammy hands of the Corpulants pulling him along. Waves of Despair smothered his conscious thoughts, fading him in and out. He couldn't tell if the others fared any better, or if he even cared. He had no urge or desire to speak of. There were brief moments of clarity, breaks in the gloom which revealed his friends: Squabbling Underkin tearing the clothes from Eliza, eager to expose her flesh; Priests dragging Valen by his hair through muddy excrement; Lileth's eyes calling out to him as Corpulants hauled her off to the shadows.

Cole found himself on a stage facing the Devotion Towers. He was immobile, buried to his chin in an urn full of hardened cement. There was no sight of the others.

"Look at you! You've got yourself a decent seat for the show now haven't you?" Kreed stepped into Cole's view. His snow-white suit bore no signs of Storn's death, though his hand was still caked with dried gore. Kreed inspected him, heels bouncing with excitement. "Angle's a bit off, but..." he grunted as he turned Cole's urn. "There we go. Now you can see all three towers. This is important you know, just as you yourself are important. I am in your debt by the way, for bringing so many of your friends here. Each one has a soul brighter than the whole herd of Underkin. Here, let me siphon some of that off for you. You ought to be present for this."

Nails scratched over Cole's cheeks as Kreed drew his fingers repeatedly to Cole's mouth. Flakes of dried blood crumbled from his gentle fingers, landing on the surface of the stone below Cole's chin. Cole felt the Despair stirring in his mind and gut. The sensation swirled too quickly, dizzying him. He heaved, vomiting dark pus into Kreed's waiting hand. The spinning stopped and he felt a measure of coherence return to him. The Fear remained, stabbing him with freezing spikes, but the Despair had lifted enough to bring clarity to the scene.

"That's much better." Kreed flung the pus at a group just off the stage, laughing as the crowd of Underkin collapsed in keening wails. "Strong stuff. You must have quite the constitution. I prefer Decreath's

Fear, but Sorronis's Despair is an incredible sight to behold. Look at them, they're... yes, they're all fainting. Your Despair was too much for their tiny hearts. You must be special indeed, Cole Carter."

A priest in crimson robes approached Kreed, hands clasped behind her back. She was short with a face locked in stony determination. A group of white-robed priests trailed behind her, looking as though they'd rather be elsewhere.

The woman's lip curled in disgust, as if she loathed Kreed from the bottom of her heart. She gestured to the group of fallen Underkin beside the stage. "Sir, it would be more prudent to *not* kill the Underkin. They are for our lords. *All* of our lords. Sorronis would be less than pleased to see such frivolous waste of his herds."

Without looking at her, Kreed wiped the Despair from his hands. He sighed, sounding bored: "Those Underkin were Chosen by me personally. They cannot die. I'd also like to inform you that Sorronis holds no sway over Costas. I do. So you'll forgive me if I don't show much favoritism for his cattle. If you're worried," he shrugged a shoulder, jabbing a thumb casually behind his back, "send one of your little minions over to collect what is owed before the Corpulants clean them up."

The female priest nodded to one of her followers, who leapt from the stage and started working over them just as Kreed had done to Storn. Cole shut his eyes and looked away, wincing as each scream pierced the din of the writhing crowds.

"What do you want anyway?" Kreed asked. "Can't you see I'm entertaining our special guest?"

"Your undue affinity for Decreath is no great mystery to us, Father Kreed." She gave a derisive bow as she said his name. "You will be pleased to know that your Master has arrived early, and alone. It's strange. It seems Decreath knew of your special guest before Sorronis and Grotton." Her eyes and voice sharpened. "I do wonder how this came to be."

"Let's not labor over the litany of things you priests wonder about. I haven't the time or the tolerance." He shot her a look that put an end to the subject. "Is that all?"

The red priest's head dropped at the weight of his glare. "No, Father Kreed, that is not all. Decreath captured one of the elders from The Sill. It was the Bone-breaker, Roth. He was found above the city, watching us from the back of a baileen. The beast escaped during the struggle, but we have Roth. Grotton's Domina are bringing him in now."

"Outstanding!" Kreed gushed, clapping his hands. Shame the baileen got away, but the Bone-breaker is the boon of boons. Where is the elder now?"

The priest extended an arm, pointing across the square. The crowd parted and revealed a squad of elephantine Domina dragging a massive two-wheeled structure. The wheels were made of solid metal, each the size of a large house. In place of the axle was Roth, locked in a thick yoke that secured his limbs inside the massive wheels. Chains coiled around his torso led to a pair of mountainous Domina that pulled the whole structure. Roth's face was blank, though his eyes were alert and calculating. The black armor shroud was gone, revealing soft blond hair and bleeding wounds. The great warrior was defeated.

Cole's chin fell to the stone. There was nothing now. No chance for anyone. Roth was supposed to be this unbreakable monolith of Rage and power. Yet here he was, laid low by just one of The Three. The Sill would fall soon enough. The only hope now was that Roth somehow had sent message to Chiron and Alvani, warning them not to come. He couldn't feel the bonds between Goran or Eliza and himself anymore. It didn't matter anyway.

"Stars above, he's bigger than I remember." Kreed's teeth came out again with his greedy smile. "With any luck Decreath might let me have a bite of his fire. I do hope he shows up to the party soon. Where is the Feared now?" Kreed clapped his hands again, sounding as if he might explode with excitement.

"Decreath is here now, Father Kreed." the priest replied, pointing to a void in the stars.

Kreed took a deep breath as he gazed up at the void. His voice dropped, wet and gravelly. "So he is. Begin the Devotion."

Priests in black robes appeared on the stage in puffs of smoke. They descended to the crowds of Underkin, shooting murky olive clouds from their hands as if watering a garden. Priests throughout the square followed suit, covering the entire area in a putrid haze.

"Kreed don't you dare!" The woman in crimson gripped her robes, her eyes wild. "Grotton and Sorronis are not here!"

Kreed ignored her, walking behind Cole and dragging something heavy into his peripheral vision. With a renewed pang of Despair, Cole saw Habbad buried up to his neck in his own stone vat. His lifeless eyes rested on the stone, puffy and pink.

"You're going to watch this, Habbad. You owe me that much." Kreed raked his nails over Habbad's skull. Invisible hooks pulled Habbad's eyelids open and snapped his head upright. "Pay close attention to the tower on the left. She'll be right on the bottom. First to burn. First to scream."

Cole thrashed against the Fear, flexing against the stone. He reached for the power Roth had given him. It was still there, waiting in his marrow, but his grip was feeble and slippery. The Fear was too powerful.

The Underkin began dousing themselves with the odium as they climbed the spiral walkways up the towers. A rotten, flowery odor like a dead woman's perfume wafted over the stage. Desperation, the likes of which he had never felt, fueled his racing heart. Cole gave a helpless groan. He flexed against the stone tub, smashing his chin over and over.

"This isn't right!" Cole wailed, "This isn't how it's supposed to be. You can't do this! Please, don't kill her."

Kreed clucked his tongue. "Come now Cole, don't fret. This is just the natural way of things here. What you are watching is no different than the butchery of livestock so that the superior life can flourish. I do believe you humans practice something similar with your own cattle, do they not?"

"They're suffering!" Cole spat, bloody spit flying. "This is evil! You're evil!"

Kreed giggled, bringing his mouth close to Cole's ear. "You haven't seen suffering yet, Wisdom Walker. Wait till they realize they cannot die, no matter how the fire burns them. Wait till you see how many shades a person can suffer when the odium takes them. First is the Fear, because they still have hope. Then when the hope melts, some time after the skin, there is Despair. My word, is there *Despair*. Roiling oceans of the stuff." Air rushed into Kreed's teeth as he tasted the words. "Then there's my favorite part. The Hatred. The Hatred saves them. It strips them of their emotions, their memories, their very identities. It gives them strength, purpose, even pleasure. They become something else entirely, something…divine. Its beauty is still beyond my comprehension." Kreed gasped, his breath rapid and feathery. Another faint squeak fluttered from his lips. With a slippery whisper, he hissed, "That is the suffering you are about to witness. That is what sweet Lexy is about to become."

Cole's chin hit the pale stone with a final thud. He could hear Habbad's choking cries as he struggled against his bonds. He too had heard every word.

"Kreed, stop this!" the red priest shouted. "This is most inappropriate! We must wait for Sorronis."

Kreed ignored her once more, drumming a playful beat on the rim of Cole's stone tub before turning to the towers. "Oh excellent! They're nearly ready for us. Ah, and there's sweet Lexy now! Front and center! She looks adorable in that dress, I must say. Picked it out myself." His sharp nails raked Cole's scalp, voice dripping with menace: "Behold her, Cole Carter. BEHOLD HER!"

Hooks yanked Cole's head back, cracking his neck and peeling his eyelids open. There she was. Right in front of them. The weight of her dwindling mortality pulling her down, never to dance again. She wore a frilly pearl gown with gold trim, just like Kreed's suit. With somber, vacant eyes, she looked to Cole and Habbad as she poured the oil over her head.

"NOOO!" Cole bellowed, voice breaking.

A long, high moan rushed through Habbad's gritted teeth before tapering off into defeated sobs.

"Kreed! Stop this at once or I will!" the red priest shrieked, delirious with ire. "Decreath be damned, I'll cast you down, Kreed. I swear it!"

Kreed brought his hand over his head, signaling to his priests below the towers, who awaited his final command with torches in hand. "Do what you feel is right in your heart, Baedine." He locked eyes with her, voice softening with endearment. "It's all a person can do."

With a flourish, Kreed snapped his hand downwards. Cole watched in helpless horror as thick straps wound up the spiral walkway, slamming into the cattle and pulling them snug to the tower.

The grim spell dissolved from the Underkin's minds as they suddenly realized where they were and what was about to happen. The first screams stung at Cole's ears. They were screams of Fear because they still had hope. Lexi's screams were not the loudest, but he heard them above everything else.

With a pained expression and tears bubbling in her eyes, the red priest Baedine twisted her hand, forming a purple needle in midair. "I'm sorry, brother."

Baedine flicked the needle, sending it screaming into Kreed's chest. Kreed fell to his knees, life draining from his face as he looked to his sister with pale adoration.

"I'm so sorry." Baedine's tears dripped into her mouth as she bawled.

The heat of the flames lashed at Cole's cheeks. The din of screams rose exponentially as the fire climbed up the tower, burning every ounce of flesh and every facet of soul on its way.

Baedine's sobs came to an abrupt halt as Kreed rose to the tips of his toes. His head lolled as he arched back at an impossible angle. He floated into the air, his fancy leather shoes dangling as he hovered a foot off the ground.

"This is not right, something is amiss." Baedine took a step towards her brother, dread in her eyes. She signaled to her priests, backing them away from Kreed.

Baedine's eyes snapped to the sky. A dark tendril descended from the void in the stars, bathing the stage in a rancid cloud of Fear.

A freezing wind burned at Cole's still-open eyes as the Fear filled his lungs. He knew this was the end, that this was death. His every instinct demanded he escape, but the stone tub held him fast, forcing him to embrace the wild terror. Just as he thought the sensation would surely smother him, the cloud thinned. The stage reappeared and the fog lifted. The void above swirled its way down into Kreed's open mouth.

There was silence for a moment as Kreed floated back down to the stage. His chest was several times its normal size, all of the buttons gone from his pearly jacket and vest. Air whistled out through his pursed lips, giving over to a sound that didn't belong in the world of the living. The sensation crippled every fiber of Cole's body and filled every corner of his mind with undiluted terror. There was no hiding from it. It was Fear in its purest form, It was the voice of Decreath.

The noise subsided, giving over to the scabbed yowls from the towers. Cole moved his eyes as far from the towers as he could, but his eyes were still locked to Lexi by Kreed's spell. The billowing flames were painfully bright now.

"Kreed... what have you done?" Baedine's voice trembled between terror and awe. "What are you?"

Kreed returned to the stage, his mouth stained with soot. He opened his eyes, revealing empty, burnt sockets. His lips parted, revealing gaps and jagged crags of shattered teeth. A child-like smile tugged at the corners of his lips. Kreed exhaled, long and low while something flapped from inside his throat.

"D-Decreath?" Baedine fell to her knees, hands open in surrender.

Kreed approached Baedine, chest heaving in ragged, weak breaths. He clasped her hands, entwining his fingers in hers as he pulled her upright. Her jaw quivered as she came up to meet him. She stared into his empty eyes. Blood leaked from the sockets as he tilted his head down to her, dripping over her cheeks and mouth. Baedine shut her eyes as Kreed brought his burnt lips to hers, kissing her tenderly. She resisted, then begrudgingly gave in, returning the kiss with a slight nudge. She made to pull away, but his hands pulled her closer. Baedine wriggled and beat her fists against his arms, but Kreed pulled her closer still.

Baedine's eyes popped open as she stopped struggling. The left side of her body convulsed as her chest rose and fell in violent jerks. Her left leg went limp, sagging at an odd angle like an empty balloon. Kreed threw a hand around her waist and caught her. Baedine moaned as her mouth stretched wide, her neck swelling as something large worked its way up and out. Kreed's jaws closed and he pulled back steadily. In between his broken teeth was a long bone covered in blood and fascia. Baedine's tibia had torn through her throat, cracking her jaw on the way out. Her fibula came next, connected by hanging ropes of tendon and ligament. Her left arm fell limp next, fingers bouncing off her side like a rubber glove. Kreed let her fall, pulling yet more bones from her mouth as she landed in a heap on the stage. When the final bone slipped between her ripped maw, Kreed threw the lot into a pile beside her.

Baedine tried to stand, but only the right side of her body seemed to want to. With her right hand she patted the left side of her head, which drooped like a loose mask.

Rasping breath still leaking from his mouth, Kreed stirred a hand over the pile of bones. The bundle rattled and rolled over itself as the bones formed the skeleton of a patchwork creature. It stretched its asymmetrical legs and wings, clicking its finger-bone teeth together. Baedine cried out, dragging her broken body away from it. Sensing movement, the creature cocked its head, curious. It took a hesitant step towards Baedine, teeth clicking.

Baedine threw herself down on her boneless side, wailing in agony. Her right arm waved in the air, purple glow flaring in her hand. The creature cantered forward as it gained confidence. Baedine fired a violet needle at the hobbling bone creature, missing it entirely. She fired a few more, one of which passed harmlessly through the gaps in the creature's structure.

Cole winced as a needle shattered against the rim of his tub. The stage became a hail of purple shards. Priests dodged and jumped, clearing the platform. Kreed stood in the middle of the bombardment, unharmed, the creature pausing with its jaw wide. It looked back to Kreed, who nodded with approval. The bone child pounced. Baedine screamed as it tore at her. She waved her hand shooting needles blindly over the stage.

Cole saw the flash of purple from his periphery. He wrenched against his invisible bonds, but to no avail. Something smacked his neck, hard. His exposed skin felt hot and wet. There was a quiet pitter patter near his head. Cole looked down to see spurts of bright red shooting from below his chin. Afraid to make it worse, he stopped struggling, but it was worse already. The surface of the stone basin became a pool of crimson around him as he grew dizzy. He could no longer hear his blood hit the pool, and Baedine had gone quiet. Most odd was the sudden silence of the towers. A vague concept swam to the fore of his mind, which explained why he couldn't hear anything at all.

He was dying. As his vision faded to a thin tunnel, the last thing Cole saw was a pair of bloody holes staring into his soul.

Cole had lost; the game was over. He'd tried harder than anyone and made the best choices he could. Yet here he was, broken, bleeding, and defeated. Whether it was the whims of fate, or an underhanded blow, it mattered not. Here he sat, frozen and unable to hold onto his own life as the heart that battled to keep him alive pumped more of his blood out of him. His breath, which was once oh so essential, no longer seemed important. He couldn't even hear the scraping of air in his throat anymore. He couldn't hear anything except for the void as it rushed to greet him. As the deafening roar filled his ears, he couldn't recall what he was just looking at, or where he was, or who he was supposed to be. He was sinking, quickly now, far beneath the world, beneath himself. Nothing mattered. Everything was gone. He was not. The void welcomed him with lover's arms, whispering eternal respite as it pulled him ever deeper. He was the blackness, the darkness, the nothingness.

No

No

Somewhere in the void, a spark ever so faintly flickered. Light? Can light exist in such a place? No, it's gone now. Far too weak and feeble, surely snuffed out. The void darkened as Cole darkened, and laughed as Cole laughed. But there it was again, stronger than before. The impossible spark became a minute flame, living and breathing. That such a flame could exist in the crushing emptiness was inconceivable, yet there it was, Raging against the darkness. With every miniscule breath the fire grew. The flame was now a thing, the only thing, and it was alive. The flame rebelled against the blackness, tiny and weak, yet hot and fierce. The void would not be denied. It deepened as Cole deepened, their suffocating presence choking from the inside out. They would not be denied the depths of their hollow.

No

NO!

There was someone else in the void now, an alien yet familiar presence that Cole half recognized from another life. *He* was there. Crouched in the darkness *He* stoked the tiny flame, breathing life into it. With *His* encouragement, the baby flame refused to go gently into the crushing abyss. The flame Raged, burning brighter and hotter until it no longer flickered, but roared. The sound filled the void, reverberating off its skin. It was the bellow of the soul outright defying death. It would not be silenced. There was no alternative. The flame was blaring now, tearing at the void, bending, twisting it asunder.

For the first time, their faces met in full, *His* eyes locking with Cole's. An iron link of vengeful wrath joined the two.

YOU EXIST! YOU EXIST THEREFORE THE VOID CANNOT EXIST! YOU SHALL NOT BE SILENCED! THERE IS NO ALTERNATIVE! ARISE, COLE CARTER!

ARISE!

His final word faded from Cole's mind, replaced by the pounding of blood in his ears. Cole's eyes snapped open, heart punching his ribcage like a bull trying to escape. Red hot Rage prickled down his neck, filling his limbs with power he had never known. The sensation was intoxicating, but it was too much. He needed a purpose for the power lest it destroy him. Without a moment to spare, his vision returned and Cole realized where and who he was. He blinked and turned his neck, snapping the invisible hooks like dried cobwebs. Fueled by utmost need the power came forth, joining Cole in body and mind, armor and claw. He became Rage incarnate.

The stone prison exploded, sending sparks and stone in every direction. Cole emerged from the cloud of dust shrouded in ebony armor inside and out, munisica flexing in the starlight.

"Kreed!" Cole shouted at the sky. "Get down here and face me!"

Kreed floated far above him, watching with empty eyes and cradling his bone child, which now sported new organs and a fresh layer of skinless muscle.

"Have it your way, coward. I'll come to you," Cole said to himself, preparing to jump. There was no doubt he could make the distance.

Just as he readied to spring his legs, he heard a scuffling of footsteps and swishing of robes. Dozens of priests flooded the stage brandishing long, sweeping daggers and hands that shone with purple light. Cole took a deep breath and sheathed his desire for vengeance. The priests would make a fine outlet for now.

"Stand down, human!" A red priest shuffled to the fore of the crowd, cramming his sleeves up to his elbows. "The Three may have deemed you useful, but not necessary. So by all means resist us. You will make a fine meal with all that Rage burning in you."

With calm purpose, Cole walked towards the priests, bladed hair clinking with every step.

The red priest let out a shrill laugh. "How brave! Do you mean to fight us all, child? Ha! Very well, let's see how you fare against your own Fear!" He flung out his crooked fingers, blasting Cole with a misty bolt of olive magic.

Cole felt something brush against his mind, a fleeting thing, weak and crying. It was more of an annoyance, like the wails of a hungry baby. The sensation flared and burned to ashes before his Rage. He placed one clawed foot in front of the other, the wooden stage creaking and splintering under his feet.

The priest winced as his spell broke and died; he stepped back and regarded Cole with a confused look. He signaled to the priests at either side of him and they readied their spells. Fingers dripping with the same black foulness that had felled Eliza and Sitra, they whipped their arms out, showering Cole with a putrid rain. The droplets covered Cole from head to toe, but he didn't break stride. The black shroud protected him, inside and out.

The red priest readied another spell, but before his hands could weave it he looked down to see Cole's arm buried to the elbow in his chest. The priest crumpled to the stage. The others wasted no time, circling around Cole with their spells at the ready.

"Where is he?"

"He's only a human, find him!"

"He was right here not two seconds ago."

"He couldn't have vanished."

Bursts of violence added to their confusion as severed limbs joined their leader on the stage. The priests barely had time to react to one attack before one of their number met a bloody end from the other side of the group.

"He's too fast! I can't-"

"Dammit! How many are there! There he is! Grab-"

The priests' conviction dissolved commensurately with their number. Through the growing gaps in the circle, flashes of black armor and clouds of blood could be seen, but Cole was too quick for them. In the confusion, several of their spells missed, hitting their allies instead. When only three priests remained, they lost all resolve and fled for nearby alleys.

Cole watched them go, Rage building and throbbing in his muscles. He panted, not in exertion but in frustration. He had wasted precious time dispatching the priests and Kreed was now far above him, barely visible. He would not be denied. Crouching, Cole dug in his claws and readied for the jump. He bent down low as his blood lust rose. His legs snapped straight with an explosion of power, but he didn't rise an inch. Confused, he saw splintered wood tumble upwards as he himself began to fall. The staging couldn't handle the force. He landed on all fours, hitting the bloody soil. He loosed a furious roar before jumping again with all his might, smashing through the broken flooring. The wind whistled over his ears, his bladed hair tinkling as he flew.

He was only a heartbeat above the stage when he knew he had missed his mark. He missed Kreed by a wide margin, sailing right past him with all his useless Rage and power. As he fell he saw Kreed's hollow eyes staring at him, sooty lips pulled tight in his manic broken grin. Cole fell like an unbalanced axe below the tops of the smoldering towers, arms and legs flailing to right himself. He smashed against the top of a stone building, landing on his back in a shower of crumbling rock and mortar. The square reverberated with Cole's screaming, drowning out the morbid chorus of the three towers. The fall did not harm him, but Kreed was now too high for him to see. He swiped at the base of the stone building, carving out a large chunk as the entire wall fell away.

The Rage continued to build. The magic demanded challenge. Kreed was too far away now, no longer an option. Cole's blackened eyes darted about, searching for an outlet before the magic destroyed him. He considered the wall he had just collided with. That could work, but what purpose would it serve? The towers? They were important for a reason Cole couldn't recall. Was he supposed to destroy them, or rescue someone? He crossed the distance in two long strides, skidding to a halt and covering the thrashing bodies with dirt. The stench of burnt meat was thick enough to taste. The things on the towers were no longer worth saving, that much was certain. They were charred beyond recognition, beating their flailing arms at everything they could reach while their scabbed vocal cords cried for revenge. Cole saw a flash of white above him; the torso and head of a priest passed between brutal hands. Cole recognized the woman as one of the priests who had escaped his wrath on the stage. She must have run too close to the towers in her haste.

The Rage flared again, stretching and burning. His muscles popped with hot power. It was too much. He needed an outlet now. The towers would have to do. Hopefully they would be enough. He planted a foot behind him and prepared to charge through the base.

"Cole!"

The voice sounded familiar. Familiar enough to give him reason to pause at least. Shaking with agonizing restraint, he turned his head towards the source.

"Cole! Over here!"

With a sudden jolt, he found Lileth, Sitra, and Eliza trapped by the stage, their heads poking out of their own stone tubs. His Rage became purpose and his purpose became action. He charged towards the urns, moving so quickly that his feet barely touched the ground.

"Is that...What's wrong with him?" Sitra asked, slurring her speech.

"It's him," Eliza said. "His Rage has severed our bond, but I'm sure it's him. I just hope *he* knows who *we* are."

The magic boiled Cole's bones, his vision flashing red and black as the Rage tore at his flesh. He recognized these people, but the magic demanded violence, demanded he kill them. He gnashed his munisica together in an attempt to tear his own hands off. His eyes flicked back to the stage, reveling in the bloody fruits of his new power. The Rage was intoxicating, and he wanted more. His munisica stretched and creaked longer by the second.

"Cole! Look at me!" Lileth shouted, grabbing hold of his wandering gaze. "You know us. You know who we are. Use your strength to free us. The poison still blocks our magics. You must free us from the stone."

Her echoing words barely reached through the maelstrom of his Rage, but they were enough. Without a word Cole kicked at each of their rock tubs, careful not to follow through and injure them. They all emerged from their prisons with a drunken stumble, backing away and putting space between them and Cole. They looked at him as if he were some wild animal who might lunge at any second. Cole considered the strangers for a moment before lunging for a man trapped between two massive wheels. The man was important as well. Cole had to free him before his dwindling clarity succumbed to the Rage.

"Don't you dare smash the wheels," Roth growled. He almost looked soft without his shroud and bladed hair. "Steady your munisica and remove the tubes from my arms first. Gentle now, or I'll remove your hands."

Cole knew this person. He was important. Cole would save him before giving into the demands of his Rage. Rubber lines ran from a tank on the yoke to the man's chest and arms. A dingy yellow liquid flowed through the tubes, each buried into a large vein. Cole's bladed fingers clinked on the metal needle, tugging slowly. Cole stopped, eyeing the man. The needle was barbed, hooking the vein from the inside.

"Do it," Roth ordered.

Cole felt an odd sense of danger at his hesitation. He jerked the needle out, blood squirting over his shoulder. He pulled out five more needles, turning the man into a fountain of blood. With a pang of worry Cole recognized the man before him.

Roth threw his head back and filled the air with a thundering bellow. The bleeding stopped abruptly as Roth's shroud flowed over the wounds. The ebony armor covered his upper arms and thighs, transforming his hair and eyebrows into straight blades.

Roth lowered his head wearing an amused grin. "Back up. Or don't. This wouldn't hurt you anyway."

Roth flexed his arms and legs, snapping the yoke in half as the two massive wheels rolled forward. Cole had already jumped back and was scanning the area for another outlet. His Rage was in control, blocking out all thought and reason.

The wheels smashed together twice; the second time, Roth's arms and legs came free from the mangled scrap. He landed on his feet and shot straight for Cole, stopping in front of him.

"You have a master's power but you lack a master's control. Release it," Roth said, bringing his hulking frame in between Cole and the towers.

"No," Cole growled as he eyed Roth's unarmored torso. "Get out of my way."

Roth smiled a little wider. "Fine then, let's have it."

Cole didn't know what Roth was talking about, and he didn't much care. The demand for violence was too great. There was no alternative. He would break those towers, and then the buildings. And if anyone got in his way he would break them too. He shot forward, diving in between Roth's legs.

His momentum came to a crashing halt as two dragon's claws wrapped around his chest, squeezing and crushing. Roth's munisica couldn't harm him, but they were enough to stop him. Cole's roar echoed off the surrounding buildings, drowning out even the tortured screams from the towers. Sparks flew from Roth's bladed hands as Cole broke free, landing like a cat. Cole bared his teeth in a grin. He had his outlet.

Quick as lightning, Cole snatched a bladed finger from each of Roth's hands, wrenching them inwards and bringing his Master to his knees.

"Don't hold back," Roth chuckled through a grimace.

Cole's Rage ignited into an unrestrained inferno. He roared again, locking claws and pushing Roth back a few paces, twisting his fingers all the while. The fingers wouldn't break, so he roared again, releasing them and shooting his munisica for something without armor. Roth's hands came down, catching Cole's just in time.

"A low blow, but I would have done the same thing." Roth's bladed hands set like vice grips over Cole's. "Now stop screaming like a child and let your Rage out! Let's have it boy!"

Cole thrashed, flexing his arms with everything he had, but his claws were locked in Roth's. He dug his bladed feet in and pushed, shoving Roth through the marble pavement like a plough. Throwing his legs up, Cole planted his bladed feet into Roth's unarmored chest. Gripping Roth's claws, Cole thrust his legs with all his might, intent on ripping his master's arms off. They remained locked for a moment, Cole's feet cutting deeper and deeper. Cole pulled again and again, each time with less force than before as the Rage expended itself. Eventually Cole stopped fighting, slowly bringing his legs back down to the broken marble. Confusion and shame replaced his Rage as the shroud receded.

Roth cocked his head. "Better?"

"Yes." Cole's eyes snapped wide as he beheld the damage to Roth's chest. Ribs and muscle poked through the skin. "Master Roth, I'm so sorry! Are you ok?"

"I'm fine. It's been awhile since someone's done a job like that on me. Don't worry, if you were doing any real damage I would have thrown you out of the City. And don't be sorry. Being sorry has never helped anyone. You should be proud." He stood, bringing his head up towards the sky. "We'll talk about this later. Decreath's stink is still in the air, and from what I overheard there's a Colossus on the way to collect the towers. We don't want to be here when that happens. Not to mention Grotton and Sorronis could be here any minute. Release the rest of your Rage, before it boils up again."

Cole looked down at his body. His cloth armor was nearly disintegrated and the shroud had flowed from his belly and chest. He relaxed his mind as Chiron had taught him, feeling the tension uncoil as the Rage dissipated. He swayed as his hands and feet returned to their normal state, feeling drained and drunk.

"You gonna make it?" Roth asked.

"Yeah. I think so." Cole looked to his Master, who was busy healing the wounds on his chest with snow-colored webs from his munisica.

"Go grab Habbad while I find Valen and Storn. The girls look stable enough for now," Roth grumbled.

"Storn… He's…" Cole's eyes fell, his silence saying exactly what Storn was.

"You positive?" Roth asked.

Cole nodded at the ground.

Roth made a noise Cole had never heard before. Cole looked up, but he was already walking away.

"Go, grab Habbad," he barked over his shoulder.

Cole didn't hesitate.

Cole ran up the broken stairs of the stage. Habbad was still there, trapped in his stone tub, eyes peeled back and bloodshot.

"Habbad?" Cole stepped slowly into his view, bringing his eyes to his line of sight.

Habbad didn't move. His eyes remained locked at the bottom of the left tower.

"Habbad, I'm going to get you out of here, just hold your head still. I don't know how to remove that magic on your face so let me know if I'm hurting you." Cole summoned the Rage, surprised at how quickly it came. He throttled it back as much as he could, stopping the shroud at his wrists. He hacked at the stone tub, breaking off chunks until Habbad was free to move. "You're good bud, you can climb out now."

Habbad didn't move. Cole bent down and retracted his munisica, scooping Habbad out of the broken stone. Habbad's head rested on Cole's shoulder as he came free.

"I will never forgive you." Habbad's voice was hoarse and weak, but his words were crystal clear.

Cole's vision blurred as a wave of shame broke across his heart. "I know."

He carried Habbad over to Eliza, Sitra, and Lileth, who were huddled together in an alcove, waiting for the effects of the Corpulant's flies to wear off. He placed Habbad gently next to them, hiding his view of Lexy's thrashing body. There was no saving her now, she was no longer the sweet girl they once knew.

"What's wrong with him?" Eliza asked. "Was he poisoned as well?"

"It's not the poison." Cole's jaw trembled as his stomach lurched. "It's Lexy, his sister. Kreed made us watch her burn. She's still over there. I can't even tell which one she is anymore."

"Oberon help him." Eliza reached for Habbad, but recoiled as if something had stung her hand.

"Where's Roth?" Lileth asked.

"He went to find Valen," Cole replied, rubbing his fingertips into his temples. "Can any of you use magic yet? My mind feels rotten and weak right now. I don't know how we're going to get out of here."

"No, the venom from the Corpulant's flies still taints our blood." Lileth took a hesitant step closer to him. "How did you manage to overcome the Rage? The shroud, you were covered from head to toe. Even your eyes…Cole, you mastered it. You mastered Rage. Not even Roth…" Her voice trailed off as her eyes darted between his. "I've never seen anything like it. For a moment I thought you were going to kill us."

Cole wrapped his fingers around her arm, gently squeezing her taut skin. "I'm better now, I promise. When Roth gets back we'll make for The Sill. He'll know what happened to me."

Lileth's face softened and she gave him a weak smile, placing a hand over his. "You were incredible."

Cole lost himself in her stare. Guilt clawed at his insides as he recalled the lust of the Rage, how it had consumed his every thought and desire. He'd been very close to killing them all.

"There you are." Roth's hulking form appeared at the mouth of their hiding spot. Valen hung over his shoulder, unconscious but breathing. "Unless you feel up for another fight I suggest you get off your asses and follow me."

They stumbled to their feet and started after him. Cole scooped Habbad off the ground and carried him. They rounded the corner and followed Roth to a three-story building a few blocks away. He kicked down the door and cast a sparkling ingot of white light into the darkened room.

"Head to the roof," Roth said as he pointed with a claw. "The baileen should be back any minute. Hopefully Decreath's too busy with the towers to notice us slipping off."

They wound their way up the flights of stairs, Roth's ball of light bobbing over their heads. Habbad grew heavy in Cole's arms and he fell behind. Eliza took him instead, whispering soft words into his ears as he hung like an infant in her arms. Roth smashed the final door off its frame and they stepped out onto the roof.

"We're too late." He snarled, snuffing out his light with a clawed hand. "The Colossus is here. Dammit, that's the biggest one I've ever seen."

They crouched down on the roof, trying to stay below the half-wall that bordered it. Cole peeked over the edge, wondering what the hell a Colossus was supposed to be. His mouth fell open. An impossibly monolithic figure strode through the cityscape. The surrounding buildings looked like low shrubs, barely coming up to its knees. Its size belied how fast it moved. It grew measurably larger with every stride, sending faint shockwaves into Cole's feet.

Roth called out to the sky opposite the towers, cupping his claws around his mouth, "Move your fat leathery ass!"

An urgent keen echoed from over a mile away. The baileen flapped its tail with a burst of speed. After a few seconds, however, the beast dropped its tail and slowed to a dead stop, blasting a terrified cry. The Colossus was in the Devotion square now, knocking over buildings as if they were made of porcelain. Cole craned his neck, dumbstruck by the enormity of the giant. It didn't seem to have noticed them yet.

"The coward won't come any closer," Roth barked as the baileen swam in circles a few blocks away. "There's no time." Without a word, Roth planted a foot and launched Valen at the baileen, his limp form spinning slowly through the air.

"Master Roth, No!" Eliza cried as she attempted to wrestle out of Roth's grip.

"Don't worry, he'll catch you," Roth said before casting her off like a shot put. Ignoring their protests, he tossed Sitra and Lileth as well.

Cole balled his fists and whooped as each of his friends landed safely on the baileen. He thought he could make out Goran on its back too. He reached for the link with his furry friend, but something else crept out of the shadows in his mind. His heart quickened with his breath as a stench of rancid flesh wafted up his nose. The groans from the towers became muffled, as if something had blocked them. Cole turned, feeling as if someone were watching him. The hand of the Colossus rested against the roof next to his feet. Cole yelped, jumping behind Roth.

"Habbad!" Cole cried, covering his mouth. The stench stung his eyes.

Habbad stood with Kreed in the palm of the Colossus, which Cole could now see was made from charred bodies, just like the ones that now lined the towers. The entire form of the Colossus appeared to be made from broken corpses. Decreath placed Kreed's arms around Habbad, pulling him into a fatherly embrace. Habbad looked back over his shoulder, his eyes containing an entire world of agony. An evil smile spread across his wrinkled face. Habbad was no more.

"Habbad! I'm sorry," Cole wailed, inching closer. "I couldn't save her. I'm so sorry."

Habbad's grin deepened, revealing teeth Cole had never seen as he glared up at Cole with Hunger in his eyes. The fingers of the Colossus came up like a massive drawbridge as the form pulled Habbad into the night. A whistling hum cut through the air as the giant's other hand came rushing down to obliterate him. Cole fumbled for the Rage that would save him, but there was nothing there. A rough hand grabbed Cole around the middle as his back slammed against something hard.

"Hold on," Roth thundered, pulling him closer.

Cole sank into Roth's chest as the wind buffeted his eyes. The giant fist crashed behind them as Costas became nothing but a blur of passing lights. They were gone.

End of Book 1

If you enjoyed your journey to Aeneria and want to help make it a real place, please take a moment and give this book an honest review.

For all Hate mail and love letters:

www.AeneriaIsComing.com/contact/

From the World of Aeneria

Website
www.AeneriaIsComing.com

FROM THE AUTHOR

Greetings Traveler!

I've been writing sporadically for most of my life. However, it wasn't until January 2016 that I began to take it seriously thanks to one of my closest friends. While I'd like to be writing full-time, I (like most independent authors) have a day job, which is a logistician position in the National Guard. I joined in 2005, deployed twice, and have been active duty since 2012. The military lifestyle has had a tremendous impact on my life, filling it with more ups and downs than I can keep track of, as well as some lifelong friends.

My days are spent at a desk or bumbling around in a humongous truck. After work I get myself to a gym and do battle with my inner fat kid for a couple of hours, then rush home and hopefully start writing before 8 pm. I nurture a love for performance arts, especially plays and local stand-up. During summers I don't ride my motorcycle nearly enough, and the same goes for my snowboard during the winters. At least once a year I'll go abroad, usually your typical over-indulgent Caribbean cruise, though recently I spent a week in France, where I had the privilege of officiating at a wedding for two dear friends.

The stories I enjoy the most usually leave me shaken for a few days, not because I'm a glutton for masochism, but because they resonate with the wounded parts of me that I wouldn't ordinarily take notice of. With a somewhat busy lifestyle where stoicism has become my go-to survival tool, I need those stories that derail me from my daily grind, that kick me in the gut and make me feel something.

As of writing this I'm 30 years old and live in Manchester, New Hampshire.

- Joe

www.ingramcontent.com/pod-product-compliance
Lightning Source LLC
Chambersburg PA
CBHW071143100726
47908CB00002B/236